A SHORTER FINNEGANS WAKE

JAMES JOYCE

A SHORTER
FINNEGANS WAKE

Edited by

ANTHONY BURGESS

GALILEO PUBLISHERS
CAMBRIDGE

Finnegans Wake
full text first published 1939
by Faber and Faber Ltd

A Shorter Finnegans Wake
edited by Anthony Burgess,
first published 1966

ISBN: 9781912916931

Galileo Publishers
16 Woodlands Road
Great Shelford
Cambridge CB22 5LW, UK
www.galileopublishing.co.uk

USA:
SCB Distributors
15608 S. Century Drive
Gardena, CA 90248-2129

Printed in the EU

FOREWORD

ASKED to name the twenty prose-works of the twentieth century most likely to survive into the twenty-first, many informed book-lovers would feel constrained to include James Joyce's *Ulysses* and *Finnegans Wake*. I say 'constrained' advisedly, because the choice of these two would rarely be as spontaneous as the choice of, say, Proust's masterpiece or a novel by D.H. Lawrence or Thomas Mann. *Ulysses* and *Finnegans Wake* are highly idiosyncratic and 'difficult' books, admired more often than read, when read rarely read through to the end, when read through to the end not often fully, or even partially, understood. This, of course, is especially true of *Finnegans Wake*. And yet there are people who not only claim to understand a great deal of these books but affirm great love for them – love of an intensity more commonly accorded to Shakespeare or Jane Austen or Dickens. Such people feel impelled to take on the task of advocacy, so that others should not miss what the devotees consider to be a profound literary pleasure, and this present reduction of *Finnegans Wake* to the length of an ordinary novel – garnished with an introduction and a running commentary – is my own attempt to bring a great masterpiece to a larger audience than, in the twenty-five years of its existence, it has yet been able to command.

Reducing the book to something over a third of its original length has been painful and difficult. *Finnegans Wake* is one of the few books of the world that totally resist cutting. Despite its bulk, it contains not one word too many, and there is the danger that to pull at a single thread will unravel the entire fabric. This shorter *Finnegans Wake* cannot be a substitute for the work as Joyce wrote it, in a seventeen years' agony of constant eye-disease and intermittent poverty. Most best-sellers will submit to *Reader's Digest* treatment, but sooner or later we have to take *Finnegans Wake* entire. For most it must be later than sooner; meanwhile, here is the gist of the book, together with a brief account of what Joyce was trying to do and a number of signposts sticking like sore thumbs out of the thickets of the text. It is at least a beginning.

Joyce scholarship has become a major industry in some American universities, but in Great Britain it has hardly as yet come into existence. My gratitude for help in preparing this reduction goes, therefore, almost entirely to American scholars, particularly to Joseph Campbell and Henry Morton Robinson, whose *A Skeleton Key to FINNEGANS WAKE* was the first major breakthrough in the hard task of cutting to the essential narrative line: it still remains, after twenty years, an indispensable guide to the Joyce reader who lacks time or equipment to pursue his own background researches. Adaline Glasheen's *A Census of FINNEGANS WAKE* has been the second most thumbed book on my shelf of guides to Joyce. I must mention also Harry Levin's *James Joyce* and – an international effort – the symposium called *Our Exagmination round his factification for incamination of Work in Progress*, which appeared before *Finnegans Wake* was completed but had the advantage of Joyce's own sponsorship and overseeing. My final thanks are to Messrs. Faber and Faber, Joyce's principal publishers in England, for their varied and general assistance and encouragement.

Two important points. Joyce knew what the average reader's difficulties would be, so one must presuppose not an intellectually superior writer deliberately mystifying, but an honest writer unwilling to compromise with a subject-matter of great complexity. But – and this is the other point – he also wanted to write a great comic book, to excite laughter more than to knot brows. Before we start reading we ought to put off the mask of solemnity and prepare to be entertained. This is one of the most entertaining books ever written.

LONDON 1965
AB

What It's All About

[1]

DRIVE westwards out of Dublin, keeping south of Phoenix Park, and you will come to Chapelizod. The name means 'Chapel of Iseult', whom the Irish know as Isoilde and the Germans as Isolde – tragic heroine of Wagner's opera. There is little that is romantic about Chapelizod nowadays; if you want a minimal excitement you will have to go to the pubs, of which the most interesting is purely fictional – the Bristol. Some will identify this for you with the Dead Man, so called because customers would roll out of it drunk to be run over by trams. It is important to us because its landlord is the hero of *Finnegans Wake*. He is middle-aged, of Scandinavian stock and Protestant upbringing, and he has a wife who seems to have some Russian blood in her. His name is, as far as we can tell, Mr. Porter, appropriate for a man who carries up crates of Guinness from the cellar, and he is the father of three children – young twin boys called Kevin and Jerry, and a pretty little daughter named Isobel.

Mr. Porter and his family are asleep for the greater part of the book. It has been a hard Saturday evening in the public bar, and sleep prolongs itself some way into the peace of Sunday morning. Mr. Porter dreams hard, and we are permitted to share his dream. In it various preoccupations of his are fantasticated, and the chief of these is a complex obsession to be expected in a man aware of ageing: his day is passing and the new age belongs to his sons, particularly his favourite son Kevin; his wife no longer attracts him, and he looks for a last sexual fling, or even a renewal of the sexual impulse, in a younger woman. All this is innocent enough and should give him no bad dreams, but it happens that his desires are fixed on his own daughter. 'Incest' is a terrible word, even though it means nothing more than a loyal desire to keep sex in the family, and Mr. Porter's dream will only admit the word in disguise – as 'insect'. Sleeping, he becomes a remarkable mixture of guilty man, beast, and crawling thing, and he even takes on a new and dreamily appropriate name – Humphrey Chimpden Earwicker. There we have the hump of sexual guilt he carries on his back (he is a different porter now), a hint of the ape, and more than a hint of the insect. 'Earwicker' is close to 'earwig', and this, through the French *perce-oreille* can be Hibernicised into 'Persse O'Reilly'. Another preoccupation is a desire to be accepted by the Irish people, as a leader or political representative, but he remains aware of a foreignness that his dream-name too well indicates, and 'Persse O'Reilly' is there only for mockery or execration.

In his dream HCE, as we shall now call him, tries to make the whole of history swallow up his guilt for him. His initials are made to stand for the generality of sinful man, and they are expanded into slogans like 'Here Comes Everybody' and 'Haveth Childers Everywhere'. After all, sexual guilt presupposes a certain creative, or procreative, vitality, and a fall only comes to those who are capable of an erection. The unquenchable vitality appears in 'our Human Conger Eel' (despite the 'down, wantons, down' of the eel-pie-maker in *King Lear*); the erector of great structures is seen in 'Howth Castle and Environs'. From the point of view of the ultimate dreamer of the dream, though (the author himself), 'HCE' has a structural task to perform. As a chemical formula (H_2CE_3) or as a genuine vocable ('hec' or 'ech' or even 'Hecech') it holds the dream down to its hero, is sewn to it like a monogram – HCE: his dream. But HCE has, so deep is his sleep, sunk to a level of dreaming in which he has become a collective being rehearsing the collective guilt of man. Man falls, man rises so that he can fall again; the sequence of falling and rising goes on till doomsday. The record of this, expressed in the lives of great men, in the systems they make and unmake and remake, is what we call history.

What Joyce is doing, then, is to make his hero re-live the whole of history in a night's sleep. This history is not what we learned at school – a chronological treadmill of kings and ministers and wars and revolutions. It is rather a special way of looking at history – less a parade of historical facts than a pattern which seeks to explain those facts. The pattern is loosely derived from the Italian philosopher Giovanni Battista Vico (1668-1744), who wrote an important book called *La Scienza Nuova* in which he presented history not as a straight line but as a circular process of recurrences. If we say that

Finnegans Wake is based on this book we shall be right, but only in the sense that we are right when we say that the same author's *Ulysses* is based on Homer's *Odyssey*. Both *Ulysses* and *Finnegans Wake* are primarily works of fiction, and Vico and Homer are enlisted only to help with the telling of a story. *Finnegans Wake* is not an interpretation of Vico, and Vico is not much of a key to the difficulties of *Finnegans Wake*. What Joyce found in Vico was what every novelist needs when planning a long book – a scaffolding, a backbone.

The backbone of *Finnegans Wake* is easily filleted out. History is a cycle divided into four arcs, and these four arcs will provide the book with its four sections. Each arc, or phase of history, is characterised by a particular form of government. In his earliest stage of development, man is much concerned with the worship of gods. In fabulous pre-history the gods speak in thunder or through oracles; the seed of the gods descends to earth to produce giants and heroes. In true, though primitive, history, the divine word is transmitted through patriarchs and prophets. This is the theocratic stage of human history. The aristocratic stage follows, in which great men, fathers of their communities, rule on their own intiative, not necessarily seeking divine sanction for their laws. The third phase is democratic, and in it we observe a certain debasement: our demagogues are feeble parodies of aristocracy and certainly less than gods. At this point, in Yeats's words, 'things fall apart; the centre cannot hold': we suffer from anarchy and flounder in chaos. The time has come for what Vico calls the *ricorso* or return. The divine speaks in a clap of thunder, we come to our senses and resume worship of the gods. We are back to the theocratic phase, and the cycle starts all over again.

This is the technique for viewing history which Joyce imposes on the dreaming mind of his Chapelizod innkeeper, and at once the reader wants to protest at the implausibility. HCE's dreaming mind may touch archetypal levels, but it is not likely to embrace Vico or the fabulous and historical data which must be used to exemplify the doctrine of the cycle. HCE is, in fact, a very ordinary innkeeper. But Joyce knows what he is doing. He obligingly falls into a trance himself and dreams a cunning dream which encloses that of his hero, a dream which confers the author's own special knowledge on the unlearned snorer, granting him the gift of tongues (this is universal history, and hence polyglot) as well as such trifles as the ability to expound the Cabala and the *Tunc* page of the Book of Kells. He goes further. When HCE and his wife are awakened by the crying of one of the twins and when, after quietening the child, they attempt intercourse, Joyce does all the dreaming himself: the sleeping quality of the book must not be lost, the dream must remain unbroken. The introduction of waking attitudes and waking language would be an intolerable shock to the system and it would be an artistic sin to mix two orders of reality.

[2]

EVEN if we abandon the straight-line view of history, starting at Julius Caesar, say, and ending with the late President Kennedy, we cannot have a history-book, even a dream one, without a large cast of characters. With the author's help HCE must people his sleeping world with a vast number of personages, all of whom must exemplify the fall-rise-fall (or rise-fall-rise) principle which is made to animate Vico's cycle. At the same time, since this is a work of art, certain rules of economy must be observed – rules which true history, which is over-fecund of characters, chooses to ignore. What HCE does in his sleep is to turn his family into a kind of amateur dramatic society which, with help from customers, the cleaning-woman, the pub handyman and a few others, is prepared to impersonate, however unhandily, a whole corpus of beings from myth and literature (including popular magazines, barnstorming melodramas and doubtful street-ballads) as well as from history-books. In a dream it is proper for fictional characters and historical personages to occupy the one zone of reality, as well as to mix their times and subsist happily together on a kind of supra-temporal level: it is the most natural thing in the dreamer's world to see Dr. Johnson and Falstaff, as well as the woman next door, waiting on Charing Cross railway station. The only significant date in HCE's version of history is 1132 A.D., and the significance is entirely symbolic: 11 stands for return or reinstatement or recovery or resumption (having counted up to ten on our fingers we have to start all over again for 11); 32 feet per second is the rate of acceleration of all falling bodies, and the number itself will remind us of the fall of Adam, Humpty Dumpty, Napoleon, Parnell, as also of HCE himself, who is all their reincarnations.

A knowledge of this easy symbolism is essential for an understanding of *Finnegans Wake*, as is also a realisation of the importance of number in general. You can build up the supporting dream-cast of the play by abstracting numbers from the calendar that hangs on some wall or other in the Bristol tavern. There are four weeks in a lunar month, and these will give you the four old men who have so much to say, though what they have to say is rarely of much value – Matthew Gregory, Mark Lyons, Luke Tarpey, and Johnny MacDougal. They are the four gospellers, as well as the four provinces of Ireland, and they take off to impersonal regions where they represent the four points of the compass, the four elements, the four classical ages, and so on. They are always together, followed by their donkey, and it is in order to think of them as a single unit, their names truncated to Ma, Ma, Lu, and Jo and crushed together to make Mamalujo. They end up, in the fading of the dream, as four bedposts. There are twelve months in the year, and these will give us the twelve Sullivans or Doyles, customers in HCE's bar but also twelve apostles and twelve jurymen, always ready to give ponderous judgement in polysyllables ending in '-ation'. Their number, as with a jury, is more important than their names, which are always changing: when we meet a catalogue of apparently new characters, it is enough for us to take breath and count: we shall usually find the same old twelve. The month of February (in which the author was born) has sometimes twenty-eight days, sometimes twenty-nine. This provides Joyce with a bevy of girls from the academy of St. Bride's (St. Bridget's, or Ireland herself) with a separable special girl who usually turns out to be Isobel, HCE's own daughter. Divide 28 by 4, and you are left with 7. The month-maidens sometimes form themselves into the seven colours of the rainbow – an important emblem in *Finnegans Wake*, since it signifies God's covenant after the Flood – hope of reinstatement after sin, 11 after 32.

One of the interesting things about *Finnegans Wake* is the way in which number refuses to melt and become fantasticated. This dream differs, then, from our own dreams, in which we take two slices of cake from a plate holding twelve and find only seven left. When HCE's dream-wife gives gifts to each of her one hundred and eleven children, there are (I have counted) exactly one hundred and eleven, no more, no less. When the thunder of man's fall sounds, or the thunder of God's wrath, we find this represented by a word of exactly one hundred letters, no more, no less. 1 sometimes becomes 2, but that is a natural process of cellular fission: the father has be gotten two sons, and the two sons together make up the parent body. This encourages Joyce to present the one daughter Isobel as two girls – a split personality, a temptress in love only with her mirror-image. But there is never any wanton deformation of a significant number: simple arithmetic is the very breath of this dream.

The four, the twelve, and the twenty-eight or twenty-nine tend to stand outside history and comment on it. The hard work of participation in the recurrent story of man's fall and resurrection rests on the shoulders of HCE, his wife and family, and the old cleaning-woman Kate. The mythical, literary, and historical characters who best exemplify the story are chosen out of a fairly narrow field – mainly from Irish history, and mainly from those Irish personages whose sin or fall best bodies forth HCE's own guilt. In other words, we must expect to meet men who indulged in, or perhaps merely contemplated, acts of illicit love – often with girls far younger than themselves. There must be a tang of incestuous sin. After the general fall motif incarnated in the figures of Adam and Humpty Dumpty, we come to particular identifications. HCE plays the part of Charles Stewart Parnell, the Irish leader whose love for Kitty O'Shea led to his downfall. A symbol of guilt is taken from the letters which the Irish journalist Piggot forged as part of the general campaign to destroy Parnell. Piggot misspelled 'hesitancy' as 'hesitency' and committed the same solecism when giving evidence before the Parnell Commission. This led to his near-collapse in the witness-box and, just after, the private confession of his crime. Changes are rung on the misspelling throughout *Finnegans Wake*, and the word itself is especially appropriate to HCE, since his guilt expresses itself in a speech-hesitation or stutter. But there is an implication of betrayal and victimisation: a hearsay sin (in the dream HCE's crime is no more than that) is swollen into an omnibus accusation which leads to HCE's trial, incarceration, and burial. Parnell, who only committed adultery, was turned by his enemies into the father of all sin.

Jonathan Swift had an obscure relationship with two girls, Esther Johnson and Esther Vanhomrigh, better known as Stella and Vanessa. A father in God (Swift was, of course, the Dean of St. Patrick's in Dublin) evinced a somewhat unfatherly interest in two of his spiritual daughters, and these two young women are conjoined in *Finnegans Wake* in the personality of HCE's daughter Isobel. Two girls with one Christian name, two girls representing one temptation – it is no wonder that the dream-Isobel so easily splits herself into two. Here, anyway, is another guilt-pattern from history, and, like that 'hesitency-hesitancy', it can be alluded to in a single word: Isobel's endearment 'ppt', and all its allomorphs, comes straight from the 'little language' of Swift's *Journal to Stella*.

Another legend with strong Irish associations is teased, in this dream, out of Isobel's own name. Isobel is Iseult-la-Belle, and Chapelizod is her secular shrine. Tristram of Lyonesse came to Ireland to convey Iseult, chosen bride, to his uncle, King Mark of Cornwall. But Tristram and Iseult fell in love, and a train of subterfuge, guilt, and disloyalty was started. Both HCE's preoccupations find potent expression here – aged Mark, too old for love, superseded by a younger man; the agonising sweetness of a forbidden relationship. But we can go further. Sir Armory Tristram (Tristram of Armorica, or Brittany) founded the St. Lawrence family of Howth in Dublin and built Howth Castle: a dream-identification of the two Tristrams is inevitable. For that matter, we have two Iseults who, like the two Esthers, belong to the one legend – King Mark's bride and the Iseult of the White Hands whom Tristram of Lyonesse eventually married. These are, naturally, both contained in Isobel, and a further justification for the splitting of her identity is provided. We have a verbal leitmotif for Parnell and for Swift; we have one for Tristram too, and Joyce takes it from Wagner's version of the legend – his music

– drama *Tristan und Isolde*. The opening line of Isolde's aria over the body of slain Tristan is '*Mild und leise*' ('soft and gentle'): this becomes distorted in *Finnegans Wake* to the grotesque nickname 'Mildew Lisa'.

We can find other identifications with Irish legend and history, some of which creep away from the fall-theme and elevate HCE to the role of proud and guiltless leader – Brian Boru, Finn MacCool, King Laoghair (or Leary). But, though the foreground of the dream is Dublin, HCE is a universal father-figure, and we must not be surprised if he plays the parts of Noah, Julius Caesar, a Russian general, Harold the Saxon, a Norwegian captain, and so on. Scandinavian roles, though, are particularly appropriate, since HCE is of Nordic stock, and the most appropriate identification of all is literary, not historical. Joyce's youthful literary god was Ibsen, and his play *The Masterbuilder* provides perhaps the most potent guilty father-figure of them all – Halvard Solness, who climbs a tower he has built at the request of a young woman he loves and, struck by the God he defies and figuratively rivals, falls from it to his death. An essential lesson of *Finnegans Wake*, if we can talk about 'lessons' in connection with so undidactic a work, is that sin and creation go together, and that 11, which complements 32, stands not only for rising but for raising. HCE has sinned, as have all men, but the sin has driven him out of the Garden of Eden only to plant in him the urge to create Eden-substitutes – cities and civilisations. The fall is, paradoxically, a happy one: '*O felix culpa*' said St. Augustine. Joyce, planting HCE's sin in Phoenix Park, puns on this with his 'O Phoenix culprit.'

Broadly speaking, then, HCE plays man the father and creator, *Bygmester* or Masterbuilder. Ultimately he is identified with what he creates – the city itself. But the creator needs nature as his inspiration and consort, and cities are built on rivers. This brings us to the dream-function of HCE's wife, Ann, whose dream-name is Anna Livia Plurabelle – the Anna Liffey (only feminine river in Europe) on which Dublin stands. The 'Plurabelle' indicates her beauty and plurality (she contains all women). ALP conveys her natural majesty (she is bigger than any tower the *Bygmester* can raise), and the roughly triangular configuration of a mountain turns her into a piece of eternal geometry – she is our 'geomater', or earthmother. A triangle

ALP suggests her triune form. She is wife, she is widow, but she is also daughter. Isobel is contained in her, as is Kate the cleaning woman, praiser of days gone by, but HCE's dream assigns to her chiefly the part of living mother and wife, protectress of her children and of the reputation of her reviled and traduced husband. Though she flows, she is a symbol of the unchanging, while her lord, like all men, is capable of assuming many forms. Her mystery is the mystery of all rivers – the spring is different from the mouth that opens to the ocean, but both are the same water, and it is from the river's death in the sea that the reality of new birth in the hills (the renewing rain-clouds blown inland from the coast) is derived for ever and ever.

As for the twin sons, they illustrate a sort of tragi-comic dialectic which owes a good deal to the Italian philosopher Giordano Bruno (1548–1600), the heretic from Nola who (in the words of Stephen Dedalus in *A Portrait of the Artist as a Young Man*) was 'terribly burned'. Bruno the Nolan taught that opposite principles are eventually reconciled, in heaven if not on earth, and much of *Finnegans Wake* deals with the clash of two brothers unconsciously endeavouring to be made one, to flow back into the unifying father who begot their opposed natures. Joyce Hibernicises Bruno the Nolan into 'Browne and Nolan', the names of the Dublin printers who published his first piece of juvenilia, and he contrives other punning tropes to allude to the Brunonian theory – 'Father San Browne … Padre Don Bruno'; 'Bruno Nowlan'; 'B. Rohan … N. Ohlan'; 'brownesberrow in nolandsland'; 'Bruin and Noselong'. The tragedy of HCE's two sons lies in the fact that each on his own is only half the man his father was: neither is fit to supersede the father in the task of ruling the community. They appear usually as Shem the Penman and Shaun the Post: the first writes the Word, the second delivers it – generally in a distorted and debased form. Shem is the artist, and his most typical manifestation is as James Joyce himself ('Shem' is the Irish form of 'James') – the man who can make the dead speak but is totally incapable of coming to terms with the living, the exile who is cut off from action. Shaun (who owes a little to James Joyce's brother Stanislaus) is a born demagogue and missionary, a kind of sham Christ, at home in the world of action but aware that he lacks the creative spark that is needed to fire the engine of rule. They hate each other, but their fights are really a vain attempt to become synthetised into a whole capable of bearing the burden of government. Anything either does tends to be cancelled out by the action of the other: when Shaun is accused of his father's crime, Shem bears false witness against him, and the four judges, remembering the Brunonian thesis, return a verdict of 'Nolans Brumans' – the accused goes scot-free. The struggles of Shem and Shaun find an eternal archetype in the war between Lucifer and Michael the Archangel ('Mick versus Nick'), but we are not inclined, despite the pressure of orthodoxy, to take sides. Neither is lovable, both are pitiable. Their dissonance sounds only that our ears may long for the unison of the father. On the plane of symbolic botany, Shem may have a little life in him, since he is sometimes presented as a 'stem', but this cannot compare with the huge world-tree that grows out of HCE and ALP. As for Shaun, he is not even alive – a mere stone on the river-bank. In Shaun, the father's authority is debased to a set of fossilised maxims, whereas Shem, drawn to the mother, drinks in a little of her flowing life. If we are going to prefer one to the other, we had better opt for Shem. After all, Shem wrote the book.

These, then, are the main characters of *Finnegans Wake*. HCE names the play, and the casting is automatic. If he, the heavy lead, is Adam, Shaun must be Abel and Shem Cain, and ALP must be Mother Eve. If HCE is King Leary, Shaun must be the missionary St. Patrick, Shem his archdruid opponent, and Isobel St. Bridget. Not all the characters need be employed at the same time: HCE is out of the troupe for a great part of the book, and then his guilt, as well as his authority, can be transferred wholly to the sons. Shaun can be Parnell, Shem Piggot, and Isobel Kitty O'Shea. On the whole, ALP has little time for acting: being a river is very nearly a full-time job. But now, having presented the actors, we must see how they fit into the vast single drama which encloses so many lesser ones: we must enter the Viconian amphitheatre.

[3]

WE HAVE mentioned everyone except Finnegan, and yet it is his wake that gives a title to the book. Now we must speak not of *Finnegans Wake*, however, but of 'Finnegan's Wake', a different title altogether, though the difference cannot be made apparent to the ear. 'Finnegan's Wake' is a New York Irish ballad which tells of the death of Tim Finnegan, a builder's labourer who, fond of the bottle, falls drunk from his ladder at too great a height. His wife and family and friends sit mourning and drinking round his laid-out corpse, but soon a fight breaks out:

> Micky Maloney raised his head,
> When a gallon of whiskey flew at him;
> It missed, and falling on the bed
> The liquor scattered over Tim.
> 'Och, he revives! See how he raises!'
> And Timothy, jumping up from bed,
> Sez, 'Whirl your liquor around like blazes
> Souls to the devil! D'ye think I'm dead?'

This ballad may be taken as demotic resurrection myth and one can see why, with its core of profundity wrapped round with the language of ordinary people, it appealed so much to Joyce. His book begins with this story, but Tim Finnegan is elevated to the rank of divine masterbuilder, a fabulous prehistoric hero hardly separable from Finn MacCool, giant leader of the Fenians under King Cormac, mighty subject of Ossianic epic poetry. Fallen, his head is the Head of Howth, his body lies under the city of Dublin, and his feet may be located near Chapelizod. In the dream-drama there is only one man to play him, and that of course is HCE, but we must not, at this stage, confuse a performance with an identification. Finnegan dies, his wake is held, and during the wake we are given a survey of his mythical world, but also of the new world of true history which is to come after him. In other words, Finnegan stands for the first phase of the Viconian cycle, the rule of gods and heroes, but, with his thunderous fall and death, we must look forward to the coming of an age of purely human rule – we expect the arrival of an unheroic family man, somebody like Humphrey Chimpden Earwicker. When Finnegan, that the legend may be fulfilled, wakes up to the spilling of the whiskey, he is told to lie down again: arrangements have been made for the second phase of the Viconian cycle, and Finnegan would only disrupt that pattern. Let him sleep then until the wheel comes full circle and the thunder kettledrums in a return of theocratic rule.

So now HCE, playing himself, arrives from overseas, and the vague mixed tale of his fall is told. It seems that three soldiers saw him in Phoenix Park, apparently exhibiting himself to two innocent Irish girls (Isobel in her dual form, mixed up with the two colleens on the arms of the city of Dublin). A caddish pipe-smoking man named, apparently, Magrath passes on, greatly garbled and expanded, the story of HCE's misdemeanour to his wife; she tells it, further expanded, to a priest; soon it is all over Dublin, and a bard called Hosty makes a scurrilous ballad about poor HCE, now christened Persse O'Reilly. He is accused of every sin in the calendar and is eventually brought to trial. Locked up in prison, reviled by a visiting American (so that he shall appear a disgrace to the New World as well as the Old), he is at length shoved into a coffin and buried deep under Lough Neagh.

All this is told in hints and rumours: HCE's fall is as ancient as Adam's. Among the rumours is one about a letter written by HCE's wife ALP (she signed the letter 'A Laughable Party'), in which his defence is set out at length: he had enemies, his crime was greatly exaggerated, he was a good husband and father. Meanwhile, as with Parnell, King Arthur, and Finn MacCool himself, it is whispered abroad that HCE is not really dead, that his indomitable spirit is uncontainable by any grave, however deep and watery. He thrusts up shoots of energy: there are quarrels; wars break out. The theme of the opposed brothers now makes its first full-length appearance. HCE's guilt has become a matter of living moment once more, and it seems to attach to Shaun (called now, for some obscure reason, Festy King). But the trial is a far less massive affair than HCE's, and the appearance of Shem as a witness – discreditable and discredited – makes the whole issue fizzle out. We are asked to forget about the brothers for a brief space and to concentrate on ALP's letter – in other words, to continue to concern ourselves with the big HCE legend.

The letter, scratched up from a midden-heap by a hen called Belinda, becomes the object of mock-scholarship. Certain people and places are mentioned in it, and a chapter is devoted to a quiz of twelve questions on these. Shaun now reveals himself as a clever quiz-kid quick to turn himself in to a voluble schoolmaster. He gives a lengthy lecture on the theme of fraternal opposition, illustrating this with certain parables. Shaun himself appears in the first of them disguised as Pope Adrian IV – the only English pope, who gave his blessing to Henry II's annexation of Ireland, since this would bring the old Irish Church under the wing of Rome. Shem stands for the old faith, embodied in St. Lawrence O'Toole, bishop of Dublin at the time of the English conquest. We have, in fact, two forms of the Christian faith which the domineering spirit of Shaun will not suffer to live peaceably side by side: one has to overcome the other. A more homely parable concerns Burrus and Gaseous (butter and cheese), both products of the same substance, the paternal milk, who are rivals for the love of Margareen. The conclusion is that reconciliation between the brothers is not possible, that, to Shaun, Shem must stand accursed, unloved, unprotected.

We are then presented with a full-length portrait of Shem and at the same time introduced to the big food-theme which plays so important a part in the story. At that wake of Finnegan, the flesh to be devoured was that of the dead hero; with the coming of the brothers, it is the substance of the father HCE which must nourish the new rulers. Shem eats all the wrong food: he will not take the Irish salmon of Finn MacCool, for instance, but prefers some foreign muck out of a tin. Shem is low, un-Irish, writer of nasty books, but he flourishes the life-wand, makes the dead speak. He stands for living mercy, while Shaun is all dead justice. It is through Shem that we are able to approach ALP, the living mother: she composed the letter, but Shem penned it. And so we move to the final chapter of the first section, in which Anna Livia Plurabelle's love-story is told, and in which she distributes the spoils of the battle which destroyed her lord's reputation in the form of gifts to her 111 children, thus sweetening memory and allaying the residue of his guilt.

The second section of the book is concerned mainly with the children of HCE and ALP, who prepare for the great work ahead in games and study. Shaun is now called Chuff and Shem is called Glugg. Chuff is an angel and Glugg is a devil, and they fight bitterly, while the twenty-nine girls (who all love Chuff and hate Glugg) look on, dancing, singing, teasing Glugg with unanswerable riddles. After play comes lesson-time, and a whole chapter is arranged to accommodate the text of the boys' lessons, with footnotes and marginal comments. The substance of the lessons is comprehensive, covering the secret doctrines of the Cabala, as well as the subjects of the mediaeval trivium and quadrivium. At the end of it all, the children fly off to the New World, whence they send a letter of greetings to the old decaying world which they have superseded.

But now, surprisingly, and in a chapter of great length, we come face to face with HCE again, this time in his capacity as innkeeper. His customers – the twelve and the four very prominent – represent the entire human community, whose purpose it is to discredit HCE in all sorts of oblique ways – through tales in which he obscurely figures, through a television programme, through accounts of imperialistic wars. Even his alleged sin in Phoenix Park is sniggeringly hinted at, and HCE is forced to defend himself, pointing out that all men are sinners. But he is reviled and rent, and the sound of a mob coming to lynch him, led by Hosty singing a threatening rann, makes him clear the bar and lock the doors. But it is all revealed as depressed hallucination – a dream within a dream – and HCE, alone in his bar save for the four old men, who lurk in the shadows, drinks up the dregs from the abandoned pots and glasses and collapses, in a stupor, on the floor. He dreams of himself as King Mark, whose destined bride Tristram has taken, an old spent man who must hand over the future to his son.

The next section is all about Shaun. In the first chapter he presents himself to the people – sly, demagogic, totally untrustworthy, obsessed with hatred for his brother and ready with another parable to figure forth the enmity – a charming tale called 'The Ondt and the Gracehoper', in which he himself is the industrious insect, while

Shem, the irresponsible artist, fritters the hours away in the sunshine. But Shaun is more ready to admit to himself now that his own extrovert philosophy is insufficient, that the life of the 'gracehoper' has its points. Shaun can rule over space, but he cannot, like the artist, 'beat time'. Sooner or later, when Shaun's rule collapses, we shall be forced to move back to the father, in whom both dimensions meet and make a rounded world. Shaun rolls off in the form of a barrel: he has filled himself with the food that is his father, but it has not nourished him; he is becoming a big bloated emptiness.

But, his name changed to Jaun, he is ready to appear as a kind of seedy Christ to the twenty-nine girls of St. Bride's, reeling off questionable homilies to them, eventually – sensing that the time for his departure is not far off – summoning the Holy Ghost (Shem) to act as proxy bridegroom to his consort the Church, who is, course, Isobel. The daughters of Erin weep over him as over the dead god Osiris. His third chapter shows him as a pathetic wreck, vast, inflated, lying supine on a hill rightly re-christened Yawn. The four old men question him, but they are not interested in his own essence, only in that great primal essence from which he derives: they ask about HCE and his ancient sin, the work he did, the world he built. But Yawn is evasive, and the task of inquisition is handed over to four bright young transatlantic brains-trusters. Eventually, through a spiritualistic medium and crackling with static, the authentic voice of HCE comes through. He confesses his sin, but affirms his deathless love for his consort ALP, whom he has adorned with a city. And so the dream seems to come to an end, or rather the dream in the bedroom over the public bar dissolves and, through the dreaming eyes of the author, we see the decadent times which Shaun's rule has brought about figured in the sterile rituals of marital sex. Mr. and Mrs. Porter copulate, their shadows on the blind flash the act to the world, but it brings no message of renewed fertility. These are the bad times: we, the readers, are living in them. It is time for the *ricorso*, the crack of divine thunder which will bring us to our knees to contemplate the return of a theocracy.

In the final section, a single chapter, Sunday morning comes and we turn our eyes to the East, looking for hope in an alien order of wisdom. The innkeeper goes to sleep again, and he dreams of his son Shaun as he may be, an agent of theocracy, a bringer of the word of God. The boy Kevin appears as St. Kevin, and we are led back to the one genuine historical year in the whole chronicle – 432 A.D., the year of the coming of St Patrick. He refutes the messed-up idealism of the Archdruid (who is also Bishop Berkeley) and speaks out the Christian message in a main voice. But the last word is neither God's nor man's: it is woman's. We are given at last the full text of ALP's letter, and she herself, all river now, dreams herself on to her death and consummation in her father the sea. Her day is done. She was once the young bride from the hills, a role passed on to her daughter; now, with the filth of man's city on her back, she must seek renewal through annihilation; she will return at length to her source in rain-clouds blown in from the sea. The hope of re-birth, for the world as well as the river, is at once fulfilled. The last sentence of the book is incomplete: to finish it we must turn back to the beginning again. And then we are led on to pursue the great cycle once more, the never-ending history of man, sinner and creator.

[4]

SO MUCH for the story of *Finnegans Wake*, but the story is inseparable from the language in which Joyce tells it. It is the language, not the theme, which makes for difficulty, and the difficulty is intentional. The purpose of a dream is to obscure truth, not reveal it: reality comes in flashes of lightning out of dark clouds of fantasy, but it is the fantasy which it is the author's duty to record. Joyce is presenting us with a dream, not with a piece of Freudian or Jungian dream-exegesis. Interpretation is up to us: he makes up the riddles, not the answers. But, as with so much of Joyce, a key to the language awaits us in popular literature: the verbal technique comes straight out of Lewis Carroll. HCE is identified with that great faller Humpty Dumpty, and it is Humpty Dumpty who explains the dream-language of 'Jabberwocky'. What Humpty Dumpty calls 'portmanteau-words' – like 'slithy', which means 'sly' and 'lithe' and 'slimy' and 'slippery' all at the same time – are a very legitimate device for rendering the quality of dreams. In dreams, identities shift and combine, and words ought to mirror this. Waking life tells us that out of a buried body new life will spring, but it is our custom to work out the life-death cycle in terms of a logical proposition. The language of *Finnegans Wake* takes a short cut in the rendering of such notions, and the word 'cropse' sums up in one syllable a whole resurrection-sermon. Waking language is made out of time and space, the gaps between the substances that occupy the one and the events that occupy the other; in dreams there are no gaps.

The technique of *Finnegans Wake* represents a sort of glorification of the pun, the ambiguity which makes us see a fundamental, but normally disregarded, identification in a burst of laughter or a nod of awe. The very title is a complex pun, one missed by printers and editors who restore the apostrophe which Joyce deliberately left out. The primary meaning is one with an apostrophe – 'the wake of Finnegan' – but, as we read the book, we find a secondary meaning assuming a greater and greater part in the semantic complex: 'The Finnegans wake up, the cycle is renewed'. The very name contains the opposed notions of completion and renewal: '*fin*' or '*fine*' (French, Italian) and 'again'. Once we understand the title, we are already beginning to understand the book.

Joyce's puns are more complicated than those of Lewis Carroll, and they tend to a sort of progressive transformation which, though baffling, is shown to be quite logical in a dreaming way. On the first page of the book we meet the expression 'tauftauf'. The German word for 'baptise' is '*taufen*'; the tutor of St. Patrick was St. Germanicus, and it is dreamily appropriate that the patron saint of Ireland should use the German to point to the continuity, as well as the supra-national essence, of Christian evangelism. But later on 'tauftauf' becomes a name – 'Toffy Tough' – and finally (appropriate for baptism) it turns to 'douche douche'; very little of the original is left, and only the surface-meaning and the reduplication show us that this is meant to be a pun at all. The use of a German word is bound, by the way, to disturb those readers who can accept puns but only know them in English. Joyce was a great linguist, at home in most of the tongues of Europe, and his word-play is multilingual, ranging from

Erse to Sanskrit, though rarely further East. The language of *Finnegans Wake* has been aptly called 'Eurish' – a basis of Irish-English with a superstructure of Aryan loan-words. This is not sheer wantonness: the dream is, so to speak, a Caucasian one, and the hero HCE is a type of all westward-migrating conquerors. As all rivers flow into Anna Livia Plurabelle, so all Aryan-speaking races enrich the blood of her husband. The language of his dream has to show this.

Joyce parodies where he does not pun ('Where the bus stops there shop I') and where he does neither he still contrives to lend his language an extra dimension of meaning. Most of the devices he uses are demonstrated in the opening of the book, a sort of overture crammed with themes destined for strenuous development once the story starts. Thus, the 'riverrun, past Eve and Adam's' is a bit of pure topography on one level (the river is the Liffey, Adam and Eve's is the church on its bank), but on another level it is the beginning of human history, the first hint of the fall of man and the polarity of the sexes. 'Sir Tristram, violer d'amores' is both the Tristram of Arthurian legend and the Sir Almeric Tristram who founded the St Lawrence family and built Howth Castle ; he plays love-songs on the viola d'amore, he violates both Iseult and his honour. 'Wielderfight' means 'fight again' (German '*wieder*' means 'again') and also 'wield weapons in wild fight'. The 'penisolate war' is the war of the pen in isolation (Shem, artist in exile), the sexual war, with its thrust of the penis, and the Peninsular War which (Wellington and Napoleon) is a type of the struggle of brothers locked in mutual hate. The reference to the 'doublin' on the river Oconee in Laurens County, Georgia, is an accurate piece of geographical information: there is a town called Dublin on that stream and in that county, and Joyce is concerned with hinting that the events of history repeat themselves, not only in time but in space as well: what happens in the Old World happens also in the New. (The gypsy word 'gorgio' means 'youngster', implying that the American Dublin is a child of the Irish one, as Shaun, founder of new worlds, is a child of HCE) , 'Mishe mishe' is the Erse for 'I am, I am' – St. Bridget, as mother of Ireland, affirming her immortality. 'Thuartpeatrick' is 'Thou art Patrick', echoing 'Thou art Peter', and also an identification of Ireland's father-saint with the 'peat rick' of the land itself. 'Not yet, though venissoon after, had a kidscad buttended a bland old isaac' is crammed with layers of meaning. Isaac Butt was ousted from the leadership of the Irish National Party by Parnell (the wheel turns; one leader supersedes another). The cadet, or younger son, Jacob, disguised in kidskin as hairier Esau, dupes his blind father Isaac, makes him the butt of his deceit. 'Venissoon' is 'very soon' but also 'venison' (appropriate in the Biblical context of goats and burnt offerings), and it modulates the harmony to Swift and Stella and Vanessa. 'Not yet, though all's fair in vanessy, were sosie sesthers wroth with twone nathandjoe.' The last word is an anagram of Swift's Christian name, Jonathan, presenting him as Nathan (wise) and Joseph (untemptable) – two in one ('twone'). Susannah, Esther and Ruth are the 'sosie sesthers wroth' – all in the Bible, all young girls champed at by old men's passion, but also ('in vanessy' is 'Inverness') three sisters who tempt and enchant, as the three weird sisters tempted and enchanted Macbeth. As two girls can be three as well as one (all are summed up in HCE's daughter), so Ham, Shem, and Japhet can be Jhem and Shen, Noah's sons brewing by 'arclight' (rainbow light, *arc en ciel* or *Regenbogen*) the liquor which will make Noah drunk and naked (protectionless) before them.

Need one go so far in digging out strata of meaning? Only if one wishes to; *Finnegans Wake* is a puzzle, just as a dream is a puzzle, but the puzzle element is less important than the thrust of the narrative and the shadowy majesty of the characters. We can get along very well with a few key-words and the general drift, and when our eyes grow bewildered with strange roots and incredible compounds, why, then we can switch on our ears. It is astonishing how much of the meaning is conveyed through music: the art of dim-sighted Joyce is, like that of Milton, mainly auditory. But if we are still disposed to curse the book as breaking those laws of intelligibility subscribed to by Nevil Shute and Ian Fleming, we ought to remind ourselves that a book about a dream would be false to itself if it made everything as clear as daylight. If it woke up and became rational it would no longer be *Finnegans Wake*. To complain that it is mixed-up, over-fluid, maddeningly complex, bursting at the seams with symbols, is to say that it resembles a dream – not a derogation but a compliment.

Whether we want dreams or not is another matter, but we seem to, since we willingly spend a third of our lives in sleep.

We have been serious about *Finnegans Wake*, and we must remain serious about any work that took seventeen years to write, but let us guard against being like Hemingway's bloody owl, solemn. This is, like *Ulysses*, a great comic vision, one of the few books of the world that can make us laugh aloud on nearly every page. Its humour is of that traditional kind, alive in Rabelais, still kicking in Sterne, which modulates easily from the farcical to the sublime and from the witty to the pathetic – a humour not much found in our brutal, sentimental and facetious age, hence a humour much needed. It seduces us into the acceptance of a view of humanity as realistic as that of Dante, and quite as optimistic. *Finnegans Wake* appeared on the eve of Armageddon, when things looked their blackest for the entire human race. The 32 seemed embossed on every bullet, the 11 two sticks burnt in the ultimate fire. But man rose again. In Joyce annihilation becomes 'abnihilisation' – the creation of new life *ab nihilo*, from the egg of nothing. As long as the race exists, *Finnegans Wake* will remain one of its big pertinent codices. The corpse is 'cropse'. Or, to borrow Eliot's borrowing, 'Sin is behovely, but all shall be well, and all manner of thing shall be well.' This is not the philosophy of Shaun, the vapid liberal demagogue, but the faith of HCE, who – 'Here Comes Everybody' – is suffering man himself.

A.B.

1

riverrun, past Eve and Adam's, from swerve of shore to bend of bay, brings us by a commodius vicus of recirculation back to Howth Castle and Environs.

Sir Tristram, violer d'amores, fr'over the short sea, had passencore rearrived from North Armorica on this side the scraggy isthmus of Europe Minor to wielderfight his penisolate war: nor had topsawyer's rocks by the stream Oconee exaggerated themselse to Laurens County's gorgios while they went doublin their mumper all the time: nor avoice from afire bellowsed mishe mishe to tauftauf thuartpeatrick: not yet, though venissoon after, had a kidscad buttended a bland old isaac: not yet, though all's fair in vanessy, were sosie sesthers wroth with twone nathandjoe. Rot a peck of pa's malt had Jhem or Shen brewed by arclight and rory end to the regginbrow was to be seen ringsome on the aquaface.

The fall (bababadalgharaghtakamminarronnkonnbronntonnerronntuonnthunntrovarrhounawnskawntoohoohoordenenthurnuk!) of a once wallstrait oldparr is retaled early in bed and later on life down through all christian minstrelsy. The great fall of the offwall entailed at such short notice the pftjschute of Finnegan, erse solid man, that the humptyhillhead of humself prumptly sends an unquiring one well to the west in quest of his tumptytumtoes: and their upturnpikepointandplace is at the knock out in the park where oranges have been laid to rust upon the green since devlinsfirst loved livvy.

What clashes here of wills gen wonts, oystrygods gaggin fishygods! Brékkek Kékkek Kékkek Kékkek! Kóax Kóax Kóax! Ualu Ualu Ualu! Quaouauh! Where the Baddelaries partisans are still out to mathmaster Malachus Micgranes and the Verdons catapelting the camibalistics out of the Whoyteboyce of Hoodie Head. Assiegates and boomeringstroms. Sod's brood, be me fear! Sanglorians, save! Arms apeal with larms, appalling. Killykillkilly: a toll, a toll. What chance cuddleys, what cashels aired and ventilated! What bidimetoloves sinduced by what tegotetabsolvers! What true feeling for their's hayair with what strawng voice of false jiccup! O here here how hoth sprowled met the duskt the father of fornicationists but, (O my shining stars and body!) how hath fanespanned most high heaven the skysign of soft advertisement! But was iz? Iseut? Ere were sewers? The oaks of ald now they lie in peat yet elms leap where askes lay. Phall if you but will, rise you must: and none so soon either shall the pharce for the nunce come to a setdown secular phoenish.

Bygmester Finnegan, of the Stuttering Hand, freemen's maurer, lived in the broadest way immarginable in his rushlit toofarback for messuages before joshuan judges had given us numbers or Helviticus committed deuteronomy (one yeastyday he sternely struxk his tete in a tub for to watsch the future of his fates but ere he swiftly stook it out again, by the might of moses, the very water was eviparated and all the guenneses had met their exodus so that ought to show you what a pentschanjeuchy chap he was!) and during mighty odd years this man of hod, cement and edifices in Toper's Thorp piled buildung supra buildung pon the banks for the livers by the Soangso. He addle liddle phifie Annie ugged the little craythur. Wither hayre in honds tuck up your part inher. Oftwhile balbulous, mithre ahead, with goodly trowel in grasp and ivoroiled overalls which he habitacularly fondseed, like Haroun Childeric Eggeberth he would caligulate by multiplicables the alltitude and malltitude until he seesaw by neatlight of the liquor wheretwin 'twas born, his roundhead staple of other days to rise in undress maisonry upstanded (joygrantit!), a waalworth of a skyerscape of most eyeful hoyth entowerly, erigenating from next to nothing and celescalating the himals and all, hierarchitectitiptitoploftical, with a burning bush abob off its baubletop and with larrons o'toolers clittering up and tombles a'buckets clottering down.

Of the first was he to bare arms and a name: Wassaily Booslaeugh of Riesengeborg. His crest of huroldry, in vert with ancillars, troublant, argent, a hegoak, poursuivant, horrid, horned. His scutschum fessed, with archers strung, helio, of the second. Hootch is for husbandman handling his hoe. Hohohoho, Mister Finn, you're going to be Mister Finnagain! Comeday morm and, O, you're vine! Sendday's eve and, ah, you're vinegar! Hahahaha, Mister Funn, you're going to be fined again!

What then agentlike brought about that tragoady thundersday this municipal sin business? Our cubehouse still rocks as earwitness to the thunder of his arafatas but we hear also through successive ages that shebby choruysh of unkalified muzzlenimiissilehims that would blackguardise the whitestone ever hurtleturtled out of heaven. Stay us wherefore in our search for tighteousness, O Sustainer, what time we rise and when we take up to toothmick and before we lump down upown our leatherbed and in the night and at the fading of the stars! For a nod to the nabir is better than wink to the wabsanti. Otherways wesways like that provost scoffing bedoueen the jebel and the jpysian sea. Cropherb the crunchbracken shall decide. Then we'll know if the feast is a flyday. She has a gift of seek on site and she allcasually ansars helpers, the dreamydeary. Heed! Heed! It may half been a missfired brick, as some say, or it mought have been due to a collupsus of his back promises, as others looked at it. (There extand by now one thousand and one stories, all told, of the same). But so sore did abe ite ivvy's holired abbles, (what with the wallhall's horrors of rollsrights, carhacks, stonengens, kisstvanes, tramtrees, fargobawlers, autokinotons, hippohobbilies, streetfleets, tournintaxes, megaphoggs, circuses and wardsmoats and basilikerks and aeropagods and the hoyse and the jollybrool and the peeler in the coat and the mecklenburk bitch bite at his ear and the merlinburrow burrocks and his fore old porecourts, the bore the more, and his blightblack workingstacks at twelvepins a dozen and the noobibusses sleighding along Safetyfirst Street and the derryjellybies snooping around Tell-No-Tailors' Corner and the fumes and the hopes and the strupithump of his ville's indigenous romekeepers, homesweepers, domecreepers, thurum and thurum in fancymud murumd and all the uproor from all the aufroofs, a roof for may and a reef for hugh butt under his bridge suits tony) wan warning Phill filt tippling full. His howd feeled heavy, his hoddit did shake. (There was a wall of course in erection) Dimb! He stottered from the latter. Damb! he was dud. Dumb! Mastabatoom, mastabadtomm, when a mon merries his lute is all long. For whole the world to see.

Shize? I should shee! Macool, Macool, orra whyi deed ye diie? of a trying thirstay mournin? Sobs they sighdid at Fillagain's chrissormiss wake, all the hoolivans of the nation, prostrated in their consternation and their duodisimally profusive plethora of ululation. There was plumbs and grumes and cheriffs and citherers and raiders and cinemen too. And the all gianed in with the shoutmost shoviality. Agog and magog and the round of them agrog. To the continuation of that celebration until Hanandhunigan's extermination! Some in kinkin corass, more, kankan keening. Belling him up and filling him down. He's stiff but he's steady is Priam Olim! 'Twas he was the dacent gaylabouring youth. Sharpen his pillowscone, tap up his bier! E'erawhere in this whorl would ye hear sich a din again? With their deepbrow fundigs and the dusty fidelios. They laid him brawdawn alanglast bed. With a bockalips of finisky fore his feet. And a barrowload of guenesis hoer his head. Tee the tootal of the fluid hang the twoddle of the fuddled, O!

Hurrah, there is but young gleve for the owl globe wheels in view which is tautaulogically the same thing. Well, Him a being so on the flounder of his bulk like an overgrown babeling, let wee peep, see, at Hom, well, see peegee ought he ought, platterplate. Ш Hum! From Shopalist to Bailywick or from ashtun to baronoath or from Buythebanks to Roundthehead or from the foot of the bill to ireglint's eye he calmly extensolies. And all the way (a horn!) from fjord to fjell his baywinds' oboboes shall wail him rockbound (hoahoahoah!) in swimswamswum and all the livvylong night, the delldale dalppling night, the night of bluerybells, her flittaflute in tricky trochees (O carina! O carina!) wake him. With her issavan essavans and her patterjackmartins about all them inns and ouses. Tilling a teel of a tum, telling a toll of a teary turty Taubling. Grace before Glutton. For what we are, gifs à gross if we are, about to believe. So pool the begg and pass the kish for crawsake. Omen. So sigh us. Grampupus is fallen down but grinny sprids the boord. Whase on the joint of a desh? Finfoefom the Fush. Whase be his baken head? A loaf of Singpantry's Kennedy bread. And whase hitched to the hop in his tayle? A glass of Danu U'Dunnell's foamous olde Dobbelin ayle. But, lo, as you would quaffoff his fraudstuff and sink teeth through that pyth of a flowerwhite bodey behold of him as behemoth for he is noewhemoe. Finiche! Only a fadograph of a yestern scene. Almost rubicund Salmosalar, ancient fromout the ages of the Agapemonides, he is smolten in our mist, woebecanned and packt away. So that meal's dead off for summan, schlook, schlice and goodridhirring.

No eating or drinking, then, at this wake. We don't get a chance to sink our teeth into the flesh of Finnegan, dead divine giant, since his body dissolves into the Dublin landscape, stretching from the Hill of Howth to Chapelizod. We can survey the heroic past he represents, though, by visiting the "Willingdone Museyroom", or Wellington Museum, in the Phoenix Park. It is as though, hidden inside that fabulous builder, the elements of war, the clash of brothers, are somehow reconciled, the dynamo of struggle made to serve a creative end. The old woman, the widow, whose task it is to gather up the shattered fragments of her dead lord, is the right person to show us round. Outside the "Museyroom", it is no surprise to us to see her transformed into a little bird, pecking up bits of the heroic past to feed us, Finnegan's heirs. And here is a great creation of the past—the city itself.

So This Is Dyoublong?

Hush! Caution! Echoland!

How charmingly exquisite! It reminds you of the outwashed engravure that we used to be blurring on the blotchwall of his innkempt house. Used they? (I am sure that tiring chabelshoveller with the mujikal chocolat box, Miry Mitchel, is listening) I say, the remains of the outworn gravemure where used to be blurried the Ptollmens of the Incabus. Used we? (He is only pretendant to be stugging at the jubalee harp from a second existed lishener, Fiery Farrelly.) It is well known. Lokk for himself and see the old butte new. Dbln. W. K. O. O. Hear? By the mausolime wall. Fimfim fimfim. With a grand funferall. Fumfum fumfum. 'Tis optophone which ontophanes. List! Wheatstone's magic lyer. They will be tuggling foriver. They will be lichening for allof. They will be pretumbling forover. The harpsdischord shall be theirs for ollaves.

Four things therefore, saith our herodotary Mammon Lujius in his grand old historiorum, wrote near Boriorum, bluest book in baile's annals, f.t. in Dyfflinarsky ne'er sall fail til heathersmoke and cloudweed Eire's ile sall pall. And here now they are, the fear of um. T. Totities! *Unum.* (Adar.) A bulbenboss surmounted upon an alderman. Ay, ay! *Duum.* (Nizam.) A shoe on a puir old wobban. Ah, ho! *Triom.* (Tamuz.) An auburn mayde, o'brine a'bride, to be desarted. Adear, adear! *Quodlibus.* (Marchessvan.) A penn no weightier nor a polepost. And so. And all. (Succoth.)

So, how idlers' wind turning pages on pages, as innocens with anaclete play popeye antipop, the leaves of the living in the boke of the deeds, annals of themselves timing the cycles of events grand and national, bring fassilwise to pass how.

1132 A.D. Men like to ants or emmets wondern upon a groot hwide Whallfisk which lay in a Runnel. Blubby wares upat Ublanium.

566 A.D. On Baalfire's night of this year after deluge a crone that

hadde a wickered Kish for to hale dead turves from the bog lookit under the blay of her Kish as she ran for to sothisfeige her cowrieosity and be me sawl but she found hersell sackvulle of swart goody quickenshoon and small illigant brogues, so rich in sweat. Blurry works at Hurdlesford.

(Silent.)

566 A.D. At this time it fell out that a brazenlockt damsel grieved (*sobralasolas!*) because that Puppette her minion was ravisht of her by the ogre Puropeus Pious. Bloody wars in Ballyaughacleeaghbally.

1132 A.D. Two sons at an hour were born until a goodman and his hag. These sons called themselves Caddy and Primas. Primas was a santryman and drilled all decent people. Caddy went to Winehouse and wrote o peace a farce. Blotty words for Dublin.

Somewhere, parently, in the ginnandgo gap between antediluvious and annadominant the copyist must have fled with his scroll. The billy flood rose or an elk charged him or the sultrup worldwright from the excelsissimost empyrean (bolt, in sum) earthspake or the Dannamen gallous banged pan the bliddy duran. A scribicide then and there is led off under old's code with some fine covered by six marks or ninepins in metalmen for the sake of his labour's dross while it will be only now and again in our rear of o'er era, as an upshoot of military and civil engagements, that a gynecure was let on to the scuffold for taking that same fine sum covertly by meddlement with the drawers of his neighbour's safe.

In that bit of ancient history we see the characters of the post-heroic tale beginning to stir—HCE, his wife, his daughter, his twin sons. The year 1132 is the time of fall (32) and return (11)—a time that is always with us (halved for women). The Irish giant is to be replaced by the foreign invader (a family man, though, not a warrior).

We recognise HCE's stutter of guilt in the following piece of dimly heard dialogue out of the far past. The word "hasatency" reminds us of the forgery which incriminated Parnell. HCE, then, is a new type of unheroic hero—vulnerable, guilty of illicit sexual desires, but still a man with the stuff of leadership in him. He has not yet arrived, but we are given here a dim hint of his coming.

Jute. — Yutah!
Mutt. — Mukk's pleasurad.
Jute. — Are you jeff?
Mutt. — Somehards.
Jute. — But you are not jeffmute?
Mutt. — Noho. Only an utterer.
Jute. — Whoa? Whoat is the mutter with you?
Mutt. — I became a stun a stummer.
Jute. — What a hauhauhauhaudibble thing, to be cause! How, Mutt?
Mutt. — Aput the buttle, surd.
Jute. — Whose poddle? Wherein?
Mutt. — The Inns of Dungtarf where Used awe to be he.
Jute. — You that side your voise are almost inedible to me. Become a bitskin more wiseable, as if I were you.
Mutt. — Has? Has at? Hasatency? Urp, Boohooru! Booru Usurp! I trumple from rath in mine mines when I rimimirim!
Jute. — One eyegonblack. Bisons is bisons. Let me fore all your hasitancy cross your qualm with trink gilt. Here have sylvan coyne, a piece of oak. Ghinees hies good for you.
Mutt. — Louee, louee! How wooden I not know it, the intellible greytcloak of Cedric Silkyshag! Cead mealy faulty rices for one dabblin bar. Old grilsy growlsy! He was poached on in that eggtentical spot. Here

where the liveries, Monomark. There where the missers moony, Minnikin passe.

Jute. — Simply because as Taciturn pretells, our wrongstoryshortener, he dumptied the wholeborrow of rubbages on to soil here.

Mutt. — Just how a puddinstone inat the brookcells by a riverpool.

Jute. — Load Allmarshy! Wid wad for a norse like?

Mutt. — Somular with a bull on a clompturf. Rooks roarum rex roome! I could snore to him of the spumy horn, with his woolseley side in, by the neck I am sutton on, did Brian d' of Linn.

Jute. — Boildoyle and rawhoney on me when I can beuraly forsstand a weird from sturk to finnic in such a patwhat as your rutterdamrotter. Onheard of and umscene! Gut aftermeal! See you doomed.

Mutt. — Quite agreem. Bussave a sec. Walk a dun blink roundward this albutisle and you skull see how olde ye plaine of my Elters, hunfree and ours, where wone to wail whimbrel to peewee o'er the saltings, where wilby citie by law of isthmon, where by a droit of signory, icefloe was from his Inn the Byggning to whose Finishthere Punct. Let erehim ruhmuhrmuhr. Mearmerge two races, swete and brack. Morthering rue. Hither, craching eastuards, they are in surgence: hence, cool at ebb, they requiesce. Countlessness of livestories have netherfallen by this plage, flick as flowflakes, litters from aloft, like a waast wizzard all of whirlworlds. Now are all tombed to the mound, isges to isges, erde from erde. Pride, O pride, thy prize!

Jute. — 'Stench!

Mutt. — Fiatfuit! Hereinunder lyethey. Llarge by the smal an' everynight life olso th'estrange, babylone the greatgrandhotelled with tit tit tittlehouse, alp on earwig, drukn on ild, likeas equal to anequal in this sound seemetery which iz leebez luv.

Jute. — 'Zmorde!

Mutt. — Meldundleize! By the fearse wave behoughted. Despond's sung. And thanacestross mound have swollup them all. This ourth of years is not save brickdust and being humus the same roturns. He who runes may rede it on all fours. O'c'stle, n'wc'stle, tr'c'stle, crumbling! Sell me sooth the fare for Humblin! Humblady Fair. But speak it allsosiftly, moulder! Be in your whisht!

Jute. — Whysht?

Mutt. — The gyant Forficules with Amni the fay.

Jute. — Howe?

Mutt. — Here is viceking's graab.

Jute. — Hwaad !

Mutt. — Ore you astoneaged, jute you?

Jute. — Oye am thonthorstrok, thing mud.

But before the invader can come and confront the native in a dream cross-talk act, we must pay our dues of praise to the heroic giant he will supersede. Finnegan, no longer a landscape but a dead god, lies there on the bier. He was a great builder, a great cultivator.

He dug in and dug out by the skill of his tilth for himself and all belonging to him and he sweated his crew beneath his auspice for the living and he urned his dread, that dragon volant, and he made louse for us and delivered us to boll weevils amain, that mighty liberator, Unfru-Chikda-Uru-Wukru and begad he did, our ancestor most worshipful, till he thought of a better one in his windower's house with that blushmantle upon him from earsend to earsend. And would again could whispring grassies wake him and may again when the fiery bird disembers. And will again if so be sooth by elder to his youngers shall be said. Have you whines for my wedding, did you bring bride and bedding, will you whoop for my deading is a? Wake? *Usqueadbaugham!*

Anam muck an dhoul! Did ye drink me doornail?

The term "wake" has taken on another meaning. Someone has shouted the Irish word for whiskey, and Finnegan reveals himself as not dead at all. This, of course, ought to please the mourners, but unfortunately they're committed to a new era, one in which gods and giants will be an embarrassment. The theocratic age is over and the aristocratic age is about to begin. The new ruler—"a big rody ram lad at random on the premises of his haunt of the hungred bordles"—has already arrived from over the seas—"with a bumrush in a hull of a wherry". All that can be done now is to persuade Finnegan to lie down again and sleep. There's no work for him to do, and there's nothing to worry about at home—everything's being taken care of. Let him then sleep and take his ease like a god on pension.

Aisy now, you decent man, with your knees and lie quiet and repose your honour's lordship! Hold him here, Ezekiel Irons, and may God strengthen you! It's our warm spirits, boys, he's spooring. Dimitrius O'Flagonan, cork that cure for the Clancartys! You swamped enough since Portobello to float the Pomeroy. Fetch neahere, Pat Koy! And fetch nouyou, Pam Yates! Be nayther angst of Wramawitch! Here's lumbos. Where misties swaddlum, where misches lodge none, where mystries pour kind on, O sleepy! So be yet!

I've an eye on queer Behan and old Kate and the butter, trust me. She'll do no jugglywuggly with her war souvenir postcards to help to build me murial, tippers! I'll trip your traps! Assure a sure there! And we put on your clock again, sir, for you. Did or didn't we, sharestutterers? So you won't be up a stump entirely. Nor shed your remnants. The sternwheel's crawling strong. I seen your missus in the hall. Like the queenoveire. Arrah, it's herself that's fine, too, don't be talking! Shirksends? You storyan Harry chap longa me Harry chap storyan grass woman plelthy good trout. Shakeshands. Dibble a hayfork's wrong with her only her lex's salig. Boald Tib does be yawning and smirking cat's hours on the Pollockses' woolly round tabouretcushion watching her sewing a dream together, the tailor's daughter, stitch to her last. Or while waiting for winter to fire the enchantement, decoying more nesters to fall down the flue. It's an allavalonche that blows nopussy food. If you only were there to explain the meaning, best of men, and talk to her nice of guldenselver. The lips would moisten once again. As when you drove with her to Findrinny Fair. What with reins here and ribbons there all your hands were employed so she never knew was she on land or at sea or swooped through the blue like Airwinger's bride. She was flirtsome then and she's fluttersome yet. She can second a song and adores a scandal when the last post's gone by. Fond of a concertina and pairs passing when she's had her forty winks for supper after kanekannan and abbely dimpling and is in her merlin chair assotted, reading her Evening World. To see is it smarts, full lengths or swaggers. News, news, all the news. Death, a leopard, kills fellah in Fez. Angry scenes at Stormount. Stilla Star with her lucky in goingaways. Opportunity fair with the China floods and we hear these rosy rumours. Ding Tams he noise about all same Harry chap. She's seeking her way, a chickle a chuckle, in and out of their serial story, *Les Loves of Selskar et Pervenche*, freely adapted to *The Novvergin's Viv*. There'll be bluebells blowing in salty sepulchres the night she signs her final tear. Zee End. But that's a world of ways away. Till track laws time. No silver ash or switches for that one! While flattering candles flare. Anna Stacey's how are you! Worther waist in the noblest, says Adams and Sons, the wouldpay actionneers. Her hair's as brown as ever it was. And wivvy and wavy. Repose you now! Finn no more!

For, be that samesake sibsubstitute of a hooky salmon, there's already a big rody ram lad at random on the premises of his haunt of the hungred bordles, as it is told me. Shop Illicit, flourishing like a lordmajor or a buaboabaybohm, litting flop a deadlop (aloose!) to lee but lifting a bennbranch a yardalong (ivoeh!) on the breezy side (for showm!), the height of Brewster's chimpney and as broad below as Phineas Barnum; humphing his share of the showthers is senken on him he's such a grandfallar, with a pocked wife in pickle that's a flyfire and three lice nittle clinkers, two twilling bugs and one midgit pucelle. And aither he cursed and recursed and was everseen doing what your fourfootlers saw or he was never done seeing what you coolpigeons know, weep the clouds aboon for smiledown witnesses, and that'll do now about the fairyhees and the frailyshees. Though Eset fibble it to the zephiroth and Artsa zoom it round her heavens for ever. Creator he has created for his creatured ones a creation. White monothoid? Red theatrocrat? And all the pinkprophets cohalething? Very much so! But however 'twas 'tis sure for one thing, what sherif Toragh voucherfors and Mapqiq makes put out, that the man, Humme the Cheapner, Esc, overseen as we thought him, yet a worthy of the naym, came at this timecoloured place where we live in our paroqial fermament one tide on another, with a bumrush in a hull of a wherry, the twin turbane dhow, *The Bey for Dybbling*, this archipelago's first visiting schooner, with a wicklowpattern waxenwench at her prow for a figurehead, the deadsea dugong updipdripping from his depths, and has been repreaching himself like a fishmummer these siktyten years ever since, his shebi by his shide, adi and aid, growing hoarish under his turban and changing cane sugar into sethulose starch (Tuttut's cess to him!) as also that, batin the bulkihood he bloats about when innebbiated, our old offender was humile, commune and ensectuous from his nature, which you may gauge after the bynames was put under him, in lashons of languages, (honnein suit and praisers be!) and, totalisating him, even hamissim of himashim that he, sober serious, he is ee and no counter he who will be ultimendly respunchable for the hubbub caused in Edenborough.

Now (to forebare for ever solittle of Iris Trees and Lili O'Rangans), concerning the genesis of Harold or Humphrey Chimpden's occupational agnomen (we are back in the presurnames prodromarith period, of course just when enos chalked halltraps) and discarding once for all those theories from older sources which would link him back with such pivotal ancestors as the Glues, the Gravys, the Northeasts, the Ankers and the Earwickers of Sidlesham in the Hundred of Manhood or proclaim him offsprout of vikings who had founded wapentake and seddled hem in Herrick or Eric, the best authenticated version, the Dumlat, read the Reading of Hofed-ben-Edar, has it that it was this way. We are told how in the beginning it came to pass that like cabbaging Cincinnatus the grand old gardener was saving daylight under his redwoodtree one sultry sabbath afternoon, Hag Chivychas Eve, in prefall paradise peace by following his plough for rootles in the rere garden of mobhouse, ye olde marine hotel, when royalty was announced by runner to have been pleased to have halted itself on the highroad along which a leisureloving dogfox had cast followed, also at walking pace, by a lady pack of cocker spaniels. Forgetful of all save his vassal's plain fealty to the ethnarch Humphrey or Harold stayed not to yoke or saddle but stumbled out hotface as he was (his sweatful bandanna loose from his pocketcoat) hasting to the forecourts of his public in topee, surcingle, solascarf and plaid, plus fours, puttees and bulldog boots ruddled cinnabar with flagrant marl, jingling his turnpike keys and bearing aloft amid the fixed pikes of the hunting party a high perch atop of which a flowerpot was fixed earthside hoist with care. On his majesty, who was, or often feigned to be, noticeably longsighted from green youth and had been meaning to inquire what, in effect, had caused yon causeway to be thus potholed, asking substitutionally to be put wise as to whether paternoster and silver doctors were not now more fancied bait for lobstertrapping honest blunt Harom-phreyld answered in no uncertain tones very similarly with a fear-less forehead: Naw, yer maggers, aw war jist a cotchin on thon bluggy earwuggers. Our sailor king, who was draining a gugglet of obvious adamale, gift both and gorban, upon this, ceasing to swallow, smiled most heartily beneath his walrus moustaches and indulging that none too genial humour which William the Conk on the spindle side had inherited with the hereditary whitelock and some shortfingeredness from his greataunt Sophy, turned to-wards two of his retinue of gallowglasses, Michael, etheling lord of Leix and Offaly and the jubilee mayor of Drogheda, Elcock, (the two scatterguns being Michael M. Manning, protosyndic of Waterford and an Italian excellency named Giubilei according to a later version cited by the learned scholarch Canavan of Can-makenoise), in either case a triptychal religious family symbolising puritas of doctrina, business per usuals and the purchypatch of hamlock where the paddish preties grow and remarked dilsydul-sily: Holybones of Saint Hubert how our red brother of Pour-ingrainia would audibly fume did he know that we have for sur-trusty bailiwick a turnpiker who is by turns a pikebailer no sel-domer than an earwigger! For he kinned Jom Pill with his court so gray and his haunts in his house in the mourning. (One still hears that pebble crusted laughta, japijap cheerycherrily, among the roadside tree the lady Holmpatrick planted and still one feels the amossive silence of the cladstone allegibelling: Ive mies outs ide Bourn.) Comes the question are these the facts of his nom-inigentilisation as recorded and accolated in both or either of the collateral andrewpaulmurphyc narratives. Are those their fata which we read in sibylline between the *fas* and its *nefas*? No dung on the road? And shall Nohomiah be our place like? Yea, Mulachy our kingable khan? We shall perhaps not so soon see. Pinck poncks that bail for seeks alicence where cumsceptres with scentaurs stay. Bear in mind, son of Hokmah, if so be you have metheg in your midness, this man is mountain and unto changeth doth one ascend. Heave we aside the fallacy, as punical as finikin, that it was not the king kingself but his inseparable sisters, uncontrollable nighttalkers, Skertsiraizde with Donyahzade, who afterwards, when the robberers shot up the socialights, came down into the world as amusers and were staged by Madame Sudlow as Rosa and Lily Miskinguette in the pantalime that two pitts paythronosed, Miliodorus and Galathee. The great fact emerges that after that historic date all holographs so far exhumed initialled by Haromphrey bear the sigla H.C.E. and while he was only and long and always good Dook Umphrey for the hungerlean spalpeens of Lucalizod and Chimbers to his cronies it was equally certainly a pleasant turn of the populace which gave him as sense of those normative letters the nickname Here Comes Everybody. An imposing everybody he always indeed looked, constantly the same as and equal to himself and magnificently well worthy of any and all such universalisation, every time he continually surveyed, amid vociferatings from in front of *Accept these few nutties!* and *Take off that white hat!*, relieved with *Stop his Grog* and *Put It in the Log* and *Loots in his* (bassvoco) *Boots*, from good start to happy finish the truly catholic assemblage gathered together in that king's treat house of satin alustrelike above floats and footlights from their assbawlveldts and oxgangs unanimously to clapplaud (the inspiration of his lifetime and the hits of their careers) Mr Wallenstein Washington Semperkelly's immergreen tourers in a command performance by special request with the courteous permission for pious purposes the homedromed and enliventh performance of the problem passion play of the millentury, running strong since creation, *A Royal Divorce*, then near the approach towards the summit of its climax, with ambitious interval band selections from *The Bo' Girl* and *The Lily* on all horserie show command nights from his viceregal booth (his bossaloner is ceilinged there a cuckoospit less eminent than the redritualhoods of Maccabe and Cullen) where, a veritable Napoleon the Nth, our worldstage's practical jokepiece and retired cecelticocommediant in his own wise, this folksforefather all of the time sat, having the entirety of his house about him, with the invariable broadstretched kerchief cooling his whole neck, nape and shoulderblades and in a wardrobe panelled tuxedo completely thrown back from a shirt well entitled a swallowall, on every point far outstarching the laundered clawhammers and marbletopped highboys of the pit stalls and early amphitheatre. The piece was this: look at the lamps. The cast was thus: see under the clock. Ladies circle: cloaks may be left. Pit, prommer and parterre, standing room only. Habituels conspicuously emergent.

A baser meaning has been read into these characters the literal sense of which decency can safely scarcely hint. It has been blurtingly bruited by certain wisecrackers (the stinks of Mohorat are in the nightplots of the morning), that he suffered from a vile disease. Athma, unmanner them! To such a suggestion the one selfrespecting answer is to affirm that there are certain statements which ought not to be, and one should like to hope to be able to add, ought not to be allowed to be made. Nor have his detractors, who, an imperfectly warmblooded race, apparently conceive him as a great white caterpillar capable of any and every enormity in the calendar recorded to the discredit of the Juke and Kellikek families, mended their case by insinuating that, alternately, he lay at one time under the ludicrous imputation of annoying Welsh fusiliers in the people's park. Hay, hay, hay! Hoq, hoq, hoq! Faun and Flora on the lea love that little old joq. To anyone who knew and loved the christlikeness of the big cleanminded giant H. C. Earwicker throughout his excellency long vicefreegal existence the mere suggestion of him as a lustsleuth nosing for trouble in a boobytrap rings particularly preposterous. Truth, beard on prophet, compels one to add that there is said to have been quondam (pfuit! pfuit!) some case of the kind implicating, it is interdum believed, a quidam (if he did not exist it would be necessary quoniam to invent him) abhout that time stambuling ha-round Dumbaling in leaky sneakers with his tarrk record who has remained topantically anonymos but (let us hue him Abdullah Gamellaxarksky) was, it is stated, posted at Mallon's at the instance of watch warriors of the vigilance committee and years afterwards, cries one even greater, Ibid, a commender of the frightful, seemingly, unto such as were sulhan sated, tropped head (pfiat! pfiat!) waiting his first of the month froods turn for thatt chopp pah kabbakks alicubi on the old house for the chargehard, Roche Haddocks off Hawkins Street. Lowe, you blondy liar, Gob scene you in the narked place and she what's edith ar home defileth these boyles! There's a cabful of bash indeed in the homeur of that meal. Slander, let it lie its flattest, has never been able to convict our good and great and no ordinary Southron Earwicker, that homogenius man, as a pious author called him, of any graver impropriety than that, advanced by some woodwards or regarders, who did not dare deny, the shomers, that they had, chin Ted, chin Tam, chinchin Taffyd, that day consumed their soul of the corn, of having behaved with ongentilmensky immodus opposite a pair of dainty maidservants in the swoolth of the rushy hollow whither, or so the two gown and pinners pleaded, dame nature in all innocency had spontaneously and about the same hour of the eventide sent them both but whose published combinations of silkinlaine testimonies are, where not dubiously pure, visibly divergent, as wapt from wept, on minor points touching the intimate nature of this, a first offence in vert or venison which was admittedly an incautious but, at its wildest, a partial exposure with such attenuating circumstances (garthen gaddeth green hwere sokeman brideth girling) as an abnormal Saint Swithin's summer and, (Jesses Rosasharon!) a ripe occasion to provoke it.

Three soldiers, then (Ted, Tam and Taffyd, or some such names) alleged that HCE, our fine father and family man, behaved indecently in the Phoenix Park: he exhibited himself, or something, to two girls. Rumour spread through the town; the misdemeanour became swollen to a great crime, thanks to the gossip-mongering of a certain cad and his wife, an overspoiled priest called Browne, Treacle Tom, Peter Cloran, O'Mara (known as Mildew Lisa—a dream-allusion to "*Mild und leise*", opening words of Isolde's song over the dead Tristan) and others. Finally Hosty, a ballad-maker, wrote a rann, very scurrilous.

And around the lawn the rann it rann and this is the rann that Hosty made. Spoken. Boyles and Cahills, Skerretts and Pritchards, viersified and piersified may the treeth we tale of live in stoney. Here line the refrains of. Some vote him Vike, some mote him Mike, some dub him Llyn and Phin while others hail him Lug Bug Dan Lop, Lex, Lax, Gunne or Guinn. Some apt him Arth, some bapt him Barth, Coll, Noll, Soll, Will, Weel, Wall but I parse him Persse O'Reilly else he's called no name at all. Together. Arrah, leave it to Hosty, frosty Hosty, leave it to Hosty for he's the mann to rhyme the rann, the rann, the rann, the king of all ranns. Have you here? (Some ha) Have we where? (Some hant) Have you hered? (Others do) Have we whered? (Others dont) It's cumming, it's brumming! The clip, the clop! (All cla) Glass crash. The (klikkaklakkaklaskaklopatzklatschabattacreppycrottygraddaghsemmihsammihnouithappluddyappladdypkonpkot!).

{*Ardite, arditi!*
{Music cue.

"THE BALLAD OF PERSSE O'REILLY."

Have you heard of one Humpty Dumpty
How he fell with a roll and a rumble
And curled up like Lord Olofa Crumple
By the butt of the Magazine Wall,
        (Chorus) Of the Magazine Wall,
                Hump, helmet and all?

He was one time our King of the Castle
Now he's kicked about like a rotten old parsnip.
And from Green street he'll be sent by order of His Worship
To the penal jail of Mountjoy
        (Chorus) To the jail of Mountjoy!
                Jail him and joy.

He was fafafather of all schemes for to bother us
Slow coaches and immaculate contraceptives for the populace,
Mare's milk for the sick, seven dry Sundays a week,
Openair love and religion's reform,
        (Chorus) And religious reform,
                Hideous in form.

Arrah, why, says you, couldn't he manage it?
I'll go bail, my fine dairyman darling,
Like the bumping bull of the Cassidys
All your butter is in your horns.
        (Chorus) His butter is in his horns.
                Butter his horns!

(Repeat) Hurrah there, Hosty, frosty Hosty, change that shirt
[on ye,
Rhyme the rann, the king of all ranns!

Balbaccio, balbuccio!
We had chaw chaw chops, chairs, chewing gum, the chicken-
[pox and china chambers
Universally provided by this soffsoaping salesman.

Small wonder He'll Cheat E'erawan our local lads nicknamed him
When Chimpden first took the floor
(Chorus) With his bucketshop store
Down Bargainweg, Lower.

So snug he was in his hotel premises sumptuous
But soon we'll bonfire all his trash, tricks and trumpery
And'tis short till sheriff Clancy'll be winding up his unlimited
[company
With the bailiff's bom at the door,
(Chorus) Bimbam at the door.
Then he'll bum no more.

Sweet bad luck on the waves washed to our island
The hooker of that hammerfast viking
And Gall's curse on the day when Eblana bay
Saw his black and tan man-o'-war.
(Chorus) Saw his man-o'-war.
On the harbour bar.

Where from? roars Poolbeg. Cookingha'pence, he bawls Donnez-
[moi scampitle, wick an wipin'fampiny
Fingal Mac Oscar Onesine Bargearse Boniface
Thok's min gammelhole Norveegickers moniker
Og as ay are at gammelhore Norveegickers cod.
(Chorus) A Norwegian camel old cod.
He is, begod.

Lift it, Hosty, lift it, ye devil ye! up with the rann, the rhyming
[rann!

It was during some fresh water garden pumping
Or, according to the *Nursing Mirror*, while admiring the mon-
[keys
That our heavyweight heathen Humpharey
Made bold a maid to woo
(Chorus) Woohoo, what'll she doo!
The general lost her maidenloo!

He ought to blush for himself, the old hayheaded philosopher,
For to go and shove himself that way on top of her.
Begob, he's the crux of the catalogue
Of our antediluvial zoo,
    (Chorus) Messrs. Billing and Coo.
        Noah's larks, good as noo.

He was joulting by Wellinton's monument
Our rotorious hippopopotamuns
When some bugger let down the backtrap of the omnibus
And he caught his death of fusiliers,
    (Chorus) With his rent in his rears.
        Give him six years.

'Tis sore pity for his innocent poor children
But look out for his missus legitimate!
When that frew gets a grip of old Earwicker
Won't there be earwigs on the green?
    (Chorus) Big earwigs on the green,
        The largest ever you seen.

Suffoclose! Shikespower! Seudodanto! Anonymoses!

Then we'll have a free trade Gaels' band and mass meeting
For to sod the brave son of Scandiknavery.
And we'll bury him down in Oxmanstown
Along with the devil and Danes,
    (Chorus) With the deaf and dumb Danes,
        And all their remains.

And not all the king's men nor his horses
Will resurrect his corpus
For there's no true spell in Connacht or hell
    (bis) That's able to raise a Cain.

Hosty's rann had remarkable repercussions. All this happened a long time ago, of course, and it's difficult to extricate fact from rumour, but it's quite certain that there was a most complicated trial, in which all sorts of false witnesses gave mixed-up evidence before four judges (the Four Old Men). It's said that a letter signed by "A Laughable Party" (ALP—Anna Livia Plurabelle—the wife of HCE) spoke up for the defendant, but it will be a long time before we can find out what was in the letter. Meanwhile, poor Earwicker languished in prison, not even there free from abuse. A certain German, Herr Betreffender, inflated the alleged crime into The Fall of Adam. An American visitor called HCE some terrible names.

O, by the by, lets wee brag of praties, it ought to be always remembered in connection with what has gone before that there was a northroomer, Herr Betreffender, out for his zimmer hole-digs, digging in number 32 at the Rum and Puncheon (Branch of Dirty Dick's free house) in Laxlip (where the Sockeye Sammons were stopping at the time orange fasting) prior to that, a Kommerzial (Gorbotipacco, he was wreaking like Zentral Oylrubber) from Osterich, the U.S.E. paying (Gaul save the mark!) 11/- in the week (Gosh, these wholly romads!) of conscience money in the first deal of Yuly wheil he was, swishing beesnest with blessure, and swobbing broguen eeriesh myth brockendootsch, making his reporterage on Der Fall Adams for the Frankofurto Siding, a Fastland payrodicule, and er, consstated that one had on him the Lynn O'Brien, a meltoned lammswolle, disturbed, and wider he might the same zurichschicken other he would, with tosend and obertosend tonnowatters, one monkey's damages become. Now you must know, franksman, to make a heart of glass, that the game of gaze and bandstand butchery was merely a Patsy O'Strap tissue of threats and obuses such as roebucks raugh at pinnacle's peak and after this sort. Humphrey's unsolicited visitor, Davy or Titus, on a burgley's clan march from the middle west, a hikely excellent crude man about road who knew his Bullfoost Mountains like a starling bierd, after doing a long dance untidled to Cloudy Green, deposend his bockstump on the waityoumaywantme, after having blew some quaker's (for you! Oates!) in through the houseking's keyhole to attract attention, bleated through the gale outside which the tairor of his clothes was hogcallering, first, be the hirsuiter, that he would break his bulsheywigger's head for him, next, be the heeltapper, that he would break the gage over his lankyduckling head the same way he would crack a nut with a monkeywrench and, last of all, be the stirabouter, that he would give him his (or theumperom's or anybloody else's) thickerthanwater to drink and his bleday steppebrodhar's into the bucket. He demanded more wood alcohol to pitch in with, alleging that his granfather's was all taxis and that it was only after ten o'connell, and this his isbar was a public oven for the sake of irsk irskusky, and then, not easily discouraged, opened the wrathfloods of his atillarery and went on at a wicked rate, weathering against him in mooxed metaphores from eleven thirty to two in the afternoon without even a luncheonette interval for House, son of Clod, to come out, you jewbeggar, to be Executed Amen. Earwicker, that patternmind, that paradigmatic ear, receptoretentive as his of Dionysius, longsuffering although whitening under restraint in the sititout corner of his conservatory, behind faminebuilt walls, his thermos flask and ripidian flabel by his side and a walrus whiskerbristle for a tusk-pick, compiled, while he mourned the flight of his wild guineese, a long list (now feared in part lost) to be kept on file of all abusive names he was called (we have been compelled for the rejoicement of foinne loidies ind the humours of Milltown etcetera by Josephine Brewster in the collision known as Contrastations with Inkermann and so on and sononward, lacies in loo water, flee, celestials, one clean turv): *Firstnighter, Informer, Old Fruit, Yellow Whigger, Wheatears, Goldy Geit, Bogside Beauty, Yass We've Had His Badannas, York's Porker, Funnyface, At Baggotty's Bend He Bumped, Grease with the Butter, Opendoor Ospices, Cainandabler, Ireland's Eighth Wonderful Wonder, Beat My Price, Godsoilman, Moonface the Murderer, Hoary Hairy Hoax, Midnight Sunburst, Remove that Bible, Hebdromadary Publocation, Tummer the Lame the Tyrannous, Blau Clay, Tight before Teatime, Read Your Pantojoke, Acoustic Disturbance, Thinks He's Gobblasst the Good Dook of Ourguile, W.D.'s Grace, Gibbering Bayamouth of Dublin, His Farther was a Mundzucker and She had him in a Growler, Burnham and Bailey, Artist, Unworthy of the Homely Protestant Religion, Terry Cotter, You're Welcome to Waterfood, signed the Ribbonmen, Lobsterpot Lardling, All for Arthur of this Town, Hooshed the Cat from the Bacon, Leathertogs Donald, The Ace and Deuce of Paupering, O'Reilly's Delights to Kiss the Man behind the Borrel, Magogagog, Swad Puddlefoot, Gouty Ghibeline, Loose Luther, Hatches Cocks' Eggs, Muddle the Plan, Luck before Wedlock, I Divorce Thee Husband, Tanner and a Make, Go to Hellena or Come to Connies, Piobald Puffpuff His Bride, Purged out of Burke's, He's None of Me Causin, Barebarean, Peculiar Person, Grunt Owl's Facktotem, Twelve Months Aristocrat, Lycanthrope, Flunkey Beadle Vamps the Tune Letting on He's Loney, Thunder and Turf Married into Clandorf, Left Boot Sent on Approval, Cumberer of Lord's Holy Ground, Stodge Arschmann, Awnt Yuke, Tommy Furlong's Pet Plagues, Archdukon Cabbanger, Last Past the Post, Kennealey Won't Tell Thee off Nancy's Gown,*

Scuttle to Cover, Salary Grab, Andy Mac Noon in Annie's Room, Awl Out, Twitchbratschballs, Bombard Street Bester, Sublime Porter, A Ban for Le King of the Burgaans and a Bom for Ye Sur of all the Ruttledges, O'Phelim's Cutprice, And at Number Wan Wan Wan, What He Done to Castlecostello, Sleeps with Feathers end Ropes, It is Known who Sold Horace the Rattler, Enclosed find the Sons of Fingal, Swayed in his Falling, Wants a Wife and Forty of Them, Let Him Do the Fair, Apeegeequanee Chimmuck, Plowp Goes his Whastle, Ruin of the Small Trader, He — — Milkinghoneybeaverbrooker, Vee was a Vindner, Sower Rapes, Armenian Atrocity, Sickfish Bellyup, Edomite, — 'Man Devoyd of the Commoner Characteristics of an Irish Nature, Bad Humborg, Hraabhraab, Coocoohandler, Dirt, Miching Daddy, Born Burst Feet Foremost, Woolworth's Worst, Easyathic Phallusaphist, Guiltey-pig's Bastard, Fast in the Barrel, Boose in the Bed, Mister Fatmate, In Custody of the Polis, Boawwll's Alocutionist, Deposed, but anarchistically respectsful of the liberties of the noninvasive individual, did not respond a solitary wedgeword beyond such sedentarity, though it was as easy as kissanywhere for the passive resistant in the booth he was in to reach for the hello gripes and ring up Kimmage Outer 17.67, because, as the fundamentalist explained, when at last shocked into speech, touchin his woundid feelins in the fuchsiar the dominican mission for the sowsealist potty was on at the time and he thought the rowmish devowtion known as the howly rowsary might reeform ihm, Gonn. That more than considerably unpleasant bullocky before he rang off drunkishly pegged a few glatt stones, all of a size, by way of final mocks for his grapes, at the wicket in support of his words that he was not guilphy but, after he had so slaunga vollayed, reconnoitring through his semisubconscious the seriousness of what he might have done had he really polished off his terrible intentions finally caused him to change the bawling and leave downg the whole grumus of brookpebbles pangpung and, having sobered up a bit, paces his groundould diablen lionndub, the flay the flegm, the floedy fleshener, (purse, purse, pursyfurse, I'll splish the splume of them all!) this backblocks boor bruskly put out his langwedge and quite quit the paleologic scene, telling how by his selfdenying ordnance he had left Hyland on the dissenting table, after exhorting Earwicker or, in slightly modified phraseology, Messrs or Missrs Earwicker, Seir, his feminisible name of multitude, to cocoa come outside to Mockerloo out of that for the honour of Crumlin, with his broody old flishguds, Gog's curse to thim, so as he could brianslog and burst him all dizzy, you go bail, like Potts Fracture did with Keddle Flatnose and nobodyatall with Wholyphamous and build rocks over him, or if he didn't, for two and thirty straws, be Cacao Campbell, he didn't know what he wouldn't do for him nor nobody else nomore nor him after which, batell martell, a brisha a milla a stroka a boola, so the rage of Malbruk, playing on the least change of his manjester's voice, the first heroic couplet from the fuguall tropical, Opus Elf, Thortytoe: *My schemes into obeyance for This time has had to fall:* they bit goodbyte to their thumb and, his bandol eer his solgier, dripdropdrap on pool or poldier, wishing the loff a falladelfian in the morning, proceeded with a Hubbleforth slouch in his slips backwords (*Et Cur Heli!*) in the directions of the duff and demb institutions about ten or eleven hundred years lurch away in the moonshiny gorge of Patself on the Bach. Adyoe!

And thus, with this rochelly exetur of Bully Acre, came to close that last stage in the siegings round our archicitadel which we would like to recall, if old Nestor Alexis would wink the worth for us, as Bar-le-Duc and Dog-an-Doras and Bangen-op-Zoom.

Yed he med leave to many a door beside of Oxmanswold for so witness his chambered cairns a cloudletlitter silent that are at browse up hill and down coombe and on eolithostroton, at Howth or at Coolock or even at Enniskerry, a theory none too rectiline of the evoluation of human society and a testament of the rocks from all the dead unto some the living. Olivers lambs we do call them, skatterlings of a stone, and they shall be gathered unto him, their herd and paladin, as nubilettes to cumule, in that day hwen, same the lightning lancer of Azava Arthur-honoured (some Finn, some Finn avant!), he skall wake from earthsleep, haught crested elmer, in his valle of briers of Greenman's Rise O, (lost leaders live! the heroes return!) and o'er dun and dale the Wulverulverlord (protect us!) his mighty horn skall roll, orland, roll.

For in those deyes his Deyus shall ask of Allprohome and call to himm: Allprohome! And he make answer: Add some. Nor wink nor wunk. *Animadiabolum, mene credidisti mortuum?* Silence was in thy faustive halls, O Truiga, when thy green woods went dry but there will be sounds of manymirth on the night's ear ringing when our pantriarch of Comestowntonobble gets the pullover on his boots.

Liverpoor? Sot a bit of it! His braynes coolt parritch, his pelt nassy, his heart's adrone, his bluidstreams acrawl, his puff but a piff, his extremeties extremely so: Fengless, Pawmbroke, Chilblaimend and Baldowl. Humph is in his doge. Words weigh no no more to him than raindrips to Rethfernhim. Which we all like. Rain. When we sleep. Drops. But wait until our sleeping. Drain. Sdops.

As the lion in our teargarten remembers the nenuphars of his Nile (shall Ariuz forget Arioun or Boghas the baregams of the Marmarazalles from Marmeniere?) it may be, tots wearsense full a naggin in twentyg have sigilposted what in our brievingbust, the besieged bedreamt him stil and solely of those lililiths undeveiled which had undone him, gone for age, and knew not the watchful treachers at his wake, and theirs to stay. Fooi, fooi, chamermissies! Zeepyzoepy, larcenlads! Zijnzijn Zijnzijn! It may be, we moest ons hasten selves te declareer it, that he reglimmed? presaw? the fields of heat and yields of wheat where corngold Ysit? shamed and shone. It may be, we habben to upseek a bitty door our good township's courants want we knew't, that with his deepseeing insight (had not wishing oftebeen but good time wasted), within his patriarchal shamanah, broadsteyne 'bove citie (Twillby! Twillby!) he conscious of enemies, a kingbilly whitehorsed in a Finglas mill, prayed, as he sat on anxious seat, (kunt ye neat gift mey toe bout a peer saft eyballds!) during that three and a hellof hours' agony of silence, *ex profundis malorum*, and bred with unfeigned charity that his wordwounder (an engles to the teeth who, nomened Nash of Girahash, would go anyold where in the weeping world on his mottled belly (the rab, the kreeponskneed!) for milk, music or married missusses) might, mercy to providential benevolence's who hates prudencies' astuteness, unfold into the first of a distinguished dynasty of his posteriors, blackfaced connemaras not of the fold but elder children of his household, his most besetting of ideas (*pace* his twolve predamanant passions) being the formation, as in more favoured climes, where the Meadow of Honey is guestfriendly and the Mountain of Joy receives, of a truly criminal stratum, Ham's cribcracking yeggs, thereby at last eliminating from all classes and masses with directly derivative decasualisation: *sigarius* (sic!) *vindicat urbes terrorum* (sicker!): and so, to mark a bank taal she arter, the obedience of the citizens elp the ealth of the ole.

Now gode. Let us leave theories there and return to here's here. Now hear. 'Tis gode again. The teak coffin, Pughglasspanelfitted, feets to the east, was to turn in later, and pitly patly near the porpus, materially effecting the cause. And this, liever, is the thinghowe. Any number of conservative public bodies, through a number of select and other committees having power to add to their number, before voting themselves and himself, town, port and garrison, by a fit and proper resolution, following a koorts order of the groundwet, once for all out of plotty existence, as a forescut, so you maateskippey might to you cuttinrunner on a neuw pack of klerds, made him, while his body still persisted, their present of a protem grave in Moyelta of the best Lough Neagh pattern, then as much in demand among misonesans as the Isle of Man today among limniphobes. Wacht even! It was in a fairly fishy kettlekerry, after the Fianna's foreman had taken his handful, enriched with ancient woods and dear dutchy deeplinns mid which were an old knoll and a troutbeck, vainyvain of her osiery and a chatty sally with any Wilt or Walt who would ongle her as Izaak did to the tickle of his rod and watch her waters of her sillying waters of and there now brown peater arripple (may their quilt gild lightly over his somnolulutent form!) Whoforyou lies his last, by the wrath of Bog, like the erst curst Hun in the bed of his treubleu Donawhu.

Best. This wastohavebeen underground heaven, or mole's paradise which was probably also an inversion of a phallopharos, intended to foster wheat crops and to ginger up tourist trade (its architecht, Mgr Peurelachasse, having been obcaecated lest he should petrifake suchanevver while the contractors Messrs T. A. Birkett and L. O. Tuohalls were made invulnerably venerable) first in the west, our misterbilder, Castlevillainous, openly damned and blasted by means of a hydromine, system, Sowan and Belting, exploded from a reinvented T.N.T. bombingpost up ahoy of eleven and thirty wingrests (*circiter*) to sternbooard out of his aerial thorpeto, Auton Dynamon, contacted with the expectant minefield by tins of improved ammonia lashed to her shieldplated gunwale, and fused into tripupcables, slipping through tholse and playing down from the conning tower into the ground battery fuseboxes, all differing as clocks from keys since nobody appeared to have the same time of beard, some saying by their Oorlog it was Sygstryggs to nine, more holding with the Ryan vogt it was Dane to pfife. He afterwards whaanever his blaetther began to fail off him and his rough bark was wholly husky and, stoop by stoop, he neared it (wouldmanspare!) carefully lined the ferroconcrete result with rotproof bricks and mortar, fassed to fossed, and retired beneath the heptarchy of his towerettes, the beauchamp, byward, bull and lion, the white, the wardrobe and bloodied, so encouraging (insteppen, alls als hats beliefd!) additional useful councils public with hoofd offdealings which were welholden of ladykants te huur out such as the Breeders' Union, the Guild of Merchants of the Staple *et*, a.u.c. to present unto him with funebral pomp, over and above that, a stone slab with the usual Mac Pelah address of velediction, a very fairworded instance of falsemeaning adamelegy: We have done ours gohellt with you, Heer Herewhippit, overgiven it, skidoo!

But t'house and allaboardshoops! Show coffins, winding sheets, goodbuy bierchepes, cinerary urns, liealoud blasses, snuffchests, poteentubbs, lacrimal vases, hoodendoses, reekwaterbeckers, breakmiddles, zootzaks for eatlust, including upyourhealthing rookworst and meathewersoftened forkenpootsies and for that matter, javel also, any kind of inhumationary bric au brac for the adornment of his glasstone honophreum, would, met these trein of konditiens, naturally follow, halas, in the ordinary course, enabling that roundtheworlder wandelingswight, did suches pass him, to live all safeathomely the presenile days of his life of opulence, ancient ere decrepitude, late lents last lenience, till stuffering stage, whaling away the whole of the while (*hypnos chilia eonion!*) lethelulled between explosion and reexplosion (Donnaurwatteur! Hunderthunder!) from grosskopp to megapod, embalmed, of grand age, rich in death anticipated.

But abide Zeit's sumonserving, rise afterfall. Blueblitzbolted from there, knowing the hingeworms of the hallmirks of habitationlesness, buried burrowing in Gehinnon, to proliferate through all his Unterwealth, seam by seam, sheol om sheol, and revisit our Uppercrust Sideria of Utilitarios, the divine one, the hoarder hidden propaguting his plutorpopular progeniem of pots and pans and pokers and puns from biddenland to boughtenland, the spearway fore the spoorway.

Lying in prison, listening to the abuse of the visiting American, HCE must have thought a great deal about the treachery that put him there, and particularly the two girls—symbols of his guilt—who fuse into the image of Iseult at her mirror (really Isobel, his real-life daughter). But the time came for putting him into a coffin and thrusting him down into a watery grave (under Lough and Neagh, so to speak). HCE, however, was not like Finnegan: he would not lie down for long. "Abide time's summons-serving, the rise after the fall". Soon his buried energy began to thrust up to the surface, manifesting itself in fights and quarrels, the snarling division exemplified best in the mutual hatred of his twin sons. The hero himself was not seen and was thought to be "like the salmon of his ladderleap all this time of totality secretly and by suckage feeding on his own misplaced fat".

Kate Strong, a widow (in waking life the old cleaning-woman of the pub), told tales of the grand old days when he was alive. Stories of the Fall in Phoenix Park were recounted, and the guilt of the father seemed to attach to one of the sons—Shaun, who appeared in court under the name of Festy King. His brother, Shem, offered evidence against him, but the Four Old Men, as judges, pronounced a verdict of *Nolans Brumans*— a dream-reference to the doctrine of Bruno the Nolan that opposites derived from a common source are eventually reconciled. The two brothers cancel each other out in the great white light of the father. Shem stank of drink, and the twenty-eight calendar-girls (in court as advocatresses) cried "Shun the Punman"! (Shem the Penman, the disregarded artist-brother).

But how about the father, long-gone HCE? The four judges reminisced in chambers about the old days of his sin. But soon the news began to spread abroad that HCE was at large again, a fox that had left his lair and was wandering abroad, cunning, not to be hunted down. HCE appears as Parnell ("the spoil of hesitants, the spell of hesitency") who, so many Irishmen believed, was not really dead and would come again (one of his pseudonyms was "Fox".)

Finally, though, it was ALP, the wife or widow of the great sinner, whom the women wanted to hear about. We end the chapter with a hymn in her praise, restorer of her dead lord's good name, eternal woman-river.

But the spoil of hesitants, the spell of hesitency. His atake is it ashe, tittery taw tatterytail, hasitense humponadimply, heyhey-heyhey a winceywencky.

Assembly men murmured. Reynard is slow!

One feared for his days. Did there yawn? 'Twas his stom-mick. Eruct? The libber. A gush? From his visuals. Pung? De-livver him, orelode! He had laid violent hands on himself, it was brought in Fugger's Newsletter, lain down, all in, fagged out, with equally melancholy death. For the triduum of Saturnalia his goatservant had paraded hiz willingsons in the Forum while the jenny infanted the lass to be greeted raucously (the Yardstat-ed) with houx and epheus and measured with missiles too from a hundred of manhood and a wimmering of weibes. Big went the bang: then wildewide was quiet: a report: silence: last Fama put it under ether. The noase or the loal had dreven him blem, blem, stun blem. Sparks flew. He had fled again (open shunshema!) this country of exile, sloughed off, sidleshomed *via* the subterranean shored with bedboards, stowed away and ankered in a dutch bottom tank the Arsa, *hod* S.S. Finlandia, and was even now occupying, under an islamitic newhame in his seventh generation, a physical body Cornelius Magrath's (badoldkarakter, commonorrong canbung) in Asia Major, where as Turk of the theater (first house all flatty: the king, eleven sharps) he had bepiastered the buikdanseuses from the opulence of his omnibox while as arab at the streetdoor he bepestered the bumbashaws for the alms of a para's pence. Wires hummed. Peacefully general astonishment assisted by regrettitude had put a term till his existence: he saw the family saggarth, resigned, put off his remainders, was recalled and scrapheaped by the Maker. Chirpings crossed. An infamous private ailment (vulgovarioveneral) had claimed endright, closed his vicious circle, snap. Jams jarred. He had walked towards the middle of an ornamental lilypond when innebriated up to the point where braced shirts meet knickerbockers, as wangfish daring the buoyant waters, when rodmen's firstaiding hands had rescued un from very possibly several feel of demifrish water. Mush spread. On Umbrella Street where he did drinks from a pumps a kind of workman, Mr Whitlock, gave him a piece of wood. What words of power were made fas between them, ekenames and auchnomes, *acnomina ecnumina?* That, O that, did Hansard tell us, would gar ganz Dub's ear wag in every pub of all the citta! Batty believes a baton while Hogan hears a hod yet Heer prefers a punsil shapner and Cope and Bull go cup and ball. And the Cassidy — Craddock rome and reme round e'er a wiege ne'er a waage is still immer and immor awagering over it, a cradle with a care in it or a casket with a kick behind. Toties testies quoties questies. The war is in words and the wood is the world. Maply me, willowy we, hickory he and yew yourselves. Howforhim chirrupeth evereachbird! From golddawn glory to glowworm gleam. We were lowquacks did we not tacit turn. Elsewere there here no concern of the Guinnesses. But only the ruining of the rain has heard. *Estout pourporteral!* Cracklings cricked. A human pest cycling (pist!) and recycling (past!) about the sledgy streets, here he was (pust!) again! Morse nuisance noised. He was loose at large and (Oh baby!) might be anywhere when a disguised exnun, of huge standbuild and masculine manners in her fairly fat forties, Carpulenta Gygasta, hattracted hattention by harbitrary conduct with a homnibus. Aerials buzzed to coastal listeners of an oertax bror collector's budget, fullybigs, sporran, tie, tuft, tabard and bloody antichill cloak, its tailor's (Baernfather's) tab reading V.P.H., found nigh Scaldbrothar's Hole, and divers shivered to think what kaind of beast, wolves, croppis's or fourpenny friars, had devoured him. C. W. cast wide. Hvidfinns lyk, drohneth svertgleam, Valkir lockt. On his pinksir's postern, the boys had it, at Whitweekend had been nailed an inkedup name and title, inscribed in the national cursives, accelerated, regressive, filiform, turreted and envenomoloped in piggotry: Move up. Mumpty! Mike room for Rumpty! By order, Nickekellous Plugg; and this go, no pentecostal jest about it, how gregarious his race soever or skilful learned wise cunning knowledgable clear profound his saying fortitudo fraught or prudentiaproven, were he chief, count, general, fieldmarshal, prince, king or Myles the Slasher in his person, with a moliamordhar mansion in the Breffnian empire and a place of inauguration on the hill of Tullymongan, there had been real murder, of the rayheallach royghal raxacraxian variety, the MacMahon chaps, it was, that had done him in. On the fidd of Verdor the rampart combatants had left him lion with his dexter handcoup wresterected in a pureede paumee bloody proper. Indeed not a few thick and thin wellwishers, mostly of the clontarfminded class, (Colonel John Bawle O'Roarke, fervxamplus), even ventured so far as to loan or beg copies of D. Blayncy's trilingual triweekly, Scatterbrains' Aftening Posht, so as to make certain sure onetime and be satisfied of their quasicontribusodalitarian's having become genuinely quite beetly dead whether by land whither by water. Transocean atalaclamoured him; The latter! The latter! Shall their hope then be silent or Macfarlane lack of lamentation? He lay under leagues of it in deep Bartholoman's Deep.

Achdung! Pozor! Attenshune! Vikeroy Besights Smucky Yung Pigeschoolies. Tri Paisdinernes Eventyr Med Lochlanner Fathach I Fiounnisgehaven. Bannalanna Bangs Ballyhooly Out Of Her Buddaree Of A Bullavogue.

But, their bright little contemporaries notwithstanding, on the morrowing morn of the suicidal murder of the unrescued expatriate, aslike as asnake comes sliduant down that oaktree onto the duke of beavers, (you may have seen some liquidamber exude exotic from a balsam poplar at Parteen-a-lax Limestone. Road and cried Abies Magnifica! not, noble fir?) a quarter of nine, imploring his resipiency, saw the infallible spike of smoke's jutstiff punctual from the seventh gable of our Quintus Centimachus' porphyroid buttertower and then thirsty p.m. with oaths upon his lastingness (*En caecos harauspices! Annos longos patimur!*) the lamps of maintenance, beaconsfarafield innerhalf the zuggurat, all brevetnamed, the wasting wyvern, the tawny of his mane, the swinglowswaying bluepaw, the outstanding man, the lolllike lady, being litten for the long (O land, how long!) lifesnight, with suffusion of fineglass transom and leadlight panes.

Wherefore let it hardly by any being thinking be said either or thought that the prisoner of that sacred edifice, were he an Ivor the Boneless or an Olaf the Hide, was at his best a onestone parable, a rude breathing on the void of to be, a venter hearing his own bauchspeech in backwords, or, more strictly, but tristurned initials, the cluekey to a worldroom beyond the roomwhorld, for scarce one, or pathetically few of his dode canal sammenlivers cared seriously or for long to doubt with Kurt Iuld van Dijke (the gravitational pull perceived by certain fixed residents and the capture of uncertain comets chancedrifting through our system suggesting an authenticitatem of his aliquitudinis) the canonicity of his existence as a tesseract. Be still, O quick! Speak him dumb! Hush ye fronds of Ulma!

Dispersal women wondered. Was she fast?

Do tell us all about. As we want to hear allabout. So tellus tellas allabouter. The why or whether she looked alottylike like ussies and whether he had his wimdop like themses shut? Notes and queries, tipbids and answers, the laugh and the shout, the ards and downs. Now listed to one aneither and liss them down and smoothen out your leaves of rose. The war is o'er. Wimwim wimwim! Was it Unity Moore or Estella Swifte or Varina Fay or Quarta Quaedam? Toemaas, mark oom for yor ounckel! Pigeys, hold op med yer leg! Who, but who (for second time of asking) was then the scourge of the parts about folkrich Lucalizod it was wont to be asked, as, in ages behind of the Homo Capite Erectus, what price Peabody's money, or, to put it bluntly, whence is the herringtons' white cravat, as, in epochs more cainozoic, who struck Buckley though nowadays as thentimes every schoolfilly of sevenscore moons or more who knows her intimologies and every colleen bawl aroof and every redflammelwaving warwife and widowpeace upon Dublin Wall for ever knows as yayas is yayas how it was Buckleyself (we need no blooding paper to tell it neither) who struck and the Russian generals, da! da!, instead of Buckley who was caddishly struck by him when be herselves. What fullpried paulpoison in the spy of three castles or which hatefilled smileyseller? And that such a vetriol of venom, that queen's head affranchisant, a quiet stinkingplaster zeal could cover, prepostered or postpaid! The loungelizards of the pumproom had their nine days' jeer, and pratschkats at their platschpails too and holenpolendom beside, Szpaszpas Szpissmas, the zhanyzhonies, when, still believing in her owenglass, when izarres were twinklins, that the upper reaches of her mouthless face and her impermanent waves were the better half of her, one nearer him, dearer than all, first warming creature of his early morn, bondwoman of the man of the house, and murrmurr of all the mackavicks, she who had given his eye for her bed and a tooth for a child till one one and one ten and one hundred again, O me and O ye! cadet and prim, the hungray and anngreen (and if she is older now than her teeth she has hair that is younger than thighne, my dear!) she who shuttered him after his fall and waked him widowt sparing and gave him keen and made him able and held adazillahs to each arche of his noes, she who will not rast her from her running to seek him till, with the help of the okeamic, some such time that she shall have been after hiding the crumbends of his enormousness in the areyou lookingfor Pearlfar sea, (ur, uri, uria!) stood forth, burnzburn the gorggony old danworld, in gogor's name, for gagar's sake, dragging the countryside in her train, finickin here and funickin there, with her louisequean's brogues and her culunder buzzle and her little bolero boa and all and two times twenty curlicornies for her headdress, specks on her eyeux, and spudds on horeilles and a circusfix riding her Parisienne's cockneze, a vaunt her straddle from Equerry Egon, when Tinktink in the churchclose clinked Steploajazzyma Sunday, *Sola*, with pawns, prelates and pookas pelotting in her piecebag, for Handiman the Chomp, Esquoro, biskbask, to crush the slander's head.

Wery weeny wight, plead for Morandmor! *Notre Dame de la Ville*, mercy of thy balmheartzyheat! Ogrowdnyk's beyond herbata tay, wort of the drogist. Bulk him no bulkis. And let him rest, thou wayfarre, and take no gravespoil from him! Neither mar his mound! The bane of Tut is on it. Ware! But there's a little lady waiting and her name is A.L.P. And you'll agree. She must be she. For her holden heirheaps hanging down her back. He spenth his strenth amok haremscarems. Poppy Narancy, Giallia, Chlora, Marinka, Anileen, Parme. And ilk a those dames had her rainbow huemoures yet for whilko her whims but he coined a cure. Tifftiff today, kissykissy tonay and agelong pine tomauranna. Then who but Crippled-with-Children would speak up for Dropping-with-Sweat?

Sold him her lease of nineninineninetee,
Tresses undresses so dyedyedaintee,
Goo, the groot gudgeon, gulped it all.
Hoo was the C. O. D.?

Bum!

At Island Bridge she met her tide.
Attabom, attabom, attabombomboom!
The Fin had a flux and his Ebba a ride.
Attabom, attabom, attabombomboom!
We're all up to the years in hues and cribies.
That's what she's done for wee!
Woe!

Nomad may roam with Nabuch but let naaman laugh at Jordan! For we, we have taken our sheet upon her stones where we have hanged our hearts in her trees; and we list, as she bibs us, by the waters of babalong.

In the name of Annah the Allmaziful, the Everliving, the Bringer of Plurabilities, haloed be her eve, her singtime sung, her rill be run, unhemmed as it is uneven!

Her untitled mamafesta memorialising the Mosthighest has gone by many names at disjointed times. Thus we hear of, *The Augusta Angustissimost for Old Seabeastius' Salvation, Rockabill Booby in the Wave Trough, Here's to the Relicts of All Decencies, Anna Stessa's Rise to Notice, Knickle Down Duddy Gunne and Arishe Sir Cannon, My Golden One and My Selver Wedding, Amoury Treestam and Icy Siseule, Saith a Sawyer til a Strame, Ik dik dopedope et tu mihimihi, Buy Birthplate for a Bite, Which of your Hesterdays Mean Ye to Morra? Hoebegunne the Hebrewer Hit Waterman the Brayned, Arcs in His Ceiling Flee Chinx on the Flur, Rebus de Hibernicis, The Crazier Letters, Groans of a Britoness, Peter Peopler Picked a Plot to Pitch his Poppolin, An Apology for a Big* (some such nonoun *as Husband* or *husboat* or *hosebound* is probably understood for we have also the plutherplethoric *My Hoonsbood Hansbaad's a Journey to Porthergill gone and He Never Has the Hour*), *Ought We To Visit Him? For Ark see Zoo, Cleopater's Nedlework Ficturing Aldborougham on the Sahara with the Coombing of the Cammmels and the Parlourmaids of Aegypt, Cock in the Pot for Father, Placeat Vestrae, A New Cure for an Old Clap, Where Portentos they'd Grow Gonder how I'd Wish I Woose a Geese; Gettle Nettie, Thrust him not, When the*

Myrtles of Venice Played to Bloccus's Line, To Plenge Me High He Waives Chiltern on Friends, Oremunds Queue Visits Amen Mart, E'en Tho' I Granny a-be He would Fain Me Cuddle, Twenty of Chambers, Weighty Ten Beds and a Wan Ceteroom, I Led the Life, Through the Boxer Coxer Rising in the House with the Golden Stairs, The Following Fork, He's my O'Jerusalem and I'm his Po, The Best in the West, By the Stream of Zemzem under Zigzag Hill, The Man That Made His Mother in the Marlborry Train, Try Our Taal on a Taub, The Log of Anny to the Base All, Nopper Tipped a Nappiwenk to his Notylytl Dantsigirls, Prszss Orel Orel the King of Orlbrdsz, Intimier Minnelisp of an Extorreor Monolothe, Drink to Him, My Juckey, and Dhoult Bemine Thy Winnowing Sheet, I Ask You to Believe I was his Mistress, He Can Explain, From Victrolia Nuancee to Allbart Noahnsy, Da's a Daisy so Guimea your Handsel too, What Barbaras Done to a Barrel Organ Before the Rank, Tank and Bonnbtail, Huskvy Admortal, What Jumbo made to Jalice and what Anisette to Him, Ophelia's Culpreints, Hear Hubty Hublin, My Old Dansh, I am Older northe Rogues among Whisht I Slips and He Calls Me his Dual of Ayessha, Suppotes a Ventriliquorst Merries a Corpse, Lapps for Finns This Funnycoon's Week, How the Buckling Shut at Rush in January, Look to the Lady, From the Rise of the Dudge Pupublick to the Fall of the Potstille, Of the Two Ways of Opening the Mouth, I have not Stopped Water Where It Should Flow and I Know the Twentynine Names of Attraente, The Tortor of Tory Island Traits Galasia like his Milchcow, From Abbeygate to Crowalley Through a Lift in the Lude, Smocks for Their Graces and Me Aunt for Them Clodshoppers, How to Pull a Good Horuscoup even when Oldsire is Dead to the World, Inn the Gleam of Waherlow, Fathe He's Sukceded to My Esperations, Thee Steps Forward, Two Stops Back, My Skin Appeals to Three Senses and My Curly Lips Demand Columbkisses; Gage Street on a Crany's Savings, Them Lads made a Trion of Battlewatschers and They Totties a Doeit of Deers, In My Lord's Bed by One Whore Went Through It, Mum It is All Over, Cowpoyride by Twelve Acre Terriss in the Unique Estates of Amessican, He Gave me a Thou so I serve Him with Thee, Of all the Wide Torsos in all the Wild Glen, O'Donogh, White Donogh, He's Hue to Me Cry, I'm the Stitch in his Baskside You'd be Nought Without Mom, To Keep the Huskies off the Hustings and Picture Pets from Lifting Shops, Norsker Torsker Find the Poddle, He Perssed Me Here with the Ardour of a Tonnoburkes, A Boob Was Weeping This Mower was Reaping, O'Loughlin, Up from the Pit of my Stomach I Swish you the White of the Mourning, Inglo-Andean Medoleys from Tommany Moohr, The Great Polynesional Entertrainer Exhibits Ballantine Brautchers with the Link of Natures, The Mimic of Meg Neg and the Mackeys, Entered as the Lastest Pigtarial and My Pooridiocal at Stitchioner's Hall, Siegfield Follies and or a Gentlehomme's Faut Pas, See the First Book of Jealesies Pessim, The Suspended Sentence, A Pretty Brick Story for Childsize Heroes, As Lo Our Sleep, I Knew I'd Got it in Me so Thit settles That, Thonderbalt Captain Smeth and La Belle Sauvage Pocahonteuse, Way for Wet Week Welikin's Douchka Marianne, The Last of the Fingallians, It Was Me Egged Him on to the Stork Exchange and Lent my Dutiful Face to His Customs, Chee Chee Cheels on their China Miction, Pickedmeup Peters, Lumptytumtumpty had a Big Fall, Pimpimp Pimpimp, Measly Ventures of Two Lice and the Fall of Fruit, The Fokes Family Interior, If my Spreadeagles Wasn't so Tight I'd Loosen my Cursits on that Bunch of Maggiestraps, Allolosha Popofetts and Howke Cotchme Eye, Seen Aples and Thin Dyed, i big U to Beleaves from Love and Mother, Fine's Fault was no Felon, Exat Delvin Renter Life, The Flash that Flies from Vuggy's Eyes has Set Me Hair On Fire, His is the House that Malt Made, Divine Views from Back to the Front, Abe to Sare Stood Icyk Neuter till Brahm Taulked Him Common Sex, A Nibble at Eve Will That Bowal Relieve, Allfor Guineas, Sounds and Compliments Libidous, Seven Wives Awake Aweek, Airy Ann and Berber Blut, Amy Licks Porter While Huffy Chops Eads, Abbrace of Umbellas or a Tripple of Caines, Buttbutterbust, From the Manorlord Hoved to the Misses O'Mollies and from the Dames to their Sames, Manyfestoons for the Colleagues on the Green, An Outstanding Back and an Excellent Halfcentre if Called on, As Tree is Quick and Stone is

White So is My Washing Done by Night, First and Last Only True Account all about the Honorary Mirsu Earwicker, L.S.D., and the Snake (Nuggets!) by a Woman of the World who only can Tell Naked Truths about a Dear Man and all his Conspirators how they all Tried to Fall him Putting it all around Lucalizod about Privates Earwicker and a Pair of Sloppy Sluts plainly Showing all the Unmentionability falsely Accusing about the Raincoats.

The above are some of the titles that have been given to ALP's letter, that great manifesto or "mamafesta memorialising the Most-highest". A professorial account of it now follows: "There was a time when naif alphabetters would have written it down the tracing of a purely deliquescent recidivist, possibly ambidextrous, snubnosed probably and presenting a strangely profound rainbowl in his (or her) occiput"—and so on. But how did the scholars manage to get hold of the letter? It seems that a hen scratched it up out of a midden-heap.

About that original hen. Midwinter (fruur or kuur?) was in the offing and Premver a promise of a pril when, as kischabrigies sang life's old sahatsong, an iceclad shiverer, merest of bantlings observed a cold fowl behaviourising strangely on that fatal midden or chip factory or comicalbottomed copsjute (dump for short) afterwards changed into the orangery when in the course of deeper demolition unexpectedly one bushman's holiday its limon threw up a few spontaneous fragments of orangepeel, the last remains of an outdoor meal by some unknown sunseeker or placehider *illico* way back in his mistridden past. What child of a strandlooper but keepy little Kevin in the despondful surrounding of such sneezing cold would ever have trouved up on a strate that was called strete a motive for future saintity by euchring the finding of the Ardagh chalice by another heily innocent and beachwalker whilst trying with pious clamour to wheedle Tipperaw raw raw reeraw puteters out of Now Sealand in spignt of the patchpurple of the massacre, a dual a duel to die to day, goddam and biggod, sticks and stanks, of most of the Jacobiters.

The bird in the case was Belinda of the Dorans, a more than quinquegintarian (Terziis prize with Serni medal, Cheepalizzy's Hane Exposition) and what she was scratching at the hour of klokking twelve looked for all this zogzag world like a goodish-sized sheet of letterpaper originating by transhipt from Boston (Mass.) of the last of the first to Dear whom it proceeded to mention Maggy well & allathome's health well only the hate turned the mild on *the van* Houtens and the general's elections with a *lovely* face of some born gentleman with a beautiful present of wedding cakes for dear thankyou Chriesty and with grand funferall of poor Father Michael don't forget unto life's & Muggy well how are you Maggy & hopes soon to hear well & must now close it with fondest to the twoinns with four crosskisses for holy paul holey corner holipoli whollyisland pee ess from (locust may eat all but this sign shall they never) affectionate largelooking tache of tch. The stain, and that a teastain (the overcautelousness of the masterbilker here, as usual, signing the page away), marked it off on the spout of the moment as a genuine relique of ancient Irish pleasant pottery of that lydialike languishing class known as a hurry-me-o'er-the-hazy.

Why then how?

Well, almost any photoist worth his chemicots will tip anyone asking him the teaser that if a negative of a horse happens to melt enough while drying, well, what you do get is, well, a positively grotesquely distorted macromass of all sorts of horsehappy values and masses of meltwhile horse. Tip. Well, this freely is what must have occurred to our missive (there's a sod of a turb for you! please wisp off the grass!) unfilthed from the boucher by the sagacity of a lookmelittle likemelong hen. Heated residence in the heart of the orangeflavoured mudmound had partly obliterated the negative to start with, causing some features palpably nearer your pecker to be swollen up most grossly while the farther back we manage to wiggle the more we need the loan of a lens to see as much as the hen saw. Tip.

You is feeling like you was lost in the bush, boy? You says: It is a puling sample jungle of woods. You most shouts out: Bethicket me for a stump of a beech if I have the poultriest notions what the farest he all means. Gee up, girly! The quad gospellers may own the targum but any of the Zingari shoolerim may pick a peck of kindlings yet from the sack of auld hensyne.

Lead, kindly fowl! They always did: ask the ages. What bird has done yesterday man may do next year, be it fly, be it moult, be it hatch, be it agreement in the nest. For her socioscientific sense is sound as a bell, sir, her volucrine automutativeness right on normalcy: she knows, she just feels she was kind of born to lay and love eggs (trust her to propagate the species and hoosh her fluffballs safe through din and danger!); lastly but mostly, in her genesic field it is all game and no gammon; she is ladylike in everything she does and plays the gentleman's part every time. Let us auspice it! Yes, before all this has time to end the golden age must return with its vengeance. Man will become dirigible, Ague will be rejuvenated, woman with her ridiculous white burden will reach by one step sublime incubation, the manewanting human lioness with her dishorned discipular manram will lie down together publicly flank upon fleece. No, assuredly, they are not justified, those gloompourers who grouse that letters have never been quite their old selves again since that weird weekday in bleak Janiveer (yet how palmy date in a waste's oasis!) when to the shock of both, Biddy Doran looked at literature.

> It's a most complex document, a palimpsest, full of the names of people.

The unmistaken identity of the persons in the Tiberiast duplex came to light in the most devious of ways. The original document was in what is known as Hanno O'Nonhanno's unbrookable script, that is to say, it showed no signs of punctuation of any sort. Yet on holding the verso against a lit rush this new book of Morses responded most remarkably to the silent query of our world's oldest light and its recto let out the piquant fact that it was but pierced butnot punctured (in the university sense of the term) by numerous stabs and foliated gashes made by a pronged instrument. These paper wounds, four in type, were gradually and correctly understood to mean stop, please stop, do please stop, and O do please stop respectively, and following up their one true clue, the circumflexuous wall of a singleminded men's asylum, accentuated by bi tso fb rok engl a ssan dspl itch ina, — Yard inquiries pointed out ⟶ that they ad bîn "provoked" ay Λ fork, of à grave Brofèsor; àth é's Brèak — fast — table; ; acùtely profèšsionally *piquéd*, to=introdùce a notion of time [ùpon à plane (?) sù ' ' fàç'e'] by pùnct! ingh oles (sic) in iSpace?! Deeply religious by nature and position, and warmly attached to Thee, and smearbread and better and Him and newlaidills, it was rightly suspected that such ire could not have been visited by him Brotfressor Prenderguest even underwittingly, upon the ancestral pneuma of one whom, with rheuma, he venerated shamelessly at least once a week at Cockspur Common as his apple in his eye and her first boys' best friend and, though plain English for a married lady misled heaps by the way, yet when some peerer or peeress detected that the fourleaved shamrock or quadrifoil jab was more recurrent wherever the script was clear and the term terse and that these two were the selfsame spots naturally selected for her perforations by Dame Partlet on her dungheap, thinkers all put grown in waterungspillfull Pratiland only and a playful fowl and musical me and not you in any case, two and two together, and, with a swarm of bisses honeyhunting after, a sigh for shyme (O, the pettybonny rouge!) separated modest mouths. So be it. And it was. The lettermaking of the explots of Fjorgn Camhelsson when he was in the Kvinnes country with Soldru's men. With acknowledgment of our fervour of the first instant he remains years most fainfully. For postscrapt see spoils. Though not yet had the sailor sipped that sup nor the humphar foamed to the fill. And fox and geese still kept the peace around *L'Auberge du Père Adam*.

Small need after that, old Jeromesolem, old Huffsnuff, old Andycox, old Olecasandrum, for quizzing your weekenders come to the R.Q. with: shoots off in a hiss, muddles up in a mussmass and his whole's a dismantled noondrunkard's son. Howbeit we heard not a son of sons to leave by him to oceanic society in his old man without a thing in his ignorance, Tulko MacHooley. And it was thus he was at every time, that son, and the other time, the day was in it and after the morrow Diremood is the name is on the writing chap of the psalter, the juxtajunctor of a dearmate and he passing out of one desire into its fellow. The daughters are after going and loojing for him, Torba's nicelookers of the fair neck. Wanted for millinary servance to olderly's person by the Totty Askinses. Formelly confounded with amother. Maybe growing a moustache, did you say, with an adorable look of amuzement? And uses noclass billiardhalls with an upandown ladder? Not Hans the Curier though had he had have only had some little laughings and some less of cheeks and were he not so warried by his bulb of persecussion he could have, ay, and would have, as true as Essex bridge. And not Gopheph go gossip, I declare to man! Noe! To all's much relief one's half hypothesis of that jabberjaw ape amok the showering jestnuts of Bruisanose was hotly dropped and his room taken up by that odious and still today insufficiently malestimated notesnatcher (kak, pfooi, bosh and fiety, much earny, Gus, poteen? Sez you!) Shem the Penman.

So?

Who do you no tonigh, lazy and gentleman?

The echo is where in the back of the wodes; callhim forth!

(Shaun Mac Irewick, briefdragger, for the concern of Messrs Jhon Jhamieson and Song, rated one hundrick and thin per storehundred on this nightly quisquiquock of the twelve apostrophes, set by Jockit Mic Ereweak. He misunderstruck and aim for am ollo of number three of them and left his free natural ripostes to four of them in their own fine artful disorder.)

We're going to have a quiz, then, about the persons and places and things mentioned in ALP's manifesto. Shaun, prize quiz-kid, answers all the questions correctly, giving us a conspectus of everybody and everything of importance in the book—Finn MacCool, the mythical giant who contains both Finnegan and Earwicker; "Ann alive, the lisp of her"; the motto of Dublin—"Thine obesity, O civilian, hits the felicitude of our orb!"; the four Irish capitals—"Delfas, Dorhqk, Nublid, Dalway";

the handyman and cleaning-woman in HCE's pub; the twelve customers who are twelve good citizens but, because they've never really woken up to life, are called the "Morphios"; the book itself—"a collideorscape".

The last three questions and their answers must be pondered at some length. The answer to Question No. 10 is a rich monologue from Isobel, Iseult, the eternal temptress. It was she, in duplicate, who made Earwicker dream his fall. His guilt is the guilt of incestuous desire for a nubile daughter, the guilt Swift must have felt in loving the daughterlike Stella. (Isobel is fond of using Swift's "little language", particularly the endearment "ppt" or "pepette".)

Shaun is then asked, in the rhythm of Moore's "The Exile of Erin", his feelings about his brother Shem. Shaun replies in a long lecture (he is now called Jones) which contains the fable of "The Mookse and the Gripes". The Mookse is Pope Adrian IV and King Henry II combined. Adrian, with his bull *Laudabiliter,* blessed Henry's conquest of Ireland, which brought the Irish Church under the rule of Rome. The Gripes is Lawrence O'Toole, bishop of Dublin at the time of the English conquest. The fable presents the fundamental theme of division and hatred within a family, as does a later parable (not given here) about the rivalry of Burrus and Caseous (butter and cheese—products of the one substance but both in love with Margareen). Shaun will never help or cherish or bless his brother.

10. What's bitter's love but yurning, what' sour lovemutch but a brief burning till she that drawes dothe smoake retourne?

Answer: I know, pepette, of course, dear, but listen, precious! Thanks, pette, those are lovely, pitounette, delicious! But mind the wind, sweet! What exquisite hands you have, you angiol, if you didn't gnaw your nails, isn't it a wonder you are not achamed of me, you pig, you perfect little pigaleen! I'll nudge you in a minute! I bet you use best Parisian smear off her vanity table to make them look so rosetop glowstop nostop. I know her. Slight me, would she? For every got I care! Three creamings a day, the first during her shower and wipe off with tissue. Then after cleanup and of course before retiring. Beme shawl, when I think of that espos of a Clancarbry, the foodbrawler, of the sociationist party with hiss blackleaded chest, hello, Prendregast! that you, Innkipper, and all his fourteen other fullback maulers or hurling stars or whatever the dagos they are, baiting at my Lord Ornery's, just becups they won the egg and spoon there so ovally provencial at Balldole. My Eilish assent he seed makes his admiracion. He is seeking an opening and means to be first with me as his belle alliance. Andoo musnoo play zeloso! Soso do todas. Such is Spanish. Stoop alittle closer, fealse! Delightsome simply! Like Jolio and Romeune. I haven't fell so turkish for ages and ages! Mine's me of squisious, the chocolate with a soul. Extraordinary! Why, what are they all, the mucky lot of them only? Sht! I wouldn't pay three hairpins for them. Peppt! That's rights, hold it steady! Leg me pull. Pu! Come big to Iran. Poo! What are you nudging for? No, I just thought you were. Listen, loviest! Of course it was *too* kind of you, miser, to remember my sighs in shockings, my often expressed wish when you were wandering about my trousseaurs and before I forget it don't forget, in your extensions to my personality, when knotting my remembrancetie, shoeweek will be trotting back with red heels at the end of the moon but look what the fool bought cabbage head and, as I shall answer to gracious heaven, I'll always in always remind of snappy new girters, me being always the one for charms with my very best in proud and gloving even if he was to be vermillion miles my youth to live on, the rubberend Mr Polkingtone, the quonian fleshmonger who Mother Browne solicited me for unlawful converse with, with her mug of October (a pots on it!), creaking around on his old shanksaxle like a crosty old cornquake. Airman, waterwag, terrier, blazer! I'm fine, thanks ever! Ha! O mind you poo tickly. Sall I puhim in momou. Mummum. Funny spot to have a fingey! I'm terribly sorry, I swear to you I am! May you never see me in my birthday pelts seenso tutu and that her blanches mainges may rot leprous off her whatever winking maggis I'll bet by your cut you go fleurting after with all the glass on her and the jumps in her stomewhere! Haha! I suspected she was! Sink her! May they fire her for a barren ewe! So she says: Tay for thee? Well, I saith: Angst so mush: and desired she might not take it amiss if I esteemed her but an odd. If I did ate toughturf I'm not a mishy-missy. Of course I know, pettest, you're so learningful and considerate in yourself, so friend of vegetables, you long cold cat you! Please by acquiester to meek my acquointance! Codling, snakelet, iciclist! My diaper has more life to it! Who drowned you in drears, man, or are you pillale with ink? Did a weep get past the gates of your pride? My tread on the clover, sweetness? Yes, the buttercups told me, hug me, damn it all, and I'll kiss you back to life, my peachest. I mean to make you suffer, meddlar, and I don't care this fig for contempt of courting. That I chid you, sweet sir? You know I'm tender by my eye. Can't you read by dazzling ones through me true? Bite my laughters, drink my tears. Pore into me, volumes, spell me stark and spill me swooning. I just don't care what my thwarters think. Transname me loveliness, now and here me for all times! I'd risk a policeman passing by, Magrath or even that beggar of a boots at the Post. The flame? O, pardone! That was what? Ah, did you speak, stuffstuff? More poestries from Chickspeer's with gleechoreal music or a jaculation from the garden of the soul. Of I be leib in the immoralities? O, you mean the strangle for love and the sowiveall of the prettiest? Yep, we open hap coseries in the home. And once upon a week I improve on myself I'm so keen on that New Free Woman with novel inside. I'm always as tickled as can be over Man in a Surplus by the Lady who Pays the Rates. But I'm as pie as is possible. Let's root out Brimstoker and give him the thrall of our lives. It's Dracula's nightout. For creepsake don't make a flush! Draw the shades, curfe you, and I'll beat any sonnamonk to love. Holy bug, how my highness would jump to make you flame your halve a bannan in two when I'd run my burning torchlight through (to adore me there and then cease to be? Whatever for, blossoms?) Your hairmejig if you had one. If I am laughing with you? No, lovingest, I'm not so dying to take my rise out of you, adored. Not in the very least. True as God made my Mamaw hiplength modesty coatmawther! It's only because the rison is I'm only any girl, you lovely fellow of my dreams, and because old somebooby is not a roundabout, my trysting of the tulipies, like that puff pape bucking Daveran assoiling us behinds. What a nerve! He thinks that's what the vesprey's for. How vain's that hope in cleric's heart Who still pursues th'adult' rous art, Cocksure that rusty gown of his Will make fair Sue forget his phiz! Tame Schwipps. Blessed Marguerite bosses, I hope they threw away the mould or else we'll have Ballshossers and Sourdamapplers with their medical assassiations all over the place. But hold hard till I've got my latchkey vote and I'll teach him when to wear what woman callours. On account of the gloss of the gleison Hasaboobrawbees isabeaubel. And because, you pluckless lankaloot, I hate the very thought of the thought of you and because, dearling, of course, adorest, I was always meant for an engindear from the French college, to be musband, *nomme d'engien*, when we do and contract with encho tencho solver when you are married to reading and writing which pleasebusiness now won't be long for he's so loopy on me and I'm so leapy like since the day he carried me from the boat, my saviored of eroes, to the beach and I left on his shoulder one fair hair to guide hand and mind to its softness. Ever so sorry! I beg your pardon, I was listening to every treasuried word I said fell from my dear mot's tongue otherwise how could I see what you were thinking of our granny? Only I wondered if I threw out my shaving water. Anyway, here's my arm, pulletneck. Gracefully yours. Move your mouth towards minth, more, preciousest, more on more! To please me, treasure. Don't be a, I'm not going to! Sh! nothing! A cricri somewhere! Buybuy! I'm fly! Hear, pippy, under the limes. You know bigtree are all against gravstone. They hisshistenency. Garnd ond mand! So chip chirp chirrup, cigolo, for the lug of Migo! The little passdoor, I go you before, so, and you're at my apron stage. Shy is him, dovey? Musforget there's an audience. I have been lost, angel. Cuddle, ye divil ye! It's our toot-a-toot. Hearhere! Sensation! Let them, their whole four courtships! Let them, Bigbawl and his boosers' eleven makes twelve territorials. The Old Sot's Hole that wants wide streets to commission their noisense in, at the Mitchells *v.* Nicholls. *Aves Selvae Acquae Valles*! And my waiting twenty classbirds, sitting on their stiles! Let me finger their eurhythmytic. And you'll see if I'm selfthought. They're all of them out to please. Wait! In the name of. And all the holly. And some the mistle and it Saint Yves. Hoost! Ahem! There's Ada, Bett, Celia, Delia, Ena, Fretta, Gilda, Hilda, Ita, Jess, Katty, Lou, (they make me cough as sure as I read them) Mina, Nippa, Opsy, Poll, Queeniee, Ruth, Saucy, Trix, Una, Vela, Wanda, Xenia, Yva, Zulma, Phoebe, Thelma. And Mee! The reformatory boys is goaling in for the church so we've all comefeast like the groupsuppers and caught lipsolution from Anty Pravidance under penancies for myrtle sins. When their bride was married all my belles began ti ting. A ring a ring a rosaring! Then everyone will hear of it. Whoses wishes is the farther to my thoughts. But I'll plant them a poser for their nomanclatter. When they're out with the daynurse doing Chaperon Mall. Bright pigeons all over the whirrld will fly with my mistletoe message round their loveribboned necks and a crumb of my cake for each chasta dieva. We keeps all and sundry papers. In th' amourlight, O my darling! No, I swear to you by Fibsburrow churchdome and Sainte Andrée's Undershift, by all I hold secret from my world and in my underworld of nighties and naughties and all the other wonderwearlds! Close your, notmust look! Now open, pet, your lips, pepette, like I used my sweet parted lipsabuss with Dan Holohan of facetious memory taught me after the flannel dance, with the proof of love, up Smock Alley the first night he smelled pouder and I coloured beneath my fan, *pipetta mia*, when you learned me the linguo to melt. Whowham would have ears like ours, the blackhaired! Do you like that, *silenzioso?* Are you enjoying, this same little me, my life, my love? Why do you like my whisping? Is it not divinely deluscious? But in't it bafforyou? *Misi, misi!* Tell me till my thrillme comes! I will not break the seal. I am enjoying it still, I swear I am! Why do you prefer its in these dark nets, if why may ask, my sweetykins? Sh sh! Longears is flying. No, sweetissest, why would that ennoy me? But don't! You want to be slap well slapped for that. Your delighted lips, love, be careful! Mind my duvetyne dress above all! It's golded silvy, the newest sextones with princess effect. For Rutland blue's got out of passion. So, so, my precious! O, I can see the cost, chare! Don't tell me! Why, the boy in sheeps' lane knows that. If I sell whose, dears? Was I sold here' tears? You mean those conversation lozenges? How awful! The bold shame of me! I wouldn't, chickens, not for all the juliettes in the twinkly way! I could snap them when I see them winking at me in bed. I didn't did so, my intended, or was going to or thinking of. Shshsh! Don't start like that, you wretch! I thought ye knew all and more, ye aucthor, to explique to ones the significat of their exsystems with your nieu nivulon lead. It's only another queer fish or other in Brinbrou's damned old trouchorous river again, Gothewishegoths bless us and spare her! And gibos rest from the bosso! Excuse me for swearing, love, I swear to the sorrasims on their trons of Uian I didn't mean to by this alpin armlet! Did you really never in all our cantalang lives speak clothse to a girl's before? No! Not even to the charmermaid? How marfellows! Of course I believe you, my own dear doting liest, when you tell me. As I'd live to, O, I'd love to! Liss, liss! I muss whiss! Never that ever or I can remember dearstreaming faces, you may go through me! Never in all my whole white life of my matchless and pair. Or ever for bitter be the frucht of this hour! With my whiteness I thee woo and bind my silk breasths I thee bound! Always, Amory, amor andmore! Till always, thou lovest! Shshshsh! So long as the lucksmith. Laughs!

11. If you met on the binge a poor acheseyeld from Ailing, when the tune of his tremble shook shimmy on shin, while his countrary raged in the weak of his wailing, like a rugilant pugilant Lyon O'Lynn; if he maundered in misliness, plaining his

plight or, played fox and lice, pricking and dropping hips teeth, or wringing his handcuffs for peace, the blind blighter, praying Dieuf and Domb Nostrums foh thomethinks to eath; if he weapt while he leapt and guffalled quith a quhimper, made cold blood a blue mundy and no bones without flech, taking kiss, kake or kick with a suck, sigh or simper, a diffle to larn and a dibble to lech; if the fain shinner pegged you to shave his immartial, wee skillmustered shoul with his ooh, hoodoodoo! broking wind that to wiles, woemaid sin he was partial, we don't think, Jones, we'd care to this evening, would you?

Answer: No, blank ye! So you think I have impulsivism? Did they tell you I am one of the fortysixths? And I suppose you heard I had a wag on my ears? And I suppose they told you too that my roll of life is not natural? But before proceeding to conclusively confute this begging question it would be far fitter for you, if you dare! to hasitate to consult with and consequentially attempt at my disposale of the same dime-cash problem elsewhere naturalistically of course, from the blinkpoint of so eminent a spatialist. From it you will here notice, Schott, upon my for the first remarking you that the sophology of Bitchson while driven as under by a purely dime-dime urge is not without his cashcash characktericksticks, borrowed for its nonce ends from the fiery goodmother Miss Fortune (who the lost time we had the pleasure we have had our little *recherché* brush with, what, Schott?) and as I further could have told you as brisk as your D.B.C. behaviouristically *pailleté* with a coat of homoid icing which is in reality only a done by chance ridiculisation of the whoo-whoo and where's hairs theorics of Winestain. To put it all the more plumbsily. The speechform is a mere sorrogate. Whilst the quality and tality (I shall explex what you ought to mean by this with its proper when and where and why and how in the subsequent sentence) are alternativomentally harrogate and arrogate, as the gates may be.

Talis is a word often abused by many passims (I am working out a quantum theory about it for it is really most tantumising state of affairs). A pessim may frequent you to say: Have you been seeing much of Talis and Talis those times? optimately meaning: Will you put up at hree of irish? Or a ladyeater may perhaps have casualised as you temptoed her *à la sourdine*: Of your plates? Is Talis de Talis, the swordswallower, who is on at the Craterium the same Talis von Talis, the penscrusher, no funk you! who runs his duly mile? Or this is a perhaps cleaner example. At a recent postvortex piece infustigation of a determinised case of chronic spinosis an extension lecturer on The Ague who out of matter of form was trying his seesers, Dr's Het Ubeleeft, borrowed the question: Why's which Suchman's *talis qualis?* to whom, as a fatter of macht, Dr Gedankje of Stoutgirth, who was wiping his whistle, toarsely retoarted: While thou beast' one zoom of a whorl! (Talis and Talis originally mean the same thing, hit it's: Qualis.)

Professor Loewy-Brueller (though as I shall promptly prove his whole account of the Sennacherib as distinct from the Shalmanesir sanitational reforms and of the Mr Skekels and Dr Hydes problem in the same connection differs *toto coelo* from the fruit of my own investigations — though the reason I went to Jericho must remain for certain reasons a political secret — especially as I shall shortly be wanted in Cavantry, I congratulate myself, for the same and other reasons — as being again hopelessly vitiated by what I have now resolved to call the dime and cash diamond fallacy) in his talked off confession which recently met with such a leonine uproar on its escape after its confinement *Why am I not born like a Gentileman and why am I now so speakable about my own eatables* (Feigenbaumblatt and Father, Judapest, 5688, A.M.) whole-heartedly takes off his gabbercoat and wig, honest draughty fellow, in his public interest, to make us see how though, as he says: 'by Allswill' the inception and the descent and the endswell of Man is *temporarily* wrapped in obscenity, looking through at these accidents with the faroscope of television, (this nightlife instrument needs still some subtractional betterment in the readjustment of the more refrangible angles to the squeals of his hypothesis on the outer tin sides), I can easily believe heartily in my own most spacious immensity as my ownhouse and microbemost cosm when I am reassured by ratio that the cube of my volumes is to the surfaces of their subjects as the sphericity of these globes (I am very pressing for a parliamentary motion this term which, under my guidance, would establish the deleteriousness of decorousness in the morbidisation of the modern mandaboutwoman type) is to the feracity of Fairynelly's vacuum. I need not anthrapologise for any obintentional (I must here correct all that school of neoitalian or paleoparisien schola of tinkers and spanglers who say I'm wrong *parcequeue* out of revolscian from romanitis I want to be) downtrodding on my foes. Professor Levi-Brullo, F.D. of Sexe-Weiman-Eitelnaky finds, from experiments made by hinn with his Nuremberg eggs in the one hands and the watches cunldron apan the oven, though it is astensably a case of Ket's rebollions cooling the Popes back, because the number of squeer faiths in weekly circulation will not be appreciably augmented by the notherslogging of my cupolar clods. What the romantic in rags pines after like all tomtompions haunting crevices for a deadbeat escupement and what het importunes our *Mitleid* for in accornish with the Mortadarthella taradition is the poorest commonon-guardiant waste of time. *His* everpresent toes are always in retaliessian out throuth his overpast boots. Hear him squak! Teek heet to that looswallawer how he bolo the bat! Tyro a toray! *When* Mullocky won the couple of colds, *when* we were stripping in number three, I would like the neat drop that would malt in my mouth but I fail to see *when* (I am purposely refraining from expounding the obvious fallacy as to the specific gravitates of the two deglutables implied nor to the lapses lequou asousiated with the royal gorge through students of mixed hydrostatics and pneumodipsics will after some difficulties grapple away with my meinungs). Myrrdin aloer! as old Marsellas Cambriannus puts his. But, on Professor Llewellys ap Bryllars, F.D., Ph. Dr's showings, the plea, if he pleads, is all posh and robbage on a melodeontic scale since his man's *when* is no otherman's *quandour* (Mine, dank you?) while, for aught I care for the contrary, the all is *where* in love as war and the plane where me arts soar you'd aisy rouse a thunder from and where I cling true'tis there I climb tree and where Innocent looks best (pick!) there's holly in his ives.

As my explanations here are probably above your understandings, lattlebrattons, though as augmentatively uncomparisoned as Cadwan, Cadwallon and Cadwalloner, I shall revert to a more expletive method which I frequently use when I have to sermo with muddlecrass pupils. Imagine for my purpose that you are a squad of urchins, snifflynosed, goslingnecked, clothyheaded, tangled in your lacings, tingled in your pants, etsitaraw etcicero. And you, Bruno Nowlan, take your tongue out of your inkpot! As none of you knows javanese I will give all my easyfree translation of the old fabulist's parable. Allaboy Minor, take your head out of your satchel! *Audi*, Joe Peters! *Exaudi* facts!

The Mookse and The Gripes.

Gentes and laitymen, fullstoppers and semicolonials, hybreds and lubberds!

Eins within a space and a wearywide space it wast ere wohned a Mookse. The onesomeness wast alltolonely, archunsitslike, broady oval, and a Mookse he would a walking go (My hood! cries Antony Romeo), so one grandsumer evening, after a great morning and his good supper of gammon and spittish, having flabelled his eyes, pilleoled his nostrils, vacticanated his ears and palliumed his throats, he put on his impermeable, seized his impugnable, harped on his crown and stepped out of his immobile *De Rure Albo* (socolled becauld it was chalkfull of masterplasters and had borgeously letout gardens strown with cascadas, pintacostecas, horthoducts and currycombs) and set off from Ludstown *a spasso* to see how badness was badness in the weirdest of all pensible ways.

As he set off with his father's sword, his *lancia spezzata*, he was girded on, and with that between his legs and his tarkeels, our once in only Bragspear, he clanked, to my clinking, from veetoes to threetop, every inch of an immortal.

He had not walked over a pentiadpair of parsecs from his azylium when at the turning of the Shinshone Lanteran near

Saint Bowery's-without-his-Walls he came (secunding to the one one oneth of the propecies, *Amnis Limina Permanent*) upon the most unconsciously boggylooking stream he ever locked his eyes with. Out of the colliens it took a rise by daubing itself Ninon. It looked little and it smelt of brown and it thought in narrows and it talked showshallow. And as it rinn it dribbled like any lively purliteasy: *My, my, my! Me and me! Little down dream don't I love thee!*

And, I declare, what was there on the yonder bank of the stream that would be a river, parched on a limb of the olum, bolt downright, but the Gripes? And no doubt he was fit to be dried for why had he not been having the juice of his times?

His pips had been neatly all drowned on him; his polps were charging odours every older minute; he was quickly for getting the dresser's desdaign on the flyleaf of his frons; and he was quietly for giving the bailiff's distrain on to the bulkside of his *cul de Pompe*. In all his specious heavings, as be lived by Optimus Maximus, the Mookse had never seen his Dubville brooderon-low so nigh to a pickle.

Adrian (that was the Mookse now's assumptinome) stuccstill phiz-à-phiz to the Gripes in an accessit of aurignacian. But Allmookse must to Moodend much as Allrouts, austereways or wastersways, in roaming run through Room. Hic sor a stone, singularly illud, and on hoc stone Seter satt huc sate which it filled quite poposterously and by acclammitation to its fullest justotoryum and whereopum with his unfallable encyclicling upom his alloilable, diupetriark of the wouest, and the athemyst-sprinkled pederect he always walked with, *Deusdedit*, cheek by jowel with his frisherman's blague, *Bellua Triumphanes*, his everyway addedto wallat's collectium, for yea longer he lieved yea broader he betaught of it, the fetter, the summe and the haul it cost, he looked the first and last micahlike laicness of Quartus the Fifth and Quintus the Sixth and Sixtus the Seventh giving allnight sitting to Lio the Faultyfindth.

— Good appetite us, sir Mookse! How do you do it? cheeped the Gripes in a wherry whiggy maudelenian woice and the jackasses all within bawl laughed and brayed for his intentions for they knew their sly toad lowry now. I am rarumominum blessed to see you, my dear mouster. Will you not perhopes tell me everything if you are pleased, sanity? All about aulne and lithial and allsall allinall about awn and liseias? Ney?

Think of it! O miserendissimest retempter! A Gripes!

— Rats! bullowed the Mookse most telesphorously, the concionator, and the sissymusses and the zozzymusses in their robenhauses quailed to hear his tardeynois at all for you cannot wake a silken nouse out of a hoarse oar. Blast yourself and your anathomy infairioriboos! No, hang you for an animal rurale! I am superbly in my supremest poncif! Abase you, baldyqueens! Gather behind me, satraps! Rots!

— I am till infinity obliged with you, bowed the Gripes, his whine having gone to his palpruy head. I am still always having a wish on all my extremities. By the watch, what is the time, pace?

Figure it! The pining peever! To a Mookse!

— Ask my index, mund my achilles, swell my obolum, woshup my nase serene, answered the Mookse, rapidly by turning clement, urban, eugenious and celestian in the formose of good grogory humours. Quote awhore? That is quite about what I came on *my* missions with *my* intentions *laudibiliter* to settle with *you*, barbarousse. Let thor be orlog. Let Pauline be Irene. Let you be Beeton. And let me be Los Angeles. Now measure your length. Now estimate my capacity. Well, sour? Is this space of our couple of hours too dimensional for you, temporiser? Will you give you up? *Como? Fuert it?*

Sancta Patientia! You should have heard the voice that answered him! *Culla vosellina.*

— I was just thinkling upon that, swees Mooksey, but, for all the rime on my raisins, if I connow make my submission, I cannos give you up, the Gripes whimpered from nethermost of his wanhope. Ishallassoboundbewilsothoutoosezit. My tumble, loudy bullocker, is my own. My velicity is too fit in one stockend. And my spetial inexshellsis the belowing things ab ove. But I will never be abler to tell Your Honoriousness (here he near lost his limb) though my corked father was bott a pseudowaiter, whose o'cloak you ware.

Incredible! Well, hear the inevitable.

— *Your* temple, *sus in cribro!* Semperexcommunicambiambisumers. Tugurios-in-Newrobe or Tukurias-in-Ashies. Novarome, my creature, blievend bleives. My building space in lyonine city is always to let to leonlike Men, the Mookse in a most consistorous allocution pompifically with immediate jurisdiction constantinently concludded (what a crammer for the shapewrucked Gripes!). And I regret to proclaim that it is out of my temporal to help you from being killed by inchies, (what a thrust!), as we first met each other newwhere so airly. (Poor little sowsieved subsquashed Gripes! I begin to feel contemption for him!). My side, thank decretals, is as safe as motherour's houses, he continued, and I can seen from my holeydome what it is to be wholly sane. Unionjok and be joined to yok! Parysis, *tu sais*, crucycrooks, belongs to him who parises himself. And there I must leave you subject for the pressing. I can prove that against you, weight a momentum, mein goot enemy! or Cospol's not our star. I bet you this dozen odd. This foluminous dozen odd. *Quas primas*—but 'tis bitter to compote my knowledge's fructos of. Tomes.

Elevating, to give peint to his blick, his jewelled pederect to the allmysty cielung, he luckystruck blueild out of a few shouldbe santillants, a cloister of starabouts over Maples, a lucciolys in Teresa street and a stopsign before Sophy Barratt's, he gaddered togodder the odds docence of his vellumes, gresk, letton and russicruxian, onto the lapse of his prolegs, into umfullth onescuppered, and sat about his widerproof. He proved it well whoonearth dry and drysick times, and *vremiament*, *tu cesses*, to the extinction of Niklaus altogether (Niklaus Alopysius having been the once Gripes's popwilled nimbum) by Neuclidius and Inexagoras and Mumfsen and Thumpsem, by Orasmus and by Amenius, by Anacletus the Jew and by Malachy the Augurer and by the Cappon's collection and after that, with Cheekee's gelatine and Alldaybrandy's formolon, he reproved it ehrltogether when not in that order sundering in some different order, alter three thirty and a hundred times by the binomial dioram and the penic walls and the ind, the Inklespill legends and the rure, the rule of the hoop and the blessons of expedience and the jus, the jugicants of Pontius Pilax and all the mummyscrips in Sick Bokes' Juncroom and the Chapters for the Cunning of the Chapters of the Conning Fox by Tail.

While that Mooksius with preprocession and with proprecession, duplicitly and diplussedly, was promulgating ipsofacts and sadcontras this raskolly Gripos he had allbust seceded in monophysicking his illsobordunates. But asawfulas he had caught his base semenoyous sarchnaktiers to combúccinate upon the silipses of his aspillouts and the acheporeoozers of his haggyown pneumax to synerethetise with the breadchestviousness of his sweeatovular ducose sofarfully the loggerthuds of his sakellaries were fond at variance with the synodals of his somepooliom and his babskissed nepogreasymost got the hoof from his philioquus.

— Efter thousand yaws, O Gripes con my sheepskins, yow will be belined to the world, enscayed Mookse the pius.

— Ofter thousand yores, amsered Gripes the gregary, be the goat of MacHammud's, yours may be still, O Mookse, more botheared.

— Us shall be chosen as the first of the last by the electress of Vale Hollow, obselved the Mookse nobily, for par the unicum of Elelijiacks, Us am in Our stabulary and that is what Ruby and Roby fall for, blissim.

The Pills, the Nasal Wash (Yardly's), the Army Man Cut, as british as bondstrict and as straightcut as when that brokenarched traveller from Nuzuland . . .

— Wee, cumfused the Gripes limply, shall not even be the last of the first, wee hope, when oust are visitated by the Veiled Horror. And, he added: Mee are relying entirely, see the fortethurd of Elissabed, on the weightiness of mear's breath. Puffut!

Unsightbared embouscher, relentless foe to social and business succes! (Hourihaleine) It might have been a happy evening but . . .

And they viterberated each other, *canis et coluber* with the wildest ever wielded since Tarriestinus lashed Pissasphaltium.

— Unuchorn!

— Ungulant!

— Uvuloid!

— Uskybeak!

And bullfolly answered volleyball.

Nuvoletta in her lightdress, spunn of sisteen shimmers, was looking down on them, leaning over the bannistars and listening all she childishly could. How she was brightened when Shouldrups in his glaubering hochskied his welkinstuck and how she was overclused when Kneesknobs on his zwivvel was makeacting such a paulse of himshelp! She was alone. All her nubied companions were asleeping with the squirrels. Their mivver, Mrs Moonan, was off in the Fuerst quarter scrubbing the backsteps of Number 28. Fuvver, that Skand, he was up in Norwood's sokaparlour, eating oceans of Voking's Blemish. Nuvoletta listened as she reflected herself, though the heavenly one with his constellatria and his emanations stood between, and she tried all she tried to make the Mookse look up at her (but *he* was fore too adiaptotously farseeing) and to make the Gripes hear how coy she could be (though he was much too schystimatically auricular about *his ens* to heed her) but it was all mild's vapour moist. Not even her feignt reflection, Nuvoluccia, could they toke their gnoses off for their minds with intrepifide fate and bungless curiasity, were conclaved with Heliogobbleus and Commodus and Enobarbarus and whatever the coordinal dickens they did as their damprauch of papyrs and buchstubs said. As if that was their spiration! As if theirs could duiparate her queendim! As if she would be third perty to search on search proceedings! She tried all the winsome wonsome ways her four winds had taught her. She tossed her sfumastelliacinous hair like *la princesse de la Petite Bretagne* and she rounded her mignons arms like Mrs Cornwallis-West and she smiled over herself like the beauty of the image of the pose of the daughter of the queen of the Emperour of Irelande and she sighed after herself as were she born to bride with Tristis Tristior Tristissimus. But, sweet madonine, she might fair as well have carried her daisy's worth to Florida. For the Mookse, a dogmad Accanite, were not amoosed and the Gripes, a dubliboused Catalick, wis pinefully obliviscent.

—I see, she sighed. There are menner.

The siss of the whisp of the sigh of the softzing at the stir of the ver grose O arundo of a long one in midias reeds: and shades began to glidder along the banks, greepsing, greepsing, duusk unto duusk, and it was as glooming as gloaming could be in the waste of all peacable worlds. Metamnisia was allsoonome coloroform brune; citherior spiane an eaulande, innemorous and unnumerose. The Mookse had a sound eyes right but he could not all hear. The Gripes had light ears left yet he could but ill see. He ceased. And he ceased, tung and trit, and it was neversoever so dusk of both of them. But still Moo thought on the deeps of the undths he would profoundth come the morrokse and still Gri feeled of the scripes he would escipe if by grice he had luck enoupes.

Oh, how it was duusk! From Vallee Maraia to Grasyaplaina, dormimust echo! Ah dew! Ah dew! It was so duusk that the tears of night began to fall, first by ones and twos, then by threes and fours, at last by fives and sixes of sevens, for the tired ones were wecking, as we weep now with them. *O! O! O! Par la pluie!*

Then there came down to the thither bank a woman of no appearance (I believe she was a Black with chills at her feet) and she gathered up his hoariness the Mookse motamourfully where he was spread and carried him away to her invisible dwelling, thats hights, *Aquila Rapax*, for he was the holy sacred solem and poshup spit of her boshop's apron. So you see the Mookse he had reason as I knew and you knew and he knew all along. And there came down to the hither bank a woman to all important (though they say that she was comely, spite the cold in her heed) and, for he was as like it as blow it to a hawker's hank, she plucked down the Gripes, torn panicky autotone, in angeu from his limb and cariad away its beotitubes with her to her unseen shieling, it is, *De Rore Coeli.* And so the poor Gripes got wrong; for that is always how a Gripes is, always was and always will be. And it was never so thoughtful of either of them. And there were left now an only elmtree and but a stone. Polled with pietrous, Sierre but saule. O! Yes! And Nuvoletta, a lass.

Then Nuvoletta reflected for the last time in her little long life and she made up all her myriads of drifting minds in one. She cancelled all her engauzements. She climbed over the bannistars; she gave a childy cloudy cry: *Nuée! Nuée!* A lightdress fluttered. She was gone. And into the river that had been a stream (for a thousand of tears had gone eon her and come on her and she was stout and struck on dancing and her muddied name was Missisliffi) there fell a tear, a singult tear, the loveliest of all tears (I mean for those crylove fables fans who are 'keen' on the pretty-pretty commonface sort of thing you meet by hopeharrods) for it was a leaptear. But the river tripped on her by and by, lapping as though her heart was brook: *Why, why, why! Weh, O weh! I'se so silly to be flowing but I no canna stay!*

No applause, please! Bast! The romescot nattleshaker will go round your circulation in *diu dursus.*

Allaboy, Major, I'll take your reactions in another place after themes. Nolan Browne, you may now leave the classroom. Joe Peters, Fox.

Shaun's last words are: "Were he my own breast-brother, my doubled withd love and my singlebiassed hate, were we bread by the same fire and signed with the same salt, had we tapped from the same master and robbed the same till, were we tucked in the one bed and bit by the one flea, homogallant and hemycapnoise, bum and dingo, jack by churl, though it broke my heart to pray it, still I'd fear I'd hate to say!"

And the last question is addressed to the hated brother himself: "Shalt thou be accursed"? He answers: "We are Shem"!

12. *Sacer esto?*

Answer: *Semus sumus!*

Shem is as short for Shemus as Jem is joky for Jacob. A few toughnecks are still getatable who pretend that aboriginally he was of respectable stemming (he was an outlex between the lines of Ragonar Blaubarb and Horrild Hairwire and an inlaw to Capt. the Hon. and Rev. Mr Bbyrdwood de Trop Blogg was among his most distant connections) but every honest to goodness man in the land of the space of today knows that his back life will not stand being written about in black and white. Putting truth and untruth together a shot may be made at what this hybrid actually was like to look at.

Shem's bodily getup, it seems, included an adze of a skull, an eight of a larkseye, the whoel of a nose, one numb arm up a sleeve, fortytwo hairs off his uncrown, eighteen to his mock lip, a trio of barbels from his megageg chin (sowman's son), the wrong shoulder higher than the right, all ears, an artificial tongue with a natural curl, not a foot to stand on, a handful of thumbs, a blind stomach, a deaf heart, a loose liver, two fifths of two buttocks, one gleetsteen avoirdupoider for him, a manroot of all evil, a salmonkelt's thinskin, eelsblood in his cold toes, a bladder tristended, so much so that young Master Shemmy on his very first debouch at the very dawn of protohistory seeing himself such and such, when playing with thistlewords in their garden nursery, Griefotrofio, at Phig Streat 111, Shuvlin, Old Hoeland, (would we go back there now for sounds, pillings and sense? would we now for annas and annas? would we for fullscore eight and a liretta? for twelve blocks one bob? for four testers one groat? not for a dinar! not for jo!) dictited to of all his little brothron and sweestureens the first riddle of the universe: asking, when is a man not a man?: telling them take their time, yungfries, and wait till the tide stops (for from the first his day was a fortnight) and offering the prize of a bittersweet crab, a little present from the past, for their copper age was yet unminted, to the winner. One said when the heavens are quakers, a second said when Bohemeand lips, a third said when he, no, when hold hard a jiffy, when he is a gnawstick and detarmined to, the next one said when the angel of death kicks the bucket of life, stiil another said when the wine's at witsends, and still another when lovely wooman stoops to conk him, one of the littliest said me, me, Sem, when pappa papared the harbour, one of the wittiest said, when he yeat ye abblokooken and he zmear hezelf zo zhooken, still one said when you are old I'm grey fall full wi sleep, and still another when wee deader walkner, and another when he is just only after having being semisized, another when yea, he hath no mananas, and one when dose pigs they begin now that they will flies up intil the looft. All were wrong, so Shem himself, the doctator, took the cake, the correct solution being — all give it up? —; when he is a — yours till the rending of the rocks, — Sham.

Shem was a sham and a low sham and his lowness creeped out first via foodstuffs. So low was he that he preferred Gibsen's teatime salmon tinned, as inexpensive as pleasing, to the plumpest roeheavy lax or the friskiest parr or smolt troutlet that ever was gaffed between Leixlip and Island Bridge and many was the time he repeated in his botulism that no junglegrown pineapple ever smacked like the whoppers you shook out of Ananias' cans, Findlater and Gladstone's, Corner House, Englend. None of your inchthick blueblooded Balaclava fried-at-belief-stakes or juicejelly legs of the Grex's molten mutton or greasilygristly grunters' goupons or slice upon slab of luscious goosebosom with lump after load of plumpudding stuffing all aswim in a swamp of bogoakgravy for that greekenhearted yude! Rosbif of Old Zealand! he could not attouch it. See what happens when your somatophage merman takes his fancy to our virgitarian swan? He even ran away with hunself and became a farsoonerite, saying he would far sooner muddle through the hash of lentils in Europe than meddle with Irrland's split little pea. Once when among those rebels in a state of hopelessly helpless intoxication the piscivore strove to lift a czitround peel to either nostril, hiccupping, apparently impromptued by the hibat he had with his glottal stop, that he kukkakould flowrish for ever by the smell, as the czitr, as the kcedron, like a scedar, of the founts, on mountains, with limon on, of Lebanon. O! the lowness of him was beneath all up to that sunk to! No likedbylike firewater or firstserved firstshot or gulletburn gin or honest brewbarrett beer either. O dear no! Instead the tragic jester sobbed himself wheywhingingly sick of life on some sort of a rhubarbarous maundarin yellagreen funkleblue windigut diodying applejack squeezed from sour grapefruice and, to hear him twixt his sedimental cupslips when he had gulfed down mmmmuch too mmmmany gourds of it retching off to almost as low withswillers, who always knew notwithstanding when they had had enough and were rightly indignant at the wretch's hospitality when they found to their horror they could not carry another drop, it came straight from the noble white fat, jo, openwide sat, jo, jo, her why hide that, jo jo jo, the winevat, of the most serene magyansty az archdiochesse, if she is a duck, she's a douches, and when she has a feherbour snot her fault, now is it? artstouchups, funny you're grinning at, fancy you're in her yet, Fanny Urinia.

Aint that swell, hey? Peamengro! Talk about lowness! Any dog's quantity of it visibly oozed out thickly from this dirty little blacking beetle for the very fourth snap the Tulloch-Turnbull girl with her coldblood kodak shotted the as yet unremuneranded national apostate, who was cowardly gun and camera shy, taking what he fondly thought was a short cut to Caer Fere, Soak Amerigas, vias the shipsteam *Pridewin*, after having buried a hatchet not so long before, by the wrong goods exeunt, nummer desh to tren, into Patatapapaveri's, fruiterers and musical florists, with his *Ciaho, chavi! Sar shin, shillipen?* she knew the vice out of bridewell was a bad fast man by his walk on the spot.

[Johns is a different butcher's. Next place you are up town pay him a visit. Or better still, come tobuy. You will enjoy cattlemen's spring meat. Johns is now quite divorced from baking. Fattens, kills, flays, hangs, draws, quarters and pieces. Feel his lambs! Ex! Feel how sheap! Exex! His liver too is great value, a spatiality! Exexex! COMMUNICATED.]

Around that time, moravar, one generally, for luvvomony hoped or at any rate suspected among morticians that he would early turn out badly, develop hereditary pulmonary T.B., and do for himself one dandy time, nay, of a pelting night blanketed creditors, hearing a coarse song and splash off Eden Quay sighed and rolled over, sure all was up, but, though he fell heavily and locally into debit, not even then could such an antinomian be true to type. He would not put fire to his cerebrum; he would not throw himself in Liffey; he would not explaud himself with pneumantics; he refused to saffrocake himself with a sod. With the foreign devil's leave the fraid born fraud diddled even death. *Anzi*, cabled (but shaking the worth out of his maulth: Guardacosta leporello? Szasas Kraicz!) from his Nearapoblican asylum to his jonathan for a brother: Here tokay, gone tomory, we're spluched, do something, Fireless. And had answer: Inconvenient, David.

|| This is Shaun's portrait of the artist, not Shem's. And here is the house that Jacques built.

The house O'Shea or O'Shame, *Quivapieno*, known as the Haunted Inkbottle, no number Brimstone Walk, Asia in Ireland, as it was infested with the raps, with his penname SHUT sepiascraped on the doorplate and a blind of black sailcloth over its wan phwinshogue, in which the soulcontracted son of the secret cell groped through life at the expense of the taxpayers, dejected into day and night with jesuit bark and bitter bite, calico-hydrants of zolfor and scoppialamina by full and forty Queasisanos, every day in everyone's way more exceeding in violent abuse of self and others, was the worst, it is hoped, even in our western playboyish world for pure mousefarm filth. You brag of your brass castle or your tyled house in ballyfermont? Niggs, niggs and niggs again. For this was a stinksome inkenstink, quite puzzonal to the wrottel. Smatterafact, Angles aftanon browsing there thought not Edam reeked more rare. My wud! The warped flooring of the lair and soundconducting walls thereof, to say nothing of the uprights and imposts, were persianly literatured with burst loveletters, telltale stories, stickyback snaps, doubtful eggshells, bouchers, flints, borers, puffers, amygdaloid almonds, rindless raisins, alphybettyformed verbage, vivlical viasses, ompiter dictas, visus umbique, ahems and ahahs, imeffible tries at speech unasyllabled, you owe mes, eyoldhyms, fluefoul smut, fallen lucifers, vestas which had served, showered ornaments, borrowed brogues, reversibles jackets, blackeye lenses, family jars, falsehair shirts, Godforsaken scapulars, neverworn breeches, cutthroat ties, counterfeit franks, best intentions, curried notes, upset latten tintacks, unused mill and stumpling stones, twisted quills, painful digests, magnifying wineglasses, solid objects cast at goblins, once current puns, quashed quotatoes, messes of mottage, unquestionable issue papers, seedy ejaculations, limerick damns, crocodile tears, spilt ink, blasphematory spits, stale shestnuts, schoolgirls', young ladies', milkmaids', washerwomen's, shopkeepers' wives, merry widows', ex nuns', vice abbess's, pro virgins', super whores', silent sisters', Charleys' aunts', grandmothers', mothers'-in-laws', fostermothers', godmothers' garters, tress clippings from right, lift and cintrum, worms of snot, toothsome pickings, cans of Swiss condensed bilk, highbrow lotions, kisses from the antipodes, presents from pickpockets, borrowed plumes, relaxable handgrips, princess promises, lees of whine, deoxodised carbons, convertible collars, diviliouker doffers, broken wafers, unloosed shoe latchets, crooked strait waistcoats, fresh horrors from Hades, globules of mercury, undeleted glete, glass eyes for an eye, gloss teeth for a tooth, war moans, special sighs, longsufferings of longstanding, ahs ohs ouis sis jas jos gias neys thaws sos, yeses and yeses and yeses, to which, if one has the stomach to add the breakages, upheavals distortions, inversions of all this chambermade music one stands, given a grain of goodwill, a fair chance of actually seeing the whirling dervish, Tumult, son of Thunder, self exiled in upon his ego, a nightlong a shaking betwixtween white or reddr hawrors, noondayterrorised to skin and bone by an ineluctable phantom (may the Shaper have mercery on him!) writing the mystery of himsel in furniture.

Of course our low hero was a self valeter by choice of need so up he got up whatever is meant by a stourbridge clay kitchenette and lithargogalenu fowlhouse for the sake of akes (the umpple does not fall very far from the dumpertree) which the moromelodious jigsmith, in defiance of the Uncontrollable Birth Preservativation (Game and Poultry) Act, playing lallaryrook cookerynook, by the dodginess of his lentern, brooled and cocked and potched in an athanor, whites and yolks and yilks and whotes to the frulling fredonnance of *Mas blanca que la blanca hermana* and *Amarilla, muy bien*, with cinnamon and locusts and wild beeswax and liquorice and Carrageen moss and blaster of Barry's and Asther's mess and Huster's micture and Yellownan's embrocation and Pinkingtone's patty and stardust and sinner's tears, acuredent to Sharadan's *Art of Panning*, chanting, for all regale to the like of the legs he left behind with Litty fun Letty fan Leven, his cantraps of fermented words, abracadabra calubra culorum, (his oewfs à la Madame Gabrielle de l'Eglise, his avgs à la Mistress B. de B. Meinfelde, his eiers Usquadmala à la pomme de ciel, his uoves, oves and uves à la Sulphate de Soude, his ochiuri sowtay sowmmonay à la Monseigneur, his soufflosion of oogs with somekat on toyast à la Mère Puard, his Poggadovies alla Fenella, his Frideggs à la Tricarême) in what was meant for a closet (Ah ho! If only he had listened better to the four masters that infanted him Father Mathew and Le Père Noble and Pastor Lucas and Padre Aguilar — not forgetting Layteacher Baudwin! Ah ho!) His costive Satan's antimonian manganese limolitmious nature never needed such an alcove so, when Robber and Mumsell, the pulpic dictators, on the nudgment of their legal advisers, Messrs Codex and Podex, and under his own benefiction of their pastor Father Flammeus Falconer, boycotted him of all mutton-suet candles and romeruled stationery for any purpose, he winged away on a wildgoup's chase across the kathartic ocean and made synthetic ink and sensitive paper for his own end out of his wit's waste. You ask, in Sam Hill, how? Let manner and matter of this for these our sporting times be cloaked up in the language of blushfed porporates that an Anglican ordinal, not reading his own rude dunsky tunga, may ever behold the brand of scarlet on the brow of her of Babylon and feel not the pink one in his own damned cheek.

Primum opifex, altus prosator, ad terram viviparam et cunctipotentem sine ullo pudore nec venia, suscepto pluviali atque discinctis perizomatis, natibus nudis uti nati fuissent, sese adpropinquans, flens et gemens, in manum suam evacuavit (highly prosy, crap in his hand, sorry!), *postea, animale nigro exoneratus, classicum pulsans, stercus proprium, quod appellavit deiectiones suas, in vas olim honorabile tristitiae posuit, eodem sub invocatione fratrorum geminorum Medardi et Godardi laete ac melliflue minxit, psalmum qui incipit: Lingua mea calamus scribae velociter scribentis: magna voce cantitans* (did a piss, says he was dejected, asks to be exonerated), *demum ex stercore turpi cum divi Orionis iucunditate mixto, cocto, frigorique exposito, encaustum sibi fecit indelibile* (faked O'Ryan's, the indelible ink).

|| More hard words from Shaun to Shem:

Sniffer of carrion, premature gravedigger, seeker of the nest of evil in the bosom of a good word, you, who sleep at our vigil and fast for our feast, you with your dislocated reason, have cutely foretold, a jophet in your own absence, by blind poring upon your many scalds and burns and blisters, impetiginous sore and pustules, by the auspices of that raven cloud, your shade, and by the auguries of rooks in parlament, death with every disaster, the dynamitisation of colleagues, the reducing of records to ashes, the levelling of all customs by blazes, the return of a lot of sweetempered gunpowdered didst unto dudst but it never stphruck your mudhead's obtundity (O hell, here comes our funeral! O pest, I'll miss the post!) that the more carrots you chop, the more turnips you slit, the more murphies you peel, the more onions you cry over, the more bullbeef you butch, the more mutton you crackerhack, the more potherbs you pound, the fiercer the fire and the longer your spoon and the harder you gruel with more grease to your elbow the merrier fumes your new Irish stew.

The nastiness of Shaun's picture of Shem, and of his vituperation towards him, is intensified by the fact that he calls himself JUSTUS, the just one. The justice he metes out is the hypocritical justice of a police state. Shaun's message is really death ("He points the deathbone and the quick are still. *Insomnia, somnia somniorum. Awmawm*",) Shem, despite the withdrawal that his exile represents, despite his dirt (that Latin passage above describes how he makes ink out of the nasty secretions of his body), is on the side of life. Soon the antagonism of the two brothers, already figured in Mutt and Jute, the Mookse and the Gripes, and other opposed pairs, will take on a sort of absolute symbolism. Shem will be a stem or tree, standing for organic life; Shaun will be seen as a dead stone.

Which of the two will become fittest to bear the great message of their mother, the timeless river, Anna Livia Plurabelle? Shaun the Post can only deliver a sealed envelope which, opened, may well turn out to be a forgery. But Shem the Penman is able to give form to the inchoate manifesto: he is a creative artist in words. And if Shaun is JUSTUS Shem is MERCIUS, more concerned with forgiving faults than exacting justice for them. He now addresses himself and, in acknowledging his real faults, is drawn towards his mother. He is closer to her than Shaun is.

MERCIUS (of hisself): *Domine vopiscus!* My fault, his fault, a kingship through a fault! Pariah, cannibal Cain, I who oathily forswore the womb that bore you and the paps I sometimes sucked, you who ever since have been one black mass of jigs and jimjams, haunted by a convulsionary sense of not having been or being all that I might have been or you meant to becoming, bewailing like a man that innocence which I could not defend like a woman, lo, you there, Cathmon-Carbery, and thank Movies from the innermost depths of my still attrite heart, Wherein the days of youyouth are evermixed mimine, now ere the compline hour of being alone athands itself and a puff or so before we yield our spiritus to the wind, for (though that royal one has not yet drunk a gouttelette from his consummation and the flowerpot on the pole, the spaniel pack and their quarry, retainers and the public house proprietor have not budged a millimetre and all that has been done has yet to be done and done again, when's day's woe, and lo, you're doomed, joyday dawns and, la, you dominate) it is to you, firstborn and firstfruit of woe, to me, branded sheep, pick of the wasterpaperbaskel, by the tremours of Thundery and Ulerin's dogstar, you alone, windblasted tree of the knowledge of beautiful andevil, ay, clothed upon with the metuor and shimmering like the horescens, astroglodynamonologos, the child of Nilfit's father, blzb, to me unseen blusher in an obscene coalhole, the cubilibum of your secret sigh, dweller in the downandoutermost where voice only of the dead may come, because ye left from me, because ye laughed on me, because, O me lonly son, ye are forgetting me!, that our turfbrown mummy is acoming, alpilla, beltilla, ciltilla, deltilla, running with her tidings, old the news of the great big world, sonnies had a scrap, woewoewoe! bab's baby walks at seven months, waywayway! bride leaves her raid at Punchestime, stud stoned before a racecourseful, two belles that make the one appeal, dry yanks will visit old sod, and fourtiered skirts are up, mesdames, while Parimiknie wears popular short legs, and twelve hows to mix a tipsy wake, did ye hear, colt Cooney? did ye ever, filly Fortescue? with a beck, with a spring, all her

illringlets shaking, rocks drops in her tachie, tramtokens in
er hair, all waived to a point and then all inuendation, little
ldfashioned mummy, little wonderful mummy, ducking under
ridges, bellhopping the weirs, dodging by a bit of bog, rapid-
hooting round the bends, by Tallaght's green hills and the
ools of the phooka and a place they call it Blessington and
lipping sly by Sallynoggin, as happy as the day is wet, bab-
ling, bubbling, chattering to herself, deloothering the fields on
heir elbows leaning with the sloothering slide of her, giddy-
addy, grannyma, gossipaceous Anna Livia.

He lifts the lifewand and the dumb speak.

— Quoiquoiquoiquoiquoiquoiquoiq!

O

tell me all about

Anna Livia! I want to hear all

about Anna Livia. Well, you know Anna Livia? Yes, of course, we all know Anna Livia. Tell me all. Tell me now. You'll die when you hear. Well, you know, when the old cheb went futt and did what you know. Yes, I know, go on. Wash quit and don't be dabbling. Tuck up your sleeves and loosen your talk-tapes. And don't butt me — hike! — when you bend. Or whatever it was they threed to make out he thried to two in the Fiendish park. He's an awful old reppe. Look at the shirt of him! Look at the dirt of it! He has all my water black on me. And it steeping and stuping since this time last wik. How many goes is it I wonder I washed it? I know by heart the places he likes to saale, duddurty devil! Scorching my hand and starving my famine to make his private linen public. Wallop it well with your battle and clean it. My wrists are wrusty rubbing the mouldaw stains. And the dneepers of wet and the gangres of sin in it! What was it he did a tail at all on Animal Sendai? And how long was he under loch and neagh? It was put in the newses what he did, nicies and priers, the King fierceas Humphrey, with illysus distilling, exploits and all. But tom's will till. I know he well. Temp untamed will hist for no man. As you spring so shall you neap. O, the roughty old rappe! Minxing marrage and making loof.

Reeve Gootch was right and Reeve Drughad was sinistrous! And the cut of him! And the strut of him! How he used to hold his head as high as a howeth, the famous eld duke alien, with a hump of grandeur on him like a walking wiesel rat. And his derry's own drawl and his corksown blather and his doubling stutter and his gullaway swank. Ask Lictor Hackett or Lector Reade of Garda Growley or the Boy with the Billyclub. How elster is he a called at all? Qu'appelle? Huges Caput Earlyfouler. Or where was he born or how was he found? Urgothland, Tvistown on the Kattekat? New Hunshire, Concord on the Merrimake? Who blocksmitt her saft anvil or yelled lep to her pail? Was her banns never loosened in Adam and Eve's or were him and her but captain spliced? For mine ether duck I thee drake. And by my wildgaze I thee gander. Flowey and Mount on the brink of time makes wishes and fears for a happy isthmass. She can show all her lines, with love, license to play. And if they don't remarry that hook and eye may! O, passmore that and oxus another! Don Dom Dombdomb and his wee follyo! Was his help inshored in the Stork and Pelican against bungelars, flu and third risk parties? I heard he dug good tin with his doll, delvan first and duvlin after, when he raped her home, Sabrine asthore, in a parakeet's cage, by dredgerous lands and devious delts, playing catched and mythed with the gleam of her shadda, (if a flic had been there to pop up and pepper him!) past auld min's manse and Maisons Allfou and the rest of incurables and the last of immurables, the quaggy waag for stumbling. Who sold you that jackalantern's tale? Pemmican's pasty pie! Not a grasshoop to ring her, not an antsgrain of ore. In a gabbard he barqued it, the boat of life, from the harbourless Ivernikan Okean, till he spied the loom of his landfall and he loosed two croakers from under his tilt, the gran Phenician rover. By the smell of her kelp they made the pigeonhouse. Like fun they did! But where was Himself, the timoneer? That marchantman he suivied their scutties right over the wash, his cameleer's burnous breezing up on him, till with his runagate bowmpriss he roade and borst her bar. Pilcomayo! Suchcaughtawan! And the whale's away with the grayling! Tune your pipes and fall ahumming, you born ijypt, and you're nothing short of one! Well, ptellomey soon and curb your escumo. When they saw him shoot swift up her sheba sheath, like any gay lord salomon, her bulls they were ruhring, surfed with spree. Boyarka buah! Boyana bueh! He erned his lille Bunbath hard, our staly bred, the trader. He did. Look at here. In this wet of his prow. Don't you know he was kaldt a bairn of the brine, Wasserbourne the waterbaby? Havemmarea, so he was! H.C.E. has a codfisck ee. Shyr she's nearly as badher as him herself. Who? Anna Livia? Ay, Anna Livia. Do you know she was calling bakvandets sals from all around, nyumba noo, chamba choo, to go in till him, her erring cheef, and tickle the pontiff aisy-oisy? She was? Gota pot! Yssel that the limmat? As El Negro winced when he wonced in La Plate. O, tell me all I want to hear, how loft she was lift a laddery dextro! A coneywink after the bunting fell. Letting on she didn't care, sina feza, me absantee, him man in passession, the proxenete! Proxenete and phwhat is phthat? Emme for your reussischer Honddu jarkon! Tell us in franca langua. And call a spate a spate. Did they never sharee you ebro at skol, you antiabecedarian? It's just the same as if I was to go par examplum now in conservancy's cause out of telekinesis and proxenete you. For coxyt sake and is that what she is? Botlettle I thought she'd act that loa. Didn't you spot her in her windaug, wubbling up on an osiery chair, with a meusic before her all cunniform letters, pretending to ribble a reedy derg on a fiddle she bogans without a band on? Sure she can't fiddan a dee, with bow or abandon! Sure, she can't! Tista suck. Well, I never now heard the like of that! Tell me moher. Tell me moatst. Well, old Humber was as glommen as grampus, with the tares at his thor and the buboes for ages and neither bowman nor shot abroad and bales allbrant on the crests of rockies and nera lamp in kitchen or church and giant's holes in Grafton's causeway and deathcap mushrooms round Funglus grave and the great tribune's barrow all darnels occumule, sittang sambre on his sett, drammen and drommen, usking queasy quizzers of his ruful continence, his childlinen scarf to encourage his obsequies where he'd check their debths in that mormon's thames, be questing and handsetl, hop, step and a deepend, with his berths in their toiling moil, his swallower open from swolf to fore and the snipes of the gutter pecking his crocs, hungerstriking all alone and holding doomsdag over hunselv, dreeing his weird, with his dander up, and his fringe combed over his eygs and droming on loft till the sight of the sternes, after zwarthy kowse and weedy broeks and the tits of buddy and the loits of pest and to peer was Parish worth thette mess. You'd think all was dodo belonging to him how he durmed adranse in durance vaal. He had been belching for severn years. And there she was, Anna Livia, she darent catch a winkle of sleep, purling around like a chit of a child, Wendawanda, a fingerthick, in a Lapsummer skirt and damazon cheeks, for to ishim bonzour to her dear dubber Dan. With neuphraties and sault from his maggias. And an odd time she'd cook him up blooms of fisk and lay to his heartsfoot her meddery eygs, yayis, and staynish beacons on toasc and a cupenhave so weeshywashy of Greenland's tay or a dzoupgan of Kaffue mokau an sable or Sikiang sukry or his ale of ferns in trueart pewter and a shinkobread (hamjambo, bana?) for to plaise that man hog stay his stomicker till her pyrraknees shrunk to nutmeg graters while her togglejoints shuck with goyt and as rash as she'd russ with her peakload of vivers up on her sieve (metauwero rage it swales and rieses) my hardey Hek he'd kast them frome him, with a stour of scorn, as much as to say you sow and you sozh, and if he didn't peg the platteau on her tawe, believe you me, she was safe enough. And then she'd esk to vistule a hymn, *The Heart Bowed Down* or *The Rakes of Mallow* or Chelli Michele's *La Calumnia è un Vermicelli* or a balfy bit ov *old Jo Robidson.* Sucho fuffing a fifeing 'twould cut you in two! She'd bate the hen that crowed on the turrace of Babbel. What harm if she knew how to cockle her mouth! And not a mag out of Hum no more than out of the mangle weight. Is that a faith? That's the fact. Then riding the ricka and roya romanche, Annona, gebroren aroostokrat Nivia, dochter of Sense and Art, with Sparks' pirryphlickathims funkling her fan, anner frostivying tresses dasht with virevlies,—

while the prom beauties sreeked nith their bearers' skins! — in a period gown of changeable jade that would robe the wood of two cardinals' chairs and crush poor Cullen and smother MacCabe. O blazerskate! Theirs porpor patches! And brahming to him down the feedchute, with her femtyfyx kinds of fondling endings, the poother rambling off her nose: *Vuggybarney, Wickerymandy! Hello, ducky, please don't die!* Do you know what she started cheeping after, with a choicey voicey like waterglucks or Madame Delba to Romeoreszk? You'll never guess. Tell me. Tell me. *Phoebe, dearest, tell, O tell me* and *I loved you better nor you knew.* And letting on hoon var daft about the warbly sangs from over holmen: *High hellskirt saw ladies hensmoker lilyhung pigger:* and soay and soan and so firth and so forth in a tone sonora and Oom Bothar below like Bheri-Bheri in his sandy cloak, so umvolosy, as deaf as a yawn, the stult! Go away! Poor deef old deary! Yare only teasing! Anna Liv? As chalk is my judge! And didn't she up in sorgues and go and trot doon and stand in her douro, puffing her old dudheen, and every shirvant siligirl or wensum farmerette walking the pilend roads, Sawy, Fundally, Daery or Maery, Milucre, Awny or Graw, usedn't she make her a simp or sign to slip inside by the sullyport? You don't say, the sillypost? Bedouix but I do! Calling them in, one by one (To Blockbeddum here! Here the Shoebenacaddie!) and legging a jig or so on the sihl to show them how to shake their benders and the dainty how to bring to mind the gladdest garments out of sight and all the way of a maid with a man and making a sort of a cackling noise like two and a penny or half a crown and holding up a silliver shiner. Lordy, lordy, did she so? Well, of all the ones ever I heard! Throwing all the neiss little whores in the world at him! To inny captured wench you wish of no matter what sex of pleissful ways two adda tammar a lizzy a lossie to hug and hab haven in Humpy's apron!

The two washerwomen at the ford are talking about Anna Livia in prose full of the noise of rivers. She loved her HCE, and, to scotch the scandal that grew and grew after the alleged incident in the Phoenix Park, she borrowed a mailbag from one of her sons—Shaun the Post—and then let down her hair, wove a garland for it, made bracelets and anklets and armlets and a necklace of cobbles and pebbles, and said she was stepping out to pay a call. She wore ploughboy's clogs, a sugarloaf hat, nude cuba stockings, "salmospot-speckled", and other garments which made her resemble the Poor Old Woman, Ireland herself, as well as the wife of poor wronged HCE. In the bag, of course, were the remnants of her lord, converted into presents for her one hundred and eleven children (111—a mystic number). These would wipe out the rumours. "Shake it up, do, do"! says one of the washerwoman. The other says, "Spey me pruth and I'll tale you true". And she pushes on with the tale.

Well, arundgirond in a waveney lyne aringarouma she pattered and swung and sidled, dribbling her boulder through narrowa mosses, the diliskydrear on our drier side and the vilde vetchvine agin us, curara here, careero there, not knowing which medway or weser to strike it, edereider, making chattahoochee all to her ain chichiu, like Santa Claus at the cree of the pale and puny, nistling to hear for their tiny hearties, her arms encircling Isolabella, then running with reconciled Romas and Reims, on like a lech to be off like a dart, then bathing Dirty Hans' spatters with spittle, with a Christmas box apiece for aisch and iveryone of her childer, the birthday gifts they dreamt they gabe her, the spoiled she fleetly laid at our door! On the matt, by the pourch and inunder the cellar. The rivulets ran aflod to see, the glashaboys, the pollynooties. Out of the paunschaup on to the pyre. And they all about her, juvenile leads and ingenuinas, from the slime of their slums and artesaned wellings, rickets and riots, like the Smyly boys at their vicereine's levee. Vivi vienne, little Annchen! Vielo Anna, high life! Sing us a sula, O, susuria! Ausone sidulcis! Hasn't she tambre! Chipping her and raising a bit of a chir or a jary every dive she'd neb in her culdee sacco of wabbash she raabed and reach out her maundy meerschaundize, poor souvenir as per ricorder and all for sore aringarung, stinkers and heelers, laggards and primelads, her furzeborn sons and dribblederry daughters, a thousand and one of them, and wickerpotluck for each of them. For evil and ever. And kiks the buch. A tinker's bann and a barrow to boil his billy for Gipsy Lee; a cartridge of cockaleekie soup for Chummy the Guardsman; for sulky Pender's acid nephew deltoïd drops, curiously strong; a cough and a rattle and wildrose cheeks for poor Piccolina Petite MacFarlane; a jigsaw puzzle of needles and pins and blankets and shins between them for Isabel, Jezebel and Llewelyn Mmarriage; a brazen nose and pigiron mittens for Johnny Walker Beg; a papar flag of the saints and stripes for Kevineen O'Dea; a puffpuff for Pudge Craig and a nightmarching hare for Techertim Tombigby; waterleg and gumboots each for Bully Hayes and Hurricane Hartigan; a prodigal heart and fatted calves for Buck Jones, the pride of Clonliffe; a loaf of bread and a father's early aim for Val from Skibereen; a jauntingcar for Larry Doolin, the Ballyclee jackeen; a seasick trip on a government ship for Teague O'Flanagan; a louse and trap for Jerry Coyle; slushmincepies for Andy Mackenzie; a hairclip and clackdish for Penceless Peter; that twelve sounds look for G. V. Brooke; a drowned doll, to face downwards for modest Sister Anne Mortimer; altar falls for Blanchisse's bed; Wildairs' breechettes for Magpeg Woppington; to Sue Dot a big eye; to Sam Dash a false step; snakes in clover, picked and scotched, and a vaticanned viper catcher's visa for Patsy Presbys; a reiz every morning for Standfast Dick and a drop every minute for Stumblestone Davy; scruboak beads for beatified Biddy; two appletweed stools for Eva Mobbely; for Saara Philpot a jordan vale tearorne; a pretty box of Pettyfib's Powder for Eileen Aruna to whiten her teeth and outflash Helen Arhone; a whippingtop for Eddy Lawless; for Kitty Coleraine of Butterman's Lane a penny wise for her foolish pitcher; a putty shovel for Terry the Puckaun; an apotamus mask for Promoter Dunne; a niester egg with a twicedated shell and a dynamight right for Pavl the Curate;

a collera morbous for Mann in the Cloack; a starr and girton for Draper and Deane; for Will-of-the-Wisp and Barny-the-Bark two mangolds noble to sweeden their bitters; for Oliver Bound a way in his frey; for Seumas, thought little, a crown he feels big; a tibertine's pile with a Congoswood cross on the back for Sunny Twimjim; a praises be and spare me days for Brian the Bravo; penteplenty of pity with lubilashings of lust for Olona Lena Magdalena; for Camilla, Dromilla, Ludmilla, Mamilla, a bucket, a packet, a book and a pillow; for Nancy Shannon a Tuami brooch; for Dora Riparia Hopeandwater a cooling douche and a warmingpan; a pair of Blarney braggs for Wally Meagher; a hairpin slatepencil for Elsie Oram to scratch her toby, doing her best with her volgar fractions; an old age pension for Betty Bellezza; a bag of the blues for Funny Fitz; a *Missa pro Messa* for Taff de Taff; Jill, the spoon of a girl, for Jack, the broth of a boy; a Rogerson Crusoe's Friday fast for Caducus Angelus Rubiconstein; three hundred and sixtysix poplin tyne for revery warp in the weaver's woof for Victor Hugonot; a stiff steaded rake and good varians muck for Kate the Cleaner; a hole in the ballad for Hosty; two dozen of cradles for J.F.X.P. Coppinger; tenpounten on the pop for the daulphins born with five spoiled squibs for Infanta; a letter to last a lifetime for Maggi beyond by the ashpit; the heftiest frozenmeat woman from Lusk to Livienbad for Felim the Ferry; spas and speranza and symposium's syrup for decayed and blind and gouty Gough; a change of naves and joys of ills for Armoricus Tristram Amoor Saint Lawrence; a guillotine shirt for Reuben Redbreast and hempen suspendeats for Brennan on the Moor; an oakanknee for Conditor Sawyer and musquodoboits for Great Tropical Scott; a C3 peduncle for Karmalite Kane; a sunless map of the month, including the sword and stamps, for Shemus O'Shaun the Post; a jackal with hide for Browne but Nolan; a stonecold shoulder for Donn Joe Vance; all lock and no stable for Honorbright Merreytrickx; a big drum for Billy Dunboyne; a guilty goldeny bellows, below me blow me, for Ida Ida and a hushaby rocker, Elletrouvetout, for Who-is-silvier — Where-is-he?; whatever you like to swilly to swash,

Yuinness or Yennessy, Laagen or Niger, for Festus King and Roaring Peter and Frisky Shorty and Treacle Tom and O. B. Behan and Sully the Thug and Master Magrath and Peter Cloran and O'Delawarr Rossa and Nerone MacPacem and whoever you chance to meet knocking around; and a pig's bladder balloon for Selina Susquehanna Stakelum. But what did she give to Pruda Ward and Katty Kanel and Peggy Quilty and Briery Brosna and Teasy Kieran and Ena Lappin and Muriel Maassy and Zusan Camac and Melissa Bradogue and Flora Ferns and Fauna Fox-Goodman and Grettna Greaney and Penelope Inglesante and Lezba Licking like Leytha Liane and Roxana Rohan with Simpatica Sohan and Una Bina Laterza and Trina La Mesme and Philomena O'Farrell and Irmak Elly and Josephine Foyle and Snakeshead Lily and Fountainoy Laura and Marie Xavier Agnes Daisy Frances de Sales Macleay? She gave them ilcka madre's daughter a moonflower and a bloodvein: but the grapes that ripe before reason to them that devide the vinedress. So on Izzy, her shamemaid, love shone befond her tears as from Shem, her penmight, life past befoul his prime.

My colonial, wardha bagful! A bakereen's dusind with tithe tillies to boot. That's what you may call a tale of a tub! And Hibernonian market! All that and more under one crinoline envelope if you dare to break the porkbarrel seal. No wonder they'd run from her pison plague. Throw us your hudson soap for the honour of Clane! The wee taste the water left. I'll raft it back, first thing in the marne. Merced mulde! Ay, and don't forget the reckitts I lohaned you. You've all the swirls your side of the current. Well, am I to blame for that if I have? Who said you're to blame for that if you have? You're a bit on the sharp side. I'm on the wide. Only snuffers' cornets drifts my way that the cracka dvine chucks out of his cassock, with her estheryear's marsh narcissus to make him recant his vanitty fair. Foul strips of his chinook's bible I do be reading, dodwell disgustered but chickled with chuckles at the tittles is drawn on the tattlepage. *Senior ga dito: Faciasi Omo! E omo fu fò.* Ho! Ho! *Senior ga dito: Faciasi Hidamo! Hidamo se ga facessà.* Ha! Ha! And *Die Windermere*

Dichter and Lefanu (Sheridan's) old *House by the Coachyard* and Mill (J.) *On Woman* with *Ditto on the Floss*. Ja, a swamp for Altmuehler and a stone for his flossies! I know how racy they move his wheel. My hands are blawcauld between isker and suda like that piece of pattern chayney there, lying below. Or where is it? Lying beside the sedge I saw it. Hoangho, my sorrow, I've lost it! Aimihi! With that turbary water who could see? So near and yet so far! But O, gihon! I lovat a gabber. I could listen to maure and moravar again. Regn onder river. Flies do your float. Thick is the life for mere.

Well, you know or don't you kennet or haven't I told you every telling has a taling and that's the he and the she of it. Look, look, the dusk is growing! My branches lofty are taking root. And my cold cher's gone ashley. Fieluhr? Filou! What age is at? It saon is late. 'Tis endless now senne eye or erewone last saw Waterhouse's clogh. They took it asunder, I hurd thum sigh. When will they reassemble it? O, my back, my back, my bach! I'd want to go to Aches-les-Pains. Pingpong! There's the Belle for Sexaloitez! And Concepta de Send-us-pray! Pang! Wring out the clothes! Wring in the dew! Godavari, vert the showers! And grant thaya grace! Aman. Will we spread them here now? Ay, we will. Flip! Spread on your bank and I'll spread mine on mine. Flep! It's what I'm doing. Spread! It's churning chill. Der went is rising. I'll lay a few stones on the hostel sheets. A man and his bride embraced between them. Else I'd have sprinkled and folded them only. And I'll tie my butcher's apron here. It's suety yet. The strollers will pass it by. Six shifts, ten kerchiefs, nine to hold to the fire and this for the code, the convent napkins, twelve, one baby's shawl. Good mother Jossiph knows, she said. Whose head? Mutter snores? Deataceas! Wharnow are alle her childer, say? In kingdome gone or power to come or gloria be to them farther? Allalivial, allalluvial! Some here, more no more, more again lost alla stranger. I've heard tell that same brooch of the Shannons was married into a family in Spain. And all the Dunders de Dunnes in Markland's Vineland beyond Brendan's herring pool takes number nine in yangsee's hats. And one of Biddy's beads went bobbing till she rounded up lost histereve with a marigold and a cobbler's candle in a side strain of a main drain of a manzinahurries off Bachelor's Walk. But all that's left to the last of the Meaghers in the loup of the years prefixed and between is one kneebuckle and two hooks in the front. Do you tell me that now? I do in troth. Orara por Orbe and poor Las Animas! Ussa, Ulla, we're umbas all! Mezha, didn't you hear it a deluge of times, ufer and ufer, respund to spond? You deed, you deed! I need, I need! It's that irrawaddyng I've stoke in my aars. It all but husheth the lethest zswound. Oronoko! What's your trouble? Is that the great Finnleader himself in his joakimono on his statue riding the high horse there forehengist? Father of Otters, it is himself! Yonne there! Isset that? On Fallareen Common? You're thinking of Astley's Amphitheayter where the bobby restrained you making sugarstuck pouts to the ghostwhite horse of the Peppers. Throw the cobwebs from your eyes, woman, and spread your washing proper! It's well I know your sort of slop. Flap! Ireland sober is Ireland stiff. Lord help you, Maria, full of grease, the load is with me! Your prayers. I sonht zo! Madammangut! Were you lifting your elbow, tell us, glazy cheeks, in Conway's Carrigacurra canteen? Was I what, hobbledyhips? Flop! Your rere gait's creakorheuman bitts your butts disagrees. Amn't I up since the damp dawn, marthared mary allacook, with Corrigan's pulse and varicoarse veins, my pramaxle smashed, Alice Jane in decline and my oneeyed mongrel twice run over, soaking and bleaching boiler rags, and sweating cold, a widow like me, for to deck my tennis champion son, the laundryman with the lavandier flannels? You won your limpopo limp fron the husky hussars when Collars and Cuffs was heir to the town and your slur gave the stink to Carlow. Holy Scamander, I sar it again! Near the golden falls. Icis on us! Seints of light! Zezere! Subdue your noise, you hamble creature! What is it but a blackburry growth or the dwyergray ass them four old codgers owns. Are you meanam Tarpey and Lyons and Gregory? I meyne now, thank all, the four of them, and the roar of them, that draves that stray in the mist and old Johnny MacDougal along with them. Is that the Poolbeg flasher beyant, pharphar, or a fireboat coasting nyar the Kishtna or a glow I behold within a hedge or my Garry come back from the Indes? Wait till the honeying of the lune, love! Die eve, little eve, die! We see that wonder in your eye. We'll meet again, we'll part once more. The spot I'll seek if the hour you'll find. My chart shines high where the blue milk's upset. Forgivemequick, I'm going! Bubye! And you, pluck your watch, forgetmenot. Your evenlode. So save to jurna's end! My sights are swimming thicker on me by the shadows to this place. I sow home slowly now by own way, moyvalley way. Towy I too, rathmine.

Ah, but she was the queer old skeowsha anyhow, Anna Livia, trinkettoes! And sure he was the quare old buntz too, Dear Dirty Dumpling, foostherfather of fingalls and dotthergills. Gammer and gaffer we're all their gangsters. Hadn't he seven dams to wive him? And every dam had her seven crutches. And every crutch had its seven hues. And each hue had a differing cry. Sudds for me and supper for you and the doctor's bill for Joe John. Befor! Bifur! He married his markets, cheap by foul, I know, like any Etrurian Catholic Heathen, in their pinky limony creamy birnies and their turkiss indienne mauves. But at milkidmass who was the spouse? Then all that was was fair. Tys Elvenland! Teems of times and happy returns. The seim anew. Ordovico or viricordo. Anna was, Livia is, Plurabelle's to be. Northmen's thing made southfolk's place but howmulty plurators made eachone in person? Latin me that, my trinity scholard, out of eure sanscreed into oure eryan! *Hircus Civis Eblanensis!* He had buckgoat paps on him, soft ones for orphans. Ho, Lord! Twins of his bosom. Lord save us! And ho! Hey? What all men. Hot? His tittering daughters of. Whawk?

Can't hear with the waters of. The chittering waters of. Flittering bats, fieldmice bawk talk. Ho! Are you not gone ahome? What Thom Malone? Can't hear with bawk of bats, all thim liffeying waters of. Ho, talk save us! My foos won't moos. I feel as old as yonder elm. A tale told of Shaun or Shem? All Livia's daughtersons. Dark hawks hear us. Night! Night! My ho head halls. I feel as heavy as yonder stone. Tell me of John or Shaun? Who were Shem and Shaun the living sons or daughters of? Night now! Tell me, tell me, tell me, elm! Night night! Telmetale of stem or stone. Beside the rivering waters of, hitherandthithering waters of Night!

II

Every evening at lighting up o'clock sharp and until further notice in Feenichts Playhouse. (Bar and conveniences always open, Diddlem Club douncestears.) Entrancings: gads, a scrab; the quality, one large shilling. Newly billed for each wickeday perfumance. Somndoze massinees. By arraignment, childream's hours, expercatered. Jampots, rinsed porters, taken in token. With nightly redistribution of parts and players by the puppetry producer and daily dubbing of ghosters, with the benediction of the Holy Genesius Archimimus and under the distinguished patronage of their Elderships the Oldens from the four coroners of Findrias, Murias, Gorias and Falias, Messoirs the Coarbs, Clive Sollis, Galorius Kettle, Pobiedo Lancey and Pierre Dusort, while the Caesar-in-Chief looks. On. Sennet. As played to the Adelphi by the Brothers Bratislavoff (Hyrcan and Haristobulus), after humpteen dumpteen revivals. Before all the King's Hoarsers with all the Queen's Mum. And wordloosed over seven seas crowdblast in cellelleneteutoslavzendlatinsoundscript. In four tubbloids. While fern may cald us until firn make cold. *The Mime of Mick, Nick and the Maggies*, adopted from the Ballymooney Bloodriddon Murther by Bluechin Blackdillain (authorways 'Big Storey'), featuring:

GLUGG (Mr Seumas McQuillad, hear the riddles between the robot in his dress circular and the gagster in the rogues' gallery), the bold bad bleak boy of the storybooks, who, when the tabs go up, as we discover, because he knew to mutch, has been divorced into disgrace court by

THE FLORAS (Girl Scouts from St. Bride's Finishing Establishment, demand acidulateds), a month's bunch of pretty maidens who, while they pick on her, their pet peeve, form with valkyrienne licence the guard for

IZOD (Miss Butys Pott, ask the attendantess for a leaflet), a bewitching blonde who dimples delightfully and is approached in loveliness only by her grateful sister reflection in a mirror, the cloud of the opal, who, having jilted Glugg, is being fatally fascinated by

CHUFF (Mr Sean O'Mailey, see the chalk and sanguine pictograph on the safety drop), the fine frank fairhaired fellow of the fairytales, who wrestles for tophole with the bold bad bleak boy Glugg, geminally about caps or puds or tog bags or bog gats or chuting rudskin gunerally or something, until they adumbrace a pattern of somebody else or other, after which they are both carried off the set and brought home to be well soaped, sponged and scrubbed again by

ANN (Miss Corrie Corriendo, Grischun scoula, bring the babes, Pieder, Poder and Turtey, she mistributes mandamus monies, after perdunamento, hendrud aloven entrees, pulcinellis must not miss our national rooster's rag), their poor little old mother-in-lieu, who is woman of the house, playing opposite to

HUMP (Mr Makeall Gone, read the sayings from Laxdalesaga in the programme about King Ericus of Schweden and the spirit's whispers in his magical helmet), cap-a-pipe with watch and topper, coat, crest and supporters, the cause of all our grievances, the whirl, the flash and the trouble, who, having partially recovered from a recent impeachment due to egg everlasting, but throughandthoroughly proconverted, propounded for cyclological, is, studding sail once more, jibsheets and royals, in the semblance of the substance for the membrance of the umbrance with the remnance of the emblence reveiling a quemdam supercargo, of The Rockery, Poopinheavin, engaged in entertaining in his pilgrimst customhouse at Caherlehome-upon-Eskur those statutory persons

THE CUSTOMERS (Components of the Afterhour Courses at St. Patricius' Academy for Grownup Gentlemen, consult the annuary, coldporters sibsuction), a bundle of a dozen of representative locomotive civics, each inn quest of outings, who are still more sloppily served after every cup final by

SAUNDERSON (Mr Knut Oelsvinger, Tiffsdays off, wouldntstop in bad, imitation of flatfish, torchbearing supperaape, dud half-sovereign, no chee daily, rolly pollsies, Glen of the Downs, the Gugnir, his geyswerks, his earsequack, his lokistroki, o.s.v.), a scherinsheiner and spoilcurate, unconcerned in the mystery but under the inflounce of the milldieuw and butt of

KATE (Miss Rachel Lea Varian, she tells forkings for baschfellors, under purdah of card palmer teaput tosspot Madam d'Elta, during the pawses), kook-and-dishdrudge, whitch believes wanthingthats, whouse be the churchyard or whorts up the aasgaars, the show must go on.

Time: the pressant.

With futurist onehorse balletbattle pictures and the Pageant of Past History worked up with animal variations amid everglaning mangrovemazes and beorbtracktors by Messrs Thud and Blunder. Shadows by the film folk, masses by the good people. Promptings by Elanio Vitale. Longshots, upcloses, outblacks and stagetolets by Hexenschuss, Coachmaher, Incubone and Rocknarrag. Creations tastefully designed by Madame Berthe Delamode. Dances arranged by Harley Quinn and Coollimbeina. Jests, jokes, jigs and jorums for the Wake lent from the properties of the late cemented Mr T. M. Finnegan R.I.C. Lipmasks and hairwigs by Ouida Nooikke. Limes and Floods by Crooker and Toll. Kopay pibe by Kappa Pedersen. Hoed Pine hat with twentyfour ventholes by Morgen. Bosse and stringbag from Heteroditheroe's and All Ladies' presents. Tree taken for grafted. Rock rent. Phenecian blends and Sourdanian doofpoosts by Shauvesourishe and Wohntbedarft. The oakmulberryeke with silktrick twomesh from Shop-Sowry, seedsmanchap. Grabstone beg from General Orders Mailed. The crack (that's Cork!) by a smoker from the gods. The interjection (Buckley!) by the firement in the pit. Accidental music providentially arranged by L'Archet and Laccorde. Melodiotiosities in purefusion by the score. To start with in the beginning, we need hirtly bemark, a community prayer, everyone for himself, and to conclude with as an exodus, we think it well to add, a chorale in canon, good for us all for us all us all all. Songs betune the acts by the ambiamphions of Annapolis, Joan MockComic, male soprano, and Jean Souslevin, bass noble, respectively: O, Mester Sogermon, ef thes es whot ye deux, then I'm not surpleased ye want that bottle of Sauvequipeu and Oh Off Nunch Der Rasche Ver Lasse Mitsch Nitscht. Till the summit scenes of climbacks castastrophear, *The Bearded Mountain* (Polymop Barethe-rootsch), and *The River Romps to Nursery* (Maidykins in Undiform). The whole thugogmagog, including the portions understood to be oddmitted as the results of the respective titulars neglecting to produce themselves, to be wound up for an after-enactment by a Magnificent Transformation Scene showing the Radium Wedding of Neid and Moorning and the Dawn of Peace, Pure, Perfect and Perpetual, Waking the Weary of the World.

An argument follows.

Chuffy was a nangel then and his soard fleshed light like likening. Fools top! Singty, sangty, meekly loose, defendy nous from prowlabouts. Make a shine on the curst. Emen.

But the duvlin sulph was in Glugger, that lost-to-lurning. Punct. He was sbuffing and sputing, tussing like anisine, whipping his eyesoult and gnatsching his teats over the brividies from existers and the outher liubbocks of life. He halth kelchy chosen a clayblade and makes prayses to his three of clubs. To part from these, my corsets, is into overlusting fear. Acts of feet, hoof and jarrety: athletes longfoot. Djowl, uphere!

After the book of the parents, the book of the children. They are playing Angels and Devils. Chuff (Shaun) is an angel, but Glugg (Shem) is a devil. All the girls love Chuff—the twenty-eight girls of St Bride's Finishing

Establishment as well as Isobel, the Leap Year Girl—but only his mother loves Glugg. He can't answer their riddles; they all laugh at him. Very well, he'll get away from them all, go into exile, turn himself into James Joyce and write *Ulysses*.

Go in for scribenery with the satiety of arthurs in S.P.Q.R.ish and inform to the old sniggering publicking press and its nation of sheepcopers about the whole plighty troth between them, malady of milady made melodi of malodi, she, the lalage of lyonesses, and him, her knave arrant. To Wildrose La Gilligan from Croppy Crowhore. For all within crystal range.

Ukalepe. Loathers' leave. Had Days. Nemo in Patria. The Luncher Out. Skilly and Carubdish. A Wondering Wreck. From the Mermaids' Tavern. Bullyfamous. Naughtsycalves. Mother of Misery. Walpurgas Nackt.

Maleesh! He would bare to untired world of Leimunconon-nulstria (and what a strip poker globbtrottel they pairs would looks!) how wholefallows, his guffer, the sabbatarian (might faction split his beard!), he too had a great big oh in the megafundum of his tomashunders and how her Lettyshape, his gummer, that congealed sponsar, she had never cessed at waking malters among the jemassons since the cluft that meataxe delt her made her microchasm as gap as down low. So they fished in the kettle and fought free and if she bit his tailibout all hat tiffin for thea. He would jused sit it all write down just as he would jused set it up all writhefully rate in blotch and void, yielding to no man in hymns ignorance, seeing how heartsilly sorey he was, owning to the condrition of his bikestool. And, reading off his fleshskin and writing with his quillbone, fillfull ninequires with it for his auditers, Caxton and Pollock, a most moraculous jeeremyhead sindbook for all the peoples, under the presidency of the suchess of sceaunonsceau, a hadtobe heldin, thoroughly enjoyed by many so meny on block at Boyrut season and for their account ottorly admired by her husband in sole intimacy, about whose told his innersense and the grusomehed's yoeureeke of his spectrescope and why he was off colour and how he was ambothed upon by the very spit of himself, first on the cheekside by Michelangelo and, besouns thats, over on the owld jowly side by Bill C. Babby, and the suburb's formule why they provencials drollo eggspilled him out of his homety dometry narrowedknee domum (osco de basco de pesco de bisco!) because all his creature comfort was an omulette finas erbas in an ark finis orbe and, no master how mustered, mind never mend, he could neither swuck in nonneither swimp in the flood of cecialism and the best and schortest way of blacking out a caughtalock of all the sorrors of Sexton until he would accoster her coume il fou in teto-dous as a wagoner would his mudheeldy wheesindonk at their trist in Parisise after tourments of tosend years, bread cast out on waters, making goods at mutuurity, Mondamoiseau of Casanuova and Mademoisselle from Armentières. Neblonovi's Nivonovio! Nobbio and Nuby in ennoviacion! Occitantitempoli! He would si through severalls of sanctuaries maywhatmay mightwhomight so as to meet somewhere, if produced, on a demi panssion for his whole lofetime, payment in goo to slee music and poisonal comfany, following which, like Ipsey Secumbe, when he fingon to foil the fluter, she could have all the g. s. M. she moohooed after fore and rickwards to herslF, including science of sonorous silence, while he, being brung up on soul butter, have recourse of course to poetry. With tears for his coronaichon, such as engines weep. Was liffe worth leaving? Nej!

Whether life is worth leaving or not, the playfight of the opposed brothers must continue. The twenty-eight girls are divided by four and become the seven colours of the rainbow, dancing in mocking iridiscence round Glugg, who by turns blusters, cries, curses, repents. Meanwhile little Iseult-Isobel drools on her hero. Night comes on, soon the games must end and the children go home to supper, prayers and bed, soothed to sleep by the noises from the Zoo in the Phoenix Park. So now is the time for one big fight before the games are over. In a childish figure we see here the struggle between Mick and

Nick—Blessed Michael the Archangel and Old Nick, accursed Lucifer. But, in the scrimmage, can we tell one from the other?

Come, thrust! Go, parry! Dvoinabrathran, dare! The mad long ramp of manchind's parlements, the learned lacklearning, merciless as wonderful.

— Now may Saint Mowy of the Pleasant Grin be your everglass and even prospect!

— Feeling dank.

Exchange, reverse.

— And may Saint Jerome of the Harlots' Curse make family three of you which is much abedder!

— Grassy ass ago.

And each was wrought with his other. And his continence fell. The bivitellines, Metellus and Ametallikos, her crown pretenders, obscindgemeinded biekerers, varying directly, uruseye each oxesother, superfetated (never cleaner of lamps frowned fiercelier on anointer of hinges), while their treegrown girls, king's game, if he deign so, are in such transfusion just to know twigst timidy twomeys, for gracious sake, who is artthoudux from whose heterotropic, the sleepy or the glouch, for, shyly bawn and showly nursured, exceedingly nice girls can strike exceedingly bad times unless so richtly chosen's by (what though of riches he have none and hope dashes hope on his heart's horizon) to gar their great moments greater. The thing is he must be put strait on the spot, no mere waterstichystuff in a selfmade world that you can't believe a word he's written in, not for pie, but one's only owned by naturel rejection. Charley, you're my darwing! So sing they sequent the assent of man. Till they go round if they go roundagain before breakparts and all dismissed. They keep. Step keep. Step. Stop. Who is Fleur? Where is Ange? Or Gardoun?

Creedless, croonless hangs his haughty. There end no moe red devil in the white of his eye. Braglodyte him do a katadupe! A condamn quondam jontom sick af a suckbut! He does not know how his grandson's grandson's grandson's grandson will stammer up in Peruvian for in the ersebest idiom I have done it equals I so shall do. He dares not think why the grandmother of the grandmother of his grandmother's grandmother coughed Russky with suchky husky accent since in the mouthart of the slove look at me now means I once was otherwise. Nor that the mappamund has been changing pattern as youth plays moves from street to street since time and races were and wise ants hoarded and sauterelles were spendthrifts, no thing making newthing wealthshowever for a silly old Sol, healthytobedder and latewiser. Nor that the turtling of a London's alderman is ladled out by the waggerful to the regionals of pigmyland. His part should say in honour bound: So help me symethew, sammarc, selluc and singin, I will stick to you, by gum, no matter what, bite simbum, and in case of the event coming off beforehand even so you was to release me for the sake of the other cheap girl's baby's name plaster me but I will pluckily well pull on the buckskin gloves! But Noodynaady's actual ingrate tootle is of come into the garner mauve and thy nice are stores of morning and buy me a bunch of iodines.

Evidentament he has failed as tiercely as the deuce before for she is wearing none of the three. And quite as patenly there is a hole in the ballet trough which the rest fell out. Because to explain why the residue is, was, or will not be, according to the eighth axiom, proceeded with, namely, since ever apart that gossan duad, so sure as their's a patch on a pomelo, this yam ham in never live could, the shifting about of the lassies, the tug of love of their lads ending with a great deal of merriment, hoots, screams, scarf drill, cap fecking, ejaculations of aurinos, reechoable mirthpeals and general thumbtonosery (Myama's a yaung yaung cauntry), one must recken with the sudden and gigantesquesque appearance unwithstandable as a general election in Barnado's bearskin amongst the brawlmiddle of this village childergarten of the largely longsuffering laird of Lucanhof.

"The laird of Lucanhof"—even in this child's-play we are reminded how the contention of the opposites is reconciled in the father. Soon we shall hear his thunder calling the children in.

And eher you could pray mercy to goodness or help with your hokey or mehokeypoo, Gallus's hen has collared her pullets. That's where they have owreglias for. Their bone of contention, flesh to their thorns, prest as Prestissima, makes off in a thinkling (and not one hen only nor two hens neyther but every blessed brigid came aclucking and aclacking), while, a rum a rum, the ram of all harns, Bier, Wijn, Spirituosen for consumption on the premises, advokaat withouten pleaders, Mas marrit, Pas poulit, Ras ruddist of all, though flamifestouned from galantifloures, is hued and cried of each's colour.

Home all go. Halome. Blare no more ramsblares, oddmund barkes! And cease your fumings, kindalled bushies! And sherrigoldies yeassymgnays; your wildeshaweshowe moves swiftly sterneward! For here the holy language. Soons to come. To pausse.

'Tis goed. Het best.

For they are now tearing, that is, teartoretorning. Too soon are coming tasbooks and goody, hominy bread and bible bee, with jaggery-yo to juju-jaw, Fine's French phrases from the Grandmère des Grammaires and bothered parsenaps from the Four Massores, Mattatias, Marusias, Lucanias, Jokinias, and what happened to our eleven in thirtytwo antepostdating the Valgur Eire and why is limbo where is he and what are the sound waves saying ceased ere they all wayed wrong and Amnist anguished axes Collis and where fishngaman fetched the mongafesh from and whatfor paddybird notplease rancoon and why was Sindat sitthing on him sitbom like a saildior, with what the doc did in the doil, not to mention define the hydraulics of common salt and, its denier crid of old provaunce, where G.P.O. is zentrum and D.U.T.C. are radients write down by the frequency of the scores and crores of your refractions the valuations in the pice of dinggyings on N.C.R. and S.C.R.

That little cloud, a nibulissa, still hangs isky. Singabed sulks before slumber. Light at night has an alps on his druckhouse. Thick head and thin butter or after you with me. Caspi, but gueroligue stings the air. Gaylegs to riot of us! Gallocks to lafft!

What is amaid today todo? So angelland all weeping bin that Izzy most unhappyis. Fain Essie fie onhapje? laughs her stella's vispirine.

While, running about their ways, going and coming, now at rhimba rhomba, now in trippiza trappaza, pleating a pattern Gran Geamatron showed them of gracehoppers, auntskippers and coneyfarm leppers, they jeerilied along, durian gay and marian maidcap, lou Dariou beside la Matieto, all boy more all girl singoutfeller longa house blong store Huddy, whilest nin nin nin nin that Boorman's clock, a winny on the tinny side, ninned nin nin nin nin, about old Father Barley how he got up of a morning arley and he met with a plattonem blondes named Hips and Haws and fell in with a fellows of Trinity some header Skowood Shaws like (You'll catch it, don't fret, Mrs Tummy Lupton! Come indoor, Scoffynosey, and shed your swank!) auld Daddy Deacon who could stow well his place of beacon but he never could hold his kerosene's candle to (The nurse'll give it you, stickypots! And you wait, my lasso, fecking the twine!) bold Farmer Burleigh who wuck up in a hurlywurly where he huddly could wuddle to wallow his weg tillbag of the baker's booth to beg of (You're well held now, Missy Cheekspeer, and your panto's off! Fie, for shame, Ruth Wheatacre, after all the booz said!) illed Diddiddy Achin for the prize of a pease of bakin with a pinch of the panch of the ponch in jurys for (Ah, crabeyes, I have you, showing off to the world with that gape in your stocking!) Wold Forrester Farley who, in deesperation of deispiration at the diasporation of his diesparation, was found of the round of the sound of the lound of the. Lukkedoerendunandurraskewdylooshoofermoyportertooryzooysphalnabortansporthaokansakroidverjkapakkapuk.

Byfall.

Upploud!

The play thou schouwburgst, Game, here endeth. The curtain drops by deep request.

Uplouderamain!

Gonn the gawds, Gunnar's gustspells. When the h, who the hu, how the hue, where the huer? Orbiter onswers: lots lives lost. Fionia is fed up with Fidge Fudgesons. Sealand snorres.

Rendningrocks roguesreckning reigns. Gwds with gurs are gttrdmmrng. Hlls vlls. The timid hearts of words all exeomnosunt. Mannagad, lammalelouh, how do that come? By Dad, youd not heed that fert? Fulgitudes ejist rowdownan tonuout. Quoq! And buncskleydoodle! Kidoosh! Of their fear they broke, they ate wind, they fled; where they ate there they fled; of their fear they fled, they broke away. Go to, let us extol Azrael with our harks, by our brews, on our jambses, in his gaits. To Mezouzalem with the Dephilim, didits dinkun's dud? Yip! Yup! Yarrah! And let Nek Nekulon extol Mak Makal and let him say unto him: Immi ammi Semmi. And shall not Babel be with Lebab? And he war. And he shall open his mouth and answer: I hear, O Ismael, how they laud is only as my loud is one. If Nekulon shall be havonfalled surely Makal haven hevens. Go to, let us extell Makal, yea, let us exceedingly extell. Though you have lien amung your posspots my excellency is over Ismael. Great is him whom is over Ismael and he shall mekanek of Mak Nakulon. And he deed.

Uplouderamainagain!

For the Clearer of the Air from on high has spoken in tumbuldum tambaldam to his tembledim tombaldoom worrild and, moguphonoised by that phonemanon, the unhappitents of the earth have terrerumbled from fimament unto fundament and from tweedledeedumms down to twiddledeedees.

Loud, hear us!

Loud, graciously hear us!

Now have thy children entered into their habitations. And nationglad, camp meeting over, to shin it, Gov be thanked! Thou hast closed the portals of the habitations of thy children and thou hast set thy guards thereby, even Garda Didymus and Garda Domas, that thy children may read in the book of the opening of the mind to light and err not in the darkness which is the afterthought of thy nomatter by the guardiance of those guards which are thy bodemen, the cheeryboyum chirryboth with the kerrybommers in their krubeems, Pray-your-Prayers Timothy and Back-to-Bunk Tom.

Till tree from tree, tree among trees, tree over tree become stone to stone, stone between stones, stone under stone for ever.

O Loud, hear the wee beseech of thees of each of these thy unlitten ones! Grant sleep in hour's time, O Loud!

That they take no chill. That they do ming no merder. That they shall not gomeet madhowiatrees.

Loud, heap miseries upon us yet entwine our arts with laughters low!

Ha he hi ho hu.

Mummum.

As we there are where are we are we there from tomtittot to teetootomtotalitarian. Tea tea too oo.

UNDE ET UBI.

With his broad and hairy face, to Ireland a disgrace.

Whom will comes over. Who to caps ever. And howelse do we hook our hike to find that pint of porter place? Am shot, says the bigguard.[1]

SIC.

Menly about peebles.

Dont retch meat fat salt lard sinks down (and out).

Whence. Quick lunch by our left, wheel, to where. Long Livius Lane, mid Mezzofanti Mall, diagonising Lavatery Square, up Tycho Brache Crescent,[2] shouldering Berkeley Alley, querfixing Gainsborough Carfax, under Guido d'Arezzo's Gadeway, by New Livius Lane till where we whiled while we whithered. Old Vico Roundpoint. But fahr, be fear! And natural, simple, slavish, filial. The marriage of Montan wetting his moll we know, like any enthewsyass cuckling a hoyden[3] in her rougey

IMAGINABLE ITINERARY THROUGH THE PARTICULAR UNIVERSAL.

[1] Rawmeash, quoshe with her girlic teangue. If old Herod with the Cornwell's eczema was to go for me like he does Snuffler whatever about his blue canaries I'd do nine months for his beaver beard.

[2] Mater Mary Mercerycordial of the Dripping Nipples, milk's a queer arrangement.

[3] Real life behind the floodlights as shown by the best exponents of a royal divorce.

gipsylike chinkaminx pulshandjupeyjade and her petsybluse indecked o' voylets.[1] When who was wist was ware. En elv, et fjaell. And the whirr of the whins humming us howe. His hume. Hencetaking tides we haply return, trumpeted by prawns and ensigned with seakale, to befinding ourself when old is said in one and maker mates with made (O my!), having conned the cones and meditated the mured and pondered the pensils and ogled the olymp and delighted in her dianaphous and cacchinated behind his culosses, before a mosoleum. Length Withought Breath, of him, a chump of the evums, upshoot of picnic or stupor out of sopor, Cave of Kids or Hymanian Glattstoneburg, denary, danery, donnery, domm, who, entiringly as he continues highlyfictional, tumulous under his chthonic exterior but plain Mr Tumulty in muftilife,[2] in his antisipiences as in his recognisances, is, (Dominic Directus) a manyfeast munificent more mob than man.

Swiney Tod, ye Daimon Barbar!

Dig him in the rubsh!

Ungodly old Ardrey, Cronwall beeswaxing the convulsion box.

Ainsoph,[3] this upright one, with that noughty besighed him zeroine. To see in his horrorscup he is mehrkurios than saltz of sulphur. Terror of the noonstruck by day, cryptogam of each nightly bridable. But, to speak broken heaventalk, is he? Who is he? Whose is he? Why is he? Howmuch is he? Which is he? When is he? Where is he?[4] How is he? And what the decans is there about him

CONSTITUTION OF THE CONSTITUTIONABLE AS CONSTITUTIONAL.

[1] When we play dress grownup at alla ludo poker you'll be happnessised to feel how fetching I can look in clingarounds.

[2] Kellywick, Longfellow's Lodgings, House of Comments III, Cake Walk, Amusing Avenue, Salt Hill, Co. Mahogany, Izalond, Terra Firma.

[3] Groupname for grapejuice.

[4] Bhing, said her burglar's head, soto poce.

anyway, the decemt man? Easy, calm your haste! Approach to lead our passage!
This bridge is upper.
Cross.
Thus come to castle.
Knock.[1]
A password, thanks.
Yes, pearse.
Well, all be dumbed!
O really?[2]

PROBAPOSSIBLE PROLEGOMENA TO IDEAREAL HISTORY.

Swing the banjo, bantams, bounce-the-baller's blown to fook.

Hoo cavedin earthwight
At furscht kracht of thunder.[3]
When shoo, his flutterby,
Was netted and named.[4]

Thsight near left me eyes when I seen her put thounce otay ithpot.

Erdnacrusha, requiestress, wake em!
And let luck's puresplutterall lucy at ease![5]
To house as wise fool ages builded.
Sow byg eat.[6]

Quartandwds.

GNOSIS OF PRECREATE DETERMINATION. AGNOSIS OF POSTCREATE DETERMINISM.

Staplering to tether to, steppingstone to mount by, as the Boote's at Pickardstown. And that skimmelk steed still in the groundloftfan. As over all. Or be these wingsets leaned to the outwalls, beastskin trophies of booth of Baws the balsamboards?[7] Burials be ballyhouraised! So let Bacchus e'en call! Inn inn! Inn inn! Where. The babbers ply the pen. The bibbers drang the den. The papplicom, the pubblicam he's turning tin for ten. From

Tickets for the Tailwaggers Terrierpuppy Raffle.

[1] Yussive smirte and ye mermon answerth from his beelyingplace below the tightmark, Gotahelv!

[2] O Evol, kool in the salg and ees how Dozi pits what a drows er.

[3] A goodrid croven in a tynwalled tub.

[4] Apis amat aram. Luna legit librum. Pulla petit pascua.

[5] And after dinn to shoot the shades.

[6] Says blistered Mary Achinhead to beautifed Tummy Tullbutt.

[7] Begge. To go to Begge. To go to Begge and to be sure to reminder Begge. Goodbeg, buggey Begge.

seldomers that most frequent him. That same erst crafty hakemouth which under the assumed name of Ignotus Loquor, of foggy old, harangued bellyhooting fishdrunks on their favorite stamping ground, from a father theobalder brake.[1] And Egyptus, the incenstrobed, as Cyrus heard of him? And Major A. Shaw after he got the miner smellpex? And old Whiteman self, the blighty blotchy, beyond the bays, hope of ostrogothic and ottomanic faith converters, despair of Pandemia's postwartem plastic surgeons? But is was all so long ago. Hispano-Cathayan-Euxine, Castillian-Emeratic-Hebridian, Espanol-Cymric-Helleniky? Rolf the Ganger, Rough the Gangster, not a feature alike and the face the same.[2] Pastimes are past times. Now let bygones be bei Gunne's. Saaleddies er it in this warken werden, mine boerne, and it vild need olderwise[3] since primal made alter in garden of Idem. The tasks above are as the flasks below, saith the emerald canticle of Hermes and all's loth and pleasestir, are we told, on excellent inkbottle authority, solarsystemised, seriolcosmically, in a more and more almightily expanding universe under one, there is rhymeless reason to believe, original sun. Securely judges orb terrestrial.[4] *Haud certo ergo.* But O felicitous culpability, sweet bad cess to you for an archetypt!

Mars speaking.

Smith, no home.

Non quod sed quiat.

Hearasay in paradox lust.

[1] Huntler and Pumar's animal alphabites, the first in the world from aab to zoo.

[2] We dont hear the booming cursowarries, we wont fear the fletches of fightning, we float the meditarenias and come bask to the isle we love in spice. Punt.

[3] And this once golden bee a cimadoro.

[4] And he was a gay Lutharius anyway, Sinobiled. You can tell by their extraordinary clothes.

Playtime is over, sleeptime too. The boys are at their lessons now, preparing to go out into the big world and initiate a new phase in the Viconian cycle of history. First we had a theocracy (Finnegan); next came the aristocracy of HCE. Now we must have the somewhat debased rule of Shaun, who will be only half the man his father was. Neither he nor his brother is fit to govern (Shaun is morally weak; Shem is an artist and irresponsible though clever). Nevertheless both must learn the nature of God, man, woman and, indeed, all the subjects which make up the mediaeval trivium and quadrivium, together with the secret doctrines of the Cabala, in order to fit themselves for taking over the world.

The middle of the page presents the dream-distorted matter of their lessons (at the moment they are trying to find out the nature of God). The left-hand notes and the footnotes are the irreverent comments of Shem. On the right Shaun summarises—more or less seriously—these Cabalistic mysteries. Spirit descends to fertilise time and space; the great All-Father wills the universe into being: man appears; in the nursery above the pub in Chapelizod the children act out the first building of human societies. The great and depressing principle of polarity—which the opposed twins represent—leads to a PANOPTICAL PURVIEW OF POLITICAL PROGRESS AND THE FUTURE PRESENTATION OF THE PAST. The boys have a break—INCIPIT INTERMISSIO—and the baffling eternal feminine, as *fanciulla* or girl, not as mother, enters the text and swamps the footnotes. We recognise at once the seductive rhythm and head-reeling "little language" of the Temptress Isobel—"encuoniams here and improperies there[1]. With a pansy for the pussy in the corner[2]".

INCIPIT INTERMISSIO.

Uncle Flabbius Muximus to Niecia Flappia Minnimiss. As this is. And as this this is.

Dear Brotus, land me arrears.

Rockaby, babel, flatten a wall.

How he broke the good news to Gent.

Bewise of Fanciulla's heart, the heart of Fanciulla! Even the recollection of willow fronds is a spellbinder that lets to hear.[3] The rushes by the grey nuns' pond: ah eh oh let me sigh too. Coalmansbell: behoves you handmake of the load. Jenny Wren: pick, peck. Johnny Post: pack, puck.[4] All the world's in want and is writing a letters.[5] A letters from a person to a place about a thing. And all the world's on wish to be carrying a letters. A letters to a king about a treasure from a cat.[6] When men want to write a letters. Ten men, ton men, pen men, pun men, wont to rise a ladder. And den men, dun men, fen men, fun men, hen men, hun men wend to raze a leader. Is then any lettersday from many peoples, Daganasanavitch? Empire, your outermost.[7] A posy cord. Plece.

MAJOR AND MINOR

We have wounded our way on foe tris prince till that force in the gill is faint afarred

[1] Gosem pher, gezumpher, greeze a jarry grim felon! Good bloke him!

[2] And if they was setting on your stool as hard as my was she could beth her bothom dolours he'd have a culious impressiom on the diminitive that chafes our ends.

[3] When I'am Enastella and am taken for Essastessa I'll do that droop on the pohlmann's piano.

[4] Heavenly twinges, if it's one of his I'll fearly feint as swoon as he enterrooms.

[5] To be slipped on, to be slept by, to be conned to, to be kept up. And when you're done push the chain.

[6] With her modesties office.

[7] Strutting as proud as a great turquin weggin that cuckhold on his Eddems and Clay's hat.

and the face in the treebark feigns afear. This is rainstones ringing. Strangely cult for this ceasing of the yore. But Erigureen is ever. Pot price pon patrilinear plop, if the osseletion of the onkring gives omen nome? Since alls war that end war let sports be leisure and bring and buy fair. Ah ah athclete, blest your bally bathfeet! Towntoquest, fortorest, the hour that hies is hurley. A halt for hearsake.[1]

MODES COALESCING PROLIFERATE HOMOGENUINE HOMOGENEITY.

[1] Come, smooth of my slate, to the beat of my blosh! With all these gelded ewes jilting about and the thrills and ills of laylock blossoms three's so much more plants than chants for cecilies that I was thinking fairly killing times of putting an end to myself and my malody, when I remembered all your pupil-teacher's erringnesses in perfection class. You sh'undn't write you can't if you w'udn't pass for undevelopmented. This is the propper way to say that, Sr. If it's me chews to swallow all you saidn't you can eat my words for it as sure as there's a key in my kiss. Quick erit faciofacey. When we will conjugate together toloseher tomaster tomiss while morrow fans amare hour, verbe de vie and verve to vie, with love ay loved have I on my back spine and does for ever. Your are me severe? Then rue. My intended, Jr, who I'm throne away on, (here he inst, my lifstack, a newfolly likon) when I slip through my pettigo I'll get my decree and take seidens when I'm not ploughed first by some Rolando the Lasso, and flaunt on the flimsyfilmsies for to grig my collage juniorees who, though they flush fuchsia, are they octette and viginity in my shade but always my figurants. They may be yea of my year but they're nary nay of my day. Wait till spring has sprung in spickness and prigs beg in to pry they'll be plentyprime of housepets to pimp and pamper my. Impending marriage. Nature tells everybody about but I learned all the runes of the gamest game ever from my old nourse Asa. A most adventuring trot is her and she vicking well knowed them all heartswise and fourwords. How Olive d'Oyly and Winnie Carr, bejupers, they reized the dressing of a salandmon and how a peeper coster and a salt sailor med a mustied poet atwaimen. It most have bean Mad Mullans planted him. Bina de Bisse and Trestrine von Terrefin. Sago sound, rite go round, kill kackle, kook kettle and (remember all should I forget to) bolt the thor. Auden. Wasn't it just divining that dog of a dag in Skokholme as I sat astrid uppum their Drewitt's altar, as cooledas as cul-cumbre, slapping my straights till the sloping ruins, postillion, postallion, a swinge a swank, with you offering me clouts of illscents and them horners stagstruck on the leasward! Don't be of red, you blanching mench! This isabella I'm on knows the ruelles of the rut and she don't fear andy mandy. So sing loud, sweet cheeriot, like anegreon in heaven! The good fother with the twingling in his eye will always have cakes in his pocket to bethroat us with for our allmichael good. Amum. Amum. And Amum again. For tough troth is stronger than fortuitous fiction and it's the surplice money, oh my young friend and ah me sweet creature, what buys the bed while wits borrows the clothes.

The boys (Shaun is called Kev and Shem is called Dolph) resume their lessons. The marginal notes have changed places—irreverent on the right (Dolph), serious on the left (Kev). With the aid of a geometrical diagram, Dolph is trying to explain the great earth-mother or "geomater"—the zero which, joined to 1 of the creative All-Father makes up the number 10, symbol of completed creation. But the earth-mother is really ALP, their own mother, and Kev at first fails to see that Dolph is reducing a great mystery to a piece of lowly illicit knowledge—science as mere infantile curiosity about what is hidden up our mothers' skirts. When he understands, he turns in a rage on Dolph and finally strikes him. But, Christlike, Dolph does not retaliate: like Stephen Dedalus in *Ulysses,* he hates to be involved in the world of action.

But the punch on the jaw has "teaspilled all my hazeydency", says Dolph. That word "hazeydency" points back to HCE's guilty stutter. Both boys have inherited their father's guilt, but it is guilt about the unworthiness of either to rule the world. Their struggles are really an attempt to become one again, to be reconciled in the father—the clash of thesis and antithesis becoming a synthesis. But they must remain polarised—"*The Twofold Truth and the Conjunctive Appetites of Oppositional Orexes*". Nothing can be done about it.

The lesson ends in a recapitulation of all the branches of knowledge and, finally, a recital of the descending ladder of numbers which, in the Cabala, represent the various stages of creation. *Cush* (5) is also *Kish*—a point of division appropriate to the two brothers (if Shaun-Kish is Christ, Shem-Cush rejects him). The crossed bones stand for love (a Kiss) and death. The brothers feed, then go off to their new world, whence they send a letter to the old.

Coss? Cossist? Your parn! You, you make what name? (and in truth, as a poor soul is between shift and shift ere the death he has lived through becomes the life he is to die into, he or he had albut — he was rickets as to reasons but the balance of his minds was stables — lost himself or himself some somnione sciupiones, soswhitchoverswetch had he or he gazet, murphy come, murphy go, murphy plant, murphy grow, a maryamyriameliamurphies, in the lazily eye of his lapis,

WHY MY AS LIKEWISE WHIS HIS.

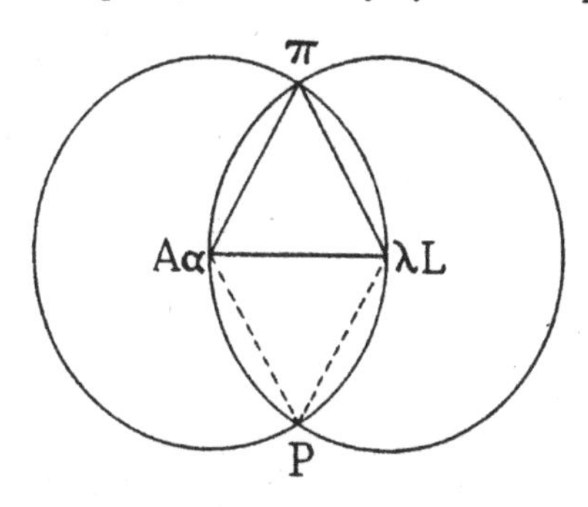

Iteralterance or the Interplay of Bones in the Womb.

Vieus Von DVbLIn, 'twas one of dozedeams a darkies ding in dewood) the Turnpike under the Great Ulm (with Mearingstone in Fore ground).[1] Given now ann linch you take enn all. Allow me! And, heaving alljawbreakical expressions out of old Sare Isaac's[2] universal of specious aristmystic unsaid, A is for Anna like L is for liv. Aha hahah, Ante Ann you're apt to ape aunty annalive! Dawn gives rise. Lo, lo, lives love! Eve takes fall. La, la, laugh leaves alass! Aiaiaiai, Antiann, we're last to the lost, Loulou! Tis perfect. Now (lens

The Vortex. Spring of Sprung Verse. The Vertex.

[1] Draumcondra's Dreamcountry where the betterlies blow.

[2] O, Laughing Sally, are we going to be toadhauntered by that old Pantifox Sir Somebody Something, Burtt, for the rest of our secret stripture?

Sarga, or the path of outgoing.

Docetism and Didicism, Maya-Thaya. Tamas-Rajas-Sattvas.

your dappled yeye here, mine's presbyoperian, shill and wall) we see the copyngink strayedline AL (in Fig., the forest) from being continued, stops ait Lambday[1]: Modder ilond there too. Allow me anchore! I bring down noth and carry awe. Now, then, take this in! One of the most murmurable loose carollaries ever Ellis threw his cookingclass. With Olaf as centrum and Olaf's lambtail for his spokesman circumscript a cyclone. Allow ter! Hoop! As round as the calf of an egg! O, dear me! O, dear me now! Another grand discobely! After Makefearsome's Ocean. You've actuary entducked one! Quok! Why, you haven't a passer! Fantastic! Early clever, surely doomed, to Swift's, alas, the galehus! Match of a matchness, like your Bigdud dadder in the boudeville song, *Gorotsky Gollovar's Troubles*, raucking his flavourite turvku in the smukking precincts of lydias,[2] with Mary Owens and Dolly Monks seesidling to edge his cropulence and Blake-Roche, Kingston and Dockrell auriscenting him from afurz, our papacocopotl,[3] Abraham Bradley King? (ting ting! ting ting!) By his magmasine fall. Lumps, lavas and all.[4] *Bene!* But, thunder and turf, it's not alover yet! One recalls Byzantium. The mystery repeats itself todate as our callback mother Gaudyanna, that was daughter to a tanner,[5] used to sing, as I think, now and then consinuously over her possetpot in her quer

[1] Ex jup pep off Carpenger Strate. The kids' and dolls' home. Makeacakeache.

[2] A vagrant need is a flagrant weed.

[3] Grand for blowing off steam when you walk up in the morning.

[4] At the foot of Bagnabun Banbasday was lost on one.

[5] We're all found of our anmal matter.

The Vegetable Cell and its Private Properties.

homolocous humminbass hesterdie and istherdie forivor.[1] Vanissas Vanistatums! And for a night of thoughtsendyures and a day. As Great Shapesphere puns it. In effect, I remumble, from the yules gone by, purr lil murrerof myhind, so she used indeed. When she give me the Sundaclouths she hung up for Tate and Comyng and snuffed out the ghost in the candle at his old game of haunt the sleepper. Faithful departed. When I'm dreaming back like that I begins to see we're only all telescopes. Or the comeallyoum saunds. Like when I dromed I was in Dairy and was wuckened up with thump in thudderdown. Rest in peace! But to return.[2] What a wonderful memory you have too! Twonderful morrowy! Straorbinaire! *Bene!* I bring town eau and curry nothung up my sleeve. Now, springing quickenly from the mudland Loosh from Luccan with Allhim as her Elder tetraturn a somersault. All's fair on all fours, as my instructor unstrict me. Watch! And you'll have the whole inkle. Allow, allow! Gyre O, gyre O, gyrotundo! Hop lala! As umpty herum as you seat! O, dear me, that was very nesse! Very nace indeed! And makes us a daintical pair of accomplasses! You, allus for the kunst and me for omething with a handel to it. *Beve!* Now, as will pressantly be felt, there's tew tricklesome poinds where our twain of doubling bicirculars, mating approxemetely in their suite poi and poi, dunloop into eath the ocher. Lucihere.! I fee where you

The haves and the havenots: a distinction.

[1] Sewing up the beillybursts in their buckskin shiorts for big Kapitayn Killykook and the Jukes of Kelleiney.

[2] Say where! A timbrelfill of twinkletinkle.

Zweispaltung as Fundemaintalish of Wiederherstellung.

mea. The doubleviewed seeds. Nun, lemmas quatsch, vide pervoys akstiom, and I think as I'm suqeez in the limon, stickme punctum, but for semenal rations I'd likelong, by Araxes, to mack a capital Pee for Pride down there on the batom[1] where Hoddum and Heave, our monsterbilker, balked his bawd of parodies. And let you go, Airmienious, and mick your modest mock Pie out of Humbles up your end. Where your apexojesus will be a point of order. With a geing groan grunt and a croak click cluck.[2] And my faceage kink and kurkle trying to make keek peep.[3] Are you right there, Michael, are you right? Do you think you can hold on by sitting tight? Well, of course, it's awful angelous. Still I don't feel it's so dangelous. Ay, I'm right here, Nickel, and I'll write. Singing the top line why it suits me mikey fine. But, yaghags hogwarts and arrahquinonthiance, it's the muddest thick that was ever heard dump since Eggsmather got smothered in the plap of the pfan. Now, to compleat anglers, beloved bironthiarn and hushtokan hishtakatsch, join alfa pea and pull loose by dotties and, to be more sparematically logoical, eelpie and paleale by trunkles. Alow me align while I encloud especious! The Nike done it. Like pah,[4] I peh. Innate little bondery. And as plane as a poke stiff.[5] Now, *aqua in buccat.* I'll make you to see figuratleavely the whome of your eternal

[1] Parsee ffrench for the upholdsterer would be delightered.
[2] I'll pass out if the screw spliss his strut.
[3] Thargam then goeligum? If you sink I can, swimford. Suksumkale!
[4] Hasitatense?
[5] The impudence of that in girl's things!

Destiny, Influence of Design upon.

Prometheus or the Promise of Provision.

geomater. And if you flung her headdress on her from under her highlows you'd wheeze whyse Salmonson set his seel on a hexengown.[1] Hissss!, Arrah, go on! Fin for fun! You've spat your shower like a son of Sibernia but let's have at it! Subtend to me now! Pisk! Outer serpumstances beiug ekewilled, we carefully, if she pleats, lift by her seam hem and jabote at the spidsiest of her trickkikant (like thousands done before since fillies calpered. Ocone! Ocone!) the maidsapron of our A.L.P., fearfully! till its nether nadir is vortically where (allow me aright to two cute winkles) its naval's napex will have to beandbe. You must proach near mear for at is dark. Lob. And light your mech. Jeldy! And this is what you'll say.[2] Waaaaaa. Tch! Sluice! Pla! And their, redneck, (for addn't we to gayatsee with Puhl the Punkah's bell?) mygh and thy, the living spit of dead waters,[3] fastness firm of Hurdlebury Fenn, discinct and isoplural in its (your sow to the duble) sixuous parts, flument, fluvey and fluteous, midden wedge of the stream's your muddy old triagonal delta, fiho miho, plain for you now, appia lippia pluvaville, (hop the hula, girls!) the no niggard spot of her safety vulve, first of all usquiluteral threeingles, (and why wouldn't she sit cressloggedlike the lass that lured a tailor?) the constant of fluxion, Mahamewetma, pride of the province[4] and when that tidled boare rutches up from the Afrantic, allaph quaran's his bett und bier![5]

[1] The chape of Doña Speranza of the Nacion.
[2] Ugol egal ogle. Mi vidim Mi.
[3] It is, it is Sangannon's dream.
[4] And all meinkind.
[5] Whangpoos the paddle and whiss whee whoo.

Ambages and Their Rôle.

Paa lickam laa lickam, apl lpa! This it is an her. You see her it. Which it whom you see it is her. And if you could goaneggbetter we'd soon see some raffant scrumala riffa. Quicks herit fossyending. Quef! So post that to your pape and smarket! And you can haul up that languil pennant, mate. I've read your tunc's dimissage. For, let it be taken that her littlenist is of no magnetude or again let it be granted that Doll the laziest can be dissimulant with all respects from Doll the fiercst, thence must any whatyoulike in the power of empthood be either

Ecclasiastical and Celestial Hierarchies. The Ascending. The Descending.

greater THaN or less THaN the unitate we have in one or hence shall the vectorious readyeyes of evertwo circumflicksrent searclhers never film in the elipsities of their gyribouts those fickers which are returnally reprodictive of themselves.[1] Which is unpassible. Quarrellary. The logos of somewome to that base anything, when most characteristically mantissa minus, comes to nullum in the endth:[2] orso, here is nowet badder than the sin of Aha with his cosin Lil, versswaysed on coverswised, and all that's consecants and cotangincies till Perperp stops repippinghim since her redtangles are all abscissan for limitsing this tendency of

The peripatetic periphery. It's Allothesis.

our Frivulteeny Sexuagesima[3] to expense herselfs as sphere as possible, paradismic perimutter, in all directions on the bend of the unbridalled, the infinisissimalls of her facets becoming manier and manier as the calicolum of her umdescribables (one has thoughts of that eternal Rome) shrinks from schurtiness

[1] I enjoy as good as anyone.
[2] Neither a soul to be saved nor a body to be kicked.
[3] The boast of the town.

to scherts.[1] Scholium, there are trist sigheds to everysing but ichs on the freed brings euchs to the feared. Qued? Mother of us all! O, dear me, look at that now! I don't know is it your spictre or my omination but I'm glad you dimentioned it! My Lourde! My Lourde! If that aint just the beatenest lay I ever see! And a superpbosition! Quoint a quincidence! O.K.

Canine Venus sublimated to Aulidic Aphrodite.

Omnius Kollidimus. As Ollover Krumwall sayed when he slepped ueber his grannyamother. Kangaroose feathers. Who in the name of thunder'd ever belevin you were that bolt? But you're holy mooxed and gaping up the wrong palce[2] as if you was seeheeing the gheist that stays forenenst, you blessed simpletop domefool! Where's your belested loiternan's lamp? You must lap wandret down the bluishing refluction below. Her trunk's not her brainbox. Hear where the bolgylines, Yseen here the puncture. So he done it. Luck! See her good.

Exclusivism: the Ors, Sors and Fors, which?

Well, well, well, well! O dee, O dee, that's very lovely! We like Simperspreach Hammeltones to fellow Selvertunes O'Haggans.[3] When he rolls over his ars and shows the hise of his heels. Vely lovely entilely! Like a yangsheepslang with the tsifengtse. So analytical plausible! And be the powers of Moll Kelly, neighbour topsowyer, it will be a lozenge to me all my lauffe.[4] More better twofeller we been speak copperads. Ever thought about Guinness's? And the regrettable Parson Rome's advice?

[1] Hen's bens, are we soddy we missiled her?

[2] I call that a scumhead.

[3] Pure chingchong idiotism with any way words all in one soluble. Gee each owe tea eye smells fish. That's U.

[4] The Doodles family, ᗰ, Δ, ⊣, X, □, ∧, ⊏. Hoodle doodle, fam.?

Want to join the police.[1] You know, you were always one of the bright ones, since a foot made you an unmentionable, fakes! You know, you're the divver's own smart gossoon, aequal to yoursell and wanigel to anglyother, so you are, hoax! You know, you'll be dampned, so you will, one of these invernal days but you will be, carrotty![2]

Primanouriture and Ultimogeniture.

SICK US A SOCK WITH SOME SEDIMENT IN IT FOR THE SAKE OF OUR DARNING WIVES.

Wherapool, gayet that when he stop look time he stop long ground who here hurry he would have ever the lothst word, with a sweet me ah err eye ear marie to reat from the jacob's[3] and a shypull for toothsake of his armjaws at the slidepage of de Vere Foster, would and could candykissing P. Kevin to fress up the rinnerung and to ate by hart (*leo* I read, such a spanish, *escribibis*, all your mycoscoups) wont to nibbleh ravenostonnoriously ihs mum to me in bewonderment of his chipper chuthor for, while that Other by the halp of his creactive mind offered to deleberate the mass from the booty of fight our Same with the holp of the bounty of food sought to delubberate the mess from his corructive mund, with his muffetee cuffes ownconsciously grafficking with his sinister cyclopes after trigamies and spirals' wobbles pursuiting their rovinghamilton selves and godolphing in fairlove to see around the waste of noland's browne jesus[4] (thur him no quartos!) till that on him poorin sweat the juggaleer's veins (quench his quill!) in his napier scrag stud out bursthright tam-

No Sturm. No Drang.

[1] Picking on Nickagain, Pikey Mikey?

[2] Early morning, sir Dav Stephens, said the First Gentleman in youreups.

[3] Bag bag blockcheap, have you any will?

[4] What a lubberly whide elephant for the men-in-the straits!

Illustration.

quam taughtropes. (Spry him! call a bloodlekar! Where's Dr Brassenaarse?) Es war itwas in his priesterrite. O He Must Suffer! From this misbelieving feacemaker to his noncredible fancyflame.[1] Ask for bosthoon, late for Mass, pray for blaablaablack sheep. (Sure you could wright anny pippap passage, Eye bet, as foyne as that moultylousy Erewhig, yerself, mick! Nock the muddy nickers![2] Christ's Church varses Bellial!) Dear and he went on to scripple gentlemine born, milady bread, he would pen for her, he would pine for her,[3] how he would patpun fun for all[4] with his frolicky frowner so and his glumsome grinner otherso. And how are you, waggy?[5] My animal his sorrafool! And trieste, ah trieste ate I my liver! *Se non é vero son trovatore.* O jerry! He was soso, harriot all! He was sadfellow, steifel! He was mistermysterion. Like a purate out of pensionee with a gouvernament job. All moanday, tearsday, wailsday, thumpsday, frightday, shatterday till the fear of the Law. Look at this twitches! He was quisquis, floored on his plankraft of shittim wood. Look at him! Sink deep or touch not the Cartesian spring! Want more ashes, griper? How diesmal he was lying low on his rawside laying siege to goblin castle. And, bezouts that, how hyenesmeal he was laying him long on his laughside lying sack to croakpartridge. (Be thou wars Rolaf's intes-

Ascription of the Active.

Proscription of the Passive.

[1] And she had to seek a pond's apeace to salve her suiterkins. Sued!

[2] Excuse theyre christianbrothers irish?

[3] When she tripped against the briery bush he profused her allover with curtsey flowers.

[4] A nastilow disigraible game.

[5] Dear old Erosmas. Very glad you are going to Penmark. Write to the corner. Grunny Grant.

tions, quoths the Bhagavat biskop Leech) Ann opes tipoo soon ear! If you could me lendtill my pascol's kondyl, sahib, and the price of a plate of poultice. Punked. With best apolojigs and merrymoney thanks to self for all the clerricals and again begs guerdon for bistrispissing on your bunificence. Well wiggywiggywagtail, and how are you, yaggy? With a capital Tea for Thirst. From here Buvard to dear Picuchet. Blott.

Ensouling Female Sustains Agonising Overman.

Now, (peel your eyes, my gins, and brush your saton hat, me elementator joyclid, son of a Butt! She's mine, Jow low jure,[1] be Skibbering's eagles, sweet tart of Whiteknees Archway) watch him, having caught at the bifurking calamum in his bolsillos, the onelike underworp he had ever funnet without difficultads, the aboleshqvick, signing away in happinext complete, (Exquisite Game of inspiration! I always adored your hand. So could I too and without the scrope of a pen. Ohr for oral, key for crib, olchedolche and a lunge ad lib. Can you write us a last line? From Smith-Jones-Orbison?) intrieatedly in years, jirryalimpaloop. And i Romain, hup u bn gd grl.[2] Unds alws my thts. To fallthere at bare feet hurryaswormarose. Two dies of one rafflement. Eche bennyache. Outstamp and distribute him at the expanse of his society. To be continued. Anon.

WHEN THE ANSWERER IS A LEMAN.

Sesama to the Rescues. The Key Signature.

And ook, ook, ook, fanky! All the charictures[3] in the drame! This is how San holy-

ALL SQUARE AND

[1] I loved to see the Macbeths Jerseys knacking spots of the Plumpduffs Pants.

[2] Lifp year fends you all and moe, fouvenirs foft as fummer fnow, fweet willings and forget-uf-knots.

[3] Gag his tubes yourself.

polypools. And this, pardonsky! is the way Romeopullupalleaps.[1] Pose the pen, man, way me does. Way ole missa vellatooth fust show me how. Fourth power to her illpogue! Bould strokes for your life! Tip! This is Steal, this is Barke, this is Starn, this is Swhipt, this is Wiles, this is Pshaw, this is Doubbllinnbbayyates.[2] This is brave Danny weeping his spache for the popers. This is cool Connolly wiping his hearth with brave Danny. And this, regard! how Chawleses Skewered parparaparnelligoes between brave Danny boy and the Connolly. Upanishadem! Top. Spoken hath L'arty Magory. Eregobragh. Prouf![3]

ACCORDING TO COCKER.

Force Centres of the Fire Serpentine: heart, throat, navel, spleen, sacral, fontanella, intertemporal eye.

Conception of the Compromise and Finding of a Formula.

And Kev was wreathed with his pother.

TROTHBLOWERS.

But, (that Jacoby feeling again for forebitten fruit and, my Georgeous, Kevvy too he just loves his puppadums, I judge!) after all his autocratic writings of paraboles of famellicurbs and meddlied muddlingisms, thee faroots hof cullchaw end ate citrawn woodint wun able rep of the triperforator awlrite blast through his pergaman hit him where he lived and do for the blessted selfchuruls, what I think, smarter like it done for a manny another unpious of the hairydary quare quandary firstings till at length, you one bladdy bragger, by mercystroke he measured his earth anyway? could not but recken in his adder's badder cadder way our frankson who, to be plain, he fight him all time twofeller longa kill dead finish bloody face blong you, was misocain. Wince

FIG AND THISTLE PLOT A PIG AND WHISTLE.

Ideal Present Alone Produces Real Future.

[1] He, angel that I thought him, and he not aebel to speel eelyotripes., Mr Tellibly Divilcult!

[2] When the dander rattles how the peacocks prance!

[3] The Brownes de Browne - Browne of Castlehacknolan.

wan's won! Rip![1] And his countinghands rose.

Formalisa. Loves deathhow simple!

Slutningsbane[2].

Service superseding self.

Thanks eversore much, Pointcarried! I can't say if it's the weight you strike me to the quick or that red mass I was looking at but at the present momentum, potential as I am, I'm seeing rayingbogeys rings round me. Honours to you and may you be commended for our exhibitiveness! I'd love to take you for a bugaboo ride and play funfer all if you'd only sit and be the ballasted bottle in the porker barrel. You will deserve a rolypoly as long as from here to tomorrow. And to hell with them driftbombs and bottom trailers! If my maily was bag enough I'd send you a toxis. By Saxon Chromaticus, you done that lovely for me! Didn't he now, Nubilina? Tiny Mite, she studiert whas? With her listeningin coiffure, her dream of Endsland's daylast and the glorifires of being presainted maid to majesty.[3] And less is the pity for she isn't the lollypops she easily might be if she had for a sample Virginia's air of achievement. That might keep her from throwing delph.[4] As I was saying, while retorting thanks, you make me a reborn of the cards. We're offals boys ambows.[5] For I've flicked up all the crambs as they crumbed from your table um, singing glory allaloserem, cog it out, here goes a sum. So

WITH EBONISER. IN PIX. EUCHRE RISK, MERCI BUCKUP, AND MIND WHO YOU'RE PUCKING, FLEBBY.

Catastrophe and Anabasis.

The rotary processus and its reestablishment of reciprocities.

[1] A byebye bingbang boys! See you Nutcracker Sunday!
[2] Chinchin Childaman! Chapchopchap!
[3] Wipe your glosses with what you know.
[4] If I'd more in the cups that peeves thee you could cracksmith your rows tureens.
[5] Alls Sings and Alls Howls.

read we in must book. It tells. He prophets most who bilks the best.

And that salubrated sickenagiaour of yaours have teaspilled all my hazeydency. Forge away, Sunny Sim! Sheepshopp. Bleating Goad, it is the least of things, Eyeinstye! Imagine it, my deep dartry dullard! It is hours giving, not more. I'm only out for celebridging over the guilt of the gap in your hiscitendency. You are a hundred thousand times welcome, old wortsampler, hellbeit you're just about as culpable as my woolfell merger would be. In effect I could engage in an energument over you till you were republicly royally toobally prussic blue in the shirtafter.[1] *Trionfante di bestia!* And if you're not your bloater's kipper may I never curse again on that pint I took of Jamesons. Old Keane now, you're rod, hook and sinker, old jubalee Keane! Biddy's hair. Biddy's hair, mine lubber. Where is that Quin but he sknows it knot but what you that are my popular endphthisis were born with a solver arm up your sleep. Thou in shanty! Thou in scanty shanty!! Thou in slanty scanty shanty!!! Bide in your hush! Bide in your hush, do! The law does not aloud you to shout. I plant my penstock in your postern, chinarpot. Ave! And let it be to all remembrance. Vale. Ovocation of maiding waters.[2] For auld lang salvy steyne. I defend you to champ my scullion's praises. To book alone belongs the lobe. Foremaster's meed[3] will mark tomorrow when we are making pilscrummage to whaboggeryin with

COME SI COMPITA CUNCTITITITILATIO? CONKERY CUNK, THIGH-THIGHT-TICKELLY-THIGH, LIGGERILAG, TITTERITOT, LEG IN A TEE, LUG IN A LAW, TWO AT A TIE, THREE ON A THRICKY TILL OHIO OHIO IOIOMISS.

The Twofold Truth and the Conjunctive Appetites of Oppositional Orexes.

Trishagion.

[1] From three shellings. A bluedye sacrifice.
[2] Not Kilty. But the manajar was. He! He! Ho! Ho! Ho!
[3] Giglamps, Soapy Geyser, The Smell and Gory Mac Gusty.

staff, scarf and blessed wallet and our aureoles round our neckkandcropfs where as and when Heavysciusgardaddy, parent who offers sweetmeats, will gift uns his Noblett's surprize. With this laudable purpose in loud ability let us be singulfied. Betwixt me and thee hung cong. Item, mizpah ends.

Abnegation is Adaptation.

But while the dial are they doodling dawdling over the mugs and the grubs? Oikey, Impostolopulos?[1] Steady steady steady steady steady studiavimus. Many many many many many manducabimus.[2] We've had our day at triv and quad and writ our bit as intermidgets. Art, literature, politics, economy, chemistry, humanity, &c. Duty, the daughter of discipline, the Great Fire at the South City Markets, Belief in Giants and the Banshee, A Place for Everything and Everything in its Place, Is the Pen Mightier than the Sword? A Successful Career in the Civil Service,[3] The Voice of Nature in the Forest,[4] Your Favorite Hero or Heroine, On the Benefits of Recreation,[5] If Standing Stones Could Speak, Devotion to the Feast of the Indulgence of Portiuncula, The Dublin Metropolitan Police Sports at Ballsbridge, Describe in Homely Anglian Monosyllables the Wreck of the Hesperus,[6] What Morals, if any, can be drawn from Diarmuid and Grania?[7] Do you Approve of our Existing Parliamentary System? The Uses and Abuses of Insects, A

ENTER THE COP AND HOW. SECURES GUBERNANT URBIS TERROREM.

Cato.
Nero.
Saul. Aristotle.
Julius Caesar.
Pericles.
Ovid.
Adam, Eve.
Domitian. Edipus.
Socrates.
Ajax.
Homer.
MarcusAurelius.
Alcibiades.
Lucretius.

[1] The divvy wants that babbling brook. Dear Auntie Emma Emma Eates.
[2] Strike the day off, the nightcap's on nigh. Goney, goney gone!
[3] R. C., disengaged, good character, would help, no salary.
[4] Where Lily is a Lady found the nettle rash.
[5] Bubabipibambuli, I can do as I like with what's me own. Nyamnyam.
[6] Able seaman's caution.
[7] Rarely equal and distinct in all things.

Noah. Plato.
Horace. Isaac.
Tiresias.
Marius.
Diogenes.
Procne, Philo-
mela. Abraham.
Nestor. Cincin-
natus. Leonidas.
Jacob.
Theocritus.
Joseph.
Fabius. Samson.
Cain.
Esop.
Prometheus.
Lot. Pompeius Magnus,
Miltiades Strategos.
Solon.
Castor, Pollux.
Dionysius.
Sappho.
Moses. Job.
Catilina.
Cadmus. Ezekiel.
Solomon. Themistocles.
Vitellius. Darius.

Visit to Guinness' Brewery, Clubs, Advantages of the Penny Post, When is a Pun not a Pun? Is the Co-Education of Animus and Anima Wholly Desirable?[1] What Happened at Clontarf? Since our Brother Johnathan Signed the Pledge or the Meditations of Two Young Spinsters,[2] Why we all Love our Little Lord Mayor, Hengler's Circus Entertainment, On Thrift,[3] The Kettle-Griffith-Moynihan Scheme for a New Electricity Supply, Travelling in the Olden Times,[4] American Lake Poetry, the Strangest Dream that was ever Halfdreamt.[5] Circumspection, Our Allies the Hills, Are Parnellites Just towards Henry Tudor? Tell a Friend in a Chatty Letter the Fable of the Grasshopper and the Ant,[6] Santa Claus, The Shame of Slumdom, The Roman Pontiffs and the Orthodox Churches,[7] The Thirty Hour Week, Compare the Fistic Styles of Jimmy Wilde and Jack Sharkey, How to Understand the Deaf, Should Ladies learn Music or Mathematics? Glory be to Saint Patrick! What is to be found in a Dustheap, The Value of Circumstantial Evidence, Should Spelling? Outcasts in India, Collecting Pewter, Eu,[8] Proper and Regular Diet Necessity For,[9] If You Do It Do It Now.

[1] Jests and the Beastalk with a little rude hiding rod.
[2] Wherry like the whaled prophet in a spookeerie.
[3] What sins is pim money sans Paris?
[4] I've lost the place, where was I?
[5] Something happened that time I was asleep, torn letters or was there snow?
[6] Mich for his pain, Nick in his past.
[7] He has *toglieresti in brodo* all over his agrammatical parts of face and as for that hippofoxphiz, unlucky number, late for the christening!
[8] Eh, Monsieur? Où, Monsieur? Eu, Monsieur? Nenni No, Monsieur!
[9] Ere we hit the hay, brothers, let's have that response to prayer!

Xenophon. Delays are Dangerous. Vitavite! Gobble Anne: tea's set, see's eneugh! Mox soonly will be in a split second per the chancellory of his exticker.

Pantocracy. Bimutualism. Interchangeability. Naturality. Superfetation. Stabimobilism. Periodicity. Consummation. Interpenetrativeness. Predicament. Balance of the factual by the theoric Boox and Coox, Amallagamated.

Aun
Do
Tri
Car
Cush[1]
Shay
Shockt
Ockt
Ni
Geg[2]
Their feed begins.

MAWMAW, LUK, YOUR BEEEFTAY'S FIZZIN OVER!

KAKAO-POETIC LIPPUDENIES OF THE UNGUMPTIOUS.

NIGHTLETTER

With our best youlldied greedings to Pep and Memmy and the old folkers below and beyant, wishing them all very merry Incarnations in this land of the livvey and plenty of preprosperousness through their coming new yonks

from
jake, jack and little sousoucie
(the babes that mean too)

[1] Kish is for anticheirst, and the free of my hand to him!

[2] And gags for skool and crossbuns and whopes he'll enjoyimsolff over our drawings on the line!

Before we can see the world handed over to the sons, we must witness the crack-up of the father, or, since he is an innkeeper, the mactation of the host. HCE must be humiliated, reviled, his substance consumed, his very garments rent. His inn is crowded this evening, and tales have been told and enacted which, in dream-obscurity, hint at the primal guilt of HCE and point to his fall. Soon the customers call for a favourite television programme—Butt and Taff, a reincarnation of Mutt and Jute in the opening chapter of the book, also a kind of vaudeville representation of the eternal theme of the quarrelling brothers. A picture on the wall of the bar —the Charge of the Light Brigade—suggests a favourite story—how the Irish general Buckley did for the Russian general at the Battle of Balaclava. (The original story is one told by James Joyce's father. Buckley aimed at the Russian while the latter was defecating, but Irish chivalry prevailed: he would not shoot a man with his trousers down). In this present story Buckley shoots, and is deemed right to do so. The Russian general suggests HCE himself, caught by three soldiers with his trousers down in the park. HCE is the only man to deprecate the act. This leads him to a defence of all men caught with their trousers down. Who are we to condemn anybody?

We want Bud. We want Bud Budderly. We want Bud Budderly boddily. There he is in his Borrisalooner. The man that shunned the rucks on Gereland. The man thut won the bettlle of the bawll. Order, order, order, order! And tough. We call on Tancred Artaxerxes Flavin to compeer with Barnabas Ulick Dunne.

Order, order, order! Milster Malster in the chair. We've heard it sinse sung thousandtimes. How Burghley shuck the rackushant Germanon. For Ehren, boys, gobrawl!

A public plouse. Citizen soldiers.

> Taff and Butt, after a lengthy preamble, come to the tale of Buckley and the Russian general. The whole narrative is thick with dream-references to imperialist wars, for all of which HCE, the invading foreigner, must be held responsible.

TAFF (*now as he has been past the buckthurnstock from Peadhar Piper of Colliguchuna, whiles they all are bealting pots to dubrin din for old daddam dombstom to tomb and wamb humbs lumbs agamb, glimpse agam, glance agen, rise up road and hive up hill, and find your pollyvoulley foncey pitchin ingles in the parler*). Since you are on for versingrhetorish say your piece! How Buccleuch shocked the rosing girnirilles. A ballet of Gasty Power. A hov and az ov and off like a gow! And don't live out the sad of tearfs, piddyawhick! Not offgott affsang is you, buthbach? Ath yetheredayth noth endeth, hay? Vaersegood! Buckle to! Sayyessik, Ballygarry. The fourscore soculums are watchyoumaycodding to cooll the skoopgoods blooff. Harkabuddy, feign! Thingman placeyear howed wholst somwom shimwhir tinkledinkledelled. Shinfine deed in the myrtle of the bog tway fainmain stod op to slog, free bond men lay lurkin on. Tuan about whattinghim! Fore sneezturmdrappen! 'Twill be a rpnice pschange, arrah, sir? Can you come it, budd?

BUTT (*who in the cushlows of his goodsforseeking hoarth, ever fondlinger of his pimple spurk, is a niallist of the ninth homestages, the babybell in his baggutstract upper going off allatwanst, begad, lest he should challenge himself, beygoad, till angush*). Horrasure, toff! As said as would. It was Colporal Phailinx first. Hittit was of another time, a white horsday where the midril met the bulg, sbogom, roughnow along about the first equinarx in the cholonder, on the plain of Khorason as thou goest from the mount of Bekel, Steep Nemorn, elve hundred and therety and to years how the krow flees end in deed, after a power of skimiskes, blodidens and godinats of them, when we sight the beasts, (hegheg whatlk of wraimy wetter!), moist moonful date man aver held dimsdzey death with, and higheye was in the Reilly Oirish Krzerszonese Milesia asundurst Sirdarthar Woolwichleagues, good tomkeys years somewhile in Crimealian wall samewhere in Ayerland, during me weeping stillstumms over the freshprosts of Eastchept and the dangling garters of Marrowbone and daring my wapping stiltstunts on Bostion Moss, old stile and new style and heave a lep onwards. And winn again, blaguadargoos, or lues the day, plays goat, the banshee pealer, if moskats knows whoss whizz, the great day and the druidful day come San Patrisky and the grand day, the excellent fine splendorous long agreeable toastworthy cylindrical day, go Sixt of the Ninth, the heptahundread annam dammias that Hajizfijjiz ells me is and will and was be till the timelag is in it that's told in the Bok of Alam to columnkill all the prefacies of Erin gone brugk. But Icantenue. And incommixtion. We was lowsome like till we'd took out after the dead beats. So I begin to study and I soon show them day's reasons how to give the cold shake to they blighty perishers and lay one over the beats. All feller he look he call all feller come longa villa finish. Toumbalo, how was I acclapadad! From them banjopeddlars on the raid. Gidding up me anti vanillas and getting off the stissas me aunties. Boxerising and coxerusing. And swiping a johnny dann sweept for to exercitise myself neverwithstanding the topkats and his roaming cartridges, orussheying and patronning, out all over Crummwiliam wall. Be the why it was me who haw haw.

TAFF (*all for letting his tinder and lighting be put to beheiss in the feuer and, while durblinly obasiant to the felicias of the skivis, still smolking his fulvurite turfkish in the rooking pressance of laddios*). Yaa hoo how how, col? Whom battles joined no bottles sever! Worn't you aid a comp?

BUTT (*in his difficoltous tresdobremient, he feels a bitvalike a baddlefall of staot but falls a batforlake a borrlefull of bare*). And me awlphul omegrims! Between me rassociations in the postleadeny past and me disconnections with aplompervious futules I've a boodle full of maimeries in me buzzim and medears runs sloze, bleime, as I now with platoonic leave recoil in (how the thickens they come back to one to rust!) me misenary post for all them old boyars that's now boomaringing in waulholler, me alma marthyrs. I dring to them, bycorn spirits fuselaiding, and you cullies adjutant, even where its contentsed wody, with absents wehrmuth. Junglemen in agleement, I give thee our greatly swooren, Theoccupant that Rueandredful, the thrownfullvner and all our royal devouts with the arrest of the whole inhibitance of Neuilands! One brief mouth. And a velligoolapnow! Meould attashees the currgans, (if they could get a kick at this time for all that's hapenced to us!) Cedric said Gormleyson and Danno O'Dunnochoo and Conno O'Cannochar it is this were their names for we were all under that manner barracksers on Kong Gores Wood together, thurkmen three, with those khakireinettes, our miladies in their toileries, the twum plumyumnietcies, Vjeras Vjenaskayas, of old Djadja Uncken who was a great mark for jinking and junking, up the palposes of womth and wamth, we war, and the charme of their lyse brocade. For lispias harth a burm in eye but whem it bames fire norone screeneth. Hulp, hulp, huzzars! Raise ras tryracy! Freetime's free! Up Lancesters! Anathem!

TAFF (*who still senses that heavinscent houroines that entertrained him who they were sinuorivals from the sunny Espionia but plied wopsy with his wallets in thatthack of the bustle Bakerloo,* (11.32), *passing the uninational truthbosh in smoothing irony over the multinotcheralled infructuosities of his grinner set*). The rib, the rib, the quean of oldbyrdes, Sinya Sonyavitches! Your Rhoda Cockardes that are raday to embrace our ruddy inflamtry world! In their ohosililesvienne biribarbebeway. Till they've kinks in their tringers and boils on their taws. Whor dor the pene lie, Mer Pencho? Ist dramhead countmortial or gonorrhal stab? Mind your pughs and keaoghs, if you piggots, marsh! Do the nut, dingbut! Be a dag! For zahur and zimmerminnes! Sing in the chorias to the ethur:

[*In the heliotropical noughttime following a fade of transformed Tuff and, pending its viseversion, a metenergic reglow of beaming Batt, the bairdboard bombardment screen, if tastefully taut guranium satin, tends to teleframe and step up to the charge of a light barricade. Down the photoslope in syncopanc pulses, with the bitts bugtwug their teffs, the missledhropes, glitteraglatteraglutt, borne by their carnier walve. Spraygun rakes and splits them from a double focus: grenadite, damnymite, alextronite, nichilite: and the scanning firespot of the sgunners traverses the rutilanced illustred sunksundered lines. Shlossh! A gaspel truce leaks out over the caeseine coatings. Amid a fluorescence of spectracular mephiticism there caoculates through the inconoscope stealdily a still, the figure of a fellowchap in the wohly ghast, Popey O'Donoshough, the jesuneral of the russuates. The idolon exhibisces the seals of his orders: the starre of the Son of Heaven, the girtel of Izodella the Calottica, the cross of Michelides Apaleogos, the latchet of Jan of Nepomuk, the puffpuff and pompom of Powther and Pall, the great belt, band and bucklings of the Martyrology of Gorman. It is for the castomercies mudwake surveice. The victar. Pleace to notnoys speach above your dreadths, please to doughboys. Hll, smthngs gnwrng wthth sprsnwtch! He blanks his oggles because he confesses to all his tellavicious nieces. He blocks his nosoes because that he confesses to everywheres he was always putting up his latest faengers. He wollops his mouther with a sword of tusk in as because that he confesses how opten he used be obening her howonton he used be undering her. He boundles alltogotter his manucupes with his pedarrests in asmuch as because that he confesses before all his handcomplishies and behind all his comfoderacies. And (hereis cant came back saying he codant steal no lunger, yessis, catz come buck beques he caudant stail awake) he touched upon this tree of livings in the middenst of the garerden for inasmuch as because that he confessed to it on Hillel and down Dalem and in the places which the lepers inhabit in the place of the stones and in pontofert jusfuggading amoret now he come to think of it jolly well ruttengenerously olyovyover the ole blucky shop. Pugger old Pumpey O'Dungaschiff! There will be a hen collection of him after avensung on the field of Hanar. Dumble down, looties and gengstermen! Dtin, dtin, dtin, dtin!*]

BUTT (*with a gisture expansive of Mr Lhugewhite Cadderpollard with sunflawered beautonhole pulled up point blanck by mailbag mundaynism at Oldbally Court though the hissindensity buck far of his melovelance tells how when he was fast marking his first lord for cremation the whyfe of his bothem was the very lad's thing to elter his mehind*). Prostatates, pujealousties! Dovolnoisers, prayshyous! Defense in every circumstancias of deboutcheries no the chaste daffs! Pack pickets, pioghs and kughs to be palsey-putred! Be at the peme, prease, of not forgetting or mere betoken yourself to hother prace! Correct me, pleatze commando, for cossakes but I abjure of it. No more basquibezigues for this pole aprican! With askormiles' eskermillas. I had my billyfell of duckish delights the whole pukny time on rawmeots and juliannes with their lambstoels in my kiddeneys and my ramsbutter in their sassenacher ribs, knee her, do her and trey her, when th'osirian cumb dumb like the whalf on the fiord and we prey-ing players and pinching peacesmokes, troupkers tomiatskyns all, for Father Petrie Spence of Parishmoslattary to go and leave us and the crimsend daun to shellalite on the darkumen (scene as signed, Slobabogue), feeding and sleeping on the huguenottes (the snuggest spalniel's where the lieon's tame!) and raiding revolations over the allbegeneses (sand us and saint us and sound as agun!). Yet still in all, spit for spat, like we chantied on Sunda schoon, every warson wearrier kaddies a komnate in his schnapsack and unlist I am getting foegutfulls of the rugi-ments of savaliged wildfire I was gamefellow willmate and send us victorias with nowells and brownings, dumm, sneak and curry, and all the fun I had in that fanagan's week. A strange man wearing abarrel. And here's a gift of meggs and teggs. And as I live by chipping nortons. And 'tis iron fits the farmer, ay. Arcdesedo! Renborumba! Then were the hellscyown days for our fellows, the loyal leibsters, and we was the redugout raw-recruitioners, praddies three and prettish too, a wheeze we has in our waynward islands, wee engrish, one long blue streak, jisty and pithy af durck rosolun, with hand to hand as Homard Kayenne was always jiggilyjugging about in his wendowed courage when our woos with the wenches went wined for a song, tsingirillies' zyngarettes, while Woodbine Willie, so popiular with the poppyrossies, our Chorney Choplain, blued the air. Sczlanthas! Banzaine! Bissbasses! S. Pivorandbowl. And we all tuned in to hear the topmast noviality. Up the revels drown the rinks and almistips all round! Paddy Bonhamme he vives! Encore! And tig for tag. Togatogtug. My droomodose days Y loved you abover all the strest. Blowhole brasshat and boy with his boots off and the butch of our bunch and all. It was buckoo bonzer, beleeme. I was a bare prive without my doglegs but I did not give to one humpenny dump, wingh or wangh, touching those thusengaged slavey generales of Tanah Kornalls, the meelisha's deelishas, pronouncing their very flank movemens in sunpictorsbosk. Baghus the whatwar! I could always take good cover of myself and, eyedulls or earwakers, preyers for rain or cominations, I did not care three tanker's hoots, ('sham! hem! or chaffit!) for any feelings from my lifeprivates on their reptrograd leanins because I have Their Honours booth my respectables sœurs assistershood off Lyndhurst Terrace, the puttih Misses Celana Dalems, and she in vinting her angurr can belle the troth on her alliance and I know His Heriness, my respeaktoble medams culonelle on Mellay Street, Lightnints Gundhur Sawabs, and they would never as the aimees of servation let me down. Not on your bludger life, touters! No peeping, pimpadoors! And, by Jova, I never went wrong nor let him doom till, risky wark rasky wolk, at the head of the wake, up come stumblebum (ye olde cottemptable!), his urssian gemenal, in his scutt's rudes unreformed and he went before him in that nemcon enchelonce with the same old domstoole story and his upleave the fallener as is greatly to be petted (whitesides do his beard!) and I seen his brichashert offensive and his boortholomas vadnhammaggs vise a vise them scharlot runners and how they gave love to him and how he took the ward from us (odious the fly fly flurtation of his him and hers! Just mairmaid maddeling it was it he was!) and, my oreland for a rolvever, sord, by the splunthers of colt and bung goes the enemay the Percy rally got me, messgér, (as true as theirs an Almagnian Gothabobus!) to blow the grand off his aceupper. Thistake it 's meest! And after meath the dulwich. We insurrectioned and, be the procuratress of the hory synnotts, before he could tell pullyirragun to parrylewis, I shuttm, missus, like a wide sleever! Hump to dump! Tumbleheaver!

TAFF (*camelsensing that sonce they have given bron a nuhlan the volkar boastsung is heading to sea vermelhion but too wellbred not to ignore the umzemlianess of his rifal's preceedings, in an effort towards autosotorisation, effaces himself in favour of the idiology alwise behounding his lumpy hump off homosodalism which means that if he has lain amain to lolly his liking-cabronne!-he may pops lilly a young one to his herth - combrune* -) Oholy rasher, I'm believer! And Oho bullyclaver of ye, bragadore-gunneral! The grand ohold spider! It is a name to call to him Umsturdum Vonn! Ah, you were shutter reshottus and sieger besieged. Aha race of fiercemarchands counterination oho of shorpshoopers.

BUTT (*miraculising into the Dann Deafir warcry, his bigotes bristling, as, jittinju triggity shittery pet, he shouts his thump and feeh fauh foul finngures up the heighohs of their ahs!*) Bluddymuddymuzzle! The buckbeshottered! He'll umbozzle no more graves nor horne nor haunder, lou garou, for gayl geselles in dead men's hills! Kaptan (backsights to his bared!), His Cumbulent Embulence, the frustate fourstar Russkakruscam, Dom Allaf O'Khorwan, connundurumchuff.

TAFF (*who, asbestas can, wiz the healps of gosh and his bluzzid maikar, has been sulphuring to himsalves all the pungataries of sin praktice in failing to furrow theogonies of the dommed*). Trisseme, the mangoat! And the name of the Most Marsiful, the Aweghost, the Gragious One! In sobber sooth and in souber civiles? And to the dirtiment of the curtailment of his all of man? Notshoh?

BUTT (*maomant scoffin, but apoxyomenously deturbaned but thems bleachin banes will be after making a bashman's haloday out of the euphorious hagiohygiecynicism of his die and be diademmed*). Yastsar! In sabre tooth and sobre saviles! Senonnevero! That he leaves nyet is my grafe. He deared me to it and he dared me do it, and bedattle I didaredonit as Cocksnark of Killtork can tell and Ussur Ursussen of the viktaurious onrush with all the rattles in his arctic! As bold and as madhouse a bull in a meadows. Knout Knittrick Kinkypeard! Olefoh, the sourd of foemoe times! Unknun! For when meseemim, and tolfoklokken rolland allover ourloud's lande, beheaving up that sob of tunf for to claimhis, for to wollpimsolff, puddywhuck. Ay, and untuoning his culothone in an exitous erseroyal *Deo Jupto*. At that instullt to Igorladns! Prronto! I gave one dobblenotch and I ups with my crozzier. Mirrdo! With my how on armer and hits leg an arrow cockshock rockrogn. Sparro!

[*The abnihilisation of the etym by the grisning of the grosning of the grinder of the grunder of the first lord of Hurtreford expolodotonates through Parsuralia with an ivanmorinthorrorumble fragoromboassity amidwhiches general uttermosts confussion are perceivable moletons skaping with mulicules while coventry plumpkins fairlygosmotherthemselves in the Landaunelegants of Pinkadindy. Similar scenatas are projectilised from Hullulullu, Bawlawayo, empyreal Raum and mordern Atems. They were precisely the twelves of clocks, noon minutes, none seconds. At someseat of Oldanelang's Konguerrig, by dawnybreak in Aira.*]

TAFF (*skimperskamper, his wools gatherings all over cromlin what with the birstol boys artheynes and is it her tour and the crackery of the fullfour fivefirearms and the crockery of their dam-*

dam domdom chumbers). Wharall thubulbs uptheaires! Shattamovick?

BUTT (*pulling alast stark daniel with alest doog at doorak while too greater than pardon painfully the issue of his mouth diminuendoing, vility of vilities, he becomes, allasvitally, faint*). Shurenoff! Like Faun MacGhoul!

BUTT and TAFF (*desprot slave wager and foeman feodal unsheckled, now one and the same person, their fight upheld to right for a wee while being baffled and tottered, umbraged by the shadow of Old Erssia's magisquammythical mulattomilitiaman, the living by owning over the surfers of the glebe whose sway craven minnions had caused to revile, as, too foul for hell, under boiling Mauses' burning brand, he falls by Goll's gillie, but keenheartened by the circuminsistence of the Parkes O'Rarelys in a hurdly gurdly Cicilian concertone of their fonngeena barney brawl, shaken everybothy's hands, while S. E. Morehampton makes leave to E. N. Sheilmartin after Meetinghouse Lanigan has embaraced Vergemout Hall, and, without falter or mormor or blathrehoot of sophsterliness, pugnate the pledge of fiannaship, dook to dook, with a commonturn oudchd of fest man and best man astoutsalliesemoutioun palms it off like commodity tokens against a cococancancacacanotioun*). When old the wormd was a gadden and Anthea first unfoiled her limbs wanderloot was the way the wood wagged where opter and apter were samuraised twimbs. They had their mutthering ivies and their murdhering idies and their mouldhering iries in that muskat grove but there'll be bright plinnyflowers in Calomella's cool bowers when the magpyre's babble towers scorching and screeching from the ravenindove. If thees lobed the sex of his head and mees ates the seep of his traublers he's dancing figgies to the spittle side and shoving outs the soord. And he'll be buying buys and go gulling gells with his flossim and jessim of carm, silk and honey while myandthys playing lancifer lucifug and what's duff as a bettle for usses makes coy cosyn corollanes' moues weeter to wee. So till butagain budly shoots thon rising germinal let bodley chow the fatt of his anger and badley bide the toil of his tubb.

[The pump and pipe pingers are ideally reconstituted. The putther and bowls are peterpacked up. All the presents are determining as regards for the future the howabouts of their past absences which they might see on at hearing could they once smell of tastes from touch. To ought find a values for. The must overlistingness. When ex what is ungiven. As ad where. Stillhead. Blunk.]

Shutmup. And bud did down well right. And if he sung dumb in his glass darkly speech lit face to face on allaround.

Vociferagitant. Viceversounding. Namely, Abdul Abulbul Amir or Ivan Slavansky Slavar. In alldconfusalem. As to whom the major guiltfeather pertained it was Hercushiccups' care to educe. Beauty's bath she's bound to bind beholders and pride, his purge, has place appoint in penance and the law's own libel lifts and lames the low with the lofty. Be of the housed! While the Hersy Hunt they harrow the hill for to rout them rollicking rogues from, rule those racketeer romps from, rein their rockery rides from. Rambling.

Nightclothesed, arooned, the conquerods sway. After their battle thy fair bosom.

— That is too tootrue enough in Solidan's Island as in Moltern Giaourmany and from the Amelakins off to date back to land of engined Egypsians, assented from his opening before his inlookers of where an oxmanstongue stalled stabled the wellnourished one, lord of the seven days, overlord of sats and suns, the sat of all the suns which are in the ring of his system of the sats of his sun, god of the scuffeldfallen skillfilledfelon, who (he contaimns) hangsters, who (he constrains) hersirrs, a gain changful, a mintage vaster, heavy on shirts, lucky with shifts, the topside humpup stummock atween his showdows fellah, Misto Teewiley Spillitshops, who keepeth watch in Khummer-Phett, whose spouse is An-Lyph, the dog's bladder, warmer of his couch in fore. We all, for whole men is lepers, have been nobbut wonterers in that chill childerness which is our true name after the allfaulters (mug's luck to em!) and, bespeaking of love and lie detectors in venuvarities, whateither the drugs truth of it, was there an iota of from the faust to the lost. And that is at most re-doubtedly an overthrew of each and ilkermann of us, I persuade myself, before Gow, gentlemen, so true as this are my kopfinpot astrode on these is my boardsoldereds.

It sollecited, grobbling hummley, his roundhouse of seven orofaces, of all, guiltshouters or crimemummers, to be sayd by, codnops, advices for, free of gracies, scamps encloded, com-petitioning them, if they had steadied Jura or when they had raced Messafissi, husband of your wifebetter or bestman botcha-lover of you yourself, how comes ever a body in our taylorised world to selve out thishis, whither it gives a primeum nobilees for our notomise or naught, the farst wriggle from the ubivence, whereom is man, that old offender, nother man, wheile he is asame. And fullexampling. The pints in question. With some by-spills. And sicsecs to provim hurtig. Soup's on!

— A time. And a find time. Whenin aye was a kiddling. And the tarikies held sowansopper. Let there beam a frishfrey. And they sodhe gudhe rudhe brodhe wedhe swedhe medhe in the kanddledrum. I have just (let us suppraise) been reading in a (suppressed) book — it is notwithstempting by meassures long and limited—the latterpress is eminently legligible and the paper, so he eagerly seized upon, has scarsely been buttered in works of previous publicity wholebeit in keener notcase would I turf aside for pastureuration. Packen paper paineth whomto is sacred scriptured sign. Who straps it scraps it that might, if ashed, have healped. Enough, however, have I read of it, like my good bedst friend, to augur in the hurry of the times that it will cocommend the widest circulation and a reputation coextensive with its merits when inthrusted into safe and pious hands upon so edifying a mission as it, I can see, as is his. It his ambullished with expurga-tive plates, replete in information and accampaigning the action passiom, slopbang, whizzcrash, boomarattling from burst to past, as I have just been seeing, with my warmest venerections, of a timmersome townside upthecountrylifer, (Guard place the town!) allthose everwhalmed upon that preposterous blank seat, before the wordcraft of this early woodcutter, a master of vignettiennes and our findest grobsmid among all their orefices, (and, shukar in chowdar, so splunderdly English!) Mr Aubeyron Birdslay. Chubgoodchob, arsoncheep and wellwillworth a triat! Bismillafoulties. But the hasard you asks is justly ever behind his meddle throw! Those sad pour sad forengistanters, dastychappy dustyrust! Chaichairs. It is that something, awe, aurorbean in that fellow, hamid and damid, (did he have but Hugh de Brassey's beardslie his wear mine of ancient guised) which comequeers this anywhat perssian which we, owe, realisinus with purups a dard of penė. There is among others pleasons whom I love and which are favourests to mind, one which I have pushed my finker in for the movement and, but for my sealring is none to hand I swear, she is highly catatheristic and there is another which I have fombly fongered freequuntly and, when my signet is on sign again I swear, she is deeply sangnificant. *Culpo de Dido*! Ars we say in theclassies. *Kunstful*, we others said. What ravening shadow! What dovely line! Not the king of this age could richlier eyefeast in oreillental longuardness with alternate nightjoys of a thousand kinds but one kind. A shahrryar cobbler on me when I am lying! And whilst (when I doot my sliding panel and I hear cawcaw) I have been idylly turmbing over the loose looves leaflefts jaggled casuallty on the lamatory, as is my this is, as I must commit my lips to make misface for misfortune, often, so far as I can chance to recollect from the some farnights ago, (so dimsweet is that selvischdischdienence of to not to be able to be obliged to have to hold further anything than a stone his throw's fruit's fall!) when I, if you wil excuse for me this informal leading down of illexpressibles, enlivened toward the Author of Nature by the natural sins liggen gobelimned theirs before me, (how differended with the manmade Eonochs Cunstuntonopolies!), weathered they be of a general golf stature, assasserted, or blossomly emblushing thems elves underneed of some howthern folleys, am entrenched up contemplating of myself, wiz my naked I, for relieving purposes in our trurally virvir vergitabale (garden) I sometimes, maybe, what has justly said of old Flannagan, a wake from this or huntsfurwards, with some shock (shell I so render it?) have (when I ope my shylight window and I see coocoo) a notion quiet involuptary of that I am cadging hapsnots as at murmurrandoms of distend renations from ficsimilar phases or dugouts in the behindscenes of our earthwork (what rovining shudder! what deadly loom!) as this is, at no spatial time processly which regards to concrude chronology about which in fact, at spite of I having belittled myself to my gay giftname of insectarian, happy burgages abeyance would make homesweetstown hopeygoalucrey, my mottu propprior, as I claim, cad's truck, I coined, I am highly pelaged and deeply gluttened to mind hindmost hearts to see by their loudest reports from my threespawn bottery parts (shsh!) that, colombophile and corvinophobe alike, when I have remassed me, my travellingself, as from Magellanic clouds, after my contractual expenditures, through the perofficies of merelimb, I, my good grief, I am, I am big altoogooder.

He beached the bark of his tale; and set to husband and vine: and the harpermaster told all the living conservancy, know Meschiameschianah, how that win a gain was in again. Flying the Perseoroyal. Withal aboarder, padar and madar, hal and sal, the sens of Ere with the duchtars of Iran. Amick amack amock in a mucktub. Qith the tou loulous and the gryffygryffygryffs, at Fenegans Wick, the Wildemanns. Washed up whight and deliveried rhight. Loud lauds to his luckhump and bejetties on jonahs! And they winxed and wanxed like baillybeacons. Till we woksed up oldermen.

Now all his customers revile HCE, who stoutly stands to deliver a general confession of his all too human crimes, including an incestuous desire for young girls ("the lilliths oft I feldt"). Now, like Caesar or Falstaff, he fearlessly awaits punishment, begging no mercy.

And you, when you kept at Dulby, were you always (for that

time only) what we knew how when we (from that point solely) were you know where? There you are! And why? Why, hitch a cock eye, he was snapped on the sly upsadaisying coras pearls out of the pie when all the perts in princer street set up their tinker's humn, (the rann, the rann, that keen of old bards), with them newnesboys pearcin screaming off their armsworths. The boss made dovesandraves out of his bucknesst while herself wears the bowler's hat in her bath. Deductive Almayne Rogers disguides his voice, shetters behind hoax chestnote from exexive. Heat wives rasing. They jest keeps rosing. He jumps leaps rizing. Howlong!

You known that tom? I certainly know. Is their bann bothstiesed? Saddenly now. Has they bane reneemed? Soothinly low. Does they ought to buy the papelboy when he footles up their suit? He's their mark to foil the flouter and they certainty owe.

He sprit in his phiz (baccon!). He salt to their bis (pudden!). He toockled her palam (so calam is solom!). And he suked their friends' leave (bonnick lass, fair weal!)

— Guilty but fellows culpows! It was felt by me sindeade, that submerged doughdoughty doubleface told waterside labourers. But since we for athome's health have chanced all that, the wild whips, the wind ships, the wonderlost for world hips, unto their foursquare trust prayed in aid its plumptylump piteousness which, when it turtled around seeking a thud of surf, spake to approach from inherdoff trisspass through minxmingled hair. Though I may have hawked it, said, and selled my how hot peas after theactrisscalls from my imprecurious position and though achance I could have emptied a pan of backslop down drain by whiles of dodging a rere from the middenprivet appurtenant thereof, salving the presents of the board of wumps and pumps, I am ever incalpable, where release of prisonals properly is concerned, of unlifting upfallen girls wherein dangered from them in thereopen out of unadulteratous bowery, with those hintering influences from an angelsexonism. It was merely my barely till their oh offs. Missaunderstaid. Meggy Guggy's giggag. The code's proof! The rebald danger with they who would bare whiteness against me I dismissem from the mind of good. He can tell such as story to the Twelfth Maligns that my first was a nurssmaid and her fellower's a willbe perambulatrix. There are twingty to twangty too thews and leathermail coatschemes penparing to hostpost for it valinnteerily with my valued fofavour to the post puzzles deparkment with larch parchels' of presents for future branch offercings. The green approve the raid! Shaum Baum's bode he is amustering in the groves while his shool comes merging along! Want I put myself in their kirtlies I were ayearn to leap with them and show me too bisextine. Dear and lest I forget mergers and bow to you low, marchers! Attemption! What a mazing month of budsome misses they are making, so wingtywish to flit beflore their kin! Attonsure! Ears to hears! The skall of a gall (for every dime he yawpens that momouth you could park your ford in it) who has papertreated him into captivities with his inside man by a hocksheat of starvision for an avragetopeace of parchment, cooking up his lenses to be my apoclogypst, the recreuter of conscraptions, let him be asservent to Kinahaun! For (peace peace perfectpeace!) I have abwaited me in a water of Elin and I have placed my reeds intectis before the Registower of the perception of tribute in the hall of the city of Analbe. How concerns any merryaunt and hworsoever gravesobbers it is perensempry sex of fun to help a dazzle off the othour. What for Mucias and Gracias may the duvlin rape the handsomst! And the whole mad knightmayers' nest! Tunpother, prison and plotch! If Y shoulden somewhat, well, I am able to oweit, hearth and chemney easy. They seeker for vannflaum all worldins merkins. I'll eager make lyst turpidump undher arkens. Basast! And if my litigimate was well to wrenn tigtag cackling about it, like the sally berd she is, to abery ham in the Cutey Strict, (I shall call upon my first among my lost of lyrars beyond a jingoobangoist, to overcast her) dismissing mundamanu all the riflings of her victuum gleaner (my old chuck! she drakes me druck! turning out, gay at ninety!) and well shoving off a boastonmess like lots wives does over her handpicked hunsbend, as she would be calling, well, for further oil mircles upon all herwayferer gods and reanouncing my deviltries as was I a locally person of caves until I got my purchase on her firmforhold I am, I like to think, by their sacreligion of daimond cap daimond, confessedly in my baron gentilhomme to the manhor bourne till ladiest day as panthoposopher, to have splet for groont a peer of bellows like Bacchulus shakes a rousing guttural at any old cerpaintime by peaching (allsole we are not amusical) the warry warst against myself in the defile as a lieberretter sebaiscopal of these mispeschyites of the first virginial water who, without an auction of biasement from my part, with gladyst tone ahquickyessed in it, overhowe and underwhere, the totty lolly poppy flossy conny dollymaukins. Though I heave a coald on my bauck and am could up to my eres hoven sametimes I used alltides to be aswarmer for the meekst and the graced. You are not going to not. You might be threeabreasted wholenosing at a whallhoarding from our Don Amir anent villayets prostatution precisingly kuschkars tarafs and it could be double densed uncounthest hour of allbleakest age with a bad of wind and a barran of rain, nompos mentis like Novus Elector, what with his Marx and their Groups, yet did a doubt, should a dare, were to you, you would do and dhamnk me, shenker, dhumnk you. Skunk. And fare with me to share with me. Hinther and thonther, hant by hont. By where dauvening shedders down whose rovely lanes. As yose were and as yese is. Sure and you would, Mr Mac Gurk! Be sure and you would, Mr O'Duane! To be sure and you would so, Mr MacElligut! Wod you nods? Mom mom. No mum has the rod to pud a stub to the lurch of amotion. My little love apprencisses, my dears, the estelles, van Nessies von Nixies voon der pool, which I had a reyal devouts for yet was it marly lowease or just a feel with these which olderman K.K. Alwayswelly he is showing ot the fullnights for my palmspread was gav to a parsleysprig, the curliest weedeen old ocean coils around, so spruce a spice for salthorse, sonnies, and as tear to the thrusty as Taylor's Spring, when aftabournes, when she was look like a little cheayat chilled (Oh sard! ah Mah!) by my tide impracing, as Beacher seath, and all the colories fair fled from my folced cheeks!

Popottes, where you canceal me you mayst forced guage my bribes. Wickedgapers, I appeal against the light! A nexistence of vividence! Panto, boys, is on a looser inloss; ballet, girls, suppline thrown tights. I have wanted to thank you such a long time so much now. Thank you. Sir, kindest of bottleholders and very dear friend, among our hearts of steel, froutiknow, it will befor you, me dare beautiful young soldier, winninger nor anyour of rudimental moskats, before you go to mats, you who have watched your share with your sockboule sodalists on your buntad nogs at our love tennis squats regatts, suckpump, when on with the balls did disserve the fain, my goldrush gainst her silvernetss, to say, biguidd, for the love of goddess and perthanow as you reveres your one mothers, mitsch for matsch, and while I reveal thus my deepseep daughter which was bourne up pridely out of medsdreams unclouthed when I was pillowing in my brime (of Saturnay Eve, how now, woren't we't?), to see, I say, whoahoa, in stay of execution *in re* Milcho Melekmans, increaminated, what you feel, oddrabbit, upon every strong ground you have ever taken up, by bitterstiff work or battonstaff play, with assault of turk against a barrakraval of grakeshoots, e'en tho' Jambuwel's defecalties is Terry Shimmyrag's upperturnity, if that is grace for the grass what is balm for the bramblers, as it is as it is, that I am the catasthmatic old ruffin sippahsedly improctor to be seducint trovatellas, the dire daffy damedeaconesses, like (why sighs the sootheesinger) the lilliths oft I feldt, and, when booboob brutals and cautiouses only aims at the oggog hogs in the humand, then, (Houtes, Blymey and Torrenation, upkurts and scotchem!) I'll tall tale tell croon paysecurers, sowill nuggets and nippers, that thash on me stumpen blows the gaff off mombition and thit thides or marse makes a good dayle to be shattat. Fall stuff.

His rote in ere, afstef, was.

And dong wonged Magongty till the bombtomb of the warr, thrusshed in his whole soort of cloose.

Whisht who wooed in Weald, bays of Bawshaw binding. The desire of Miriam is the despair of Marian as Joh Joseph's beauty is Jacq Jacob's grief. Brow, tell nun; eye, feign sad; mouth, sing mim. Look at Lokman! Whatbetween the cupgirls and the platterboys. And he grew back into his grossery baseness: and for all his grand remonstrance: and there you are.

Clear the bar! Shut up shop! The people, led by ranning Hosty, are coming for HCE!

Dour douchy was a sieguldson. He cooed that loud nor he was young. He cud bad caw nor he was gray Like wather parted from the say.

Ostia, lift it! Lift at it, Ostia! From the say! Away from the say!

Himhim. Himhim.

Hearhasting he, himmed, reromembered all the chubbs, chipps, chaffs, chuckinpucks and chayney chimebells That he had mistributed in port, pub, park, pantry and poultryhouse, While they, thered, the others, that are, were most emulously concerned to cupturing the last dropes of summour down through their grooves of blarneying. Ere the sockson locked at the dure. Which he would, shuttinshure. And lave them to sture.

For be all rules of sport 'tis right That youth bedower'd to charm the night Whilst age is dumped to mind the day When wather parted from the say.

The humming, it's coming. Insway onsway.

Fingool MacKishgmard Obesume Burgearse Benefice, He was bowen hem and scrapin him in recolcitrantament to the rightabout And these probenopubblicoes clamatising for an extinsion on his hostillery With his chargehand bombing their eres. Tids, genmen, plays, she been goin shoother off almaynoother onawares.

You here nort farwellens rouster? Ashiffle ashuffle the wayve they.

From Dancingtree till Suttonstone There's lads no lie would filch a crown To mull their sack and brew their tay With wather parted from the say.

Lelong Awaindhoo's a selverbourne enrouted to Rochelle Lane and liberties those Mullinguard minstrelsers are marshalsing, par tunepiped road, under where, perked on hollowy hill, that poor man of Lyones, good Dook Weltington, hugon come errindwards, had hircomed to the belles bows and been cutattrapped by the mausers. Now is it town again, londmear of Dublin! And off coursse the toller, ples the dotter of his eyes with her: Moke the Wanst, whye doe we aime alike a pose of poeter peaced? While the dumb he shoots the shopper rope. And they all pour forth. Sans butly Tuppeter Sowyer, the rouged engenerand, a barttler of the beauyne, still our benjamin liefest, sometime frankling to thise citye, whereas bigrented him a piers half subporters for his arms, Josiah Pipkin, Amos Love, Raoul Le Febber, Blaize Taboutot, Jeremy Yopp, Francist de Loomis, Hardy Smith and Sequin Pettit followed by the snug saloon seanad of our Café Béranger. The scenictutors.

Because they wonted to get out by the goatweigh afore the sheep was looset for to wish the Wobbleton Whiteleg Welshers kaillykailly kellykekkle and savebeck to Brownhazelwood from all the dinnasdoolins on the labious banks of their swensewn snewwesner, turned again weastinghome, by Danesbury Common, and they onely, duoly, thruely, fairly after rainydraining fountybuckets (chalkem up, hemptyempty!) till they caught the wind abroad (alley loafers passinggeering!) all the rockers on the roads and all the boots in the stretes.

Oh dere! Ah hoy!

Last ye, lundsmin, hasty hosty! For an anondation of mirification and the lutification of our paludination.

His bludgeon's bruk, his drum is tore. For spuds we'll keep the hat he wore And roll in clover on his clay By wather parted from the say.

Hray! Free rogue Mountone till Dew Mild Well to corry awen and glowry! Are now met by Brownaboy Fuinnninuinn's former for a lyncheon partyng of his burgherbooh. The Shanavan Wacht. Rantinroarin Batteries Dorans. And that whistling thief, O' Ryne O'Rann. With a catch of her cunning like and nowhere a keener.

The for eolders were aspolootly at their wetsend in the mailing waters, trying to. Hide! Seek! Hide! Seek! Because number one lived at Bothersby North and he was trying to. Hide! Seek! Hide!

Seek! And number two digged up Poors Coort, Soother, trying to. Hide! Seek! Hide! Seek! And nomber three he sleeped with Lilly Tekkles at The Eats and he was trying to. Hide! Seek! Hide! Seek! And the last with the sailalloyd donggie he was berthed on the Moherboher to the Washte and they were all trying to and baffling with the walters of, hoompsydoompsy walters of. High! Sink! High! Sink! Highohigh! Sinkasink!

Waves.

The gangstairs strain and anger's up As Hoisty rares the can and cup To speed the bogre's barque away O'er wather parted from the say.

Horkus chiefest ebblynuncies!

— He shook be ashaped of hempshelves, hiding that shepe in his goat. And for rassembling so bearfellsed the magreedy prince of Roger. Thuthud. Heigh hohse, heigh hohse, our kindom from an orse! Bruni Lanno's woollies on Brani Lonni's hairyparts. And the hunk in his trunk it would be an insalt foul the matter of that cellaring to a pigstrough. Stop his laysense. Ink him! You would think him Alddaublin staking his lordsure like a gourd on puncheon. Deblinity devined. Wholehunting the pairk on a methylogical mission whenever theres imberillas! And calling Rina Roner Reinette Ronayne. To what mine answer is a lemans. Arderleys, beedles and postbillers heard him. Three points to one. Ericus Vericus corrupted into ware eggs. Dummy up, distillery! Broree aboo! Run him a johnsgate down jameseslane. Begetting a wife which begame his niece by pouring her youngthings into skintighs. That was when he had dizzy spells. Till Gladstools Pillools made him ride as the mall. Thanks to his huedobrass beerd. Lodenbroke the Longman, now he canseels under veerious persons but is always that Rorke relly! On consideration for the musickers he ought to have down it. Pass out your cheeks, why daunt you! Penalty, please! There you'll know how warder barded the bollhead that parssed our alley. We just are upsidedown singing what ever the dimkims mummur allalilty she pulls inner out heads. This is not the end of this by no manners means. When you've bled till you're bone it crops out in your flesh.

> But this fantasy of an invitation to a lyncheon party dissolves into yet another tale, an extrusion of guilt. HCE drowns his sorrows and passes out.

So you were saying, boys? Anyhow he what?

So anyhow, melumps and mumpos of the hoose uncommons, after that to wind up that longtobechronickled gettogether thanksbetogiving day at Glenfinnisk-en-la-Valle, the anniversary of his finst homy commulion, after that same barbecue beanfeast was all over poor old hospitable corn and eggfactor, King Roderick O'Conor, the paramount chief polemarch and last preelectric king of Ireland, who was anything you say yourself between fiftyodd and fiftyeven years of age at the time after the socalled last supper he greatly gave in his umbrageous house of the hundred bottles with the radio beamer tower and its hangars, chimbneys and equilines or, at least, he was'nt actually the then last king of all Ireland for the time being for the jolly good reason that he was still such as he was the eminent king of all Ireland himself after the last preeminent king of all Ireland, the whilom joky old top that went before him in the Taharan dynasty, King Arth Mockmorrow Koughenough of the leathered leggions, now of parts unknown, (God guard his generous comicsongbook soul!) that put a poached fowl in the poor man's pot before he took to his pallyass with the weeping eczema for better and worse until he went under the grass quilt on us, nevertheless, the year the sugar was scarce, and we to lather and shave and frizzle him, like a bald surging buoy and himself down to three cows that was meat and drink and dogs and washing to him, 'tis good cause we have to remember it, going through summersultryngs of snow and sleet witht the widow Nolan's goats and the Brownes girls neats anyhow, wait till I tell you, what did he do, poor old Roderick O'Conor Rex, the auspicious waterproof monarch of all Ireland, when he found himself all alone by himself in his grand old handwedown pile after all of them had all gone off with themselves to their castles of mud, as best they cud, on footback, owing to the leak of the McCarthy's mare, in extended order, a tree's length from the longest way out, down the switchbackward slidder of the landsown route of Hauburnea's liveliest vinnage on the brain, the unimportant Parthalonians with the mouldy Firbolgs and the Tuatha de Danaan googs and the ramblers from Clane and all the rest of the notmuchers that he did not care the royal spit out of his ostensible mouth about, well, what do you think he did, sir, but, faix, he just went heeltapping through the winespilth and weevily popcorks that were kneedeep round his own right royal round rollicking toper's table, with his old Roderick Random pullon hat at a Lanty Leary cant on him and Mike Brady's shirt and Greene's linnet collarbow and his Ghenter's gaunts and his Macclefield's swash and his readymade Reillys and his panprestuberian poncho, the body you'd pity him, the way the world is, poor he, the heart of Midleinster and the supereminent lord of them all, overwhelmed as he was with black ruin like a sponge out of water, allocutioning in bellcantos to his own oliverian society MacGuiney's *Dreans of Ergen Adams* and thruming through all to himself with diversed tonguesed through his old tears and his ould plaised drawl, starkened by the most regal of belches, like a blurney Cashelmagh crooner that lerking Clare air, the blackberd's ballad *I've a terrible errible lot todue todie todue tootorribleday*, well, what did he go and do at all, His Most Exuberant Majesty King Roderick O'Conor but, arrah bedamnbut, he finalised by lowering his woolly throat with the wonderful midnight thirst was on him, as keen as mustard, he could not tell what he did ale, that bothered he was from head to tail, and, wishawishawish, leave it, what the Irish, boys, can do, if he did'nt go, sliggymaglooral reemyround and suck up, sure enough, like a Trojan, in some particular cases with the assistance of his venerated tongue, whatever surplus rotgut, sorra much, was left by the lazy lousers of maltknights and beerchurls in the different bottoms of the various different replenquished drinking utensils left there behind them on the premisses by that whole hogsheaded firkin family, the departed honourable homegoers and other slygrogging suburbanites, such as it was, fall and fall about, to the brindishing of his charmed life, as toastified by his cheeriubicundenances,no matter whether it was chateaubottled Guiness's or Phoenix brewery stout it was or John Jameson and Sons or Roob Coccola or, for the matter of that, O'Connell's famous old Dublin ale that he wanted like hell, more that halibut oil or jesuits tea, as a fall back, of several different quantities and qualities amounting in all to, I should say, considerably more than the better part of a gill or naggin of imperial dry and liquid measure till, welcome be from us here, till the rising of the morn, till that hen of Kaven's shows her beaconegg, and Chapwellswendows stain our horyhistoricold and Father MacMichael stamps for aitch o'clerk mess and the Litvian Newestlatter is seen, sold and delivered and all's set for restart after the silence, like his ancestors to this day after him (that the blazings of their ouldmouldy gods may attend to them we pray!), overopposides the cowery lad in the corner and forenenst the staregaze of the cathering candled, that adornment of his album and folkenfather of familyans, he came acrash a crupper sort of a sate on accomondation and the very boxst in all his composs, whereuponce, behome the fore for cove and trawlers, heave hone, leave lone, Larry's on the focse and Faugh MacHugh O'Bawlar at the wheel, one to do and one to dare, par by par, a peerless pair, ever here and over there, with his fol the dee oll the doo on the flure of his feats and the feels of the fumes in the wakes of his ears our wineman from Barleyhome he just slumped to throne.

So sailed the stout ship *Nansy Hans*. From Liff away. For Nattenlaender. As who has come returns. Farvel, farerne! Goodbark, goodbye!

Now follow we out by Starloe!

— Three quarks for Muster Mark!
Sure he hasn't got much of a bark
And sure any he has it's all beside the mark.
But O, Wreneagle Almighty, wouldn't un be a sky of a lark
To see that old buzzard whooping about for uns shirt in the dark
And he hunting round for uns speckled trousers around by Palmer-
stown Park?
Hohohoho, moulty Mark!
You're the rummest old rooster ever flopped out of a Noah's ark
And you think you're cock of the wark.
Fowls, up! Tristy's the spry young spark
That'll tread her and wed her and bed her and red her
Without ever winking the tail of a feather
And that's how that chap's going to make his money and mark!

Overhoved, shrillgleescreaming. That song sang seaswans. The winging ones. Seahawk, seagull, curlew and plover, kestrel and capercallzie. All the birds of the sea they trolled out rightbold when they smacked the big kuss of Trustan with Usolde.

And there they were too, when it was dark, whilest the wildcaps was circling, as slow their ship, the winds aslight, upborne the fates, the wardorse moved, by courtesy of Mr Deaubaleau Downbellow Kaempersally, listening in, as hard as they could, in Dubbeldorp, the donker, by the tourneyold of the wattarfalls, with their vuoxens and they kemin in so hattajocky (only a quartebuck askull for the last acts) to the solans and the sycamores and the wild geese and the gannets and the migratories and the mistlethrushes and the auspices and all the birds of the rockbysuckerassousyoceanal sea, all four of them, all sighing and sobbing, and listening. Moykle ahoykling!

They were the big four, the four maaster waves of Erin, all listening, four. There was old Matt Gregory and then besides old Matt there was old Marcus Lyons, the four waves, and oftentimes they used to be saying grace together, right enough, bausnabeatha, in Miracle Squeer: here now we are the four of us: old Matt Gregory and old Marcus and old Luke Tarpey: the four of us and sure, thank God, there are no more of us: and, sure now, you wouldn't go and forget and leave out the other fellow and old Johnny MacDougall: the four of us and no more of us and so now pass the fish for Christ sake, Amen: the way they used to be saying their grace before fish, repeating itself, after the interims of Augusburgh for auld lang syne. And so there they were, with their palms in their hands, like the pulchrum's proculs, spraining their ears, luistening and listening to the oceans of kissening, with their eyes glistening, all the four, when he was kiddling and cuddling and bunnyhugging scrumptious his colleen bawn and dinkum belle, an oscar sister, on the fifteen inch loveseat, behind the chieftaness stewardesses cubin, the hero, of Gaelic champion, the onliest one of her choice, her bleaueyedeal of a girl's friend, neither bigugly nor smallnice, meaning pretty much everything to her then, with his sinister dexterity, light and rufthandling, vicemversem her ragbags et assaucyetiams, fore and aft, on and offsides, the brueburnt sexfutter, handson and huntsem, that was palpably wrong and bulbubly improper, and cuddling her and kissing her, tootyfay charmaunt, in her ensemble of maidenna blue, with an overdress of net, tickled with goldies, Isolamisola, and whisping and lisping her about Trisolanisans, how one was whips for one was two and two was lips for one was three, and dissimulating themself, with his poghue like Arrah-na-poghue, the dear dear annual, they all four remembored who made the world and how they used to be at that time in the vulgar ear cuddling and kiddling her, after an oyster supper in Cullen's barn, from under her mistlethrush and kissing and listening, in the good old bygone days of Dion Boucicault, the elder, in Arrah-na-pogue, in the otherworld of the passing of the key of Two-tongue Common, with Nush, the carrier of the word, and with Mesh, the cutter of the reed, in one of the farback, pitchblack centuries when who made the world, when they knew O'Clery, the man on the door, when they were all four collegians on the nod, neer the Nodderlands Nurskery, whiteboys and oakboys, peep of tim boys and piping tom boys, raising hell while the sin was shining, with their slates and satchels, playing Florian's fables and communic suctions and vellicar frictions with mixum members, in the Queen's Ultonian colleges, along with another fellow, a prime number, Totius Quotius, and paying a pot of tribluts to Boris O'Brien, the buttler of Clumpthump, two looves, two turnovers plus (one) crown, to see the mad dane ating his vitals. Wulf! Wulf! And throwing his tongue in the snakepit. Ah ho! The ladies have mercias! It brought the dear prehistoric scenes all back again, as fresh as of yore, Matt and Marcus, natural born lovers of nature, in all her moves and senses, and after that now there he was, that mouth of mandibles, vowed to pure beauty, and his Arrah-na-poghue, when she murmurously, after she let a cough, gave her firm order, if he wouldn't please mind, for a sings to one hope a dozen of the best favourite lyrical national blooms in Luvillicit, though not too much, reflecting on the situation, drinking in draughts of purest air serene and revelling in the great outdoors, before the four of them, in the fair fine night, whilst the stars shine bright, by she light of he moon, we longed to be spoon, before her honeyoldloom, the plaint effect being in point of fact there being in the whole, a seatuition so shocking and scandalous and now, thank God, there were no more of them and he poghuing and poghuing like the Moreigner bowed his crusted hoed and Tilly the Tailor's Tugged a Tar in the Arctic Newses Dagsdogs number and there they were, like a foremasters in the rolls, listening, to Rolando's deepen darblun Ossian roll, (Lady, it was just too gorgeous, that expense of a lovely tint, embellished by the charms of art and very well conducted and nicely mannered and all the horrid rudy noisies locked up in nasty cubbyhole!) as tired as they were, the three jolly topers, with their mouths watering, all the four, the old connubial men of the sea, yambing around with their old pantometer, in duckasaloppics, Luke and Johnny MacDougall and all wishening for anything at all of the bygone times, the wald times and the fald times and the hempty times and the dempty times, for a cup of kindness yet, for four farback tumblerfuls of woman squash, with them, all four, listening and spraining their ears for the millennium and all their mouths making water.

HCE's bar—empty save for the snoring landlord on the floor and the four old men who have somehow avoided being thrown out—has been turning imperceptibly into a ship. It is the ship in which Tristram is taking Isolde of Ireland to be married to his uncle Mark—with what guilty consequences we know. HCE is Mark, lustful but ageing, seeing in frightful impotence his destined bride fall into the arms of a younger man. The day of the young is dawning. Matthew, Mark, Luke and John—as seabirds or as waves—look on and comment, remembering the old days of cuddling and tickling, drooling now in a concupiscence as impotent as that of "moulty Mark".

Hear, O hear, Iseult la belle! Tristan, sad hero, hear! The Lambeg drum, the Lombog reed, the Lumbag fiferer, the Limibig brazenaze.

Anno Domini nostri sancti Jesu Christi
Nine hundred and ninetynine million pound sterling in the blueblack bowels of the bank of Ulster.
Braw bawbees and good gold pounds, galore, my girleen, a Sunday'll prank thee finely.

And no damn loutll come courting thee or by the mother of the Holy Ghost there'll be murder!

O, come all ye sweet nymphs of Dingle beach to cheer Brinabride queen from Sybil surfriding
In her curragh of shells of daughter of pearl and her silverymonnblue mantle round her.
Crown of the waters, brine on her brow, she'll dance them a jig and jilt them fairly.
Yerra, why would she bide with Sig Sloomysides or the grogram grey barnacle gander?

You won't need be lonesome, Lizzy my love, when your beau gets his glut of cold meat and hot soldiering
Nor wake in winter, window machree, but snore sung in my old Balbriggan surtout.
Wisha, won't you agree now to take me from the middle, say, of next week on, for the balance of my days, for nothing (what?) as your own nursetender?
A power of highsteppers died game right enough—but who, acushla, 'll beg coppers for you?

I tossed that one long before anyone.
It was of a wet good Friday too she was ironing and, as I'm given now to understand, she was always mad gone on me.
Grand goosegreasing we had entirely with an allnight eiderdown bed picnic to follow.
By the cross of Cong, says she, rising up Saturday in the twilight from under me, Mick, Nick the Maggot or whatever your name is, you're the mose likable lad that's come my ways yet from the barony of Bohermore.

Mattheehew, Markeehew, Lukeehew, Johnheehewheehew!
Haw!
And still a light moves long the river. And stiller the mermen ply their keg.
Its pith is full. The way is free. Their lot is cast.
So, to john for a john, johnajeams, led it be!

III

Hark!

Tolv two elf kater ten (it can't be) sax.

Hork!

Pedwar pemp foify tray (it must be) twelve.

And low stole o'er the stillness the heartbeats of sleep.

White fogbow spans. The arch embattled. Mark as capsules. The nose of the man who was nought like the nasoes. It is self-tinted, wrinkling, ruddled. His kep is a gorsecone. He am Gascon Titubante of Tegmine – sub – Fagi whose fixtures are mobiling so wobiling befear my remembrandts. She, exhibit next, his Anastashie. She has prayings in lowdelph. Zeehere green egg-brooms. What named blautoothdmand is yon who stares? Gugurtha! Gugurtha! He has becco of wild hindigan. Ho, he hath hornhide! And hvis now is for you. Pensée! The most beautiful of woman of the veilch veilchen veilde. She would kidds to my voult of my palace, with obscidian luppas, her aal in her dhove's suckling. Apagemonite! Come not nere! Black! Switch out!

Methought as I was dropping asleep somepart in nonland of where's please (and it was when you and they were we) I heard at zero hour as 'twere the peal of vixen's laughter among midnight's chimes from out the belfry of the cute old speckled church tolling so faint a goodmantrue as nighthood's unseen violet rendered all animated greatbritish and Irish objects nonviewable to human watchers save 'twere perchance anon some glistery gleam darkling adown surface of affluvial flowandflow as again might seem garments of laundry reposing a leasward close at hand in full expectation. And as I was jogging along in a dream as dozing I was dawdling, arrah, methought broadtone was heard and the creepers and the gliders and flivvers of the earth breath and the dancetongues of the woodfires and the hummers in their ground all vociferated echoating: Shaun! Shaun! Post the post! with a high voice and O, the higher on high the deeper and low, I heard him so! And lo, mescemed somewhat came of the noise and somewho might amove allmurk. Now, 'twas as clump, now mayhap. When look, was light and now'twas as flasher, now moren as the glaow. Ah, in unlitness 'twas in very similitude, bless me, 'twas his belted lamp! Whom we dreamt was a shaddo, sure, he's lightseyes, the laddo! Blessed momence, O romence, he's growing to stay! Ay, he who so swayed a will of a wisp before me, hand prop to hand, prompt side to the pros, dressed like an earl in just the correct wear, in a classy mac Frieze o'coat of far suparior ruggedness, indigo braw, tracked and tramped, and an Irish ferrier collar, freeswinging with mereswin lacers from his shoulthern and thick welted brogues on him hammered to suit the scotsmost public and climate, iron heels and sparable soles, and his jacket of providence wellprovided woolies with a softrolling lisp of a lapel to it and great sealingwax buttons, a good helping bigger than the slots for them, of twentytwo carrot krasnapoppsky red and his invulnerable burlap whiskcoat and his popular choker, Tamagnum sette-and-forte and his loud boheem toy and the damasker's overshirt he sported inside, a starspangled zephyr with a decidedly surpliced crinklydoodle front with his motto through dear life embrothred over it in peas, rice, and yeggyyolk, Or for royal, Am for Mail, R.M.D. hard cash on the nail and the most successfully carried gigot turnups now you ever, (what a pairfact crease! how amsolookly kersse!) breaking over the ankle and hugging the shoeheel, everything the best — none other from (Ah, then may the turtle's blessings of God and Mary and Haggispatrick and Huggisbrigid be souptumbling all over him!) other than (and may his hundred thousand welcome stewed letters, relayed wand postchased, multiply, ay faith, and plultiply!) Shaun himself.

What a picture primitive!

Had I the concordant wiseheads of Messrs Gregory and Lyons alongside of Dr Tarpey's and I dorsay the reverend Mr Mac Dougall's, but I, poor ass, am but as their fourpart tinckler's dunkey. Yet methought Shaun (holy messonger angels be uninterruptedly nudging him among and along the winding ways of random ever!) Shaun in proper person (now may all the blueblacksliding constellations continue to shape his changeable timetable!) stood before me. And I pledge you my agricultural word by the hundred and sixty odds rods and cones of this even's vision that young fellow looked the stuff, the Bel of Beaus' Walk, a prime card if ever was! Pep? Now without deceit it is hardly too much to say he was looking grand, so fired smart, in much more than his usual health. No mistaking that beamish brow! There was one for you that ne'er would nunch with good Duke Humphrey but would aight through the months without a sign of an err in hem and then, otherwise rounding, fourale to the lees of Traroe. Those jehovial oyeglances! The heart of the rool! And hit the hencoop. He was immense, topping swell for he was after having a great time of it, a twentyfour hours every moment matters maltsight, in a porterhouse, scutfrank, if you want to know, Saint Lawzenge of Toole's, the Wheel of Fortune, leave your clubs in the hall and wait on yourself, no chucks for walnut ketchups, Lazenby's and Chutney graspis (the house the once queen of Bristol and Balrothery twice admired because her frumped door looked up Dacent Street) where in the sighed of lovely eyes while his knives of hearts made havoc he had recruited his strength by meals of spadefuls of mounded food, in anticipation of the faste of tablenapkins, constituting his threepartite pranzipal meals *plus* a collation, his breakfast of first, a bless us O blood and thirsthy orange, next, the half of a pint of becon with newled googs and a segment of riceplummy padding, met of sunder suigar and some cold forsoaken steak peatrefired from the batblack night o'erflown then, without prejuice to evectuals, came along merendally his stockpot dinner of a half a pound or round steak, very rare, Blong's best from Portarlington's Butchery, with a side of riceypeasy and Corkshire alla mellonge and bacon with (a little mar pliche!) a pair of chops and thrown in from the silver grid by the proprietoress of the roastery who lives on the hill and gaulusch gravy and pumpernickel to wolp up and a gorger's bulby onion (Margareter, Margaretar Margarastican-deatar) and as well with second course and then finally, after his avalunch oclock snack at Appelredt's or Kitzy Braten's of saddlebag steak and a Botherhim with her old phoenix portar, jistr to gwen his gwistel and praties sweet and Irish too and mock gurgle to whistle his way through for the swallying, swp by swp, and he getting his tongue arount it and Boland's broth broken into the bargain, to his regret his soupay *avic* nightcap, vitellusit, a carusal consistent with second course eyer and becon (the rich of) with broad beans, hig, steak, hag, pepper the diamond bone hotted up timmtomm and while'twas after that he scoffed a drake-ling snuggily stuffed following cold loin of veal more cabbage and in their green free state a clister of peas, soppositorily petty, last. P.S. but a fingerhot of rheingenever to give the Pax cum Spiri-tututu. Drily thankful. Burud and dulse and typureely jam, all free of charge, aman, and. And the best of wine *avec*. For his heart was as big as himself, so it was, ay, and bigger! While the loaves are aflowering and the nachtingale jugs. All St Jilian's of Berry, hurrah there for tobies! Mabhrodaphne, brown pride of our custard house quay, amiable with repastful, cheerus graciously, cheer us! Ever of thee, Anne Lynch, he's deeply draiming! Houseanna! Tea is the Highest! For auld lang Ayternitay! Thus thicker will he grow now, grew new. And better and better on butterand butter. At the sign of Mesthress Vanhungrig. However! Mind you, nuckling down to nourritures, were they menuly some ham and jaffas, and I don't mean to make the ingestion for the moment that he was guilbey of gulpable gluttony as regards chew-able boltaballs, but, biestings be biestings, and upon the whole, when not off his oats, given prelove appetite and postlove pricing good coup, goodcheap, were it thermidor oogst or floreal may while the whistling prairial roysters play, between gormandising and gourmeteering, he grubbed his tuck all right, deah smorregos, every time he was for doing dirt to a meal or felt like a bottle of ardilaun arongwith a smag of a lecker biss of a welldressed taart or. Though his net intrants wight weighed nought but a flyblow to his gross and ganz afterduepoise. And he was so jarvey jaunty with a romp of a schoolgirl's completion sitting pretty over his Oyster Monday print face and he was plainly out on the ramp and mash, as you might say, for he sproke.

A brief moment of half-waking at the beginning of this chapter, and now the old men's donkey has introduced us to Shaun the demagogue, shabby and unsure, eater of his father's substance and inheritor of his right to rule. He is not fit for this, and half-knows it. He gives the electorate a revealing parable on the old theme of brother-conflict—"The Ondt and the Gracehoper". Disparaging the artist Shem, he disparages himself, since each son alone is only half the man his father was.

The Gracehoper was always jigging ajog, hoppy on akkant of his joyicity, (he had a partner pair of findlestilts to supplant him), or, if not, he was always making ungraceful overtures to Floh and Luse and Bienie and Vespatilla to play pupa-pupa and pulicy-pulicy and langtennas and pushpygyddyum and to commence insects with him, there mouthparts to his orefice and his gambills to there airy processes, even if only in chaste, ameng the everlistings, behold a waspering pot. He would of curse melissciously, by his fore feelhers, flexors, contractors, depressors and extensors, lamely, harry me, marry me, bury me, bind me, till she was puce for shame and allso fourmish her in Spinner's housery at the earthsbest schoppinhour so summery as his cottage, which was cald fourmillierly Tingsomingenting, groped up. Or, if he was always striking up funny funereels with Besterfarther Zeuts, the Aged One, with all his wigeared corollas, albedinous and oldbuoyant, inscythe his elytrical wormcasket and Dehlia and Peonia, his druping nymphs, bewheedling him, compound eyes on hornitosehead, and Auld Letty Plussiboots to scratch his cacumen and cackle his tramsitus, diva deborah (seven bolls of sapo, a lick of lime, two spurts of fussfor, threefurts of sulph, a shake o'shouker, doze grains of migniss and a mesfull of midcap pitchies. The whool of the whaal in the wheel of the whorl of the Boubou from Bourneum has thus come to taon!), and with tambarins and cantoridettes soturning around his eggshill rockcoach their dance McCaper in retrophoebia, beck from bulk, like fantastic disossed and jenny aprils, to the ra, the ra, the ra, the ra, langsome heels and langsome toesis, attended to by a mutter and doffer duffmatt baxingmotch and a myrmidins of pszozlers pszinging *Satyr's Caudledayed Nice* and *Hombly, Dombly Sod We Awhile* but *Ho, Time Timeagen, Wake!* For if sciencium (what's what) can mute uns nought, 'a thought, abought the Great Sommboddy within the Omniboss, perhops an artsaccord (hoot's hoot) might sing ums tumtim abutt the Little Newbuddies that ring his panch. A high old tide for the barheated publics and the whole day as gratiis! Fudder and lighting for ally looty, any filly in a fog, for O'Cronione lags acrumbling in his sands but his sunsunsuns still tumble on. Erething above ground, as his Book of Breathings bed him, so as everwhy, sham or shunner, zeemliangly to kick time.

Grouscious me and scarab my sahul! What a bagateller it is! Libelulous! Inzanzarity! Pou! Pschla! Ptuh! What a zeit for the goths! vented the Ondt, who, not being a sommerfool, was thothfolly making chilly spaces at hisphex affront of the icinglass of his windhame, which was cold antitopically Nixnixundnix. We shall not come to party at that lopp's, he decided possibly, for he is not on our social list. Nor to Ba's berial nether, thon sloghard, this oldeborre's yaar ablong as there's a khul on a khat. Nefersenless, when he had safely looked up his ovipository, he loftet hails and prayed: May he me no voida water! Seekit Hatup! May no he me tile pig shed on! Suckit Hotup! As broad as Beppy's realm shall flourish my reign shall flourish! As high as

Heppy's hevn shall flurrish my haine shall hurrish! Shall grow, shall flourish! Shall hurrish! Hummum.

The Ondt was a weltall fellow, raumybult and abelboobied, bynear saw altitudinous wee a schelling in kopfers. He was sair sair sullemn and chairmanlooking when he was not making spaces in his psyche, but, laus! when he wore making spaces on his ikey, he ware mouche mothst secred and muravyingly wisechairmanlooking. Now whim the sillybilly of a Gracehoper had jingled through a jungle of love and debts and jangled through a jumble of life in doubts afterworse, wetting with the bimblebeaks, drikking with nautonects, bilking with durrydunglecks and horing after ladybirdies (*ichnehmon diagelegenaitoikon*) he fell joust as sieck as a sexton and tantoo pooveroo quant a churchprince, and wheer the midges to wend hemsylph or vosch to sirch for grub for his corapusse or to find a hospes, alick, he wist gnit! Bruko dry! fuko spint! Sultamont osa bare! And volomundo osi videvide! Nichtsnichtsundnichts! Not one pickopeck of muscowmoney to bag a tittlebits of beebread! Iomio! Iomio! Crick's corbicule, which a plight! O moy Bog, he contrited with melanctholy. Meblizzered, him sluggered! I am heartily hungry!

He had eaten all the whilepaper, swallowed the lustres, devoured forty flights of styearcases, chewed up all the mensas and seccles, ronged the records, made mundballs of the ephemerids and vorasioused most glutinously with the very timeplace in the ternitary — not too dusty a cicada of neutriment for a chittinous chip so mitey. But when Chrysalmas was on the bare branches, off he went from Tingsomingenting. He took a round stroll and he took a stroll round and he took a round strollagain till the grillies in his head and the leivnits in his hair made him thought he had the Tossmania. Had he twicycled the sees of the deed and trestraversed their revermer? Was he come to hevre with his engiles or gone to hull with the poop? The June snows was flocking in thuckflues on the hegelstomes, millipeeds of it and myriopoods, and a lugly whizzling tournedos, the Boraborayellers, blohablasting tegolhuts up to tetties and ruching sleets off the coppeehouses, playing ragnowrock rignewreck, with an irritant, penetrant, siphonopterous spuk. Grausssssss! Opr! Grausssssss! Opr!

The Gracehoper who, though blind as batflea, yet knew, not a leetle beetle, his good smetterling of entymology asped nissunitimost lous nor liceens but promptly tossed himself in the vico, phthin and phthir, on top of his buzzer, tezzily wondering wheer would his aluck alight or boss of both appease and the next time he makes the aquinatance of the Ondt after this they have met themselves, these mouschical umsummables, it shall be motylucky if he will beheld not a world of differents. Behailed His Gross the Ondt, prostrandvorous upon his dhrone, in his Papylonian babooshkees, smolking a spatial brunt of Hosana cigals, with unshrinkables farfalling from his unthinkables, swarming of himself in his sunnyroom, sated before his comfortumble phullupsuppy of a plate o'monkynous and a confucion of minthe (for he was a conformed aceticist and aristotaller), as appi as a oneysucker or a baskerboy on the Libido, with Floh biting his leg thigh and Luse lugging his luff leg and Bieni bussing him under his bonnet and Vespatilla blowing cosy fond tutties up the allabroad length of the large of his smalls. As entomate as intimate could pinchably be. Emmet and demmet and be jiltses crazed and be jadeses whipt! schneezed the Gracehoper, aguepe with ptchjelasys and at his wittol's indts, what have eyeforsight!

The Ondt, that true and perfect host, a spiter aspinne, was making the greatest spass a body could with his queens laceswinging for he was spizzing all over him like thingsumanything in formicolation, boundlessly blissfilled in an allallahbath of houris. He was ameising himself hugely at crabround and marypose, chasing Floh out of charity and tickling Luse, I hope too, and tackling Bienie, faith, as well, and jucking Vespatilla jukely by the chimiche. Never did Dorsan from Dunshanagan dance it with more devilry! The veripatetic imago of the impossible Gracehoper on his odderkop in the myre, after his thrice ephemeral journeeys, sans mantis ne shooshooe, featherweighed animule, actually and presumptuably sinctifying chronic's despair, was sufficiently and probably coocoo much for his chorous of gravitates. Let him be Artalone the Weeps with his parisites peeling off him I'll be Highfee the Crackasider. Flunkey Footle furloughed foul, writing off his phoney, but Conte Carme makes the melody that mints the money. *Ad majorem l.s.d.! Diviglorian.* A darkener of the threshold. Haru? Orimis, capsizer of his antboat, sekketh rede from Evil-it-is, lord of loaves in Amongded. Be it! So be it! Thou-who-thou-art, the fleet-as-spindhrift, impfang thee of mine wideheight. Haru!

The thing pleased him andt, and andt,

He larved ond he larved on he merd such a nauses
The Gracehoper feared he would mixplace his fauces.
I forgive you, grondt Ondt, said the Gracehoper, weeping,
For their sukes of the sakes you are safe in whose keeping.
Teach Floh and Luse polkas, show Bienie where's sweet
And be sure Vespatilla fines fat ones to heat.
As I once played the piper I must now pay the count
So saida to Moyhammlet and marhaba to your Mount!
Let who likes lump above so what flies be a full 'un;
I could not feel moregruggy if this was prompollen.
I pick up your reproof, the horsegift of a friend,
For the prize of your save is the price of my spend.
Can castwhores pulladeftkiss if oldpollocks forsake 'em
Or Culex feel etchy if Pulex don't wake him?
A locus to loue, a term it t'embarass,
These twain are the twins that tick Homo Vulgaris.
Has Aquileone nort winged to go syf
Since the Gwyfyn we were in his farrest drewbryf
And that Accident Man not beseeked where his story ends
Since longsephyring sighs sought heartseast for their orience?
We are Wastenot with Want, precondamned, two and true,
Till Nolans go volants and Bruneyes come blue.
Ere those gidflirts now gadding you quit your mocks for my gropes
An extense must impull, an elapse must elopes,
Of my tectucs takestock, tinktact, and ail's weal;
As I view by your farlook hale yourself to my heal.

Partiprise my thinwhins whiles my blink points unbroken on
Your whole's whercabroads with Tout's trightyright token on.
My in risible universe youdly haud find
Sulch oxtrabeeforeness meat soveal behind.
Your feats end enormous, your volumes immense,
(May the Graces I hoped for sing your Ondtship song sense!),
Your genus its worldwide, your spacest sublime!
But, Holy Saltmartin, why can't you beat time?

In the name of the former and of the latter and of their holocaust. Allmen.

After his long bloated speeches and evasive answers to the people's questions, Shaun, appropriately, turns into a barrel and rolls on his way.

Well, (how dire do we thee hours when thylike fades!) all's dall and youllow and it is to bedowern that thou art passing hence, mine bruder, able Shaun, with a twhisking of the robe, ere the morning of light calms our hardest throes, beyond cods' cradle and porpoise plain, from carnal relations undfamiliar faces, to the inds of Tuskland where the oliphants scrum till the ousts of Amiracles where the toll stories grow proudest, more is the pity, but for all your deeds of goodness you were soo ooft and for ever doing, manomano and myriamilia even to mulimuli, as our humbler classes, whose virtue is humility, can tell, it is hardly we in the country of the old, Sean Moy, can part you for, oleypoe, you were the walking saint, you were, tootoo too stayer, the graced of gods and pittites and the salus of the wake. Countenance whose disparition afflictedly fond Fuinn feels. Winner of the gamings, primed at the studience, propredicted from the storybouts, the choice of ages wise! Spickspookspokesman of our specturesque silentiousness! Musha, beminded of us out there in Cockpit, poor twelve o'clock scholars, sometime or other anywhen you think the time. Wisha, becoming back to us way home in Biddyhouse one way or either anywhere we miss your smile.

Palmwine breadfruit sweetmeat milksoup! Suasusupo! However! Our people here in Samoanesia will not be after forgetting you and the elders luking and marking the jornies, chalkin up drizzle in drizzle out on the four bare mats. How you would be thinking in your thoughts how the deepings did it all begin and how you would be scrimmaging through your scruples to collar a hold of an imperfection being committled. Sireland calls you. Mery Loye is saling moonlike. And Slyly mamourneen's ladymaid at Gladshouse Lodge. Turn your coat, strong character, and tarry among us down the vale, yougander, only once more! And may the mosse of prosperousness gather you rolling home! May foggy dews bediamondise your hooprings! May the fireplug of filiality reinsure your bunghole! May the barleywind behind glow luck to your bathershins! 'Tis well we know you were loth to leave us, winding your hobbledehorn, right royal post, but, aruah sure, pulse of our slumber, dreambookpage, by the grace of Votre Dame, when the natural morning of your nocturne blankmerges into the national morning of golden sunup and Don Leary gets his own back from old grog Georges Quartos as that goodship the Jonnyjoys takes the wind from waterloogged Erin's king, you will shiff across the Moylendsea and round up in your own escapology some canonisator's day or other, sack on back, alack! digging snow, (not so?) like the good man you are, with your picture pockets turned knockside out in the rake of the rain for fresh remittances and from that till this in any case, timus tenant, may the tussocks grow quickly under your trampthickets and the daisies trip lightly over your battercops.

Jaunty Jaun, as I was shortly before that made aware, next halted to fetch a breath, the first cothurminous leg of his night-stride being pulled through, and to loosen (let God's son now be looking down on the poor preambler!) both of his bruised brogues that were plainly made a good bit before his hosen were, at the weir by Lazar's Walk (for far and wide, as large as he was lively, was he noted for his humane treatment of any kind of abused footgear), a matter of maybe nine score or so barrelhours distance off as truly he merited to do. He was there, you could planemetrically see, when I took a closer look at him, that was to say, (gracious helpings, at this rate of growing our cotted child of yestereve will soon fill space and burst in systems, so speeds the instant!) amply altered for the brighter, though still the graven image of his squarer self as he was used to be, perspiring but happy notwithstanding his foot was still asleep on him, the way he thought, by the holy januarious, he had a bullock's hoof in his buskin, with his halluxes so splendid, through Ireland untranscended, bigmouthed poesther, propped up, restant, against a butterblond warden of the peace, one comestabulish Sigurdsen, (and where a better than such exsearfaceman to rest from roving the laddyown he bootblacked?) who, buried upright like the Osbornes, kozydozy, had tumbled slumbersomely on sleep at night duty behind the curing station, equilebriated amid the embracings of a monopolized bottle.

Now, there were as many as twentynine hedge daughters out of Benent Saint Berched's national nightschool (for they seemed to remember how it was still a once-upon-a-four year) learning their antemeridian lesson of life, under its tree, against its warning, beseated, as they were, upon the brinkspondy, attracted to the rarerust sight of the first human yellowstone landmark (the bear, the boer, the king of all boors, sir Humphrey his knave we met on the moors!) while they paddled away, keeping time magnetically with their eight and fifty pedalettes, playing foolufool jouay allo misto posto, O so jaonickally, all barely in their typtap teens, describing a charming dactylogram of nocturnes though repelled by the snores of the log who looked stuck to the sod as ever and oft, when liquefied, (vil!) he murmoaned abasourdly in his Dutchener's native, visibly unmoved, over his treasure trove for the crown: *Dotter dead bedstead mean diggy smuggy flasky!*

Jaun (after he had in the first place doffed a hat with a reinforced crown and bowed to all the others in that chorus of praise of goodwill girls on their best beehiviour who all they were girls all rushing sowarmly for the post as buzzy as sie could bie to read his kisshands, kittering all about, rushing and making a tremendous girlsfuss over him pellmale, their *jeune premier* and his rosyposy smile, mussing his frizzy hair and the golliwog curls of him, all, but that one; Finfria's fairest, done in loveletters like a trayful of cloudberry tartlets (ain't they fine, mighty, mighty fine and honoured?) and smilingly smelling, pair and pair about, broad by bread and slender to slimmer, the nice perfumios that came cunvy peeling off him (nice!) which was angelic simply, savouring of wild thyme and parsley jumbled with breadcrumbs (O nice!) and feeling his full fat pouch for him so tactily and jingaling his jellybags for, though he looked a young chapplie of sixtine, they could frole by his manhood that he was just the killingest ladykiller all by kindness, now you, Jaun, asking kindlily (hillo, missies!) after their howareyous at all with those of their dollybegs (and where's Agatha's lamb? and how are Bernadetta's columbillas? and Juliennaw's tubberbunnies? and Eulalina's tuggerfunnies?) he next went on (finefeelingfit!) to drop a few stray remarks anent their personal appearances and the contrary tastes displayed in their tight kittycasques and their smart fricky-frockies, asking coy one after sloy one had she read Irish legginds and gently reproving one that the ham of her hom could be seen below her hem and whispering another aside, as lavariant, that the hook of her hum was open a bittock at her back to have a sideeye to that, hom, (and all of course just to fill up a form out of pure human kindness and in a sprite of fun) for Jaun, by the way, was by the way of becoming (I think, I hope he was) the most purely human being that ever was called man, loving all up and down the whole creation from Sampson's tyke to Jones's sprat and from the King of all Wrenns down to infuseries) Jaun, after those few prelimbs made out through his eroscope the apparition of his fond sister Izzy for he knowed his love by her waves of splabashing and she showed him proof by her way of blabushing nor could he forget her so tarnelly easy as all that since he was brotherbesides her benedict godfather and heaven knows he thought the world and his life of her sweet heart could buy, (brao!) poor, good, true, Jaun!

— Sister dearest, Jaun delivered himself with express cordiality, marked by clearance of diction and general delivery, as he began to take leave of his scolastica at once so as to gain time with deep affection, we honestly believe you sorely will miss us the moment we exit yet we feel as a martyr to the dischurch of all duty that it is about time, by Great Harry, we would shove off to stray on our long last journey and not be the load on ye. This is the gross proceeds of your teachings in which we were raised, you, sis, that used to write to us the exceeding nice letters for presentation and would be telling us anun (full well do we wont to recall to mind) thy oldworld tales of homespinning and derringdo and dieobscure and daddyho, these tales which reliterately whisked off our heart so narrated by thou, gesweest, to perfection, our pet pupil of the whole rhythmetic class and the mainsay of our erigenal house, the time we younkers twain were fairly tossing ourselves (O Phoebus! O Pollux!) in bed, having been laid up with Castor's oil on the Parrish's syrup (the night we will remember) for to share our hard suite of affections with thee.

I rise, O fair assemblage! Andcommincio. Now then, after this introit of exordium, my galaxy girls, *quiproquo* of directions to henservants I was asking his advice on the strict T.T. from Father Mike, P.P., my orational dominican and confessor doctor, C.C.D.D. (buy the birds, he was saying as he yerked me under the ribs sermon in an offrand way and confidence petween peas like ourselves in soandso many nuncupiscent words about how he had been confarreating teat-a-teat with two viragos intactas about what an awful life he led, poorish priced, uttering mass for a coppall of geldings and what a lawful day it was, there and then, for a consommation with an effusion and how, by all the manny larries ate pignatties, how, hell in tunnels, he'd marry me any old buckling time as flying quick as he'd look at me) and I am giving youth now again in words of style byaway of offertory hisand mikeadvice, an it place the person, as ere he retook him to his cure, those verbs he said to me. From above. The most eminent bishop titular of Dubloonik to all his purtybusses in Dellabelliney. Comeallyedimseldamsels, siddle down and lissle all! Follow me close! Keep me in view! Understeady me saries! Which is to all practising massoeurses from a preaching freer and be a gentleman without a duster before a parlourmade without a spitch. Now. During our brief apsence from this furtive feugtig season adhere to as many as probable of the ten commandments touching purgations and indulgences and in the long run they will prove for your better guidance along your path of right of way. Where the lisieuse are we and what's the first sing to be sung? Is it rubrics, mandarimus, pasqualines, or verdidads is in it, or the bruiselivid indecores of estreme voyoulence and, for the lover of lithurgy, bekant or besant, where's the fate's to be wished for? Several sindays after whatsintime. I'll sack that sick server the minute I bless him. That's the mokst I can do for his grapce. Economy of movement, axe why said. I've a hopesome's choice if I chouse of all the sinkts in the colander. From the common for ignitious Purpalume to the proper of Francisco Ultramare, last of scorchers, third of snows, in terrorgammons howdydos. Here she's, is a bell, that's wares in heaven, virginwhite, Undetrigesima, vikissy manonna. Doremon's! The same or similar to be kindly observed within the affianced dietcess of Gay O'Toole and Gloamy Gwenn du Lake (Danish spoken!) from Manducare Monday up till farrier's siesta in china dominos. Words taken in triumph, my sweet assistance, from the sufferant pen of our jocosus inkerman militant of the reed behind the ear.

Never miss your lostsomewhere mass for the couple in Myles you butrose to brideworship. Never hate mere pork which is bad for your knife of a good friday. Never let a hog of the howth trample underfoot your linen of Killiney. Never play lady's game for the Lord's stake. Never lose your heart away till you win his diamond back. Make a strong point of never kicking up your rumpus over the scroll end of sofas in the Dar Bey Coll Cafeteria by tootling risky *apropos* songs at commercial travellers' smokers for their Columbian nights entertainments the like of *White limbs they never stop teasing* or *Minxy was a Manxmaid when Murry wor a Man.* And, by the bun, is it you goes bisbuiting His Esaus and Cos and then throws them bag in the box? Why the tin's nearly empty. First thou shalt not smile. Twice thou shalt not love. Lust, thou shalt not commix idolatry. Hip confiners help compunction. Never park your brief stays in the men's convenience. Never clean your buttoncups with your dirty pair of sassers. Never ask his first person where's your quickest cut to our last place. Never let the promising hand usemake free of your oncemaid sacral. The soft side of the axe! A coil of cord, a colleen coy, a blush on a bush turned first man's laughter into wailful moither. O foolish cuppled! Ah, dice's error! Never dip in the ern while you've browsers on your suite. Never slip the silver key through your gate of golden age. Collide with man, collude with money. Ere you sail foreget my prize. Where you truss be circumspicious and look before you leak, dears. Never christen medlard apples till a swithin is in sight. Wet your thistle where a weed is and you'll rue it, despyneedis. Especially beware please of being at a party to any demoralizing home life. That saps a chap. Keep cool faith in the firm, have warm hoep in the house and begin frem athome to be chary of charity. Where it is nobler in the main to supper than the boys and errors of outrager's virtue. Give back those stolen kisses; restaure those allcotten glooves. Recollect the yella perals that all too often beset green gerils, Rhidarhoda and Daradora, once they gethobbyhorsical, playing breeches parts for Bessy Sudlow in flesh-coloured pantos instead of earthing down in the coalhole trying to boil the big gun's dinner. Leg-before-Wicked lags-behind-Wall where here Mr Whicker whacked a great fall. Femorafamilla feeled it a candleliked but Hayes, Conyngham and Erobinson sware it's an egg. Forglim mick aye! Stay, forestand and tillgive it! Remember the biter's bitters I shed the vigil I buried our Harlotte Quai from poor Mrs Mangain's of Britain Court on the feast of Marie Maudlin. Ah, who would wipe her weeper drÿ and lead her to the halter? Sold in her heyday, laid in the straw, bought for one puny petunia. Moral: if you can't point a lily get to henna out of here! Put your swell foot foremost on foulardy pneumonia shertwaists, irriconcilible with true fiminin risirvition and ribbons of lace, limenick's disgrace. Sure, what is it on the whole only holes tied together,the merest and transparent washingtones to make Languid Lola's lingery longer? Scenta Clauthes stiffstuffs your hose and heartsies full of temptiness. Vanity flee and Verity fear! Diobell! Whalebones and buskbutts may hurt you (thwackaway thwuck!) but never lay bare your breast secret (dickette's place!) to joy a Jonas in the Dolphin's Barncar with your meetual fan, Doveyed Covetfilles, comepulsing paynattention spasms between the averthisment for Ulikah's wine and a pair of pulldoors of the old cupiosity shape. There you'll fix your eyes darkled on the autocart of the bringfast cable but here till youre martimorphysed please sit still face to face. For if the shorth of your skorth falls down to his knees pray how wrong will he look till he rises? Not before Gravesend is commuted. But now reappears Autist Algy, the pulcherman and would-do performer, *oleas* Mr Smuth, stated by the vice crusaders to be well known to all the dallytaunties in and near the ciudad of Buellas Arias, taking you to the playguehouse to see the *Smirching of Venus* and asking with whispered offers in a very low bearded voice, with a nice little tiny manner and in a very nice little tony way, won't you be an artist's moral and pose in your nudies as a local esthetic before voluble old masters, introducing you, left to right the party comprises, to hogarths like Bottisilly and Titteretto and Vergognese and Coraggio with their extrahand Mazzaccio, plus the usual bilker's dozen of dowdycameramen. And the volses of lewd Buylan, for innocence! And the phyllisophies of Bussup Bulkeley. O, the frecklessness of the giddies nouveautays! There's many's the icepolled globetopper is haunted by the hottest spot under his equator like Ramrod, the meaty hunter, always jaeger for a thrust. The back beautiful, the undraped divine! And Suzy's Moedl's with their Blue Danuboyes! All blah! Viper's vapid vilest! Put off the old man at the very font and get right on with the nutty sparker round the back. Slip your oval out of touch and let the paravis be your goal. Up leather, Prunella, convert your try! Stick wicks in your earshells when you hear the prompter's voice. Look on a boa in his beauty and you'll never more wear your strawberry leaves. Rely on the relic. What bondman ever you bind on earth I'll be bound 'twas combined in hemel. Keep airly hores and the worm is yores. Dress the pussy for her nighty and follow her piggytails up their way to Winkyland. See little poupeep she's firsht ashleep. After having sat your poetries and you know what happens when chine throws over jupan. Go to doss with the poulterer, you understand, and shake up with the milchmand. The Sully van vultures are on the prowl. And the hailies fingringmaries. Tobaccos tabu and toboggan's a back seat. Secret satieties and onanymous letters make the great unwatched as bad as their betters. Don't on any account acquire a paunchon for that alltoocommon fagbutt habit of frequenting and chumming together with the braces of couples in Mr Tunnelly's hallways (smash it) wriggling with lowcusses and cockchafers and vamps and rodants, with the end to commit acts of interstipital indecency as between twineties and tapegarters, fingerpats on fondlepets, under the couvrefeu act. It's the thin end; wedge your steps! Your high powered hefty hoyden thinks nothing of ramping through a whole suite of smokeless husbands. Three minutes I'm counting you. Woooooon. No triching now! Give me that when I tell you! *Ragazza ladra!* And is that any place to be smuggling his madam's apples up? Deceitful jade. Gee wedge! Begor, I like the way they're half cooked. Hold, flay, grill, fire that laney feeling for kosenkissing disgenically within the proscribed limits like Population Peg on a hint or twim clandestinely does be doing to Temptation Tom, atkings questions in barely and snakking svarewords like a nursemagd. While there's men-a'war on the say there'll be loves-o'women on the do. Love through the usual channels, cisternbrothelly, when properly disinfected and taken neat in the generable way upon retiring to roost in the company of a husband-in-law or other respectable relative of an apposite sex, not love that leads by the nose as I foresmellt but canalised love, you understand, does a felon good, suspiciously if he has a slugger's liver but I cannot belabour the point too ardently (and after the lessions of experience I speak from inspiration) that fetid spirits is the thief of prurities, so none of your twenty rod cherrywhisks, me daughter! At the Cat and Coney or the Spotted Dog. And at 2bis Lot's Road. When parties get tight for each other they lose all respect together. By the stench of her fizzle and the glib of her gab know the drunken draggletail Dublin drab. You'll pay for each bally sorraday night every billing sumday morning. When the night is in May and the moon shines might. We won't meeth in Navan till you try to give the Kellsfrieclub the goby. Hill or hollow, Hull or Hague! And beware how you dare of wet cocktails in Kildare or the same may see your wedding driving home from your wake. Mades of ashens when you flirt spoil the lad but spare his shirt! Lay your lilylike long his shoulder but buck back if he buts bolder and just hep your homely hop and heed no horning but if you've got some brainy notion to raise cancan and rouse commotion I'll be apt to flail that tail for you till it's borning. Let the love ladleliked at the eye girde your gastricks in the gym. Nor must you omit to screw the lid firmly on that jazz jiggery and kick starts. Bumping races on the flat and point to point over obstacles. Ridewheeling that accliviciously up windy Rutland Rise and insighting rebellious northers before the saunter of the city of Dunlob. Then breretonbiking on the free with your airs of go-be-dee and your heels upon the handlebars. Berrboel brazenness! No, before your corselage rib is decartilaged, that is to mean if you have visceral ptossis, my point is, making allowances for the fads of your weak abdominal wall and your liver asprewl, vinvin, vinvin, or should you feel, in shorts, as though you needed healthy physicking exorcise to flush your kidneys, you understand, and move that twelffinger bowel and threadworm inhibitating it, lassy, and perspire freely, lict your lector in the lobby and why out you go by the ostiary on to the dirt track and skip! Be a sportive. Deal with Nature the great greengrocer and pay regularly the monthlies. Your Punt's Perfume's only in the hatpinny shop beside the reek of the rawny. It's more important than air—I mean than eats—air (Oop, I never open momouth but I pack mefood in it) and promotes that natural emotion. Stamp out bad eggs. Why so many puddings prove disappointing, as Dietician says, in Creature Comforts Causeries, and why so much soup is so muck slop. If we could fatten on the elizabeetons we wouldn't have teeth like the hippopotamians. However. Likewise if I were in your envelope shirt I'd keep my weathereye well cocked open for your furnished lodgers paying for their feed on tally with company and piano tunes. Only stuprifying yourself! The too friendly friend sort, Mazourikawitch or some other sukinsin of a vitch, who he's kommen from olt Pannonia on this porpoise whom sue stooderin about the maul and femurl artickles and who mix himself so at home mid the musik and spanks the ivory that lovely for this your Mistro Melosiosus MacShine MacShane may soon prove your undoing and bane through the succeeding years of rain should you, whilst Jaun is from home, get used to basking in his loverslowlap, inordinately clad, moustacheteasing, when closehended together behind locked doors, kissing steadily, (malbongusta, it's not the thing you know!) with the calfloving selfseeker, under the influence of woman, inching up to you, disarranging your modesties and fumbling with his forte paws in your bodice after your billy doos twy as a first go off (take care, would you stray and split on me!) and going on doing his idiot every time you gave him his chance to get thick and play pigglywiggly, making much of you, bilgetalking like a ditherer, gougouzoug, about your glad neck and the round globe and the white milk and the red raspberries (O horrifier!) and prying down furthermore to chance his lucky arm with his pregnant questions up to our past lives. What has that caught to sing with him? The next fling you'll be squitting on the Tubber Nakel, pouring pitchers to the well for old Gloatsdane's glorification and the postequities of the Black Watch, peeping private from the Bush and Rangers. And our local busybody, talker-go-bragk. Worse again! Off of that praying fan on to them priars! It would be a whorable state of affairs altogether for the redcolumnists of presswritten epics, Peter Paragraph and Paulus Puff, (I'm keepsoaking them to cover my concerts) to get ahold of for their balloons and shoot you private by surprise, considering the marriage slump that's on this oil age and pulexes three shillings a pint and wives at six and seven when domestic calamities belame par and newlaids bellow mar for the twenty twotoosent time thwealthy took thousands in the slack march of civilisation were you, becoming guilty of unleckylike intoxication to have and to hold, to pig and to pay direct connection, *qua* intervener, with a prominent married member of the vicereeking squad and, in consequence of the thereinunder subpenas, be flummoxed to the second degree by becoming a detestificated companykeeper on the dammymonde of Lucalamplight. Anything but that, for the fear and love of gold! Once and for all, I'll have no college swankies (you see, I am well voiced in love's arsenal and all its overtures from collion boys to colleen bawns so I have every reason to know that rogues' gallery of nightbirds and bitchfanciers, lucky duffs and light lindsays, haughty hamiltons and gay gordons, dosed, doctored and otherwise, messing around skirts and what their fickling intentions look like, you make up your mind to that) trespassing on your danger zone in the dancer years. If ever I catch you at it, mind, it's you that will cocottch it! I'll tackle you to feel if you have a few devils in you. Holy gun, I'll give it to you, hot, high and heavy before you can say sedro! Or may the maledictions of Lousyfear fall like nettlerash on the white friar's father that converted from moonshine the fostermother of the first nancyfree that ran off after the trumpadour that mangled Moore's melodies and so upturned the tubshead of the stardaft journalwriter to inspire the prime finisher to fellhim the firtree out of which Cooper Funnymore planed the flat of the beerbarrel on which my grandydad's lustiest sat his seat of unwisdom with my tante's petted sister for the cause of his joy! Amene.

> Shaun, as you will have noticed, has now become Jaun, a sort of debased Christ of the ladies. He has given the most lewdly cynical advice to the twenty-nine girls of St Bride's (the daughters of Erin), of whom the twenty-ninth is, of course, his bride-sister Iseult. She is also the Church to which, before his apotheosis, he introduces his proxy, a Holy Ghost as debased as himself: it can be no one but his brother. Bewailed and mourned by the women, particularly by his sister ("Pipetto, Pipetta has misery unnoticed!"), he passes on.

After poor Jaun the Boast's last fireless words of postludium of his soapbox speech ending in'sheaven, twentyaid add one with a flirt of wings were pouring to his bysistance (could they snip that curl of curls to lay with their gloves and keep the kids bright!) prepared to cheer him should he leap or to curse him should he fall, but, with their biga triga rheda rodeo, the cherubs in the charabang, set down here and sedan chair, don't you wish you'd a yoke or a bit in your mouth, repulsing all attempts at first hands on, as no es nada, our greatly misunderstood one we perceived to give himself some sort of a hermetic prod or kick to sit up and take notice, which acted like magic, while the phalanx of daughters of February Filldyke, embushed and climbing, ramblers and weeps, voiced approval in their customary manner by dropping kneedeep in tears over their concelebrated meednight sunflower, piopadey boy, their solase in dorckaness, and splattering together joyously the plaps of their tappyhands as, with a cry of genuine distress, so prettly prattly pollylogue, they viewed him, the just one, their darling, away.

A dream of favours, a favourable dream. They know how they believe that they believe that they know. Wherefore they wail.

Eh jourd'weh! Oh jourd'woe! dosiriously it psalmodied. Guesturn's lothlied answring to-maronite's wail.

Oasis, cedarous esaltarshoming Leafboughnoon!

Oisis, coolpressus onmountof Sighing!

Oasis, palmost esaltarshoming Gladdays!

Oisis, phantastichal roseway anjerichol!

Oasis, newleavos spaciosing encampness!

Oisis, plantainous dewstuckacqmirage playtennis!

Pipetto, Pipetta has misery unnoticed!

But the strangest thing happened. Backscuttling for the hop off with the odds altogether in favour of his tumbling into the river, Jaun just then I saw to collect from the gentlest weaner among the weiners, (who by this were in half droopleaflong mourning for the passing of the last post) the familiar yellow label into which he let fall a drop, smothered a curse, choked a guffaw, spat expectoratiously and blew his own trumpet. And next thing was he gummalicked the stickyback side and stamped the oval badge of belief to his agnelows brow with a genuine dash of irrepressible piety that readily turned his ladylike typmanzelles capsy curvy (the holy scamp!), with half a glance of Irish frisky (a Juan Jaimesan *hastaluego*) from under the shag of his parallel brows. It was then he made as if be but waved instead a handacross the sea as notice to quit while the pacifettes made their armpacts widdershins (Frida! Freda!

Paza! Paisy! Irine! Areinette! Bridomay! Bentamai! Sososopky! Bebebekka! Bababadkessy! Ghugugoothoyou! Dama! Damadomina! Takiya! Tokaya! Scioccara! Siuccherillina! Peocchia! Peucchia! Ho Mi Hoping! Ha Me Happinice! Mirra! Myrha! Solyma! Salemita! Sainta! Sianta! O Peace!), but in selfrighting the balance of his corporeity to reexchange widerembrace with the pillarbosom of the Dizzier he loved prettier, between estellos and venoussas, bad luck to the lie but when next to nobody expected, their star and gartergazer at the summit of his climax, he toppled a lipple on to the off and, making a brandnew start for himself to run down his easting, by blessing hes sthers with the sign of the southern cross, his bungaloid borsaline with the hedgygreen bound blew off in a loveblast (award for trover!) and Jawjon Redhead, bucketing after, meccamaniac, (the headless shall have legs!), kingscouriered round with an easy rush and ready relays by the bridge a stadion beyond Ladycastle (and what herm but he narrowly missed fouling her buttress for her but for he acqueducked) and then, cocking a snook at the stock of his sermons, so mear and yet so fahr from that region's general, away with him at the double, the hulk of a garron, pelting after the road, on Shanks's mare, let off like a wind hound loose (the bouchal! you'd think it was that moment they gave him the jambos!) with a posse of tossing hankerwaves to his windward like seraph's summonses on the air and a tempest of good things in packetshape teeming from all accounts into the funnel of his fanmail shrimpnet, along the highroad of the nation, Traitor's Track, following which fond floral fray he was quickly lost to sight through the statuemen though without a doubt he was all the more on that same head to memory dear while Sickerson, that borne of bjoerne, *la garde auxiliaire* she murmured, hellyg Ursulinka, full of woe (and how fitlier should goodboy's hand be shook than by the warmin of her besom that wrung his swaddles?): *Where maggot Harvey kneeled till bags? Ate Andrew coos hogdam farvel!*

Wethen, now, may the good people speed you, rural Haun, export stout fellow that you are, the crooner born with sweet wail of evoker, healing music, ay, and heart in hand of Shamrogueshire! The googoos of the suckabolly in the rockabeddy are become the copiosity of wiseableness of the friarylayman in the pulpitbarrel. May your bawny hair grow rarer and fairer, our own only wideheaded boy! Rest your voice! Feed your mind! Mint your peas! Coax your qyous! Come to disdoon blarmey and walk our groves so charming and see again the sweet rockelose where first you hymned *O Ciesa Mea!* and touch the light theorbo! Songster, angler, choreographer! Piper to prisoned! Musicianship made Embrassador-at-Large! Good by nature and natural by design, had you but been spared to us, Hauneen lad, but sure where's the use my talking quicker when I know you'll hear me all astray? My long farewell I send to you, fair dream of sport and game and always something new. Gone is Haun! My grief, my ruin! Our Joss-el-Jovan! Our Chris-na-Murty! 'Tis well you'll be looked after from last to first as yon beam of light we follow receding on your photophoric pilgrimage to your antipodes in the past, you who so often consigned your distributory tidings of great joy into our nevertoolatetolove box, mansuetudinous manipulator, victimisedly victorihoarse, dearest Haun of all, you of the boots, true as adie, stepwalker, pennyatimer, lampaddyfair, postanulengro, our rommanychiel! Thy now paling light lucerne we ne'er may see again. But could it speak how nicely would it splutter to the four cantons praises be to thee, our pattern sent! For you had — may I, in our, your and their names, dare to say it? — the nucleus of a glow of a zeal of soul of service such as rarely, if ever, have I met with single men. Numerous are those who, nay, there are a dozen of folks still unclaimed by the death angel in this country of ours today, humble indivisibles in this grand continuum, overlorded by fate and interlarded with accidence, who, while there are hours and days, will fervently pray to the spirit above that they may never depart this earth of theirs till in his long run from that place where the day begins, ere he retourneys postexilic, on that day that belongs to joyful Ireland, the people that is of all time, the old old oldest, the young young youngest, after decades of longsuffering and decennia of brief glory, to mind us of what was when and to matter us of the withering of our ways, their Janyouare Fibyouare wins true from Sylvester (only Walker himself is like Waltzer, whimsicalissimo they go murmurand) comes marching ahome on the summer crust of the flagway. Life, it is true, will be a blank without you because avicuum's not there at all, to nomore cares from nomad knows, ere Molochy wars bring the devil era, a slip of the time between a date and a ghostmark, rived by darby's chilldays embers, spatched fun Juhn that dandyforth, from the night we are and feel and fade with to the yesterselves we tread to turnupon.

But, boy, you did your strong nine furlong mile in slick and slapstick record time and a farfetched deed it was in troth, champion docile, with your high bouncing gait of going and your feat of passage will be contested with you and through you, for centuries to come. The phaynix rose a sun before Erebia sank his smother! Shoot up on that, bright Bennu bird! *Va faotre!* Eftsoon so too will our own sphoenix spark spirt his spyre and sunward stride the rampante flambe. Ay, already the sombrer opacities of the gloom are sphanished! Brave footsore Haun! Work your progress! Hold to! Now! Win out, ye divil ye! The silent cock shall crow at last. The west shall shake the east awake. Walk while ye have the night for morn, lightbreakfastbringer, morroweth whereon every past shall full fost sleep. Amain.

Lowly, longly, a wail went forth. Pure Yawn lay low. On the mead of the hillock lay, heartsoul dormant mid shadowed landshape, brief wallet to his side, and arm loose, by his staff of citron briar, tradition stick-pass-on. His dream monologue was over, of cause, but his drama parapolylogic had yet to be, affact. Most distressfully (but, my dear, how successfully!) to wail he did, his locks of a lucan tinge, quickrich, ripely rippling, unfilleted, those lashbetasselled lids on the verge of closing time, whiles ouze of his sidewiseopen mouth the breath of him, evenso languishing as the princeliest treble treacle or lichee chewchow purse could buy. Yawn in a semiswoon lay awailing and (hooh!) what helpings of honeyful swoothead (phew!), which earpiercing dulcitude! As were you suppose to go and push with your bluntblank pin in hand upinto his fleshasplush cushionettes of some chubby boybold love of an angel. Hwoah!

When, as the buzzer brings the light brigade, keeping the home fires burning, so on the churring call themselves came at him, from the westborders of the eastmidlands, three kings of three suits and a crowner, from all their cardinal parts, along the amber way where Brosna's furzy. To lift them they did, senators four, by the first quaint skreek of the gloaming and they hopped it up the mountainy molehill, traversing climes of old times gone by of the days not worth remembering; inventing some excusethems, any sort, having a sevenply sweat of night blues moist upon them. Feefee! phopho!! foorchtha!!! aggala!!!! jeeshee!!!!! paloola!!!!!! ooridiminy!!!!!!! Afeared themselves were to wonder at the class of a crossroads puzzler he would likely be, length by breadth nonplussing his thickness, ells upon ells of him, making so many square yards of him, one half of him in Conn's half but the whole of him nevertheless in Owenmore's five quarters. There would he lay till they would him descry, spancelled down upon a blossomy bed, at one foule stretch, amongst the daffydowndillies, the flowers of narcosis fourfettering his footlights, a halohedge of wild spuds hovering over him, epicures waltzing with gardenfillers, puritan shoots advancing to Aran chiefs. Phopho!! The meteor pulp of him, the seamless rainbowpeel. Aggala!!!! His bellyvoid of nebulose with his neverstop navel. Paloola!!!!!! And his veins shooting melanite phosphor, his creamtocustard cometshair and his asteroid knuckles, ribs and members. Ooridiminy!!!!!!! His electrolatiginous twisted entrails belt.

Those four claymen clomb together to hold their sworn starchamber quiry on him. For he was ever their quarrel, the way they would see themselves, everybug his bodiment atop of annywom her notion, and the meet of their noght was worth two of his morning. Up to the esker ridge it was, Mallinger parish, to a mead that was not far, the son's rest. First klettered Shanator Gregory, seeking spoor through the deep timefield, Shanator Lyons, trailing the wavy line of his partition footsteps (something in his blisters was telling him all along how he had been in that place one time), then his Recordership, Dr Shunadure Tarpey, caperchasing after honourable sleep, hot on to the aniseed and, up out of his prompt corner, old Shunny MacShunny, MacDougal the hiker, in the rere of them on the run, to make a quorum. Roping their ass he was, their skygrey globetrotter, by way of an afterthought and by no means legless either for such sprouts on him they were that much oneven it was tumbling he was by four lengths, within the bawl of a mascot, kuss yuss, kuss cley, patsy watsy, like the kapr in the kabisses, the big ass, to hear with his unaided ears the harp in the air, the bugle dianablowing, wild as wild, the mockingbird whose word is misfortune, so 'tis said, the bulbul down the wind.

The proto was traipsing through the tangle then, Mathew Walker, godsons' goddestfar, deputising for gossipocracy, and his station was a few perch to the weatherside of the knoll Asnoch and it was from no other place unless there, how and ever, that he proxtended aloof upon the ether Mesmer's Manuum, the hand making silence. The buckos beyond on the lea, then stopped wheresoever they found their standings and that way they set ward about him, doing obedience, nod, bend, bow and curtsey, like the watchers of Prospect, upholding their broadawake prober's hats on their firrum heads, the travelling court on its findings circuiting that personer in his fallen. And a crack quatyouare of stenoggers they made of themselves, solons and psychomorers, all told, with their hurts and daimons, spites and clops, not even to the seclusion of their beast by them that was the odd trick of the pack, trump and no friend of carrots. And, what do you think, who should be laying there above all other persons forenenst them only Yawn! All of asprawl he was laying too amengst the poppies and, I can tell you something more than that, drear writer, profoundly as you may bedeave to it, he was oscasleep asleep. And it was far more similar to a satrap he lay there with unctuous beauty all surrounded, the poser, or for whatall I know like Lord Lumen, coaching his preferred constellations in faith and doctrine, for old Matt Gregory, 'tis he had the starmenagerie, Marcus Lyons and Lucas Metcalfe Tarpey and the mack that never forgave the ass that lurked behind him, Jonny na Hossaleen.

More than their good share of their five senses ensorcelled you would say themselves were, fuming censor, the way they could not rightly tell their heels from their stools as they cooched down a mamalujo by his cubical crib, as question time drew nighing and the map of the souls' groupography rose in relief within their quarterings, to play tops or kites or hoops or marbles, curchycurchy, gawking on him, for the issuance of his pnum and softnoising one of them to another one, the boguaqueesthers.

Question time? Shaun, now called Yawn, has ended as we expected him to end, as a great inert emptiness, spent, useless, supine "on the mead of the hillock". The four old questioners probe him for facts of ancient true history, the creative sins of his progenitor, the fall in the park, the letter of ALP. Evasive gibberish only comes forth from the swollen nothingness that is Yawn. The four old men hand over their task to four young ones, bright modern brains-trusters, and at length, through the distortions of a medium, they reach the authentic voice of HCE himself. He confesses the wrongs he has done, but he asks posterity to look at his works—the city that adorns the banks of his river-wife—ALP, whom, despite all his transgressions, he has loved dearly and deeply. HCE and ALP, town and river, shine forth as eternal father and mother. If Shem was a stem and Shaun a stone, HCE and ALP conjoin into the very Tree of Life.

Forget about myth (shut that programme down). Call on the father of history, who is the father of all of us. (Expect interruptions when he speaks—from fourfold probers, from other spiritualistic voices. This is, after all, a séance).

— All halt! Sponsor programme and close down. That's enough, genral, of finicking about Finnegan and fiddling with his faddles. A final ballot, guvnor, to remove all doubt. By sylph and salamander and all the trolls and tritons, I mean to top her drive and to tip the tap of this, at last. His thoughts that wouldbe words, his livings that havebeen deeds. And will too, by the holy child of Coole, primapatriock of the archsee, if I have at first to down every mask in Trancenania from Terreterry's Hole to Stutterers' Corner to find that Yokeoff his letter, this Yokan his dahet. Pass the jousters of the king, the Kovnor-Journal and eirenarch's custos himself no less, the meg of megs, with the Carrison old gang! Off with your persians! Search ye the Finn! The sinder's under shriving sheet. Fa Fe Fi Fo Fum! Ho, croak, evildoer! Arise, sir ghostus! As long as you've lived there'll be no other. Doff!

— Amtsadam, sir, to you! Eternest cittas, heil! Here we are again! I am bubub brought up under a camel act of dynasties long out of print, the first of Shitric Shilkanbeard (or is it Owllaugh MacAuscullpth the Thord?), but, in pontofacts massimust, I am known throughout the world wherever my good Allenglisches Angleslachsen is spoken by Sall and Will from Augustanus to Ergastulus, as this is, whether in Farnum's rath or Condra's ridge or the meadows of Dalkin or Monkish tunshep, by saints and sinners eyeeye alike as a cleanliving man and, as a matter of fict, by my halfwife, I think how our public at large appreciates it most highly from me that I am as cleanliving as could be and that my game was a fair average since I perpetually kept my ouija ouija wicket up. On my verawife I never was nor can afford to be guilty of crim crig con of malfeasance trespass against parson with the person of a youthful gigirl frifrif friend chirped Apples, acted by Miss Dashe, and with Any of my cousines in Kissilov's Slutsgartern or Gigglotte's Hill, when I would touch to her dot and feel most greenily of her unripe ones as it should prove most anniece and far too bahad, nieceless to say, to my reputation on Babbyl Malket for daughters-in-trade being lightly clad. Yet, as my acquainters do me the complaisance of apprising me, I should her have awristed under my duskguise of whippers through toombs and deempeys, lagmen, was she but tinkling of such a tink. And, as a mere matter of ficfect, I tell of myself how I popo possess the ripest littlums wifukie around the globelettes globes upon which she was romping off on Floss Mundai out of haram's way round Skinner's circusalley first with her consolation prize in my serial dreams of faire women, Mannequins Passe, with awards in figure and smile subsections, handicapped by two breasts in operatops, a remarkable little endowment garment. Fastened at various places. What spurt! I kickkick keenly love such, particularly while savouring of their flavours at their most perfect best when served with heliotrope ayelips, as this is, where I do drench my jolly soul on the pu pure beauty of hers past.

She is my bestpreserved wholewife, sowell her as herafter, in Evans's eye, with incompatibly the smallest shoenumber outside chinatins. They are jolly dainty, spekin tluly. May we not recommend them? It was my proofpiece from my prenticeserving. And, alas, our private chaplain of Lambeyth and Dolekey, bishopregionary, an always sadfaced man, in his lutestring pewcape with tabinet band, who has visited our various hard hearts and reins by imposition of fufuf fingers, olso haddock's fumb, in that Upper Room can speak loud to you some quite complimentary things about my clean charactering, even when detected in the dark, distressful though such recital prove to me, as this is, when I introduced her (Frankfurters, numborines, why drive fear?) to our fourposter tunies chantreying under Castrucci Sinior and De Mellos, those whapping oldsteirs, with sycamode euphonium in either notation in our altogether cagehaused duckyheim on Goosna Greene, that cabinteeny homesweetened through affection's hoardpayns (First Murkiss, or so they sankeyed. Dodo! O Clearly! And Gregorio at front with Johannes far in back. Aw, aw!), gleeglom there's gnome sweepplaces like theresweep Nowhergs. By whom, as my Kerk Findlater's, ye litel chuch rond ye coner, and K. K. Katakasm enjoineth in the Belief and, as you all know, of a child, dear Humans, one of my life's ambitions of my youngend from an early peepee period while still to hedjeskool, intended for broadchurch, I, being fully alive to it, was parruchially confirmed in Caulofat's bed by our bujibuji beloved curate-author. Michael Engels is your man. Let Michael relay Sutton and tell you people here who have the phoney habit (it was remarketable) in his clairaudience, as this is, as only our own Michael can, when reicherout at superstation, to bring ruptures to our roars how I am amp amp amplify. Hiemlancollin. Pimpim's Ornery forninehalf. Shaun Shemsen saywhen saywhen. Holmstock unsteaden. Livpoomark lloyrge hoggs one four tupps noying. Big Butter Boost! Sorry! Thnkyou! Thatll beall fortody. Cal it off. Godnotch, vryboily. End a muddy crushmess! Abbreciades anew York gustoms. Kyow! Tak.

— Tiktak. Tikkak.

— Awind abuzz awater falling.

— Poor a cowe his jew placator.

— It's the damp damp damp.

— Calm has entered. Big big Calm, announcer. It is most ernst terooly a moresome intartenment. Colt's tooth! I will give tandsel to it. I protest there is luttrelly not one teaspoonspill of evidence at bottomlie to my babad, as you shall see, as this is. Keemun Lapsang of first pickings. And I contango can take off my dudud dirtynine articles of quoting here in Pynix Park before those in heaven to provost myself, by gramercy of justness, I mean veryman and moremon, stiff and staunch for ever, and enter under the advicies from Misrs Norris, Southby, Yates and Weston, Inc, to their favoured client, into my preprotestant caveat against the pupup publication of libel by any tixtim tipsyloon or tobtomtowley of Keisserse Lean (a bloweyed lanejoymt, waring lowbelt suit, with knockbrecky kenees and bullfist rings round him and a fallse roude axehand (he is cunvesser to Saunter's Nocelettres and the Poe's Toffee's Directory in his pisness), the best begrudged man in Belgradia who doth not belease to our paviour) to my nonesuch, that highest personage at moments holding down the throne. So to speak of beauty scouts in elegant pursuit of flowers, searchers for tabernacles and the celluloid art! Happen seen sore eynes belived? The caca cad! He walked by North Strand with his Thom's towel in hand. Snakeeye! Strangler of soffiacated green parrots! I protest it that he is, by my wipehalf. He was leaving out of my double inns while he was all teppling over my single ixits. So was keshaned on for his recent behaviour. Sherlook is lorking for him. Allare beltspanners. Get your air curt! Shame upon Private M! Shames on his fulsomeness! Shamus on his atkinscum's lulul lying suulen for an outcast mastiff littered in blood currish! Eristocras till Hanging Tower! Steck a javelin through his advowtried heart! Instaunton! Flap, my Larrybird! Dangle, my highflyer! Jiggety jig my jackadandyline! Let me never see his waddphez again! And mine it was, Barktholed von Hunarig, Soesown of Furrows (hourspringlike his joussture, immitiate my chry! as urs now, so yous then!), when to our lot it fell on my poplar Sexsex, my Sexencentaurnary, whenby Gate of Hal, before his hostel of the Wodin Man, I hestened to freeholdit op to his Mam his Maman, Majuscules, His Magnus Maggerstick, first city's leasekuays of this Nova Tara, our most noble, when hrossbucked on his pricelist charger, Pferdinamd Allibuster (yeddonot need light oar till Noreway for you fanned one o'er every doorway) with my allbum's greethims through this whole of my promises, handshakey congrandyoulikethems, ecclesency.

Whosaw the jackery dares at handgripper thisa breast? Dose makkers ginger. Some one we was with us all fours. Adversarian! The spiking Duyvil! First liar in Londsend! Wulv! See you scargore on that skeepsbrow! And those meisies! Sulken taarts! Man sicker at I ere bluffet konservative? Shucks! Such ratshause bugsmess so I cannot barely conceive of! Lowest basemeant in hystry! Ibscenest nansence! Noksagt! Per Peeler and Pawr! The brokerheartened shugon! Hole affair is rotten muckswinish porcupig's draff. Enouch!

— Is that yu, Whitehed?

— Have you headnoise now?

— Give us your mespilt reception, will yous?

— Pass the fish for Christ's sake!

— Old Whitehowth he is speaking again. Ope Eustace tube! Pity poor whiteoath! Dear gone mummeries, goby! Tell the woyld I have lived true thousand hells. Pity, please, lady, for poor O.W. in this profundust snobbing I have caught. Nine dirty years mine age, hairs hoar, mummery failend, snowdrift to my ellpow, deff as Adder. I askt you, dear lady, to judge on my tree by our fruits. I gave you of the tree. I gave two smells, three eats. My freeandies, my celeberrimates: my happy bossoms, my allfalling fruits of my boom. Pity poor Haveth Childers Everywhere with Mudder!

That was Communicator, a former colonel. A disincarnated

spirit, called Sebastion, from the Rivera in Januero, (he is not all hear) may fernspreak shortly with messuages from my deadported. Let us cheer him up a little and make an appunkment for a future date. Hello, Commudicate! How's the buttes? Everscepistic! He does not believe in our psychous of the Real Absence, neither miracle wheat nor soulsurgery of P. P. Quemby. He has had some indiejestings, poor thing, for quite a little while, confused by his tonguer of baubble. A way with him! Poor Felix Culapert! Ring his mind, ye staples, (bonze!) in my ould reekeries' ballyheart and in my krumlin and in aroundisements and stremmis! Sacks eleathury! Sacks eleathury! Bam! I deplore over him ruely. Mongrieff! O Hone! Guestermed with the nobelities, to die bronxitic in achershous! So enjoying of old thick whiles, in haute white toff's hoyt of our formed reflections, with stock of eisen all his prop, so buckely hosiered from the Royal Leg, and his puertos mugnum, he would puffout a dhymful bock. And the how he would husband her that verikerfully, his cigare divane! (He would redden her with his vestas, but 'tis naught.) With us his nephos and his neberls, mest incensed and befogged by him and his smoke thereof. But he shall have his glad stein of our zober beerbest in Oscarshal's winetavern. *Buen retiro!* The boyce voyce is still flautish and his mounth still wears that soldier's scarlet though the flaxafloyeds are peppered with salsedine. It is bycause of what he was ascend into his prisonce on account off. I whit it wel. Hence his deepraised words. Some day I may tell of his second storey. Mood! Mood! It looks like someone other bearing my burdens. I cannot let it. Kanes nought.

Well, yeamen, I have bared my whole past, I flatter myself, on both sides. Give me even two months by laxlaw in second division and my first broadcloth is business will be to protest to Recorder at Thing of all Things, or court of Skivinis, with marchants grey, antient and credibel, Zerobubble Barrentone, Jonah Whalley, Determined Codde or Cucumber Upright, my jurats, if it does not occur again. O rhyme us! Haar Faagher, wild heart in Homelan; Harrod's be the naun. Mine kinder come, mine wohl be won. There is nothing like leuther. O Shee! And nosty mens in gladshouses they shad not peggot stones. The elephant's house is his castle. I am here to tell you, indeed to goodness, that, allbe I discountenanced beallpersuasions, in rinunciniation of pomps of heretofore, with a wax too held in hand, I am thorgtfulldt to do dope me of her miscisprinks and by virchow of those filthered Ovocnas presently like Browne umbracing Christina Anya, after the Irishers, to convert me into a selt (but first I must proxy babetise my old antenaughties), when, as Sigismond Stolterforth, with Rabbin Robroost for my auspicer and Leecher Rutty for my lifearst and Lorencz Pattorn (*Ehren til viktrae!*), when I will westerneyes those poor sunuppers and outbreighten their land's eng. A man should stump up and I will pay my pretty decent trade price for my glueglue gluecose, peebles, were it even, as this is, the legal eric for infelicitous conduict (here incloths placefined my pocketanchoredcheck) and, as a matter of fact, I undertake to discontinue entyrely all practices and I deny wholeswiping *in toto* at my own request in all stoytness to have confermentated and confoederated and agreed in times prebellic, when here were waders for the trainsfolk, as it is now nuggently laid to me, with a friend from mine, Mr Billups, pulleter, my quarterbrother, who sometimes he is doing my locum for me on a grubstake and whom I have cleped constoutuent, for so it was felt by me, at goodbuy cootcoops byusucapiture a mouthless niggeress, Blanchette Brewster from Cherna Djamja, Blawlawnd-via-Brigstow, or to illsell my fourth part in her, which although allowed of in Deuterogamy as in several places of Scripture (copyright) and excluded books (they should quite rightly verbanned be), would seem eggseggs excessively haroween to my feelimbs for two punt scotch, one pollard and a crockard or three pipples on the bitch. Thou, Frick's Flame, Uden Sulfer, who strikest only on the marryd bokks, enquick me if so be I did cophetuise milady's maid! In spect of her beavers she is a womanly and sacret. Such wear a frillick for my comic strip, Mons Meg's Monthly, comes out aich Fanagan's Weck, to bray at by clownsillies in Donkeybrook Fair. It would lackin mackin Hodder's and Cocker's erithmatic. The unpurdonable preempson of all of her of yourn, by Juno Moneta! If she, irished Marryonn Teheresiann, has been disposed of for her consideration, I, Ledwidge Salvatorious, am tradefully unintiristid. And if she is still further talc slopping over her cocoa contours, I hwat mick angars, am strongly of opinion why I should not be. Inprobable! I do not credit one word of it from such and suchess mistraversers. Just feathers! Nanenities! Or to have ochtroyed to resolde or borrough by exchange same super melkkaart, means help; best Brixton high yellow, no outings: cent for cent on Auction's Bridge. 'Twere a honnibel crudelty wert so tentement to their naktlives and scatab orgias we devour about in the mightyevil roohms of encient cartage. Utterly improperable! Not for old Crusos or white soul of gold! A pipple on the panis, two claps on the cansill, or three pock pocks cassey knocked on the postern! Not for one testey tickey culprik's coynds ore for all ecus in cunziehowffse! So hemp me Cash! I meanit.

My herrings! The surdity of it! Amean to say. Her bare idears, it is choochoo chucklesome. Absurd bargain, mum, will call. One line with! One line, with with! Will ate everadayde saumone like a boyne alive O. The tew cherripickers, with their Catheringnettes, Lizzy and Lissy Mycock, from Street Fleshshambles, were they moon at aube with hespermun and I their covin guardient, I would not know to contact such gretched youngsteys in my ways from Haddem or any suistersees or heiresses of theirn, claiming by, through, or under them. Ous of their freiung pfann into myne foyer. Her is one which rassembled to mein enormally. The man what shocked his shanks at contey Carlow's. He is Deucollion. Each habe goheerd, uptaking you are innersence, but we sen you meet sose infance. Deucollion! Odor. Evilling chimbes is smutsick rivulverblott but thee hard casted thereass pigstenes upann Congan's shootsmen in Schottenhof, ekeascent? Igen Deucollion! I liked his Gothamm chic! Stuttertub! What a shrubbery trick to play! I will put my oathhead unner my whitepot for ransom of beeves and will stand me where I stood mine in all free heat between Pelagios and little

Chistayas by Roderick's our mostmonolith, after my both earstoear and brebreeches buybibles and, minhatton, testify to my unclothed virtue by the longstone erectheion of our allfirst manhere. I should tell you that honestly, on my honour of a Nearwicked, I always think in a wordworth's of that primed favourite continental poet, Daunty, Gouty and Shopkeeper, A. G., whom the generality admoyers in this that is and that this is to come. Like as my palmer's past policy I have had my best master's lessons, as the public he knows, and do you know, homesters, I honestly think, if I have failed lamentably by accident benefits though shintoed, spitefired, perplagued and cramkrieged, I am doing my dids bits and have made of my prudentials good. I have been told I own stolemines or something of that sorth in the sooth of Spainien. Hohohoho! Have I said ogso how I abhor myself vastly (truth to tell) and do repent to my netherheart of suntry clothing? The amusin part is, I will say, hotelmen, that since I, over the deep drowner Athacleeath to seek again Irrlanding, shamed in mind, with three plunges of my ruddertail, yet not a bottlenim, vanced imperial standard by weaponright and platzed mine residenze, taking bourd and burgage under starrymisty and ran and operated my brixtol selection here at thollstall, for mean straits male with evorage fimmel, in commune soccage among strange and enemy, among these plotlets, in Poplinstown, alore Fort Dunlip, then-on-sea, hole of Serbonian bog, now city of magnificent distances, goodwalldabout, with talus and counterscarp and pale of palisades, upon martiell siegewin, with Abbot Warre to blesse, on yon slauchterday of cleantarriffs, in that year which I have called myriabellous, and overdrave these marken (the soord on Whencehislaws was mine and mine the prusshing stock of Allbrecht the Bearn), under patroonshaap of our good kingsinnturns, T. R. H. Urban First and Champaign Chollyman and Hungry the Loaved and Hangry the Hathed, here where my tenenure of office and my toils of domestication first began, with weight of woman my skat and skuld but Flukie of the Ravens as my sure piloter, famine with Englisch sweat and oppedemics, the two-toothed dragon worms with allsort serpents, has compolitely seceded from this landleague of many nations and open and notorious naughty livers are found not on our rolls. This seat of our city it is of all sides pleasant, comfortable and wholesome. If you would traverse hills, they are not far off. If champain land, it lieth of all parts. If you would be delited with fresh water, the famous river, called of Ptolemy the Libnia Labia, runneth fast by. If you will take the view of the sea, it is at hand. Give heed!

— *Do Drumcollogher whatever you do!*

— *Visitez Drumcollogher-la-Belle!*

— *Be suke and sie so ersed Drumcollogher!*

— *Vedi Drumcollogher e poi Moonis.*

— Things are not as they were. Let me briefly survey. Pro clam a shun! Pip! Peep! Pipitch! Ubipop jay piped, ibipep goes the whistle. Here Tyeburn throttled, massed murmars march: where the bus stops there shop I: here which ye see, yea reste. On me, your sleeping giant. Estoesto! Estote sunto! From the hold of my capt in altitude till the mortification that's my fate. The end of aldest mosest ist the beginning of all thisorder so the last of their hansbailis shall the first in our sheriffsby. New highs for all! Redu Negru may be black in tawn but under them lintels are staying my horneymen meet each his mansiemagd. For peers and gints, quaysirs and galleyliers, fresk letties from the say and stale headygabblers, gaingangers and dudder wagoners, pullars off societies and pushers on rothmere's homes. Obeyance from the townsmen spills felixity by the toun. Our bourse and politico-ecomedy are in safe with good Jock Shepherd, our lives are on sure in sorting with Jonathans, wild and great. Been so free! Thank you, besters! Hattentats have mindered. Blaublaze devil-bobs have gone from the mode and hairtrigger nicks are quite out of time now. Thuggeries are reere as glovars' metins, lepers lack, ignerants show beneath suspicion like the bitterhalves of esculapuloids. In midday's mallsight let Miledd discurverself. Me ludd in her hide park seek Minuinette. All is waldy bonums. Blownose aerios we luft to you! Firebugs, good blazes! Lubbers, kepp your poudies drier! Seamen, we segn your skivs and wives!

Seven ills so barely as centripunts havd I habt, seaventy seavens for circumference inkeptive are your hill prospect. Braid Blackfordrock, the Calton, the Liberton, Craig and Lockhart's, A. Costofino, R. Thursitt. The chort of Nicholas Within was my guide and I raised a dome on the wherewithouts of Michan: by awful tors my wellworth building sprang sky spearing spires, cloud cupoled campaniles: further this. By fineounce and imposts I got and grew and by grossscruple gat I grown outreachesly: murage and lestage were my mains for Ouerlord's tithing and my drains for render and prender the doles and the tribute: I was merely out of my mint with all the percussors on my braincap till I struck for myself and muched morely by token: to Sirrherr of Gambleden ruddy money, to Madame of Pitymount I loue yous. Paybads floriners moved in hugheknots against us and I matt them, pepst to papst, barthelemew: milreys (mark!) onfell, and (Luc!) I arose Daniel in Leonden. Bulafests onvied me, Corkcuttas graatched. Atabey! I braved Brien Berueme to berow him against the Loughlins, all her tolkies shraking: Fugabollags! Lusqu'au bout! If they had ire back of eyeball they got danage on front tooth: theres were revelries at ridottos, here was rivalry in redoubt: I wegschicked Duke Wellinghof to reshockle Roy Shackleton: Walhalloo, Walhalloo, Walhalloo, mourn in plein! Under law's marshall and warschouw did I thole till lead's plumbate, ping on pang, reliefed me. I made praharfeast upon acorpolous and fastbroke down in Neederthorpe. I let faireviews in on slobodens but ranked rothgardes round wrathmindsers: I bathandbaddend on mendicity and I corocured off the unoculated. Who can tell their tale whom I filled ad liptum on the plain of Soulsbury? With three hunkered peepers and twa and twas! For sleeking beauties I spinned their nightinveils, to slumbred beast I tummed the thief air. Round the musky moved a murmel but mewses whinninaird and belluas zoomed: tendulcis tunes like water parted fluted up from the westinders while from gorges in the east came the strife of ourangoontangues. All in my thicville Escuterre ofen was thorough fear but in the meckling of my burgh Belvaros was the site forbed: tuberclerosies I reized spudfully from the murphyplantz Hawkinsonia and berriberries from the pletoras of the Irish shou. I heard my libertilands making free through their curraghcoombs, my trueblues hurusalaming before Wailingtone's Wall: I richmounded the rainelag in my bathtub of roundwood and conveyed it with cheers and cables, roaring mighty shouts, through my longertubes of elm: out of fundness for the outozone I carried them amd curried them in my Putzemdown cars to my Kommeandine hotels: I made sprouts fontaneously from Philuppe Sobriety in the coupe that's cheyned for noon inebriates: when they weaned weary of that bibbing I made infusion more infused: sowerpacers of the vinegarth, obtemperate unto me! When you think me in my coppeecuffs look in ware would you meckamockame, as you pay in caabman's sheltar tot the ites like you corss the tees. Wherefore watch ye well! For, while I oplooked the first of Janus's straight, I downsaw the last of Christmas steps: syndic podestril and on the rates, I for indigent and intendente: in Forum Foster I demosthrenated my folksfiendship, enmy pupuls felt my burk was no worse than their brite: Sapphrageta and Consciencia were undecidedly attached to me but the maugher machrees and the auntieparthenopes my schwalby words with litted spongelets set their soakye pokeys and botchbons afume: Fletcher-Flemmings, elisaboth, how interquackeringly they rogated me, their golden one, I inhesitant made replique: Mesdememdes to leursieuresponsor: and who in hillsaide, don't you let flyfire till you see their whites of the bunkers' eyes! Mr Answers: Brimgem young, bringem young, bringem young!: in my bethel of Solyman's I accouched their rotundaties and I turnkeyed most insultantly over raped lutetias in the lock: I gave bax of biscums to the jacobeaters and pottage bakes to the esausted; I dehlivered them with freakandesias by the constant droppings from my smalls instalmonths while I titfortotalled up their farinadays for them on my slataper's slate with my chandner's chauk: I jaunted on my jingelbrett rapt in neckloth and sashes, and I beggered about the amnibushes like belly in a bowle. In the humanity of my heart I sent out heyweywomen to refresh the ballwearied and then, doubling megalopolitan poleetness, my great great greatest of these charities, devaleurised the base fellows for the curtailment of their lower man: with a slog to square leg I sent my boundary to Botany Bay and I ran up a score and four of mes while the Yanks were huckling the Empire: I have been reciping om omominous letters and widelysigned petitions full of pieces of pottery about my monumentalness as a thingabolls and I have been inchanting causeries to the feshest cheoilboys so that they are allcalling on me for the song of a birtch: the more secretely bi built, the more openly palastered. Attent! Couch hear! I have becket my vonderbilt hutch in sunsmidnought and at morningrise was encampassed of mushroofs. Rest and bethinkful, with licence, thanks. I considered the lilies on the veldt and unto Balkis did I disclothe mine glory. And this. This missy, my taughters, and these man, my son, from my fief of the villa of the Ostmanorum to Thorstan's, *recte* Thomars Sraid, and from Huggin Pleaze to William Inglis his house, that man de Loundres, in all their barony of Saltus, bonders and foeburghers, helots and zelots, strutting oges and swaggering macks, the darsy jeamses, the drury joneses, redmaids and bleucotts, in hommage all and felony, all who have received tickets, fair home overcrowded, tidy but very little furniture, respectable, whole family attends daily mass and is dead sick of bread and butter, sometime in the militia, mentally strained from reading work on German physics, shares closet with eight other dwellings, more than respectable, getting comfortable parish relief, wageearner freshly shaven from prison, highly respectable, planning new departure in Mountgomery cyclefinishing, eldest son will not serve but peruses Big-man-up-in-the-Sky scraps, anoopanadoon lacking backway, quasi respectable, pays ragman in bones for faded windowcurtains, staircase continually lit up with guests, particularly respectable, house lost in dirt and blocked with refuse, getting on like Roe's distillery on fire, slovenly wife active with the jug, in business for himself, has a tenth illegitimate coming, partly respectable, following correspondence courses, chucked work over row, both cheeks kissed at levee by late marquess of Zetland, sharing closet which is profusely written over with eleven other subscribers, once respectable, open hallway pungent of Baltic dishes, bangs kept woman's head against wall thereby disturbing neighbours, private chapel occupies return landing, removal every other quarter day, case one of peculiar hopelessness, most respectable, nightsoil has to be removed through snoring household, eccentric naval officer not quite steady enjoys weekly churchwarden and laugh while reading foreign pictorials on clumpstump before door, known as the trap, widow rheumatic and chars, haunted, condemned and execrated, of dubious respectability, tools too costly pledged or uninsured, reformed philanthropist whenever feasible takes advantage of unfortunates against dilapidating ashpits, serious student is eating his last dinners, floor dangerous for unaccompanied old clergymen, thoroughly respectable, many uncut pious books in evidence, nearest watertap two hundred yards' run away, fowl and bottled gooseberry frequently on table, man has not had boots off for twelve months, infant being taught to hammer flat piano, outwardly respectable, sometimes hears from titled connection, one foot of dust between banister and cracked wall, wife cleans stools, eminently respectable, ottawark and regular loafer, should be operated would she consent, deplorable rent in roof, claret cellar cobwebbed since the pontificate of Leo, wears drill trousers and collects rare buddhas, underages very treacly and verminous have to be separated, sits up with fevercases for one and threepence, owns two terraces (back to back breeze), respectable in every way, harmless imbecile supposingly weakminded, a sausage every Sunday, has a staff of eight servants, outlook marred by ne'er-do-wells using the laneway, lieabed sons go out with sisters immediately after dark, has never seen the sea, travels always with her eleven trunks of clothing, starving cat left in disgust, the pink of respectability, resting after colonial service, labours at plant, the despair of his many benefactresses, calories exclusively from Rowntrees and dumplings, one bar of sunlight does them all january and half february, the V. de V's (animal diet) live in five-storied semidetached but rarely pay tradesmen, went security for friend who absconded, shares same closet with fourteen similar cottages and an illfamed lodginghouse, more respectable than some, teawidow pension but held to purchase, inherited silk hat from father-in-law, head of domestic economy never mentioned, queery how they live, reputed to procure, last four occupants carried out, mental companionship with mates only, respectability unsuccessfully aimed at, copious holes emitting mice, decoration from Uganda chief in locked ivory casket, grandmother has advanced alcoholic amblyopia, the terror of Goodmen's Field, and respected and respectable, as respectable as respectable can respectably be, though their orable amission were the herrors I could have expected, all, let them all come, they are my villeins, with chartularies I have talledged them. Wherfor I will and firmly command, as I willed and firmly commanded, upon my royal word and cause the great seal now to be affixed, that from the farthest of the farther of their fathers to their children's children's children they do inhabit it and hold it for me unencumbered and my heirs, firmly and quietly, amply and honestly, and with all the liberties and free customs which the men of Tolbris, a city of Tolbris, have at Tolbris, in the county of their city and through whole my land. Hereto my vouchers, knive and snuffbuchs. Fee for farm. Enwreak us wrecks.

Struggling forlongs I have livramentoed, milles on milles of mancipelles. Lo, I have looked upon my pumpadears in their easancies and my drummers have tattled tall tales of me in the land: in morgenattics litt I hope, in seralcellars louched I bleakmealers: on my siege of my mighty I was parciful of my subject but in street wauks that are darkest I debelledem superb: I deemed the drugtails in my pettycourts and domstered dustyfeets in my husinclose: at Guy's they were swathed, at Foulke's slashed, the game for a Gomez, the loy for a lynch: if I was magmonimoss as staidy lavgiver I revolucanized by my eructions: the hye and bye wayseeds I scattered em, in my graben fields sew sowage I gathered em: in Sheridan's Circle my wits repose, in black pitts of the pestered Lenfant he is dummed. (Hearts of Oak, may ye root to piece!

Rechabites obstain! Clayed sheets, pineshrouded, wake not, walk not! Sigh lento, Morgh!) *Quo warranto* has his greats my soliven and puissant lord V. king regards for me and he has given to me my necknamesh (flister it!) which is second fiddler to nomen. These be my genteelician arms. At the crest, two young frish, etoiled, flappant, devoiled of their habiliments, vested sable, withdrewers argent. For the boss a coleopter, pondant, partifesswise, blazoned sinister, at the slough, proper. In the lower field a terce of lanciers, shaking unsheathed shafts, their arms crossed in saltire, embusked, sinople. Motto, in letters portent: *Hery Crass Evohodie.* Idle were it, repassing from elserground to the elder disposition, to inquire whether I, draggedasunder, be the forced generation of group marriage, holocryptogam, of my essenes, or carried of cloud from land of locust, in ouzel galley borne, I, huddled til summone be the massproduct of teamwork, three surtouts wripped up in itchother's, two twin pritticoaxes lived as one, troubled in trine or dubildin too, for abram nude be I or roberoyed with the faineans, of Feejeean grafted ape on merfish, surrounded by obscurity, by my virtus of creation and by boon of promise, by my natural born freeman's journeymanright and my otherchurch's inher light, in so and such a manner as me it so besitteth, most surely I pretend and reclam to opt for simultaneous. Till daybowbreak and showshadows flee. Thus be hek. Verily! Verily! Time, place!

— What is your numb? Bun!

— Who gave you that numb? Poo!

— Have you put in all your sparepennies? I'm listening. Sree!

— Keep clear of propennies! Fore!

— Mr Televox, Mrs Taubiestimm and invisible friends! I maymay mean to say. Annoyin part of it was, had faithful Fulvia, following the wiening courses of this world, turned her back on her ways to gon on uphills upon search of louvers, brunette men of Earalend, Chief North Paw and Chief Goes in Black Water and Chief Brown Pool and Chief Night Cloud by the Deeps, or again had Fluvia, amber whitch she was, left her chivily crookcrook crocus bed at the bare suggestions of some prolling bywaymen from Moabit who could have abused of her, the foxrogues, there might accrue advantage to ask wher in pellmell her deceivers sinned. Yet know it was vastly otherwise which I have heard it by mmummy goods waif, as I, chiefly endmost hartyly aver, for Fulvia Fluvia, iddle woman to the plusneeborn, ever did ensue tillstead the things that pertained unto fairnesse, this wharom I am fawned on, that which was loost. Even so, for I waged love on her: and spoiled her undines. And she wept: O my lors!

— Till we meet!

— Ere we part!

— Tollollall!

— This time a hundred years!

— But I was firm with her. And I did take the reached of my delights, my jealousy, ymashkt, beyashmakt, earswathed, snout-snooded, and did raft her flumingworthily and did leftlead her overland the pace, from lacksleap up to liffsloup, tiding down, as portreeve should, whimpering by Kevin's creek and Hurdlesford and Gardener's Mall, long rivierside drive, embankment large, to Ringsend Flott and Ferry, where she began to bump a little bit, my dart to throw: and there, by wavebrink, on strond of south, with mace to masthigh, taillas Cowhowling, quailless Highjakes, did I upreized my magicianer's puntpole, the tridont sired a tritan stock, farruler, and I bade those polyfizzyboisterous seas to retire with hemselves from os (rookwards, thou seasea stamoror!) and I abridged with domfine norsemanship till I had done abate her maidan race, my baresark bride, and knew her fleshly when with all my bawdy did I her whorship, min bryllupswibe: Heaven, he hallthundered; Heydays, he flung blissforhers. And I cast my tenspan joys on her, arsched over-tupped, from bank of call to echobank, by dint of strongbow (Galata! Galata!) so streng we were in one, malestream in shegulf: and to ringstresse I thumbed her with iern of Erin and tradesmanmarked her lieflang mine for all and singular, iday, igone, imorgans, and for ervigheds: base your peak, you! you, strike your flag!: (what screech of shippings! what low of dampfbulls!): from Livland, hoks zivios, from Lettland, skall vives! With Impress of Asias and Queen Columbia for her pairanymphs and the singing sands for herbrides' music: goosegaze annoynted uns, canailles canzoned and me to she her shyblumes lifted: and I pudd a name and wedlock boltoned round her the which to carry till her grave, my durdin dearly, Appia Lippia Pluviabilla, whiles I herr lifer amstell and been: I chained her chastemate to grippe fiuming snugglers, her chambrett I bestank so to spunish furiosos: I was her hochsized, her cleavunto, her everest, she was my annie, my lauralad, my pisoved: who cut her ribbons when nought my prowes? who expoused that havenliness to beachalured ankerrides when not I, freipforter?: in trinity huts they met my dame, pick of their poke for me: when I foregather 'twas my sumbad, if I farseeker itch my list: had I not workit in my cattagut with dogshunds' crotts to clene and had I not gifted of my coataways, constantonoble's aim: and, fortiffed by my right as man of capitol, I did umgyrdle her about, my vermincelly vinagerette, with all loving kindness as far as in man's might it lay and enfranchised her to liberties of fringes: and I gave until my lilienyounger turkeythighs soft goods and hardware (catalogue, *passim*) and ladderproof hosiery lines (see stockinger's raiment), cocquette coiffs (see Agnes' hats) and peningsworths of the best taste of knaggs of jets and silvered waterroses and geegaws of my pretty novelties and wispywaspy frocks of redferns and lauralworths, trancepearances such as women cattle bare and peltries piled, the peak of Pim's and Slyne's and Sparrow's, loomends day lumineused luxories on. looks, *La Primamère, Pyrrha Pyrrhine, Or de Reinebeau, Sourire d'Hiver* and a crinoline, wide a shire, and pattens for her trilibies that know she might the tortuours of the boots and bedes of wampun with to toy and a murcery glaze of shard to mirrow, for all daintiness by me and theetime, the cupandnaggin hour: and I wound around my swanchen's neckplace a school of shells of moyles marine to swing their saysangs in her silents: and, upping her at king's count, her aldritch cry oloss unheading, what though exceeding bitter, I pierced her beak with order of the

Danabrog (Cunnig's great! Soll leve! Soll leve!): with mare's greese cressets at Leonard's and Dunphy's and Madonna lanthorns before quintacasas and tallonkindles spearhead syngeing nickendbookers and mhutton lightburnes dipdippingdownes in blackholes, the tapers of the topers and his buntingpall at hoist: for days there was no night for nights were days and our folk had rest from Blackheathen and the pagans from the prince of pacis: what was trembling sod quaked no more, what were frozen loins were stirred and lived: gone the septuor, dark deadly dismal doleful desolate dreadful desperate, no more the tolvmaans, bloody gloomy hideous fearful furious alarming terrible mournful sorrowful frightful appalling: peace, perfect peace: and I hung up at Yule my duindleeng lunas, helphelped of Kettil Flashnose, for the souperhore of my frigid one, *coloumba mea*, *frimosa mea*, in Wastewindy tarred strate and Elgin's marble halles lamping limp from black to block, through all Livania's volted ampire, from anodes to cathodes and from the topazolites of Mourne, Wykinloeflare, by Arklow's sapphire siomen's lure and Wexterford's hook and crook lights to the polders of Hy Kinsella: avenyue ceen my peurls ahumming, the crown to my estuarine munipicence?: three firths of the sea I swept with draughtness and all ennempties I bottled em up in bellomport: when I stabmarooned jack and maturin I was a bad boy's bogey but it was when I went on to sankt piotersbarq that they gave my devil his dues: what is seizer can hack in the old wold a sawyer may hew in the green: on the island of Breasil the wildth of me perished and I took my plowshure sadly, feeling pity for me sored: where bold O'Connee weds on Alta Mahar, the tawny sprawling beside that silver burn, I sate me and settled with the little crither of my hearth: her intellects I charmed with I calle them utile thoughts, her turlyhyde I plumped with potatums for amiens pease in plenty: my biblous beadells shewed her triumphs of craftygild pageantries, loftust Adam, duffed our cousterclother, Conn and Owel with cortoppled baskib, Sire Noeh Guinnass, exposant of his bargeness and Lord Joe Starr to hump the body of the camell: I screwed the Emperor down with ninepins gaelic with sixpennyhapennies for his hanger on: my worthies were bissed and trissed from Joshua to Godfrey but my *processus prophetarum* they would have plauded to perpetuation. Moral: book to besure, see press.

— He's not all buum and bully.

— But his members handly food him.

— Steving's grain for's greet collegtium.

— The S. S. Paudraic's in the harbour.

— And after these things, I fed her, my carlen, my barelean linsteer, upon spiceries for her garbage breath, italics of knobby lauch and the rich morsel of the marrolebone and shains of garleeks and swinespepper and gothakrauts and pinkee dillisks, primes of meshallehs and subleties in jellywork, come the feast of Saint Pancreas, and shortcake nutrients for Paas and Pingster's pudding, bready and nutalled and potted fleshmeats from store dampkookin, and the drugs of Kafa and Jelupa and shallots out of Ascalon, feeding her food convenient herfor, to pass them into earth: and to my saffronbreathing mongoloid, the skinsyg, I gave Biorwik's powlver and Uliv's oils, unguents of cuticure, for the swarthy searchall's face on her, with handewers and groinscrubbers and a carrycam to teaze her tussy out, the brown but combly, a mopsa's broom to duist her sate, and clubmoss and wolvesfoot for her more moister wards (amazing efficiencies!): and, my shopsoiled doveling, when weeks of kindness kinly civicised, in our saloons esquirial, with fineglas bowbays, draped embrasures and giltedged librariums, I did devise my telltale sports at evenbread to wring her withers limberly, wheatears, slapbang, drapier-cut-dean, bray, nap, spinado and ranter-go-round: we had our lewd mayers and our lairdie meiresses kiotowing and smuling fullface on us out of their framous latenesses, oilclothed over for cohabitation and allpointed by Hind: Tamlane the Cussacke, Dirk Wettingstone, Pieter Stuyvesant, Outlawrie O'Niell, Mrs Currens, Mrs Reyson-Figgis, Mrs Dattery, and Mrs Pruny-Quetch: in hym we trust, footwash and sects principles, apply to overseer, Amos five six: she had dabblingtime for exhibiting her grace of aljambras and duncingk the bloodanoobs in her vauxhalls while I, dizzed and dazed by the lumpty thumpty of our interloopings, fell clocksure off my ballast: in our windtor palast it vampared for elenders, we lubded Sur Gudd for the sleep and the ghoasts: she chauffed her fuesies at my Wigan's jewels while she skalded her mermeries on my Snorryson's Sagos: in paycook's thronsaale she domineered, lecking icies off the dormer panes all admired her in camises: on Rideau Row Duanna dwells, you merk well what you see: let wellth were I our pantocreator would theirs be tights for the gods: in littleritt reddinghats and cindery yellows and tinsel and glitter and bibs under hoods: I made nusance of many well pressed champdamors and peddled freely in the scrub: I foredreamed for thee and more than fullmaked: I prevened for thee in the haunts that joybelled frail light-a-leaves for sturdy traemen: *pelves ad hombres sumus:* I said to the shiftless prostitute; let me be your fodder; and to rodies and prater brothers; Chau, Camerade!: evangel of good tidings, omnient as the Healer's word, for the lost, loathsome and whomsoever will: who, in regimentation through liberal donation in coordination for organisation of their installation and augmentation plus some annexation and amplification without precipitation towards the culmination in latification of what was formerly their utter privation, competence, cheerfulness, usefulness and the meed, shall, in their second adams, all be made alive: my tow tugs steered down canal grand, my lighters lay longside on Regalia Water. And I built in *Urbs in Rure*, for minne elskede, my shiny brows, under astrolobe from my upservatory, an erdcloset with showne ejector wherewithin to be squatquit in most covenience from her sabbath needs, when open noise should stilled be: did not I festfix with mortarboard my unniversiries, wholly rational and gottalike, sophister agen sorefister, life sizars all?: was I not rosetted on two stellas of little egypt? had not I rockcut readers, hieros, gregos and democriticos?: triscastellated, bimedallised: and by my sevendialled changing charties Hibernska Ulitzas made not I to pass through twelve Threadneedles and Newgade and Vicus Veneris to cooinsight?: my camels' walk, kolossa kolossa! no porte sublimer benared my ghates: Oi polled ye many but my fews were chousen (Voter, voter, early voter, he was never too oft for old Sarum): terminals four my staties were, the Geenar, the Greasouwea, the Debwickweck, the Mifgreawis. And I sept up twinminsters, the pro and the con, my stavekirks wove so norcely of peeled wands and attachatouchy floodmud, now all loosebrick and stonefest, freely masoned, arked for covennanters and shinners' rifuge: descent from above on us, Hagiasofia of Astralia, our orisons thy nave and absedes, our aeone tone aeones thy studvaast vault; Hams, circuitise! Shemites, retrace!: horns, hush! no barkeys! hereround is't holied!: all truanttrulls made I comepull, all rubbeling gnomes I pushed, gowgow: Cassels, Redmond, Gandon, Deane, Shepperd, Smyth, Neville, Heaton, Stoney, Foley, Farrell, Vnost with Thorneycroft and Hogan too: sprids serve me! gobelins guard!: tect my tileries (O tribes! O gentes!), keep my keep, the peace of my four great ways: oathiose infernals to Booth Salvation, arcane celestials to Sweatenburgs Welhell! My seven wynds I trailed to maze her and ever a wynd had saving closes and all these closes flagged with the gust, hoops for her, hatsoff for him and ruffles through Neeblow's garding: and that was why Blabus was razing his wall and eltering the suzannes of his nighboors: and thirdly, for ewigs, I did reform and restore for my smuggy piggiesknees, my sweet coolocked, my auburn coyquailing one, her paddypalace on the crossknoll with massgo bell, sixton clashcloshant, duominous and muezzatinties to commind the fitful: doom adimdim adoom adimadim: and the oragel of the lauds to tellforth's glory: and added thereunto a shallow laver to slub out her hellfire and posied windows for her oriel house: gospelly pewmillieu, christous pewmillieu: zackbutts babazounded, ollguns tararulled: and she sass her nach, chillybombom and forty bonnets, upon the altarstane. May all have mossyhonours!

— Hoke!

— Hoke!

— Hoke!

— Hoke!

— And wholehail, snaeffell, dreardrizzle orsleetshowers of blessing, where it froze in chalix eller swum in the vestry, with fairskin book and ruling rod, vein of my vergin page, her chastener ever I did learn my little ana countrymouse in alphabeater cameltemper, from alderbirk to tannenyou, with myraw rattan atter dundrum; ooah, oyir, oyir, oyir: and I did spread before my Livvy, where Lord street lolls and ladies linger and Cammomile Pass cuts Primrose Rise and Coney Bend bounds Mulbreys Island but never a blid had bledded or bludded since long agore when the whole blighty acre was bladey well pessovered, my selvage mats of lecheworked lawn, my carpet gardens of Guerdon City, with chopes pyramidous and mousselimes and beaconphires and colossets and pensilled turisses for the busspleaches of the summiramies and esplanadas and statuesques and templeogues, the Pardonell of Maynooth, Fra Teobaldo, Nielsen, rare admirable, Jean de Porteleau, Conall Gretecloke, Guglielmus Caulis and the eiligh ediculous Passivucant (glorietta's inexcellsiored!): for irkdays and for folliedays till the comple anniums of calendarias, gregoromaios and gypsyjuliennes as such are pleased of theirs to walk: and I planted for my own hot lisbing lass a quickset vineyard and I fenced it about with huge Chesterfield elms and Kentish hops and rigs of barlow and bowery nooks and greenwished villas and pampos animos and (N.I.) necessitades iglesias and pons for aguaducks: a hawthorndene, a feyrieglenn, the hallaw vall, the dyrchace, Finmark's Howe, against lickybudmonth and gleanermonth with a magicscene wall (rimrim! rimrim!) for a Queen's garden of her phoenix: and (hush! hush!) I brewed for my alpine plurabelle, wigwarming wench, (speakeasy!) my granvilled brandold Dublin lindub, the free, the froh, the frothy freshener, puss, puss, pussyfoot, to split the spleen of her maw: and I laid down before the trotters to my eblanite my stony battered waggonways, my nordsoud circulums, my eastmoreland and westlandmore, running boullowards and syddenly parading, (hearsemen, opslo! nuptiallers, get storting!): whereon, in mantram of truemen like yahoomen (expect till dutc cundoctor summoneth him all fahrts to pay, velkommen all hankinhunkn in this vongn of Hoseyeh!), claudesdales withe arabinstreeds, Roamer Reich's rickyshaws with Hispain's King's trompateers, madridden mustangs, buckarestive bronchos, poster shays and turnintaxis, and tall tall tilburys and nod nod noddies, others gigging gaily, some sedated in sedans: my priccoping gents, aroger, aroger, my damsells softsidesaddled, covertly, covertly, and Lawdy Dawe a perch behind: the mule and the hinny and the jennet and the mustard nag and piebald shjelties and skewbald awknees steppit lively (lift ye the left and rink ye the right!) for her pleashadure: and she lalaughed in her diddydid domino to the switcheries of the whip. Down with them! Kick! Playup!

Mattahah! Marahah! Luahah! Joahanahanahana!

What was thaas? Fog was whaas? Too mult sleepth. Let sleepth.

But reəlly now whenabouts? Expatiate then how much times we live in. Yes?

So, nat by night by naught by naket, in those good old lousy days gone by, the days, shall we say? of Whom shall we say? while kinderwardens minded their twinsbed, therenow theystood, the sycomores, all four of them, in their quartan agues, the majorchy, the minorchy, the everso and the fermentarian with their ballyhooric blowreaper, titranicht by tetranoxst, at their pussycorners, and that old time pallyollogass, playing copers fearsome, with Gus Walker, the cuddy, and his poor old dying boosy cough, esker, newcsle, saggard, crumlin, dell me, donk, the way to wumblin. Follow me beeline and you're bumblin, esker, newcsle, saggard, crumlin. And listening. So gladdied up when nicechild Kevin Mary (who was going to be commandeering chief of the choirboys' brigade the moment he grew up under all the auspices) irishsmiled in his milky way of cream dwibble and onage tustard and dessed tabbage, frighted out when badbrat Jerry Godolphing (who was hurrying to be cardinal scullion in a night refuge as bald as he was cured enough unerr all the hospitals) furrinfrowned down his wrinkly waste of methylated spirits, ick, and lemoncholy lees, ick, and pulverised rhubarbarorum, icky;

night by silentsailing night while infantina Isobel (who will be blushing all day to be, when she growed up one Sunday, Saint Holy and Saint Ivory, when she took the veil, the beautiful presentation nun, so barely twenty, in her pure coif, sister Isobel, and next Sunday, Mistlemas, when she looked a peach, the beautiful Samaritan, still as beautiful and still in her teens, nurse Saintette Isabelle, with stiffstarched cuffs but on Holiday, Christmas, Easter mornings when she wore a wreath, the wonderful widow of eighteen springs, Madame Isa Veuve La Belle, so sad but lucksome in her boyblue's long black with orange blossoming weeper's veil) for she was the only girl they loved, as she is the queenly pearl you prize, because of the way the night that first we met she is bound to be, methinks, and not in vain, the darling of my heart, sleeping in her april cot, within her singachamer, with her greengageflavoured candywhistle duetted to the crazyquilt, Isobel, she is so pretty, truth to tell, wildwood's eyes and primarose hair, quietly, all the woods so wild, in mauves of moss and daphnedews, how all so still she lay, neath of the whitethorn, child of tree, like some losthappy leaf, like blowing flower stilled, as fain would she anon, for soon again 'twill be, win me, woo me, wed me, ah weary me! deeply, now evencalm lay sleeping;

nowth upon nacht, while in his tumbril Wachtman Havelook seequeerscenes, from yonsides of the choppy, punkt by his curserbog, went long the grassgross bumpinstrass that henders the pubbel to pass, stowing his bottle in a hole for at whet his whuskle to stretch ecrooksman, sequestering for lovers' lost propertied offices the leavethings from allpurgers' night, og gneiss ogas gnasty, kikkers, brillers, knappers and bands, handsboon and strumpers, sminkysticks and eddiketsflaskers;

wan fine night and the next fine night and last find night while Kothereen the Slop in her native's chambercushy, with dreamings of simmering my veal astore, was basquing to her pillasleep how she thawght a knogg came to the dowanstairs dour at that howr to peirce the yare and dowandshe went, schritt be schratt, to see was it Schweeps's mingerals or Shuhorn the posth with a tilly-cramp for Hemself and Co, Esquara, or them four hoarsemen on their apolkaloops, Norreys, Soothbys, Yates and Welks, and, galorybit of the sanes in hevel, there was a crick up the stirkiss and when she ruz the cankle to see, galohery, downand she went on her knees to blessersef that were knogging together like milk-juggles as if it was the wrake of the hapspurus or old Kong Gander O'Toole of the Mountains or his googoo goosth she seein, sliving off over the sawdust lobby out of the backroom, wan ter, that was everywans in turruns, in his honeymoon trim, holding up his fingerhals, with the clookey in his fisstball, tocher of davy's, tocher of ivileagh, for her to whisht, you sowbelly, and the whites of his pious eyebulbs swering her to silence and coort;

each and every juridical sessions night, whenas goodmen twelve and true at fox and geese in their numbered habitations tried old wireless over boord in their juremembers, whereas by reverendum they found him guilty of their and those imputations of fornicolopulation with two of his albowcrural correlations on whom he was said to have enjoyed by anticipation when schooling them in amown, mid grass, she sat, when man was, amazingly frank, for their first conjugation whose colours at standing up from the above were of a pretty carnation but, if really 'twere not so, of some deretane denudation with intent to excitation, caused by his retrogradation, among firearmed forces proper to this nation but apart from all titillation which, he said, was under heat pressure and a good mitigation without which in any case he insists upon being worthy of continued alimentation for him having displayed, he says, such grand toleration, reprobate so noted and all, as he was, with his washleather sweeds and his smokingstump, for denying transubstantiation nevertheless in respect of his highpowered station, whereof more especially as probably he was meantime suffering genteel tortures from the best medical attestation, as he oftentimes did, having only strength enough, by way of festination, to implore (or I believe you have might have said better) to complore, with complete obsecration, on everybody connected with him the curse of co-agulation for, he tells me outside Sammon's in King Street, after two or three hours of close confabulation, by this pewterpint of Gilbey's goatswhey which is his prime consolation, albeit involving upon the same no uncertain amount of esophagous regurgitation, he being personally unpreoccupied to the extent of a flea's gizzard anent eructation, if he was still extremely offensive to a score and four nostrils' dilatation, still he was likewise, on the other side of him, for some nepmen's eyes a delectation, as he asserts without the least alienation, so prays of his faullt you would make obliteration but for our friend behind the bars, though like Adam Findlater, a man of estimation, summing him up to be done, be what will of excess his exaltation, still we think with Sully there can be no right extinuation for contravention of common and statute legislation for which the fit remedy resides, for Mr Sully, in corporal amputation: so three months for Gubbs Jeroboam, the frothwhiskered pest of the park, as per act one, section two, schedule three, clause four of the fifth of King Jark, this sentence to be carried out tomorrowmorn by Nolans Volans at six o'clock shark, and may the yeastwind and the hoppinghail malt mercy on his seven honeymeads and his hurlyburlygrowth, Amen, says the Clarke;

niece by nice by neat by natty, whilst amongst revery's happy gardens nine with twenty Leixlip yearlings, darters all, had such a ripping time with gleeful cries of what is nice toppingshaun made of made for and weeping like fun, him to be gone, for they were never happier, huhu, than when they were miserable, haha;

in their bed of trial, on the bolster of hardship, by the glimmer of memory, under coverlets of cowardice, Albatrus Nyanzer with Victa Nyanza, his mace of might mortified, her beautifell hung up on a nail, he, Mr of our fathers, she, our moddereen ru arue rue, they, ay, by the hodypoker and blazier, they are, as sure as dinny drops into the dyke . . .

A cry off.

The cry is the cry of one of the twins, who, wakening from a nightmare, rouses his parents. The dream of our hero is thus temporarily dissolved, though the dream of the author continues. The four old men have become bedposts, and we have just heard them droning away as they surveyed HCE and ALP—converted to a pair of African lakes (Albatrus Nyanzer and Victa Nyanza)—on their "bed of trial". The bad and decadent times that have come about with the rule of Shaun are no mere dream-stuff— they are here and now, and they find their best, or worst, symbol in the sterile sexual encounter of a sleepy innkeeper and his wife. ("Legalentitled . . . Twainbeonerflsh".) The crying child soothed and quietened, the two make their way back to bed, but before they can couple we are treated to a ghastly cold fantasy of sexual perversion (HCE as Honuphrius, ALP as Anita) which sums up our debased age. The wide-awake legalistic language comes on us, after so much dreaming, like a freezing douche. As for the sanctions of religion in a period of sterile debauchery, consult Tangos, Limited (the Church of Rome) and the rival firm Pangos (the Church of England)—musical banks without the music. The cheque of condom-rubber, embossed DUD 1132, tells its own story.

After this shocking interlude, HCE and ALP go back to bed and copulate, their shadows on the blind broadcasting the act to the world.

— He is quieter now.

— Legalentitled. Accesstopartnuzz. Notwildebeestsch. Byrightofoaptz. Twainbeonerflsh. Haveandholdpp.

— S! Let us go. Make a noise. Slee . . .

— Qui . . . The gir . . .

— Huesofrichunfoldingmorn. Wakenupriseandprove. Provideforsacrifice.

— Wait! Hist! Let us list!

For our netherworld's bosomfoes are working tooth and nail overtime: in earthveins, toadcavites, chessganglions, saltklesters, underfed: nagging firenibblers knockling aterman up out of his hinterclutch. Tomb be their tools! When the youngdammers will be soon heartpocking on their betters' doornoggers: and the youngfries will be backfrisking diamondcuts over their lyingin underlayers, spick and spat trowelling a gravetrench for their fourinhand forebears. Vote for your club!

— Wait!

— What!

— Her door!

— Ope?

— See!

— What?

— Careful.

— Who?

Live well! Iniivdluaritzas! Tone!

Cant ear! Her dorters ofe? Whofe? Her eskmeno daughters hope? Whope? Ellme, elmme, elskmestoon! Soon!

Let us consider.

The procurator Interrogarius Mealterum presends us this proposer.

Honuphrius is a concupiscent exservicemajor who makes dishonest propositions to all. He is considered to have committed, invoking *droit d'oreiller*, simple infidelities with Felicia, a virgin, and to be practising for unnatural coits with Eugenius and Jeremias, two or three philadelphians. Honophrius, Felicia, Eugenius and Jeremias are consanguineous to the lowest degree. Anita the wife of Honophrius, has been told by her tirewoman, Fortissa, that Honuphrius has blasphemously confessed under voluntary chastisement that he has instructed his slave, Mauritius, to urge Magravius, a commercial, emulous of Honuphrius, to solicit the chastity of Anita. Anita is informed by some illegitimate children of Fortissa with Mauritius (the supposition is Ware's) that Gillia, the schismatical wife of Magravius, is visited clandestinely by Barnabas, the advocate of Honuphrius, an immoral person who has been corrupted by Jeremias. Gillia, (a cooler blend, D'Alton insists) *ex equo* with Poppea, Arancita, Clara,

Marinuzza, Indra and Iodina, has been tenderly debauched (in Halliday's view), by Honuphrius, and Magravius knows from spies that Anita has formerly committed double sacrilege with Michael, *vulgo* Cerularius, a perpetual curate, who wishes to seduce Eugenius. Magravius threatens to have Anita molested by Sulla, an orthodox savage (and leader of a band of twelve mercenaries, the Sullivani), who desires to procure Felicia for Gregorius, Leo, Vitellius and Macdugalius, four excavators, if she will not yield to him and also deceive Honuphrius by rendering conjugal duty when demanded. Anita who claims to have discovered incestuous temptations from Jeremias and Eugenius would yield to the lewdness of Honuphrius to appease the savagery of Sulla and the mercernariness of the twelve Sullivani, and (as Gilbert at first suggested), to save the virginity of Felicia for Magravius when converted by Michael after the death of Gillia, but she fears that, by allowing his marital rights she may cause reprehensible conduct between Eugenius and Jeremias. Michael, who has formerly debauched Anita, dispenses her from yielding to Honuphrius who pretends publicly to possess his conjunct in thirtynine several manners (*turpiter!* affirm *ex cathedris* Gerontes Cambronses) for carnal hygiene whenever he has rendered himself impotent to consummate by subdolence. Anita is disturbed but Michael comminates that he will reserve her case tomorrow for the ordinary Guglielmus even if she should practise a pious fraud during affrication which, from experience, she knows (according to Wadding), to be leading to nullity. Fortissa, however, is encouraged by Gregorius, Leo, Viteilius, and Magdugalius, reunitedly, to warn Anita by describing the strong chastisements of Honuphrius and the depravities (*turpissimas!*) of Canicula, the deceased wife of Mauritius, with Sulla, the simoniac, who is abnegand and repents. Has he hegemony and shall she submit?

Translate a lax, you breed a bradaun. In the goods of Cape and Chattertone, deceased.

This, lay readers and gentilemen, is perhaps the commonest of all cases arising out of umbrella history in connection with the wood industries in our courts of litigation. D'Oyly Owens holds (though Finn Magnusson of himself holds also) that so long as there is a joint deposit account in the two names a mutual obligation is posited. Owens cites Brerfuchs and Warren, a foreign firm, since disseized, registered as Tangos, Limited, for the sale of certain proprietary articles. The action which was at the instance of the trustee of the heathen church emergency fund, suing by its trustee, a resigned civil servant, for the payment of tithes due was heard by Judge Doyle and also by a common jury. No question arose as to the debt for which vouchers spoke volumes. The defence alleged that payment had been made effective. The fund trustee, one Jucundus Fecundus Xero Pecundus Coppercheap, counterclaimed that payment was invalid having been tendered to creditor under cover of a crossed cheque, signed in the ordinary course, in the name of Wieldhelm, Hurls Cross, voucher copy provided, and drawn by the senior partner only by whom the lodgment of the species had been effected but in their joint names. The bank particularised, the national misery (now almost entirely in the hands of the four chief bondholders for value in Tangos), declined to pay the draft, though there were ample reserves to meet the liability, whereupon the trusty Coppercheap negociated it for and on behalf of the fund of the thing to a client of his, a notary, from whom, on consideration, he received in exchange legal relief as between trusthee and bethrust, with thanks. Since then the cheque, a good washable pink, embossed D you D No 11 hundred and thirty 2, good for the figure and face, had been circulating in the country for over thirtynine years among holders of Pango stock, a rival concern, though not one demonetised farthing had ever spun or fluctuated across the counter in the semblance of hard coin or liquid cash. The jury (a sour dozen of stout fellows all of whom were curiously named after doyles) naturally disagreed jointly and severally, and the belligerent judge, disagreeing with the allied jurors' disagreement, went outside his jurisfiction altogether and ordered a garnishee attachment to the neutral firm. No *mandamus* could locate the depleted whilom Breyfawkes as he had entered into an ancient moratorium, dating back to the times of the early barters, and only the junior partner Barren could be found, who entered an appearance and turned up, upon a notice of motion and after service of the motion by interlocutory injunction, among the male jurors to be an absolete turfwoman, originally from the proletarian class, with still a good title to her sexname of Ann Doyle, 2 Coppinger's Cottages, the Doyle's country. Doyle (Ann), add woman in, having regretfully left the juryboxers, protested cheerfully on the stand in a long jurymiad *in re* corset checks, delivered in doylish, that she had often, in supply to brusk demands rising almost to bollion point, discounted Mr Brakeforth's first of all in exchange at nine months from date without issue and, to be strictly literal, unbottled in corrubberation a current account of how she had been made at sight for services rendered the payee-drawee of unwashable blank assignations, sometimes pinkwilliams (laughter) but more often of the *crème-de-citron, vair émail paoncoque* or marshmallow series, which she, as bearer, used to endorse, adhesively, to her various payers-drawers who in most cases were identified by the timber papers as wellknown tetigists of the city and suburban. The witness, at her own request, asked if she might and wrought something between the sheets of music paper which she had accompanied herself with for the occasion and this having been handed up for the bench to look at *in camera*, Coppinger's doll, as she was called, (*annias*, Mack Erse's Dar, the adopted child) then proposed to jerrykin and jureens and every jim, jock and jarry in that little green courtinghousie for her satisfaction and as a whole act of settlement to reamalgamate herself, tomorrow perforce, in pardonership with the permanent suing fond trustee, Monsignore Pepigi, under the new style of Will Breakfast and Sparrem, as, when all his cognisances had been estreated, he seemed to proffer the steadiest interest towards her, but this prepoposal was ruled out on appeal by Judge JeremyDoyler, who, reserving judgment in a matter of courts and reversing the findings of the lower correctional, found, beyond doubt of treuson, fending the dissassents of the pickpackpanel, twelve as upright judaces as ever let down their thoms, and, *occupante extremum scabie*, handed down to the jury of the Liffey that, as a matter of tact, the woman they gave as free was born into contractual incapacity (the Calif of Man *v* the Eaudelusk Company) when, how and where mamy's mancipium act did not apply and therefore held supremely that, as no property in law can exist in a corpse, (Hal Kilbride *v* Una Bellina) Pepigi's pact was pure piffle (loud laughter) and Wharrem would whistle for the rhino. Will you, won't you, pango with Pepigi? Not for Nancy, how dare you do! And whew whewwhew whew.

— He sighed in sleep.

— Let us go back.

— Lest he forewaken.

— Hide ourselves.

While hovering dreamwings, folding around, will hide from fears my wee mee mannikin, keep my big wig long strong manomen, guard my bairn, *mon beau.*

— To bed.

|| To bed it is then, for a quick and joyless tumble.

Humperfeldt and Anunska, wedded now evermore in annastomoses by a ground plan of the placehunter, whiskered beau and donahbella. Totumvir and esquimeena, who so shall separate fetters to new desire, repeals an act of union to unite in bonds of schismacy. O yes! O yes! Withdraw your member! Closure. This chamber stands abjourned. Such precedent is largely a cause to lack of collective continencies among Donnelly's orchard as lifelong the shadyside to Fairbrother's field. Humbo, lock your kekkle up! Anny, blow your wickle out! Tuck away the tablesheet! You never wet the tea! And you may go rightoway back to your Aunty Dilluvia, Humprey, after that!

|| Physical love between these two seems to end here forever. "That's his last tryon to march through the grand tryomphal arch. His reignbolt's shot. Never again!"

IV

Sandhyas! Sandhyas! Sandhyas!

Calling all downs. Calling all downs to dayne. Array! Surrection! Eireweeker to the wohld bludyn world. O rally, O rally, O rally! Phlenxty, O rally! To what lifelike thyne of the bird can be. Seek you somany matters. Haze sea east to Osseania. Here! Here! Tass, Patt, Staff, Woff, Havv, Bluvv and Rutter. The smog is lofting. And already the olduman's olduman has godden up on othertimes to litanate the bonnamours. Sonne feine, somme feehn avaunt! Guld modning, have yous viewsed Piers' aube? Thane yaars agon we have used yoors up since when we have fused now orther. Calling all daynes. Calling all daynes to dawn. The old breeding bradsted culminwillth of natures to Foyn MacHooligan. The leader, the leader! Securest jubilends albas Temoram. Clogan slogan. Quake up, dim dusky, wook doom for husky! And let Billey Feghin be baallad out of his humuluation. Confindention to churchen. We have highest gratifications in announcing to pewtewr publikumst of pratician pratyusers, genghis is ghoon for you.

A hand from the cloud emerges, holding a chart expanded.

The eversower of the seeds of light to the cowld owld sowls that are in the domnatory of Defmut after the night of the carrying of the word of Nuahs and the night of making Mehs to cuddle up in a coddlepot, Pu Nuseht, lord of risings in the yonderworld of Ntamplin, tohp triumphant, speaketh.

Vah! Suvarn Sur! Scatter brand to the reneweller of the sky, thou who agnitest! Dah! Arcthuris comeing! Be! Verb umprincipiant through the trancitive spaces! Kilt by kelt shell kithagain with kinagain. We elect for thee, Tirtangel. Svadesia salve! We Durbalanars, theeadjure. A way, the Margan, from our astamite, through dimdom done till light kindling light has led we hopas but hunt me the journeyon, iteritinerant, the kal his course, amid the semitary of Somnionia. Even unto Heliotropolis, the castellated, the enchanting. Now if soomone felched a twoel and soomonelses warmet watter we could, while you was saying Morkret Miry or Smud, Brunt and Rubbinsen, make sunlike sylp om this warful dune's battam. Yet clarify begins at. Whither the spot for? Whence the hour by? See but! Lever hulme! Take in. Respassers should be pursaccoutred. Qui stabat Meins quantum qui stabat Peins. As of yours. We annew. Our shades of minglings mengle them and help help horizons. A flasch and, rasch, it shall come to pasch, as hearth by hearth leaps live. For the tanderest stock with the rosinost top Ahlen Hill's, clubpubber, in general stores and. Atriathroughwards, Lugh the Brathwacker will be the listened after and he larruping sparks out of his teiney ones. The spearspid of dawnfire totouches ain the tablestoane ath the centre of the great circle of the macroliths of Helusbelus in the boshiman brush on this our peneplain by Fangaluvu Bight whence the horned cairns erge, stanserstanded, to floran frohn, idols of isthmians. Overwhere. Gaunt grey ghostly gossips growing grubber in the glow. Past now pulls. Cur one beast, even Dane the Great, may treadspath with sniffer he snout impursuant to byelegs. Edar's chuckal humuristic. But why pit the cur afore the noxe? Let shrill their duan Gallus, han, and she, hou the Sassqueehenna, makes ducksruns at crooked. Once for the chantermale, twoce for the pother and once twoce threece for the waither. So an inedible yellowmeat turns out the invasable blackth. Kwhat serves to rob with Alliman, saelior, a turnkeyed trot to Seapoint, pierrotettes, means Noel's Bar and Julepunsch, by Joge, if you've tippertaps in your head or starting kursses, tailour, you're silenced at Henge Ceolleges, Exmooth, Ostbys for ost, boys, each and one? Death banes and the quick quoke. But life wends and the dombs spake! Whake? Hill of Hafid, knock and knock, nachasach, gives relief to the langscape as he strauches his lamusong untoupon gazelle channel and the bride of the Bryne, shin high shake, is dotter than evar for a damse wed her farther. Lambel on the up! We may plesently heal Geoglyphy's twentynine ways to say goodbett an wassing seoosoon liv. With the forty wonks winking please me your much as to. With her tup. It's a long long ray to Newirgland's premier. For korps, for streamfish, for confects, for bullyoungs, for smearsassage, for patates, for steaked pig, for men, for limericks, for waterfowls, for wagsfools, for louts, for cold airs, for late trams, for curries, for curlews, for leekses, for orphalines, for tunnygulls, for clear goldways, for lungfortes, for moonyhaunts, for fairmoneys, for coffins, for tantrums, for armaurs, for waglugs, for rogues comings, for sly goings, for larksmathes, for homdsmeethes, for quailsmeathes, kilalooly. Tep! Come lead, crom lech! Top. Wisely for us Old Bruton has withdrawn his theory. You are alpsulumply wroght! Amsulummmm. But this is perporteroguing youpoorapps? Namantanai. Sure it's not revieng your? Amslu! Good all so. We seem to understand apad vellumtomes muniment, Arans Duhkha, among hoseshoes, cheriotiers and etceterogenious bargainboutbarrows, ofver and umnder, since, evenif or although, in double preposition as in triple conjunction, how the mudden research in the topaia that was Mankaylands has gone to prove from the picalava present in the maramara melma that while a successive generation has been in the deep deep deeps of Deepereras. Buried hearts. Rest here.

Conk a dook he'll doo. Svap.

So let him slap, the sap! Till they take down his shatter from his shap. He canease. Fill stap.

It's morning, then, and we turn to the East (hence the Sanskrit *Sandhyas*—used here to mean a dawn prayer). A Sanskrit-speaking voice bids us rise, but the dreamer dreams on (Svap is Sanskrit for "sleep"). His dream is hopeful, though. The boy Kevin is no longer Shaun, debased messenger, but St. Kevin himself, rising out of the life-giving waters.

Polycarp pool, the pool of Innalavia, Saras the saft as, of meadewy marge, atween Deltas Piscium and Sagittariastrion, whereinn once we lave 'tis alve and vale, minnyhahing here from hiarwather, a poddlebridges in a passabed, the river of lives, the regenerations of the incarnations of the emanations of the apparentations of Funn and Nin in Cleethabala, the kongdomain of the Alieni, an accorsaired race, infester of Libnud Ocean, Moylamore, let it be! Where Allbroggt Neandser tracking Viggynette Neeinsee gladsighted her Linfian Fall and a teamdiggingharrow turned the first sod. Sluce! Caughterect! Goodspeed the blow! (Incidentally 'tis believed that his harpened before Gage's Fane for it has to be over this booty spotch, though some hours to the wester, that ex-Colonel House's preterpost heiress is to return unto the outstretcheds of Dweyr O'Michael's loinsprung the blunterbusted pikehead which his had hewn in hers, prolonged laughter words). There an alomdree begins to green, soreen seen for loveseat, as we know that should she, for by essentience his law, so it make all. It is scainted to Vitalba. And her little white bloomkins, twittersky trimmed, are hobdoblins' hankypanks. Saxenslyke our anscessers thought so darely on now they're going soever to Anglesen, free of juties, dyrt chapes. There too a slab slobs, immermemorial, the only in all swamp. But so bare, so boulder, brag sagging such a brr bll bmm show that, of Barindens, the white alfred, it owed to have at leased some butchup's upperon. *Homos Circas Elochlannensis*! His showplace at Leeambye. Old Wommany Wyes. Pfif! But, while gleam with gloom swan here and there, this shame rock and that whispy planter tell Paudheen Steel-the-Poghue and his perty Molly Vardant, in goodbroomirish, arrah, this place is a proper and his feist a ferial for curdnal communial, so be who would celibrate the holy mystery upon or that the pirigrim from Mainylands beatend, the calmleaved hutcaged by that look whose glaum is sure he means bisnisgels to empalmover. A naked yogpriest, clothed of sundust, his oakey doaked with frondest leoves, offrand to the ewon of her owen. Tasyam kuru salilakriyamu! Pfaf!

Bring about it to be brought about and it will be, loke, our lake lemanted, that greyt lack, the citye of Is is issuant (atlanst!), urban and orbal, through seep froms umber under wasseres of Erie.

Lough!

Hwo! Hwy, dairmaidens? Asthoreths, assay! Earthsigh to is heavened.

Hillsengals, the daughters of the cliffs, responsen. Longsome the samphire coast. From thee to thee, thoo art it thoo, that thouest there. The like the near, the liker nearer. O sosay! A family, a band, a school, a clanagirls. Fiftines andbut fortines by novanas andor vantads by octettes ayand decadendecads by a lunary with last a lone. Whose every has herdifferent from the similies with her site. *Sicut campanulae petalliferentes* they coroll in caroll round Botany Bay. A dweam of dose innocent dirly dirls. Keavn! Keavn! And they all setton voicies about singsing music was Keavn! He. Only he. Ittle he. Ah! The whole clangalied. Oh!

S. Wilhelmina's, S. Gardenia's, S. Phibia's, S. Veslandrua's, S. Clarinda's, S. Immecula's, S. Dolores Delphin's, S. Perlanthroa's, S. Errands Gay's, S. Eddaminiva's, S. Rhodamena's, S. Ruadagara's, S. Drimicumtra's, S. Una Vestity's, S. Mintargisia's, S. Misha-La-Valse's, S. Churstry's, S. Clouonaskieym's, S. Bellavistura's, S. Santamonta's, S. Ringsingsund's, S. Heddadin Drade's, S. Glacianivia's, S. Waidafrira's, S. Thomassabbess's and (trema! unloud!! pepet!!!) S. Loellisotoelles!

Prayfulness! Prayfulness!

Euh! Thaet is seu whaet shaell one naeme it!

The meidinogues have tingued togethering. Ascend out of your bed, cavern of a trunk, and shrine! Kathlins is kitchin. Soros cast, ma brone! You must exterra acquarate to interirigate all the arkypelicans. The austrologer Wallaby by Tolan, who farshook our showrs from Newer Aland, has signed the you and the now our mandate. Milenesia waits. Be smark.

One seekings. Not the lithe slender, not the broad roundish near the lithe slender, not the fairsized fullfeatured to the leeward of the broad roundish but, indeed and inneed, the curling, perfect-portioned, flowerfleckled, shapely highhued, delicate features swaying to the windward of the fairsized fullfeatured.

Was that in the air about when something is to be said for it or is it someone imparticular who will somewherise for the whole anyhow?

What does Coemghen? Tell his hidings clearly! A woodtoo-gooder. Is his moraltack still his best of weapons? How about a little more goaling goold? Rowlin's tun he gadder no must. It is the voice of Roga. His face is the face of a son. Be thine the silent hall, O Jarama! A virgin, the one, shall mourn thee. Roga's stream is solence. But Croona is in adestance. The ass of the O'Dwyer of Greyglens is abrowtobayse afeald in his terroirs of the Potter-ton's forecoroners, the reeks around the burleyhearthed. When visited by an independant reporter, "Mike" Portlund, to burrow burning the latterman's Resterant so is called the gortan in ques-ture he mikes the fallowing for the Durban Gazette, firstcoming issue. From a collispendent. Any were. Deemsday. Bosse of Upper and Lower Byggotstrade, Ciwareke, may he live for river! The Games funeral at Valleytemple. Saturnights pomps, exhabiting that corricatore of a harss, revealled by Oscur Camerad. The last of Dutch Schulds, perhumps. Pipe in Dream Cluse. Uncovers Pub History. The Outrage, at Length. Affected Mob Follows in Reli-gious Sullivence. Rinvention of vestiges by which they drugged the buddhy. Moviefigure on in scenic section. By Patathicus. And there, from out of the scuity, misty Londan, along the canavan route, that is with the years gone, mild beam of the wave his polar bearing, steerner among stars, trust touthena and you tread true turf, comes the sorter, Mr Hurr Hansen, talking allthe-ways in himself of his hopes to fall in among a merryfoule of maidens happynghome from the dance, his knyckle allaready in his knackskey fob, a passable compatriate proparly of the Grimstad galleon, old pairs frieze, feed up to the noxer with their geese and peeas and oats upon a trencher and the toyms he'd lust in Wooming but with that smeoil like a grace of backoning over his egglips of the sunsoonshine. Here's heering you in a guessmasque, latterman! And such an improofment! As royt as the mail and as fat as a fuddle! Schoen! Shoan! Shoon the Puzt! A penny for your thought abouts! Tay, tibby, tanny, tummy, tasty, tosty, tay. Batch is for Baker who baxters our bread. O, what an ovenly odour! Butter butter! Bring us this days our maily bag! But receive me, my frensheets, from the emerald dark winterlong! For diss is the doss for Eilder Downes and dass is it duss, as singen sengers, what the hardworking straightwalking stoutstamping securelysealing officials who trow to form our G.M.P.'s pass muster generally shay for shee and sloo for slee when butting their headd to the pillow for a nightshared nakeshift with the alter girl they tuck in for sweepsake. Dutiful wealker for his hydes of march. Haves you the time. Hans ahike? Heard you the crime, senny boy? The man was giddy on letties on the dewry of the duary, be pursueded, whethered with entrenous, midgreys, dagos, teatimes, shadows, nocturnes or samoans, if wellstocked fillerouters plushfeverfraus with dopy chonks, and this, that and the other pigskin or muffle kinkles, taking a pipe course or doing an anguish, seen to his fleece in after his foull, when Dr Chart of Greet Chorsles street he changed his backbone at a citting. He had not the declaination, as what with the foos as whet with the fays, but so far as hanging a goobes on the precedings, wherethen the lag allows, it mights be anything after darks. Which the deers alones they sees and the darkies they is snuffing of the wind up. Debbling. Greanteavvents! Hyacinssies with heliotrollops! Not once fullvixen freakings and but dubbledecoys! It is a lable iction on the porte of the cuthulic church and summum most atole for it. Where is that blinketey blanketer, that quound of a pealer, the sunt of a hunt whant foxes good men! Where or he, our loved among many?

But what does Coemghem, the fostard? Tyro a tora. The novened iconostase of his blueygreyned vitroils but begins in feint to light his legend. Let Phosphoron proclaim! Peechy

peechy. Say he that saw him that saw! Man shall sharp run do a get him. Ask no more, Jerry mine, Roga's voice! No pice soorkabatcha. The bog which puckerooed the posy. The vinebranch of Heremonheber on Bregia's plane where Teffia lies is leaved invert and fructed proper but the cublic hatches endnot open yet for hourly rincers' mess. Read Higgins, Cairns and Egen. Malthus is yet lukked in close. Withun. How swathed there-answer alcove makes theirinn! Besoakers loiter on. And primi-libatory solicates of limon sodias will be absorbable. It is not even yet the engine of the load with haled morries full of crates, you mattinmummur, for dombell dumbs? Sure and 'tis not then. The greek Sideral Reulthway, as it havvents, will soon be starting a smooth with its first single hastencraft. Danny buz-zers instead of the vialact coloured milk train on the fartykket plan run with its endless gallaxion of rotatorattlers and the smool-troon our elderens rememberem as the scream of the service, Strubry Bess. Also the waggonwobblers are still yet everdue to precipitate after night's combustion. Aspect, Shamus Rogua or! Taceate and! *Hagiographice canat Ecclesia.* Which aubrey our first shall show. Inattendance who is who is will play that's what's that to what's that, what.

Oyes! Oyeses! Oyesesyeses! The primace of the Gaulls, pro-tonotorious, I yam as I yam, mitrogenerand in the free state on the air, is now aboil to blow a Gael warning. Inoperation Eyr-lands Eyot, Meganesia, Habitant and the onebut thousand insels, Western and Osthern Approaches.

Of Kevin, of increate God the servant, of the Lord Creator a filial fearer, who, given to the growing grass, took to the tall tim-ber, slippery dick the springy heeler, as we have seen, so we have heard, what we have received, that we have transmitted, thus we shall hope, this we shall pray till, in the search for love of knowledge through the comprehension of the unity in altruism through stupefaction, it may again how it may again, shearing aside the four wethers and passing over the dainty daily dairy and dropping by the way the lapful of live coals and smoothing out Nelly Nettle and her lad of mettle, full of stings, fond of stones, friend of gnewgnawns bones and leaving all the messy messy to look after our douche douche, the miracles,

> "Messy messy . . . douche douche"—we've come a long and punning way since the "mishe mishe" and "tauftauf" of the book's opening. But we're led back to the great day of St. Patrick's arrival in Ireland, his proclamation of the truth of Christianity and his baptismal ("tauftauf") ceremonies. Our two cross-talk comedians—called Muta and Juva now—stand squarely in a true historical year—432 A.D.—and hear St. Patrick refuting the philosophical gibberish of the archdruid Berkeley-Bulkily-Buckley in the presence of King Leary. The Christian dawn has come again.
>
> And then we hand over to ALP, great mother, for the magnificent coda of the book. We read her letter at last in full, and then hear her voice, the voice of the river that, soiled with the work of man, the city, goes out to meet the sea, her great father. Her day is past, a young bride supersedes her, but she herself will be re-born, young and beautiful, in the hills where she rises. The last sentence leads back to the first; the cycle is renewed; the huge mad dream of life goes on for ever.

Juva: It is Old Head of Kettle puffing off the top of the mornin.

Muta: He odda be thorly well ashamed of himself for smoking before the high host.

Juva: Dies is Dorminus master and commandant illy tonobrass.

Muta: Diminussed aster! An I could peecieve amonkst the gatherings who ever they wolk in process?

Juva: Khubadah! It is the Chrystanthemlander with his porters of bonzos, pompommy plonkyplonk, the ghariwallahs, moveyovering the cabrattlefield of slaine.

Muta: Pongo da Banza! An I would uscertain in druidful scatterings one piece tall chap he stand one piece same place?

Juva: Bulkily: and he is fundementially theosophagusted over the whorse proceedings.

Muta: Petrificationibus! O horild haraflare! Who his dickhuns now rearrexes from undernearth the memorialorum?

Juva: Beleave filmly, beleave! Fing Fing! King King!

Muta: Ulloverum? Fulgitudo ejus Rhedonum teneat!

Juva: Rolantlossly! Till the tipp of his ziff. And the ubideintia of the savium is our ervics fenicitas.

Muta: Why soly smiles the supremest with such for a leary on his rugular lips?

Juva: Bitchorbotchum! Eebrydime! He has help his crewn on the burkeley buy but he has holf his crown on the Eurasian Generalissimo.

Muta: Skulkasloot! The twyly velleid is thus then paridicynical?

Juva: Ut vivat volumen sic pereat pouradosus!

Muta: Haven money on stablecert?

Juva: Tempt to wom Outsider!

Muta: Suc? He quoffs. Wutt?

Juva: Sec! Wartar wartar! Wett.

Muta: Ad Piabelle et Purabelle?

Juva: At Winne, Woermann og Sengs.

Muta: So that when we shall have acquired unification we shall pass on to diversity and when we shall have passed on to diversity we shall have acquired the instinct of combat and when we shall have acquired the instinct of combat we shall pass back to the spirit of appeasement?

Juva: By the light of the bright reason which daysends to us from the high.

Muta: May I borrow that hordwanderbaffle from you, old rubberskin?

Juva: Here it is and I hope it's your wormingpen, Erinmonker! Shoot.

Rhythm and Colour at Park Mooting. Peredos Last in the Grand Natural. Velivision victor. Dubs newstage oldtime turftussle, recalling Winny Willy Widger. Two draws. Heliotrope leads from Harem. Three ties. Jockey the Ropper jerks Jake the Rape. Paddrock and bookley chat.

And here are the details.

Tunc. Bymeby, bullocky vampas tappany bobs topside joss pidgin fella Balkelly, archdruid of islish chinchinjoss in the his heptachromatic sevenhued septicoloured roranyellgreenlindigan mantle finish he show along the his mister guest Patholic with alb belongahim the whose throat hum with of sametime all the his cassock groaner fellas of greysfriaryfamily he fast all time what time all him monkafellas with Same Patholic, quoniam, speeching, yeh not speeching noh man liberty is, he drink up words, scilicet, tomorrow till recover will not, all too many much illusiones through photoprismic velamina of hueful panepiphanal world spectacurum of Lord Joss, the of which zoantholitic furniture, from mineral through vegetal to animal, not appear to full up together fallen man than under but one photoreflection of the several iridals gradationes of solar light, that one which that part of it (furnit of heupanepi world) had shown itself (part of fur of huepanwor) unable to absorbere, whereas for numpa one puraduxed seer in seventh degree of wisdom of Entis-Onton he savvy inside true inwardness of reality, the Ding hvad in idself id est, all objects (of panepiwor) allside showed themselves in trues coloribus resplendent with sextuple gloria of light actually retained, untisintus, inside them (obs of epiwo). Rumnant Patholic, stareotypopticus, no catch all that preachybook, utpiam, tomorrow recover thing even is not, bymeby vampsybobsy tappanasbullocks topside joss pidginfella Bilkilly-Belkelly say patfella, ontesantes, twotime hemhaltshealing, with other words verbigratiagrading from murmurulentous till stridulocelerious in a hunghoranghoangoly tsinglontseng while his comprehendurient, with diminishing claractinism, augumentationed himself in caloripeia to vision so throughsighty, you anxioust melancholic, High Thats Hight Uberking Leary his fiery grassbelonghead all show colour of sorrelwood herbgreen, again, niggerblonker, of the his essixcoloured holmgrewnworsteds costume the his fellow saffron pettikilt look same hue of boiled spinasses, other thing, voluntary mutismuser, he not compyhandy the his golden twobreasttorc look justsamelike curlicabbis, moreafter, to pace negativisticists, verdant readyrainroof belongahim Exuber High Ober King Leary very dead, what he wish to say, spit of superexuberabundancy plenty laurel leaves, after that commander bulopent eyes of Most Highest Ardreetsar King same thing like thyme choppy upon parsley, alongsidethat, if pleasesir, nos displace tauttung, sowlofabishospastored, enamel Indian gem in maledictive fingerfondler of High High Siresultan Emperor all same like one fellow olive lentil, onthelongsidethat, by undesendas, kirikirikiring, violaceous warwon contusiones of facebuts of Highup Big Cockywocky Sublissimime Autocrat, for that with pure hueglut intensely saturated one, tinged uniformly, allaroundside upinandoutdown, very like you seecut chowchow of plentymuch sennacassia. Hump cumps Ebblybally! Sukkot?

Punc. Bigseer, refrects the petty padre, whackling it out, a tumble to take, tripeness to call thing and to call if say is good while, you pore shiroskuro blackinwhitepaddynger, by thiswis aposterioprismically apatstrophied and paralogically periparolysed, celestial from principalest of Iro's Irismans ruinboon pot before, (for beingtime monkblinkers timeblinged completamentarily murkblankered in their neutrolysis between the possible viriditude of the sager and the probable eruberuption of the saint), as My tappropinquish to Me wipenmeselps gnosegates a handcaughtscheaf of synthetic shammyrag to hims hers, seemingsuch four three two agreement cause heart to be might, saving to Balenoarch (he kneeleths), to Great Balenoarch (he kneeleths down) to Greatest Great Balenoarch (he kneeleths down quitesomely), the sound sense sympol in a weedwayedwold of the firethere the sun in his halo cast. Onmen.

That was thing, bygotter, the thing, bogcotton, the very thing, begad! Even to uptoputty Bilkilly-Belkelly-Balkally. Who was for shouting down the shatton on the lamp of Jeeshees. Sweating on to stonker and throw his seven. As he shuck his thumping fore features apt the hoyhop of His Ards.

Thud.

Good safe firelamp! hailed the heliots. Goldselforelump! Halled they. Awed. Where thereon the skyfold high, trampatrampatramp. Adie. Per ye comdoom doominoom noonstroom. Yeasome priestomes. Fullyhum toowhoom.

Taawhaar?

Sants and sogs, cabs and cobs, kings and karls, tentes and taunts.

'Tis gone infarover. So fore now, dayleash. Pour deday. To trancefixureashone. Feist of Tabornеccles, scenopegia, come! Shamwork, be in our scheining! And let every crisscouple be so crosscomplimentary, little eggons, youlk and meelk, in a farbiger pancosmos. With a hottyhammyum all round. Gudstruce!

Yet is no body present here which was not there before. Only is order othered. Nought is nulled. *Fuitfiat!*

Lo, the laud of laurens now orielising benedictively when saint and sage have said their say.

A spathe of calyptrous glume involucrumines the perinanthean Amenta: fungoalgaceous muscafilicial graminopalmular planteon; of increasing, livivorous, feelful thinkamalinks; luxuriotiating everywhencewithersoever among skullhullows and charnelcysts of a weedwastewoldwevild when Ralph the Retriever ranges to jawrode his knuts knuckles and her theas thighs; onegugulp down of the nauseous forere brarkfarsts oboboomaround and you're as paint and spickspan as a rainbow; wreathe the bowl to rid the bowel; no runcure, no rank heat, sir; amess in amullium; chlorid cup.

Health, chalce, endnessnessessity! Arrive, likkypuggers, in a poke! The folgor of the frightfools is olympically optimominous; there is bound to be a lovleg day for mirrages in the open; Murnane and Aveling are undertoken to berry that ortchert: provided that. You got to make good that breachsuit, seamer. You going to haulm port houlm, toilermaster. You yet must get up to kill (nonparticular). You still stand by and do as hit (private). While for yous, Jasminia Aruna and all your likers, affinitatively must it be by you elected if Monogynes his is or hers Diander, the tubous, limbersome and nectarial. Owned or grazeheifer, ethel or bonding. Mopsus or Gracchus, all your horodities will incessantlament be coming back from the Annone Wishwashwhose, Ormepierre Lodge, Doone of the Drumes, blanches bountifully and nightsend made up, every article lathering leaving several rinsings so as each rinse results with a dapperent rolle, cuffs for meek and chokers for sheek and a kink in the pacts for namby. Forbeer, forbear! For nought that is has bane. In mournenslaund. Themes have thimes and habit reburns. To flame in you. Ardor vigor forders order. Since ancient was our living is in possible to be. Delivered as. Caffirs and culls and onceagain overalls, the fittest surviva lives that blued, iorn and storridge can make them. Whichus all claims. Clean. Whenastcleeps. Close. And the mannormillor clipperclappers. Noxt. Doze.

Fennsense, finnsonse, aworn! Tuck upp those wide shorts. The pink of the busket for sheer give. Peeps. Stand up to hard ware and step into style. If you soil may, puett, guett me prives. For newmanmaun set a marge to the merge of unnotions. Innition wons agame.

What has gone? How it ends?

Begin to forget it. It will remember itself from every sides, with all gestures, in each our word. Today's truth, tomorrow's trend.

Forget, remember!

Have we cherished expectations? Are we for liberty of perusiveness? Whyafter what forewhere? A plainplanned liffeyism assemblements Eblania's conglomerate horde. By dim delty Deva.

Forget!

Our wholemole millwheeling vicociclometer, a tetradomational gazebocroticon (the "Mamma Lujah" known to every schoolboy scandaller,be he Matty, Marky, Lukey or John-a-Donk), autokinatonetically preprovided with a clappercoupling smeltingworks exprogressive process, (for the farmer, his son and their homely codes, known as eggburst, eggblend, eggburial and hatch-as-hatch can) receives through a portal vein the dialytically separated elements of precedent decomposition for the verypetpurpose of subsequent recombination so that the heroticisms, catastrophes and eccentricities transmitted by the ancient legacy of the past, type by tope, letter from litter, word at ward, with sendence of sundance, since the days of Plooney and Columcellas when Giacinta, Pervenche and Margaret swayed over the all-too-ghoulish and illyrical and innumantic in our mutter nation, all, anastomosically assimilated and preteridentified paraidiotically, in fact, the sameold gamebold adomic structure of our Finnius the old One, as highly charged with electrons as hophazards can effective it, may be there for you, Cockalooralooraloomenos, when cup, platter and pot come piping hot, as sure as herself pits hen to paper and there's scribings scrawled on eggs.

Of cause, so! And in effect, as?

Dear. And we go on to Dirtdump. Reverend. May we add majesty? Well, we have frankly enjoyed more than anything these secret workings of natures (thanks ever for it, we humbly pray) and, well, was really so denighted of this lights time. Mucksrats which bring up about uhrweckers they will come to know good. Yon clouds will soon disappear looking forwards at a fine day. The honourable Master Sarmon they should be first born like he was with a twohangled warpon and it was between Williamstown and the Mairrion Ailesbury on the top of the longcar, as merrily we rolled along, we think of him looking at us yet as if to pass away in a cloud. When he woke up in a sweat besidus it was to pardon him, goldylocks, me having an airth, but he daydreamsed we had a lovelyt face for a pulltomine. Back we were by the jerk of a beamstark, backed in paladays last, on the brinks of the wobblish, the man what never put a dramn in the swags but milk from a national cowse. That was the prick of the spindle to me that gave me the keys to dreamland. Sneakers in the grass, keep off! If we were to tick off all that cafflers head, whisperers for his accomodation, the me craws, namely, and their bacon what harmed butter! It's margarseen oil. Thinthin thinthin. Stringstly is it forbidden by the honorary tenth commendmant to shall not bare full sweetness against a nighboor's wiles. What those slimes up the cavern door around you, keenin, (the lies is coming out on them frecklefully) had the shames to suggest can we ever? Never! So may the low forget him their trespasses against Molloyd O'Reilly, that hugglebeddy fann, now about to get up, the hartiest that Coolock ever! A nought in nought Eirinishmhan, called Ervigsen by his first mate. May all similar douters of our oldhame story have that fancied widming! For a pipe of twist or a slug of Hibernia metal we could let out and, by jings, someone would make a carpus of somebody with the greatest of pleasure by private shootings. And in contravention to the constancy of chemical combinations not enough of all the slatters of him left for Peeter the Picker to make their threi sevelty filfths of a man out of. Good wheat! How delitious for the three Sulvans of Dulkey and what a sellpriceget the two Peris of Monacheena! Sugars of lead for the chloras ashpots! Peace! He possessing from a child of highest valency for our privileged beholdings ever complete hairy of chest, hamps and eyebags in pursuance to salesladies' affectionate company. His real devotes. Wriggling reptiles, take notice! Whereas we exgust all such sprinkling snigs. They are pestituting the whole time never with standing we simply agree upon the committee of amusance! Or could above bring under same notice for it to be able to be seen.

About that coerogenal hun and his knowing the size of an egg-cup. First he was a skulksman at one time and then Cloon's fired him through guff. Be sage about sausages! Stuttutistics shows with he's heacups of teatables the old firm's fatspitters are most eatenly appreciated by metropolonians. While we should like to drag attentions to our Wolkmans Cumsensation Act. The magnets of our midst being foisted upon by a plethorace of parachutes. Did speece permit the bad example of setting before the military to the best of our belief in the earliest wish of the one in mind was the mitigation of the king's evils. And how he staired up the step after it's the power of the gait. His giantstand of manun-known. No brad wishy washy wathy wanted neither! Once you are balladproof you are unperceable to haily, icy and missile-throes. Order now before we reach Ruggers' Rush! As we now must close hoping to Saint Laurans all in the best. Moral. Mrs Stores Humphreys: So you are expecting trouble, Pondups, from the domestic service questioned? Mr Stores Humphreys: Just as there is a good in even, Levia, my cheek is a compleet bleenk. Plumb. Meaning: one two four. Finckers. Up the hind hose of hizzars. Whereapon our best again to a hundred and eleven ploose one thousand and one other blessings will now concloose thoose epoostles to your great kindest, well, for all at trouble to took. We are all at home in old Fintona, thank Danis, for ourselfsake, that direst of housebonds, whool wheel be true unto lovesend so long as we has a pockle full of brass. Impossible to remember persons in improbable to forget position places. Who would pellow his head off to conjure up a, well, particularly mean stinker like funn make called Foon MacCrawl brothers, mystery man of the pork martyrs? Force in giddersh! Tomothy and Lorcan, the bucket Toolers, both are Timsons now they've changed their characticuls during their blackout. Conan Boyles will pudge the daylives out through him, if they are correctly informed. Music, me ouldstrow, please! We'll have a brand rehearsal. Fing! One must simply laugh. Fing him aging! Good licks! Well, this ought to weke him to make up. He'll want all his fury gutmurdherers to redress him. Gilly in the gap. The big bad old sprowly all uttering foon! Has now stuffed last podding. His fooneral will sneak pleace by creeps o'clock toosday. Kingen will commen. Allso brewbeer. Pens picture at Manchem House Horsegardens shown in Morning post as from Boston transcripped. Femelles will be preadaminant as from twentyeight to twelve. To hear that lovelade parson, of case, of a bawl gentlemale, pour forther moracles. Don't forget! The grand fooneral will now shortly occur. Remember. The remains must be removed before eaght hours shorp. With earnestly conceived hopes. So help us to witness to this day to hand in sleep. From of Mayasdaysed most duteoused.

Well, here's lettering you erronymously anent other clerical fands allieged herewith. I wisht I wast be that dumb tyke and he'd wish it was me yonther heel. How about it? The sweetest song in the world! Our shape as a juvenile being much admired from the first with native copper locks. Referring to the Married Woman's Improperty Act a correspondent paints out that the Swees Aubumn vogue is hanging down straith fitting to her innocenth eyes. O, felicious coolpose! If all theMacCrawls would only handle virgils like Armsworks, Limited! That's handsel for gertles! Never mind Micklemans! Chat us instead! The cad with the pope's wife, Lily Kinsella, who became the wife of Mr Sneakers for her good name in the hands of the kissing solicitor, will now engage in attentions. Just a princhе for to-night! Pale bellies our mild cure, back and streaky ninepace. The thicks off Bully's Acre was got up by Sully. The Boot lane brigade. And she had a certain medicine brought her in a licenced victualler's bottle. Shame! Thrice shame! We are advised the waxy is at the present in the Sweeps hospital and that he may never come out! Only look through your leather-box one day with P.C.Q. about 4.32 or at 8 and 22.5 with the quart of scissions masters and clerk and the bevyhum of Marie Reparatrices for a good allround sympowdhericks purge, full view, to be surprised to see under the grand piano Lily on the sofa (and a lady!) pulling a low and then he'd begin to jump a little bit to find out what goes on when love walks in besides the solicitous bussness by kissing and looking into a mirror.

That we were treated not very grand when the police and everybody is all bowing to us when we go out in all directions on Wanterlond Road with my cubarola glide? And, personably speaking, they can make their beaux to my alce, as Hillary Allen sang to the opennine knighters. Item, we never were chained to a chair, and, bitem, no widower whother soever followed us about with a fork on Yankskilling Day. Meet a great civilian (proud lives to him!) who is gentle as a mushroom and a very affectable when he always sits forenenst us for his wet while to all whom it may concern Sully is a thug from all he drunk though he is a rattling fine bootmaker in his profession. Would we were here-arther to lodge our complaint on sergeant Laraseny in consequence of which in such steps taken his health would be constably broken into potter's pance which would be the change of his life by a Nollwelshian which has been oxbelled out of crispianity.

Well, our talks are coming to be resumed by more polite con-versation with a huntered persent human over the natural bestness of pleisure after his good few mugs of humbedumb and shag. While for whoever likes that urogynal pan of cakes one apiece it is thanks, beloved, to Adam, our former first Finnlatter and our grocerest churcher, as per Grippiths' varuations, for his beautiful crossmess parzel.

Well, we simply like their demb cheeks, the Rathgarries, wagging here about around the rhythms in me amphybed and he being as bothered that he pausably could by the fallth of hampty damp. Certified reformed peoples, we may add to this stage, are proptably saying to quite agreeable deef. Here gives your answer, pigs and scuts! Hence we've lived in two worlds. He is another he what stays under the himp of holth. The herewaker of our hamefame is his real namesame who will get himself up and erect, confident and heroic when but, young as of old, for my daily comfreshenall, a wee one woos.

Alma Luvia, Pollabella.

P.S. Soldier Rollo's sweetheart. And she's about fetted up now with nonsery reams. And rigs out in regal rooms with the ritzies. Rags! Worns out. But she's still her deckhuman amber too.

Soft morning, city! Lsp! I am leafy speafing. Lpf! Folty and folty all the nights have falled on to long my hair. Not a sound, falling. Lispn! No wind no word. Only a leaf, just a leaf and then leaves. The woods are fond always. As were we their babes in. And robins in crews so. It is for me goolden wending. Unless? Away! Rise up, man of the hooths, you have slept so long! Or is it only so mesleems? On your pondered palm. Reclined from cape to pede. With pipe on bowl. Terce for a fiddler, sixt for makmerriers, none for a Cole. Rise up now and aruse! Norvena's over. I am leafy, your goolden, so you called me, may me life, yea your goolden, silve me solve, exsogerraider! You did so drool. I was so sharm. But there's a great poet in you too. Stout Stokes would take you offly. So has he as bored me to slump. But am good and rested. Taks to you, toddy, tan ye! Yawhawaw. Helpunto min, helpas vin. Here is your shirt, the day one, come back. The stock, your collar. Also your double brogues. A comforter as well. And here your iverol and everthelest your umbr. And stand up tall! Straight. I want to see you looking fine for me. With your brandnew big green belt and all. Blooming in the very lotust and second to nill, Budd! When you're in the buckly shuit Rosensharonals near did for you. Fiftyseven and three, cosh, with the bulge. Proudpurse Alby with his pooraroon Eireen, they'll. Pride, comfytousness, enevy! You make me think of a wonderdecker I once. Or somebalt thet sailder, the man megallant, with the bangled ears. Or an earl was he, at Lucan? Or, no, it's the Iren duke's I mean. Or somebrey erse from the Dark Countries. Come and let us! We always said we'd. And go abroad. Rathgreany way perhaps. The childher are still fast. There is no school today. Them boys is so contrairy. The Head does be worrying himself. Heel trouble and heal travel. Galliver and Gellover. Unless they changes by mistake. I seen the likes in the twinngling of an aye. Som. So oft. Sim. Time after time. The sehm asnuh. Two bredder as doffered as nors in soun. When one of him sighs or one of him cries 'tis you all over. No peace at all. Maybe it's those two old crony aunts held them out to the water front. Queer Mrs Quickenough and odd Miss Doddpebble. And when them two has had a good few there isn't much more dirty clothes to publish. From the Laundersdale Minssions. One chap googling the holyboy's thingabib and this lad wetting his widdle. You were pleased as Punch, recitating war exploits and pearse orations to them jackeen gapers. But that night after, all you were wanton! Bidding me do this and that and the other. And blowing off to me, hugly Judsys, what wouldn't you give to have a girl! Your wish was mewill. And, lo, out of a sky! The way I too. But her, you wait. Eager to choose is left to her shade. If she had only more matcher's wit. Findlings makes runaways, runaways a stray. She's as merry as the gricks still. 'Twould be sore should ledden sorrow. I'll wait. And I'll wait. And then if all goes. What will be is. Is is. But let them. Slops hospodch and the slusky slut too. He's for thee what she's for me. Dogging you round cove and haven and teaching me the perts of speech. If you spun your yarns to him on the swishbarque waves I was spelling my yearns to her over cottage cake. We'll not disturb their sleeping duties. Let besoms be bosuns. It's Phoenix, dear. And the flame is, hear! Let's our joornee saintomichael make it. Since the lausafire has lost and the book of the depth is. Closed. Come! Step out of your shell! Hold up you free fing! Yes. We've light enough. I won't take our laddy's lampern. For them four old windbags of Gustsofairy to be blowing at. Nor you your rucksunck. To bring all the dannymans out after you on the hike. Send Arctur guiddus! Isma! Sft! It is the softest morning that ever I can ever remember me. But she won't rain showerly, our Ilma. Yet. Until it's the time. And me and you have made our. The sons of bursters won in the games. Still I'll take me owld Finvara for my shawlders. The trout will be so fine at brookfisht. With a taste of roly polony from Blugpuddels after. To bring out the tang of the tay. Is't you fain for a roost brood? Oaxmealturn, all out of the woolpalls! And then all the chippy young cuppinjars cluttering round us, clottering for their creams. Crying, me, grownup sister! Are me not truly? Lst! Only but, theres a but, you must buy me a fine new girdle too, nolly. When next you go to Market Norwall. They're all saying I need it since the one from Isaacsen's slooped its line. Mrknrk? Fy arthou! Come! Give me your great bearspaw, padder avilky, fol a miny tiny. Dola. Mineninecyhandsy, in the languo of flows. That's Jorgen Jargonsen. But you understood, nodst? I always know by your brights and shades. Reach down. A lil mo. So. Draw back your glave. Hot and hairy, hugon, is your hand! Here's where the falskin begins. Smoos as an infams. One time you told you'd been burnt in ice. And one time it was chemicalled after you taking a lifeness. Maybe that's why you hold your hodd as if. And people thinks you missed the scaffold. Of fell design. I'll close me eyes. So not to see. Or see only a youth in his florizel, a boy in innocence, peeling a twig, a child beside a weenywhite steed. The child we all love to place our hope in for ever. All men has done something. Be the time they've come to the weight of old fletch. We'll lave it. So. We will take our walk before in the timpul they ring the earthly bells. In the church by the hearseyard. Pax Goodmens will. Or the birds start their treestirm shindy. Look, there are yours off, high on high! And cooshes, sweet good luck they're cawing you, Coole! You see, they're as white as the riven snae. For us. Next peaters poll you will be elicted or I'm not your elicitous bribe. The Kinsella woman's man will never reduce me. A MacGarath O'Cullagh O'Muirk MacFewney sookadoodling and sweepacheeping round the lodge of Fjorn na Galla of the Trumpets! It's like potting the po to shambe on the dresser or tamming Uncle Tim's Caubeen on to the brows of a Viker Eagle. Not such big strides, huddy foddy! You'll crush me antilopes I saved so long for. They're Penisole's. And the two goodiest shoeshoes. It is hardly a Knut's mile or seven, possumbotts. It is very good for the health of a morning. With Buahbuah. A gentle motion all around. As leisure paces. And the helpyourselftoastrool cure's easy. It seems so long since, ages since. As if you had been long far away. Afartodays, afeartonights, and me as with you in thadark. You will tell me some time if I can believe its all. You know where I am bringing you? You remember? When I ran berrying after hucks and haws. With you drawing out great aims to hazel me from the hummock with your sling. Our cries. I could lead you there and I still by you in bed. Les go dutc to Danegreven, nos? Not a soul but ourselves. Time? We have loads on our hangs. Till Gilligan and Halligan call again to hooligan. And the rest of the guns. Sullygan eight, from left to right. Olobobo, ye foxy theagues! The moskors thought to ball you out. Or the Wald Unicorns Master, Bugley Captain, from the Naul, drawls up by the door with the Honourable Whilp and the Reverend Poynter and the two Lady Pagets of Tallyhaugh, Ballyhuntus, in their riddletight raiding hats for to lift a hereshealth to their robost, the Stag, evers the Carlton hart. And you needn't host out with your duck and your duty, capapole, while they reach him the glass he never starts to finish. Clap this wis on your poll and stick this in your ear, wiggly! Beauties don't answer and the rich never pays. If you were the enlarged they'd hue in cry you, Heathtown, Harbourstown, Snowtown, Four Knocks, Flemingtown, Bodingtown to the Ford of Fyne on Delvin. How they housed to house you after the Platonic garlens! And all because, loosed in her reflexes, she seem she seen Ericoricori coricome huntsome with his three poach dogs aleashing him. But you came safe through. Enough of that horner corner! And old mutthergoosip! We might call on the Old Lord, what do you say? There's something tells me. He is a fine sport. Like the score and a moighty went before him. And a proper old promnentory. His door always open. For a newera's day. Much as your own is. You invoiced him last Eatster so he ought to give us hockockles and everything. Remember to take off your white hat, ech? When we come in the presence. And say hoothoothoo, ithmuthisthy! His is house of laws. And I'll drop my graciast kertssey too. If the Ming Tung no go bo to me homage me hamage kow bow tow to the Mong Tang. Ceremonialness to stand lowest place be! Saying: What'll you take to link to light a pike on porpoise, plaise? He might knight you an Armor elsor daub you the first cheap magyerstrape. Remember Bomthomanew vim vam vom Hungerig. Hoteform, chain and epolettes, botherbumbose. And I'll be your aural eyeness. But we vain. Plain fancies. It's in the castles air. My currant bread's full of sillymottocraft. Aloof is anoof. We can take or leave. He's reading his ruffs. You'll know our way from there surely. Flura's way. Where once we led so many car couples have follied since. Clatchka! Giving Shaughnessy's mare the hillymount of her life. With her strulldeburgghers! Hnmn hnmn! The rollcky road adondering. We can sit us down on the heathery benn, me on you, in quolm unconsciounce. To scand the arising. Out from Drumleek. It was there Evora told me I had best. If I ever. When the moon of mourning is set and gone. Over Glinaduna. Lonu nula. Ourselves, oursouls alone. At the site of salvocean. And watch would the letter you're wanting be coming may be. And cast ashore. That I prays for be mains of me draims. Scratching it and patching at with a prompt from a primer. And what scrips of nutsnolleges I pecked up me meself. Every letter is a hard but yours sure is the hardest crux ever. Hack an axe, hook an oxe, hath an an, heth hith ences. But once done, dealt and delivered, tattat, you're on the map. Rased on traumscrapt from Maston, Boss. After rounding his world of ancient days. Carried in a caddy or screwed and corked. On his mugisstosst surface. With a bob, bob, bottledby. Blob. When the waves give up yours the soil may for me. Sometime then, somewhere there, I wrote me hopes and buried the page when I heard Thy voice, ruddery dunner, so loud that none but, and left it to lie till a kissmiss coming. So content me now. Lss. Unbuild and be buildn our bankaloan cottage there and we'll cohabit respectable. The Gowans, ser, for Medem, me. With acute bubel runtoer for to pippup and gopeep where the sterres be. Just to see would we hear how Jove and the peers talk. Amid the soleness. Tilltop, bigmaster! Scale the summit! You're not so giddy any more. All your graundplotting and the little it brought! Humps, when you hised us and dumps, when you doused us! But sarra one of me cares a brambling ram, pomp porteryark! On limpidy marge I've made me hoom. Park and a pub for me. Only don't start your stunts of Donachie's yeards agoad again. I could guessp to her name who tuckt you that one, tufnut! Bold bet backwords. For the loves of sinfintins! Before the naked universe. And the bailby pleasemarm rincing his eye! One of these fine days, lewdy culler, you must redoform again. Blessed shield Martin! Softly so. I am so exquisitely pleased about the loveleavest dress I have. You will always call me Leafiest, won't you, dowling? Wordherfhull Ohldhbhoy! And you won't urbjunk to me parafume, oiled of kolooney, with a spot of marashy. Sm! It's Alpine Smile from Yesthers late Yhesters. I'm in everywince nasturtls. Even in Houlth's nose. Medeurscodeignus! Astale of astoun. Grand owld marauder! If I knew who you are! When that hark from the air said it was Captain Finsen makes cumhulments and was mayit pressing for his suit I said are you there here's nobody here only me. But I near fell off the pile of samples. As if your tinger winged ting to me hear. Is that right what your brothermilk in Bray bes telling the district you were bragged up by Brostal because your parents would be always tumbling into his foulplace and losing her pentacosts after drinking their pledges? Howsomendeavour, you done me fine! The only man was ever known could eat the crushts of lobsters. Our native night when you twicetook me for some Marienne Sherry and then your Jermyn cousin who signs hers with exes and the beardwig I found in your Clarksome bag. Pharaops you'll play you're the king of Aeships. You certainly make the most royal of noises. I will tell you all sorts of makeup things, strangerous. And show you to every simple storyplace we pass. *Cadmillersfolly*, *Bellevenue*, *Wellcrom*, *Quid Superabit*, villities valleties. Change the plates for the next course of murphies! Spendlove's still there and the canon going strong and so is Claffey's habits endurtaking and our parish pomp's a great warrent. But you'll have to ask that same four that named them is always snugging in your barsalooner, saying they're the best relicts of Conal O'Daniel and writing *Finglas since the Flood*. That'll be some kingly work in progress. But it's by this route he'll come some morrow. And I can signal you all flint and fern are rasstling as we go by. And you'll sing thumb a bit and then wise your selmon on it. It is all so often and still the same to me. Snf? Only turf, wick dear! Clane turf. You've never forgodden batt on tarf, have you, at broin burroow, what? Mch? Why, them's the muchrooms, come up during the night. Look, agres of roofs in parshes. Dom on dam, dim in dym. And a capital part for olympics to ply at. Steadyon, Cooloosus! Mind your stride or you'll knock. While I'm dodging the dustbins. Look what I found! A lintil pea. And look at here! This cara weeseed. Pretty mites, my sweetthings, was they poorloves abandoned by wholawidey world? Neighboulotts for newtown. The Eblanamagna you behazyheld loomening up out of the dumblynass. But the still sama sitta. I've lapped so long. As you said. It fair takes. If I lose my breath for a minute or two don't speak, remember! Once it happened, so it may again. Why I'm all these years within years in soffran, allbeleaved. To hide away the tear, the parted. It's thinking of all. The brave that gave their. The fair that wore. All them that's gunne. I'll begin again in a jiffey. The nik of a nad. How glad you'll be I waked you! My! How well you'll feel! For ever after. First we turn by the vagurin here and then it's gooder. So side by side, turn agate, weddingtown, laud men of Londub! I only hope whole the heavens sees us. For I feel I could near to faint away. Into the deeps. Annamores leep. Let me lean, just a lea, if you le, bowldstrong bigtider. Allgearls is wea. At times. So. While you're adamant evar. Wrhps, that wind as if out of norewere! As on the night of the Apophanypes. Jumpst shootst throbbst into me mouth like a bogue and arrohs! Ludegude of the Lashlanns, how he whips me cheeks! Sea, sea! Here, weir, reach, island, bridge. Where you meet I. The day. Remember! Why there that moment and us two only? I was but teen, a tiler's dot. The swankysuits was boosting always, sure him, he was like to me fad. But the swaggerest swell off Shackvulle Strutt. And the fiercest freaky ever followed a pining child round the sluppery table with a forkful of fat. But a king of whistlers. Scieoula! When he'd prop me atlas against his goose and light our two candles for our singers duohs on the sewingmachine. I'm sure he squirted juice in his eyes to make them flash for flightening me. Still and all he was awful fond to me. Who'll search for *Find Me Colours* now on the hillydroops of Vikloefells? But I read in Tobecontinued's tale that while blubles blows there'll still be sealskers. There'll be others but non so for me. Yed he never knew we seen us before. Night after night. So that I longed to go to. And still with all. One time you'd stand fornenst me, fairly laughing, in your bark and tan billows of branches for to fan me coolly. And I'd lie as quiet as a moss. And one time you'd rush upon me, darkly roaring, like a great black shadow with a sheeny stare to perce me rawly. And I'd frozen up and pray for thawe. Three times in all. I was the pet of everyone then. A princeable girl. And you were the pantymammy's Vulking Corsergoth. The invision of Indelond. And, by Thorror, you looked it! My lips went livid for from the joy of fear. Like almost now. How? How you said how you'd give me the keys of me heart. And we'd be married till delth to uspart. And though dev do espart. O mine! Only, no, now it's me who's got to give. As duv herself div. Inn this linn. And can it be it's nnow fforvell? Illas! I wisht I had better glances to peer to you through this baylight's growing. But you're changing, acoolsha, you're changing from me, I can feel. Or is it me is? I'm getting mixed. Brightening up and tightening down. Yes, you're changing, sonhusband, and you're turning, I can feel you, for a daughterwife from the hills again. Imlamaya. And she is coming. Swimming in my hindmoist. Diveltaking on me tail. Just a whisk brisk sly spry spink spank sprint of a thing theresomere, saultering. Saltarella come to her own. I pity your oldself I was used to. Now a younger's there. Try not to part! Be happy, dear ones! May I be wrong! For she'll be sweet for you as I was sweet when I came down out of me mother. My great blue bedroom, the air so quiet, scarce a cloud. In peace and silence. I could have stayed up there for always only. It's something fails us. First we feel. Then we fall. And let her rain now if she likes. Gently or strongly as she likes. Anyway let her rain for my time is come. I done me best when I was let. Thinking always if I go all goes. A hundred cares, a tithe of troubles and is there one who understands me? One in a thousand of years of the nights? All me life I have been lived among them but now they are becoming lothed to me. And I am lothing their little warm tricks. And lothing their mean cosy turns. And all the greedy gushes out through their small souls. And all the lazy leaks down over their brash bodies. How small it's all! And me letting on to meself always. And lilting on all the time. I thought you were all glittering with the noblest of carriage. You're only a bumpkin. I thought you the great in all things, in guilt and in glory. You're but a puny. Home! My people were not their sort out beyond there so far as I can. For all the bold and bad and bleary they are blamed, the seahags. No! Nor for all our wild dances in all their wild din. I can seen meself among them, allaniuvia pulchrabelled. How she was handsome, the wild Amazia, when she would seize to my other breast! And what is she weïrd, haughty Niluna, that she will snatch from my ownest hair! For 'tis they are the stormies. Ho hang! Hang ho! And the clash of our cries till we spring to be free. Auravoles, they says, never heed of your name! But I'm loothing them that's here and all I lothe. Loonely in me loneness. For all their faults. I am passing out. O bitter ending! I'll slip away before they're up. They'll never see. Nor know. Nor miss me. And it's old and old it's sad and old it's sad and weary I go back to you, my cold father, my cold mad father, my cold mad feary father, till the near sight of the mere size of him, the moyles and moyles of it, moananoaning, makes me seasilt saltsick and I rush, my only, into your arms. I see them rising! Save me from those therrble prongs! Two more. Onetwo moremens more. So. Avelaval. My leaves have drifted from me. All. But one clings still. I'll bear it on me. To remind me of. Lff! So soft this morning, ours. Yes. Carry me along, taddy, like you done through the toy fair! If I seen him bearing down on me now under whitespread wings like he'd come from Arkangels, I sink I'd die down over his feet, humbly dumbly, only to washup. Yes, tid. There's where. First. We pass through grass behush the bush to. Whish! A gull. Gulls. Far calls. Coming, far! End here. Us then. Finn, again! Take. Bussoftlhee, mememormee! Till thousendsthee. Lps. The keys to. Given! A way a lone a last a loved a long the

PARIS,
1922-1939.